About the Contributors

MARGARET WEIS lives in a converted barn in Wisconsin with her daughter Elizabeth Baldwin. Her two DRAGONLANCE® trilogies and her hardcover sequel *Dragons of Summer Flame*, all in collaboration with Tracy Hickman, have sold more than 13 million copies worldwide.

TRACY HICKMAN lived in Wisconsin before moving to Arizona with his wife and four children. He and Margaret Weis wrote the Chronicles and Legends trilogies and edited the first Tales trilogy. Hickman also co-wrote the best-selling Darksword Trilogy and the Rose of the Prophet series for Bantam Spectra.

MARK ANTHONY received his B.A. in Anthropology at the University of Colorado, and is completing his Ph.D. at Duke University in North Carolina. He has co-authored a DRAGONLANCE novel, *Kindred Spirits*, contributed to the Tales II series, and written the FORGOTTEN REALMS® novels *Crypt of the Shadowking* and *Escape from Undermountain*.

NANCY VARIAN BERBERICK is the author of the DRAGONLANCE novel *Stormblade, Shadow of the Seventh Moon, The Jewels of Elvish* and *A Child of Elvish*. She is presently working on her fifth novel while waiting for the wildflower gardens to bloom.

JEFF GRUBB is a former game designer for TSR. He spends most of his time working in the FORGOTTEN REALMS and adjacent territories, but he vacations on Krynn. He lives in Lake Geneva with the light of his life and novel co-writer, Kate Novak (The Finder's Stone Trilogy).

RICHARD A. KNAAK has penned short stories for Tales I and Tales II as well as two novels set in the world of Krynn, including the *New York Times* best-seller *The Legend of Huma* and its sequel, *Kaz the Minotaur*. He is also the author of an ongoing fantasy series published by Warner Books, including *Firedrake* and his latest, *Dragon Tome*.

ROGER MOORE is the editor of DRAGON® Magazine, The plot line for his story, "Dead on Target," changed two dozen times before it reached this final version. He wishes to thank Margaret Weis and Patrick McGilligan for keeping him sane and for their faith and editorial feedback.

DOUGLAS NILES, author of the best-selling Moonshae and Maztica trilogies for the FORGOTTEN REALMS, has also written several DRAGONLANCE novels and designed numerous games, including *The Hunt for Red October* and *Red Storm Rising*.

NICK O'DONOHOE has written stories in both Tales I and Tales II and the science-fiction novel, *Too, Too Solid Flesh*. He is also the author of the Nathan Phillips detective series, and has a fantasy novel, *The Magic and the Healing*, forthcoming from Berkeley. He dedicates his story to Robert Lipschitz.

DAN PARKINSON has published 25 novels in the last eight years, including best-sellers in four genres. Best known for westerns and history-fiction such as the acclaimed *Summer Land*, he also authored the Patrick Dalton series of seafaring adventures, the TSR® novel *Starsong* and the DRAGONLANCE novel, *The Gates of Thorbardin*.

MICHAEL WILLIAMS has written six novels, including *Weasel's Luck, Galen Beknighted*, and *The Oath and the Measure*. He has recently completed *The Balance of Power*, the third book in his Thief to King trilogy for Warner Books. He lives in Louisville, Kentucky, with his wife Teri.

Tales II
Trilogy
♦
Volume
Three

With an introduction by
Margaret Weis and Tracy Hickman

Cover art by Larry Elmore

Interior art by Karl Waller

First Printing: November, 1992
Printed in the United States of America
Library of Congress Catalog Card Number: 91-66490

9 8 7 6

ISBN: 1-56076-431-7

TSR, Inc.
201 Sheridan Springs Rd.
Lake Geneva, WI 53147
U.S.A.

TSR Ltd.
120 Church End, Cherry Hinton
Cambridge CB1 3LB
United Kingdom

TABLE OF CONTENTS

INTRODUCTION

The Queen of Darkness seeks to reenter the world. Her minions of evil once more grow strong and powerful. Dragons return to Krynn as war sweeps across the land. Every person is called upon to face the evil. Some rise to the challenge. Some fall. But each is, in his or her own way, a hero.

Michael Williams delves into the soul of the tortured king of Silvanesti in the epic poem, "Lorac."

"Raistlin and the Knight of Solamnia" by Margaret Weis and Tracy Hickman tells how the young mage helped a stern knight learn a hard lesson. (Originally published in DRAGON® Magazine, Issue 154, February 1990.)

Roger Moore writes about the vengeful quest of a revenant in "Dead on Target."

Mara, Queen of Thieves, sneaks into Mountain Nevermind in search of "War Machines" by Nick O'Donohoe.

Dan Parkinson continues the misadventures of the Bulp clan, as those intrepid gully dwarves search for "The Promised Place."

Jeff Grubb relates (be warned!) a gnome story in "Clockwork Hero."

"The Night Wolf" by Nancy Varian Berberick is a tale of three friends who share a dark and deadly secret.

Mark Anthony's "The Potion Sellers" have a bitter pill of their own to swallow when the wrong people come to believe in their fake cure-alls.

Richard Knaak writes the story of an evil priest of Chemosh, trying to recover dread magical artifacts from beneath the Blood Sea, in "The Hand That Feeds."

Foryth Teal, valiant scribe of Astinus, returns to provide us with an exciting account of "The Vingaard Campaign" by Douglas Niles.

And finally, Tasslehoff Burrfoot tells "The Story That Tasslehoff Promised He Would Never, Ever, Ever Tell" to the kender's good friends, Margaret Weis and Tracy Hickman.

We hope you are enjoying our return to Krynn as much as we are. Thanks to all of you for your support. You are the ones who have made this return journey possible. We look forward to traveling with you again in the future.

Margaret Weis and Tracy Hickman

Lorac

Michael Williams

The country of thought
is a pathless forest,
is an intricate night
of redoubling green,
where the best and the worst
entangle and scatter
like distant light
on the face of an emerald
like a spark on the breast
of the fallen seas.
    And yes, it is always like this,
for that country is haunted
with old supposition,
and no matter your stories,
no matter the rumors
of legend and magic
that illumine you through
the curtain of years,
you come to believe
in the web of yourself
that history twines
in the veins of your fingers,
that it knits all purpose,
all pardon and injury,
recovers the lapsed
and plausible blood,
until finally, in the midst of believing,
you contrive the story
out of the rumors,
the old convolution
of breath and forgetting,

---

and then you will say,
beyond truth and belief,
this is what it means,
for once and at last
what it always meant,
no more than I knew
from the world's beginning
is all that it means forever.
  Perhaps it was love
in the towers of thought,
in the haunts of High Sorcery,
in the towering doctrine
of moon and spell and convergence:
where the dragons dispersed
and the Kingpriest hovered
in the blind riots
of dogma and piety.
  Perhaps it was love
in the breathing radius,
in the forest of crystal
where thought tunneled into
five vanishing countries,
forging the five stones
at Istar, at Wayreth,
in lofted Palanthas.
  Perhaps it was love
but more likely thought
in the two vanished towers,
as the rioting stones
dwindled to four, then three,
three like the moons
in a fracturing orbit,
and the towers at Istar
and gabled Palanthas
echoed and shuddered
in the forgotten language,
hollow and cold
with ancient departures,
as high on their turrets
the spiders walked,
and the moth and the rust
corrupted the dream of days.

II

But before the towers
fell to abandonment,
before the fire,
the incense of destruction,
when the Tower at Istar
blossomed in magic
and durable light,
the parapets shone
in the lonely notions
of Lorac Caladon,
Speaker of Stars.
   Restless in Silvanost,
drawn by cold light,
by the intricate forest of magic,
to the North he came,
to glittering Istar
where the tests of High Sorcery
awaited his judgment,
his ordained mathematics,
and the first test past,
and the second surmounted,
he stood as if satisfied
high on the parapets
in doubtful, striated light,
the vaunt of his intellect
over the globe of the city,
where the green luminescence
of the dangered orb
called to him out of the Tower's heart.
   In the pathless forest
at the end of all centuries,
he would hear the song
as it tumbled from thought
into faceted memory,
singing, perpetually singing,
After the second
    there is no other.
O the tests are behind you
    Speaker of Suns
and the song of the orb
    is the song of your mind

in this ancient tower
>*hollow and loveless*

with long departures.
>*O the tests are behind you*

Speaker of Suns
>*but I shall lie here*

the orb said, shimmering
>*as history folds*

in these flourishing walls
>*as the Tower crumbles*

and with it the mind
>*the first high battlements*

the house of the gods
>*but I shall lie here*

as the forest withers
>*as the plains descend*

into winter and nothing
>*unless the song of your thoughts*

which is everything, is the world,
>*controls and subdues*

and informs the mystery.
>*Take me to Silvanost*

Speaker of Suns,
>*take me to freedom*

to the country of green on green.
   Perhaps it was love
in the crystal heart,
in the refraction of light
and beguiling light,
love meeting love in his long belief,
in dire mathematics,
in the mapped parabola
of the trining moons,
but there in the Tower
six reasons converged
   the hand of the prophet
      the nesting heart of his will
   the hurdling thought
      the summoning crystal
   and always the ruinous moment,
all of them settling
in grim alignment,
the orb the sixth

like a heart in his hand,
like a fluttering light
a firebrand he carried
to ignited Silvanost
in the numbered days.
  I am bringing them fire,
he said to himself,
I am bringing them light
in the old gods' story.
I am the first
    I will save them
in the rising earth
    I will save them
and the old world pivots
away from my guiding hand.
So he said to himself,
and the shapeless horizon
shaded to green
and redoubling green
as out of his last dreams
arose Silvanesti,
tangible, fractured in light.

III

And outside the forest
the world collapsed,
a mountain of fire
crashed like a comet
through jewelled Istar,
through the endless city,
and the Tower, unmanned and unhouseled,
split like a dry stalk
in the midst of the ruinous flames,
and out of the valleys
the mountains erupted,
the seas poured forever
into the graves of mountains,
the long deserts sighed
on abandoned floors of the seas,
and the highways of Krynn descended
into the paths of the dead.
  As hail and fire

in a downpour of blood
tumbled to earth,
igniting the trees and the grass,
   as the mountains were burning,
   as the sea became blood
   as above and below us
      the heavens were scattered,
   as locusts and scorpions
      wandered the face of the planet,
Silvanost floated on islands of thought,
immaculate memory
gabled in cloud and dreaming,
untouched by the fire,
by the shocks of the Rending,
and from tower to tower
from the Tower of Sorcery
down to the Tower of Stars,
drowsy in thinking, Lorac imagined
an impossible dream of salvation,
a country bartered in magic,
renewed in his mind
to a paradise won
in a ranging study.
   And so it appeared in the orb,
in the waking hours,
in the suddenly secret
lodging of light
as the globe lay buried,
masked and unfabled
in the Tower of Stars,
the ancestral tower
of Speakers, of Silvanost,
buried for centuries.
   While the continent burned
and the people of Qualinost
wandered through ash
and the outer darkness,
Silvanost floated
at the edge of their sight,
absent and glorious,
down to the edge of their dreams.
Lorac watched from the Tower of Stars,
from the heart of the crystal,

his eye on the face
of the damaged world
like a rumor of history
he was forgetting
lost in the fathomless
maze of the orb.
   But often at night
when the senses faltered
and the polished country
altered and coiled,
the shape of the dream
was the Speaker's reflection:
The estranging trees
were nests of daggers,
the streams black and clotted
under a silent moon
that mourned for the day
and the fierce definition
of sunlight and knowledge
where the trees and towns
were named and numbered
and always, implacably
intended and purposed,
far from the tangle
of nightmare, the shadow
and weave of the forest
that wrangled to light
in the dreams of Lorac,
invading the day
with the glitter of flint,
subverting the pale
and anonymous sun.

IV

Then to the North
an evil arose
in the cloud-wracked skies,
for the Dragon Highlords
sent sword and messenger,
firebrand and word
to the Tower of Stars,
to rapt Silvanesti,

to the dwindling porches
of the elf king's ear,
promising peace
and the forest's asylum
in the discord of armies,
promising Silvanost free
in exchange for the promise
of silence, inaction,
for a nodding head
on the Green Throne.
    And Lorac agreed,
his eye on the hooded orb,
where miraculous silence
promised a blessing of spears,
an end to all promise,
the dragons by summer.
    And so Silvanesti
was emptied of silver,
emptied of lives
and the long dreaming blood
of its last inhabitants
as they took to the boats,
to the skiffs, to the coracles,
aimless on water
as cloudy as oracles
and the Wildrunners fought
in the wake of the water,
where their last breath billowed
in the spreading sails.
    Alhana Starbreeze, the Speaker's daughter,
stood at the helm
in the silver passage
as they sailed to the South
on the Paths of Astralas,
on the bard's memory,
on history's spindrift,
and Lorac behind them
ordered his soldiers
to leave the unraveling land
in the last of the ships,
for there in the dark
called the forest, called Silvanost,
the elm and aeterna

choiring like nightingales,
singing this song
to his turning ear,
After the last test
 there is no other.
O the tests are behind you
 Speaker of Suns
and the song of the orb
 is the song of your mind
in this ancient tower
 hollow and loveless
with long departures.
 O the tests are behind you
Speaker of Suns
 but I shall lie here
as history folds
 in these flourishing walls
as the Tower crumbles
 and with it the mind
the first high battlements
 the house of the gods
but I shall lie here
 as the forest withers
as the plains descend
 into winter and nothing
unless the song of your thoughts
 which is everything, is the world,
controls and subdues
 and informs the mystery.
Keep me in Silvanost
 Speaker of Suns,
Keep me in freedom
 in the country of green on green.

It lay in the chambers
secret in stars,
above it the Tower
and a labyrinth of legends,
and the freedom it promised
at its crystalline heart
was green ice beckoning,
flame of the distant voice.
 And drawn by its music,

by the unearthly chiming
of crystal and shifting thought
the Speaker of Suns descended alone
to the heart of the Tower
where time and the forest
and a shaft of moonlight
collapsed on the orb,
and he reached for the crystal
as a thousand voices
rose from its brimming fire,
all of them singing
the lure of the possible,
all of them singing
the song he imagined,
and his thoughts were a fortress,
phantasmal ramparts
of maple and ash and belief,
in his daylit dreams
the armies were breaking,
the edge of the forest
bristled with leaf and invention,
and summoned, he reached
for the crystal
   as the globe and the world
   dissolved in his terrible grasp.

He knew when the bones
of his fingers ignited,
when green fire danced
on the back of his hands,
in the damage of arteries,
and he knew at once
that the fire was the heart of his error,
that neither the strength
nor the words nor the mind
could govern the magic.
   But the shadows of Silvanost
faded from green into red,
into brown and untenable gold,
the orb was a prison
and above Thon-Thalas
the long wingbeat
of the dragon approached,

and the trees bent and bowed
in a sinister wind
as Lorac beheld this
all through the light of the orb,
and the dragon, the Bloodbane,
came with its whispers,
and under its words
the old stones tilted,
and the Tower of Stars,
as white as a sepulchre,
twisted and torted
as the trees rained blood
and the animals shrieked
their cries like torn metal
in a charmed and perpetual midnight.

V

So it was as the centuries
gathered and telescoped
into the passage
of a dozen years,
as the bristling heart
of Silvanesti
festered and doubled
and hardened like crystal.
And always the promise
of Cyan Bloodbane,
of the dragon coiled
on the crystal globe,
always the promise
was nothing and nothing
and the forest the map
of a strangled country,
land of stillbirth, of fever,
of warped and gangrenous age
and of long unendurable dying,
until from the North
came another invasion
of hard light and lances
as the Heroes, the Fellowship,
the fashioned alliance
of elf and dwarf,

of human and gnome and kender
came to the forest
through the nest of nightmare,
through the growing entanglement,
through bone, through crystal,
through all the forgotten
banes and allures
of the damaged heart,
to Silvanost and the disfigured Tower,
to Lorac, to the imprisoning Orb,
and they freed the Speaker
    the Tower and town,
    the forest, the people,
    the bright orb they freed
and like a survivor
tumbled the globe through the years
through the centuries lodged
in the pale hands of others
and its old polished carapace
bright and reflecting
the hourglassed eyes
of its ultimate wielder.
    But the sands were draining
over the Speaker of Suns,
and the knowledge of Lorac,
vaulted and various,
numbered and faceted,
descended and simplified
into a knowledge of evil,
as the forest unfolded,
stripped of the long light,
bare of bedazzlement
and at last Silvanesti
was free of his mind,
torn from the labyrinth
bearing forever the scars of belief
to the last syllable of eventual time,
and Lorac died in his daughter's arms,
his thoughts in the Tower
entombed and surrendered,
his last wish a burial
underneath Silvanost,
driving the green

from the body's decay,
resolving to forest,
resolving to Silvanost
forever and ever, his enabling ghost
to ascribe and deliver
the land that he dreamt of,
as thought was translated to dream.
　　And yes, it is always like this,
for the country is haunted
with old supposition,
and no matter the stories,
no matter the rumors
of legend and magic
that illumine you through
the curtain of years,
you come to believe
in the web of yourself
that history twines
in the veins of your fingers,
that it knits all purpose,
all pardon and injury,
recovers the lapsed
and plausible blood,
until finally, in the midst of believing,
you contrive among rumors
the story, the old convolution
of breath and forgetting,
in which you will say,
beyond truth and belief,
this is what it means,
for once and at last
what it always meant,
no more than I knew
from the world's beginning
is all that it means forever.

Raistlin and the Knight of Solamnia

Margaret Weis and Tracy Hickman

It was a chill night for spring, undoubtedly the reason there were so many people in the inn. The inn wasn't accustomed to such crowds. In fact, it wasn't accustomed to any crowds, for the inn was new, so new that it still smelled of fresh-hewn wood and paint instead of stale ale and yesterday's stew. Called "Three Sheets," after a popular drinking song of the time, the inn was located in—. But where it was located doesn't matter. The inn was destroyed five years later in the Dragon Wars and never rebuilt. Small wonder, for it was on a road little traveled then and less traveled after the dragons leveled the town.

It would be some time yet before the Queen of Darkness plunged the world into what she hoped would be eternal night, but already, in these years just prior to the war, her evil shadow was spreading. Goblins had always been a problem in this realm, but suddenly what had been small bands of raiders who struck isolated farms had grown into armies attacking villages.

"What's His Lordship offering?" queried a mage clad in red robes who occupied a booth—the one nearest the fire and the most comfortable in the crowded inn—with just one companion. No one thought of joining them. Though the mage was sickly in appearance, with a hacking cough that nearly bent him double, those who had served with him in previous campaigns whispered that he was quick to anger and quicker with his spells.

15

"Standard rate—two pieces of steel a week and a bounty on goblin ears. I signed us up." The man responding was a large, burly warrior who sat down opposite his questioner. Shedding his plain, undecorated cloak in the heat of the room, the warrior revealed hard-muscled arms the size of tree trunks and a chest like a bull's. He unbuckled from around his waist a sword belt, laying on the table near at hand a sword with every appearance of having been well and skillfully used.

"When do we get our pay?"

"After we drive out the goblins. He'll make us earn it."

"Of course," said the mage, "and he won't be out any cash to those who die. What took you so long?"

"The town is packed! Every mercenary this side of Ansalon is here, not to mention horse traders, camp followers, swordmakers, and every kender not currently behind bars. We'll be lucky to find a place in a field to spread our blankets this night."

"Hullo, Caramon!" called out a leather-armor-clad man, coming over to the table and clapping the warrior on the back. "Mind if I share your booth?" he asked, starting to sit down. "It's standing room only in this place. This your twin I've heard so much about? Introduce us."

The mage lifted his head, fixed his gaze upon the stranger.

Golden eyes with pupils the shape of an hourglass glittered in the shadows of the red hood. The light in the inn glinted off golden skin. Near at hand stood a wooden staff—obviously and ominously magical—topped by a multifaceted crystal clutched in a dragon's claw. Gulping, the man rose quickly to his feet and, with a hasty farewell to Caramon, took his ale to a distant corner of the room.

"He looked at me as if he saw me on my deathbed!" muttered the man to more congenial companions.

"It's going to be a cold night tonight, Raist," said the warrior to his brother in a low voice when the two were again alone. "It smells like snow in the air. You shouldn't sleep outside."

"And where would you have me sleep, Caramon?" asked the mage in a soft, sneering voice. "In a hole in the ground, like a rabbit, for that is all we can aff—." He broke off in a fit of coughing that left him breathless.

His twin gazed at him anxiously. Pulling a coin from a shabby purse he wore at his belt, Caramon held it up. "We have this, Raist. You could sleep here tonight and the next night."

"And what would we do for food in the interim, my brother? We won't get paid for a fortnight, at least."

Caramon lowered his voice and, leaning across the table, grasped hold of his brother's arm to draw him near. "I could snare us something, if need be."

"You'd be the one to end up in a snare, you fool!" The mage jerked away from his brother's touch. "The lord's men are all over the woods, hunting for poachers with only slightly less enthusiasm than they're hunting for goblins. No, we'll return to camp tonight. Don't fuss over me. You know how I hate it. I'll be fine. I've slept in worse places."

Raistlin began to cough again, the spasms shaking his frail body until it seemed he must split apart. Pulling out a cloth, he pressed it over his mouth. Those who glanced at him in concern saw that, when the mage withdrew the cloth, it was covered with blood.

"Fix me my drink!" he ordered Caramon, his lips forming the words for he had momentarily lost the power of speech. Collapsing in a corner, he closed his eyes and concentrated on drawing breath. Those near could hear the air whistle in his lungs.

Caramon peered through the crowd, attempting to find the barmaid, and shouted for boiling hot water. Raistlin slid a pouch across the table toward his brother, who picked it up and carefully measured out some of its contents into a mug. The inn's proprietor himself came bustling over with the hot water in a steaming kettle. He was just about to pour when a sudden shouting rose up around the door.

"Hey, there! Get out you little vermin! No kender allowed!" cried several of the guests.

"Kender!" Kettle in hand, the proprietor ran off in panic.

"Hey!" shouted Caramon after the flurried innkeeper in exasperation, "you forgot our water!"

"But I tell you I have friends here!" A shrill voice rose up from the doorway. "Where? Why,"—there was a moment's pause—"there! Hi, Caramon! Remember me?"

"Name of the Abyss!" muttered Caramon, hunching up his big shoulders and ducking his head.

A short figure, about the stature of a twelve-year old human, with the face of a man of twenty and the wide-eyed innocent expression of a babe of three, was pointing gleefully at the booth of the warrior and his brother. The figure was clad in a bright green tunic and orange striped hose. A long tassel of hair was twisted round his head and hung down his back. Numerous pouches containing the possessions of everyone who had been unfortunate enough to cross his path hung from his belt.

"You're answerable for him, then," said the proprietor grimly, marching the kender across the room, one hand gripping the slight shoulders firmly. There was a wild scramble as men stuffed their purses inside their shirts, down their pants, or wherever else they thought their valuables might be safe from a kender's light and nimble fingers.

"Hey! Our water!" Caramon made a grab for the innkeeper but got a handful of kender instead.

"Earwig Lockpicker," said the kender, holding out his hand politely. "Friend of Tasslehoff Burrfoot's. We met at the Inn of the Last Home. I couldn't stay long. There was that misunderstanding over the horse. I told them I didn't steal it. I can't think how it came to follow me."

"Maybe because you were holding firmly onto the reins?" suggested Caramon.

"Do you think so? Because I—Ouch!"

"Drop it!" said Raistlin, his thin hand closing tightly over the kender's wrist.

"Oh," said Earwig meekly, releasing the pouch that had been lying on the table and was now making its way into the kender's pocket. "Is that yours?"

The mage cast a piercing, infuriated glare at his brother, who flushed and shrugged uncomfortably. "I'll get that water for you, Raist. Right now. Uh, Innkeeper!"

"Well, look over there!" said the kender, squirming around in his seat to face the front door as it closed behind a small group of travelers. "I followed those people into town. You can't imagine," he said in an indignant whisper that carried clearly across the room, "how rude that man is! He should have thanked me for finding his dagger, instead of—"

"Greetings, sir. Greetings, my lady." The proprietor bobbed and bowed officiously. The heavily cloaked man and woman were, to all appearances, well dressed. "You'll be wanting a room, no doubt, and then dinner. There's hay in the stable for your horses."

"We'll be wanting nothing," said the man in a harsh voice. He was carrying a young boy in his arms and, as he spoke, he eased the child to the floor, then flexed his arms as though they ached. "Nothing except a seat by your fire. We wouldn't have come in except that my lady-wife is not feeling well."

"Not well?" The innkeeper, backing up, held out a dish cloth in front of him as a sort of shield and eyed them askance. "Not the plague?"

"No, no!" said the woman in a low, cultivated voice. "I am not ill. I am just tired and chilled to the bone, that is all." Reaching out her hand, she drew her son near. "We have walked a great distance."

"Walked!" muttered the innkeeper, not liking the sound of that. He looked more closely at the family's dress.

Several of the men standing around the fire moved to one side. Others hurried to draw up a bench, and the overworked barmaid, ignoring her waiting customers, put her arm around the woman and helped her to a seat. The woman sank down limply.

"You're white as a ghost, milady," said the barmaid. "Let me bring you a posset of honey and brandywine."

"No," said the man, moving to stand by his wife, the child clinging to his father. "We have no money to pay for it."

"Tut, tut. Talk of money later," said the barmaid briskly. "Call it my treat."

"We'll not take charity!" The man's voice rose to a angry shout.

The boy shrank close to his mother, who glanced at her husband, then lowered her eyes. "Thank you for your kind offer," she said to the barmaid, "but I need nothing. I'm feeling much better already."

The proprietor, stalking his guests, noted that by firelight their clothes were not nearly so fine as they had first seemed. The man's cloak was frayed at the hem and travel worn and stained with mud. The woman's dress was clean and neat but many times mended. The boy, who appeared to be about five or six, was clad in shirt and trousers that had probably once been his father's, cut down to fit the boy's small, thin frame. The proprietor was about to hint broadly that only those who spent money in his inn had a right to his fire when he was distracted by a scream from inside the kitchen.

"Where's that kender?" the innkeeper cried out in alarm.

"Right here!" shouted Earwig eagerly, raising his hand and waving. "Do you want me?"

The proprietor cast him a baleful glance, then fled.

"Humpf," said Caramon in an undertone, his eyes on the woman. She had shoved the hood of her cloak back with a weary hand, revealing a pale, thin face once beautiful, now anxious and worn with care and fatigue. Her arm stole around her son, who was gazing up at her in concern, and she hugged the boy close. "I wonder when the last time was those two had anything to eat," Caramon muttered.

"I can ask them," offered Earwig helpfully. "Hey, lady, when—Ulp!"

Caramon clamped his hand over the kender's mouth.

"It's no concern of yours, my brother," snapped Raistlin irritably. "Get that imbecile innkeeper back here with the hot water!" He began to cough again.

Caramon released the wriggling kender (who had actually been silent for as long as three minutes on account of having no breath left with which to talk) and heaved his great bulk to his feet, peering over the heads of the crowd for the proprietor. Smoke was rolling out from under the kitchen door.

"I think he's going to be a while, Raist," said Caramon solemnly. "I'll get the barmaid."

He tried to catch the barmaid's eye, but she was hovering over the woman.

"I'll go and fix you a nice cup of tarbean tea, milady. No, no. It's all right. There's no charge for tarbean tea in this inn. Is there?" she said, flashing a threatening look at the other customers.

"No, no. No charge. None," chorused the men in response.

The cloaked and booted man frowned, but swallowed whatever words he might have wanted to say.

"Hey, over here!" Caramon shouted, but the barmaid was still standing in front of the woman, twisting her apron in her hands.

"Milady," she began hesitantly, in a low voice, "I've been speaking to cook. We're that busy tonight we're shorthanded. It would be a gift of charity, milady, if you could help us out. It'd be worth a night's lodging and a meal."

The woman cast a swift and pleading glance up at her husband.

His face was livid. "No wife of a Knight of Solamnia will work in an inn! We'll all three starve and go to our graves first!"

"Uh, oh," muttered Caramon and eased himself back into his seat.

Talking and bantering and laughter ceased, the silence falling gradually as word circulated. All eyes went to the man. Hot blood flooded his cheeks. He had obviously not meant to reveal such a thing about himself. His hand went to his smooth-shaven upper lip, and it seemed to those watching that they could almost see the long, flowing mustaches that marked a Knight of Solamnia. It was not unusual that he had shaved it off. For long centuries the Order had stood for justice and law on Krynn. Now the knights were hated and reviled, blamed for bringing down the wrath of the gods. What calamity had forced this knight and his family to flee their homeland without money and barely the clothes on their backs? The crowd didn't know and most of them didn't care. The proprietor now wasn't the only one who wanted the knight and his family gone.

"Come along, Aileen," said the knight gruffly. He put his hand on his wife's shoulder. "We'll not stay in this place. Not when they cater to the likes of that!" His narrowed eyes went to Raistlin, to the red robes that proclaimed him a wizard and the magical staff that stood by his side. The knight turned stiffly to the barmaid. "I understand the lord of this realm seeks men to fight the goblins. If you could tell me where to find him—"

"He's seeking fighters," sang out a man in a far corner of the common room. "Not pretty boys dressed up in fancy iron suits."

"Ho, you're wrong, Nathan," called out another. "I hear His Lordship's lookin' for someone to lead a regiment—a regiment of gully dwarves!"

There was appreciative laughter. The knight choked with fury, his hand went to the hilt of his sword. His wife laid a gentle hand restrainingly on his arm. "No, Gawain," she murmured, starting to rise to her feet. "We will go. Come."

"Stay put, milady. And as for you . . ." The barmaid glared at the boisterous crowd. "Shut your mouths or that'll be the last cold beer I draw for anyone in this inn tonight."

Quelled by this awful threat, the men quieted. Putting her arm around the woman, the barmaid looked up at the knight. "You'll find His Lordship in the sheriff's hall, about a mile down the street. Go tend to your business, Sir Knight, and let your lady-wife and the boy rest. There's a lot of rough men down there," she added, seeing the knight about to refuse. "It's no fit place for your child."

The proprietor came hurrying up. He would have liked dearly to throw all three out of his inn, but he could see the crowd was siding with his barmaid in favor of the woman. Having just put out a grease fire in the kitchen, the last thing he needed was a riot.

"Go, Sir Knight, will you, please?" pleaded the innkeeper in a low voice. "We'll take good care of your lady."

The knight seemingly had no choice. Gnawing his lip, he gave an ungracious assent. "Galeth, watch over your mother. And speak no word to anyone." Glancing meaningfully at the mage, the knight drew his cloak around his shoulders, cast his hood over his face, and stalked out of the inn.

"His Lordship'll have nothing to do with a Knight of Solamnia," prophesied Caramon. "Half the army would quit if he hired him. What did he look at you like that for, Raist? You didn't say anything."

"The knights have no love for magic. It's something they can neither control nor understand. And now, my brother, the hot water! Or are you going to watch me die here in this wretched inn?"

"Oh, uh, sure, Raist." Caramon stood up and began searching the crowd for the barmaid.

"I'll go!" Earwig leaped to his feet and skipped out of reach to disappear into the crowd.

Talk and laughter resumed. The proprietor was arguing over the tab with a couple of his patrons. The barmaid had disappeared back into the kitchen. The knight's wife, overcome by weariness, lay down upon the bench. The boy stood protectively near her, his hand on her arm. But his gaze strayed to the red-robed magic-user.

Raistlin cast a swift glance at his brother. Seeing Caramon preoccupied in attempting to capture the barmaid's attention, the mage made a slight, beckoning gesture with his hand.

Nothing appears as sweet as fruit we are forbidden to eat. The boy's eyes widened. He looked around to see if the mage meant someone else, then looked back at Raistlin, who repeated the gesture. The boy tugged gently at his mother's sleeve.

"Here, now. Let your ma sleep," scolded the barmaid, hustling past, a tray of mugs in her hands. "Be good for a few moments, and when I come back I'll bring you a treat." She vanished into the crowd.

"Hey, there! Barmaid!" Caramon was waving his arms and bellowing like a bull.

Raistlin cast him an irritated glance, then turned back to the boy.

Slowly, drawn by irresistible curiosity and fascination, the child left his mother's side and crept over to stand near the mage.

"Can you really do magic?" he asked, round-eyed with wonder.

"Here, there!" Caramon, seeing the kid apparently bothering his brother, tried to shoo him away. "Go on back to your ma."

"Caramon, shut up," said Raistlin softly. He turned his

golden-eyed gaze on the boy. "Is your name Galeth?"

"Yes, sir. I was named after my grandfather. He was a knight. I'm going to be a knight, too."

Caramon grinned at his brother. "Reminds you of Sturm, doesn't he? These knights, they're all daft," he added, making the mistake that most adults make in thinking that children—because they are small—have no feelings.

The boy flared up like dry tinder cast in the fire. "My father's not daft! He's a great man!" Galeth flushed, realizing perhaps that his father hadn't seemed all that great. "It's just that he's worried about my mother. He and I can do without food, we're men. But my mother. . ." His lower lip began to tremble, his eyes filled with tears.

"Galeth," said Raistlin, casting Caramon a glance that sent the big man back to shouting for the barmaid, "would you like to see some magic?"

The boy, too awed to speak, nodded.

"Then bring me your mother's purse."

"Her purse is empty, sir," said the boy. Even though young, he was old enough to understand that this was a shameful thing, and his cheeks flushed.

"Bring it to me," said Raistlin in his soft, whispering voice.

Galeth stood a moment, undecided, torn between what he knew he should be doing and what he longed to do. Temptation proved too strong for his six years. Turning, he ran back to his mother and gently, without disturbing her rest, slipped her purse from the pocket of her gown. He brought it back and handed it to Raistlin, who took it in his long-fingered, delicate hands and studied it carefully. It was a small leather bag embroidered with golden thread, such as fine ladies use to carry their jewels. If this one had ever had jewels in it, they had long since been sold to buy food and clothing.

The mage turned the purse inside out and shook it. It was lined with silk and was, as the boy said, pitifully empty. Then, shrugging, Raistlin handed it back to the boy. Galeth accepted it hesitantly. Where was the magic? He began to droop a little in disappointment.

"And so you are going to be a knight like your father,"

said Raistlin.

"Yes!" The boy blinked back his tears.

"Since when, then, does a future knight tell a lie?"

"I didn't lie, sir!" Galeth flushed. "That's a wicked thing!"

"But you said the purse was empty. Look inside."

Startled, the boy opened the leather bag. Whistling in astonishment, he pulled out a coin, then gazed at Raistlin in delight.

"Go put the purse back, quietly now," said the mage. "And not a word to anyone about where the coin came from, or the spell will be broken!"

"Yes, sir!" said Galeth solemnly. Scurrying back, he slipped his mother's purse into her pocket with the stealthy skill of a kender. Squatting down next to her on the floor, he began to chew on a piece of candied ginger the barmaid tossed to him, pausing every now and then to share a conspiratorial grin with the mage.

"That's all well and good," grunted Caramon, leaning his elbows on the table, "but what do *we* do now for food for the next week?"

"Something will turn up," said Raistlin calmly. Raising his frail hand, he made a weak gesture and the barmaid hurried to his side.

*   *   *   *

The soft glow of twilight darkened to night. The inn became even more crowded, hot, and noisy. The knight's wife slept through the turmoil, her exhaustion so apparent that many looked upon her with pitying eyes and muttered that she deserved a better fate. The boy fell asleep, too, curled up on the floor at his mother's feet. He never stirred when Caramon lifted him in his strong arms and tucked him near his mother. Earwig returned and sat down next to Caramon. Flushed and happy, he emptied out his bulging pouches onto the table and began to sort their contents, keeping up a nonstop, one-sided conversation at the same time.

After two hours, Sir Gawain returned. Each man in the inn who saw him enter nudged a neighbor into silence so that all were quiet and watching him attentively as he stepped into the common room.

"Where's my son?" he demanded, staring around darkly.

"Right here, safe and warm and sound asleep," answered the barmaid, pointing out the slumbering child. "We haven't made off with him, if that's what you're thinking."

The knight had grace enough to look ashamed. "I'm sorry," Gawain said gruffly. "I thank you for your kindness."

"Knight or barmaid, death takes us all alike. At least we can help one another through life. I'll wake your lady."

"No," said Gawain and put out his hand to stop her. "Let her sleep. I want to ask you"—he turned to the proprietor—"if she and my son can stay the night. I will have money to pay you in the morning," he added stiffly.

"You will?" The proprietor stared at him suspiciously. "His Lordship hired you?"

"No," answered the knight. "It seems he has all the fighters he needs to handle the goblins."

An audible sigh whispered through the room. "Told you so," said Caramon to his brother.

"Shut up, you fool!" Raistlin returned sharply. "I'm interested to know where he's planning to find money this night."

"His Lordship says that there is a woodland not far from here, and in that woodland is a fortress that is of no use to him or to anyone because there is a curse laid upon it. Only—"

"A cursed fortress? Where? What kind of curse?" demanded an excited Earwig, scrambling up onto the table to get a better view.

"The Maiden's Curse," called out several in answer. "The fortress is called Death's Keep. No one who has entered it has ever returned."

"Death's Keep!" breathed the kender, misty-eyed with rapture. "What a wonderful-sounding place!"

"A true Knight of Solamnia may enter and return. According to His Lordship, it takes a true knight to lift the curse. I plan to go there and, with the help of Paladine, perform this deed."

"I'll come wi—" Earwig was offering magnanimously,

when Caramon yanked the kender's feet out from underneath him, sending the green-clad figure sprawling face-first on the floor.

"His Lordship has promised to reward me well," concluded Gawain, ignoring the crash and the kender's protest.

"Uh, huh," sneered the proprietor, "And who's going to pay your family's bill if you don't return, Sir True Knight? You're not the first of your kind to go up there, and I've never seen a one come back!"

Nods and low voices in the crowd affirmed this.

"His Lordship has promised to provide for them if I fall," answered Gawain in a calm and steady voice.

"His Lordship? Oh, that's quite all right then," said the proprietor, happy once more. "And my best wishes to you, Sir Knight. I'll personally escort the lady and your boy—a fine child, if I may say so—to their room."

"Wait just a minute," said the barmaid, ducking beneath the proprietor's elbow and coming to stand in front of the knight. "Where's the mage who'll be going with you to Death's Keep?"

"No mage accompanies me," answered Gawain, frowning. "Now, if there is nothing further you want of me, I must leave." He looked down at his sleeping wife and, with a gentle hand, started to reach out to touch her hair. Fearing it would waken her, however, he drew back. "Good-bye, Aileen. I hope you can understand." Turning swiftly, he started to leave, but the proprietor grabbed his elbow.

"No mage! But didn't His Lordship tell you? It takes a knight *and* a mage to lift the Maiden's Curse! For it was because of a knight and a mage that the curse was placed on the keep."

"And a kender!" Earwig shouted, scrambling to his feet. "I'm positive I heard that it takes a knight and a mage and a kender!

"His Lordship mentioned some legend about a knight and a mage," said Gawain scornfully. "But a true knight with faith in his god needs the help of no other being on Krynn."

Freeing himself of the proprietor's plucking hand, the knight started toward the door.

"Are you truly so eager to throw away your life, Sir

Knight?" The sibilant whisper cut through the hubbub in the inn, bringing with it a deathlike silence. "Do you truly believe that your wife and son will be better off when you are dead?"

The knight stopped. His shoulders stiffened, his body trembled. He did not turn, but glanced back at the mage over his shoulder. "His Lordship promised. They will have food and a roof over their heads. I can buy them that, at least."

"And so, with a cry of 'My Honor is My Life' you rush off to certain defeat when, by bending that proud neck and allowing me to accompany you, you have a chance to achieve victory. How typical of you all," said Raistlin with an unpleasant smile. "No wonder your Order has fallen into ruin."

Gawain's face flushed in anger at this insult. His hand went to his sword. Caramon, growling, reached for his own sword.

"Put away your weapons," snapped Raistlin. "You are a young man, Sir Knight. Fortune has not been kind to you. It is obvious that you value your life, but, being desperate, you know no other way to escape your misfortune with honor." His lip twisted as he said the last word. "I have offered to help. Will you kill me for that?"

Gawain's hand tightened around the sword's hilt.

"Is it true that a knight and a mage are needed to lift the curse?" he asked of those in the inn. ("And a kender!" piped up a shrill voice indignantly.)

"Oh, yes. Truly," averred everyone around him.

"Have there been any who have tried it?"

At this the men in the inn glanced at each other and then looked at the ceiling or the floor or the walls or stared into their mugs.

"A few," said someone.

"How few?" asked Caramon, seeing that his brother was in earnest about accompanying the knight.

"Twenty, thirty maybe."

"Twenty or thirty! And none of them ever came back? Did you hear that, Raist? Twenty or thirty and none of them ever came back!" Caramon said emphatically.

"I heard." Using his staff to support him, Raistlin rose from the booth.

"So did I!" said Earwig, dancing with excitement.

"And we're still going, aren't we," Caramon said gloomily, buckling his sword belt around his waist. "Some of us, that is. Not you, Nosepicker."

"Nosepicker!" Hearing this foul corruption of a name long honored among kender, Earwig was momentarily paralyzed with shock and forgot to dodge Caramon's large hand. Catching hold of the kender by the long ponytail, the big warrior skillfully tied him by the hair to one of the inn's support posts. "The name's Lockpicker!" he shrieked indignantly.

"Why is it you're doing this, mage?" asked Gawain suspiciously as Raistlin walked slowly across the room.

"Yeah, Raist, why is it we're doing this?" Caramon shot out of the corner of his mouth.

"For the money, of course," said Raistlin coolly. "What other reason would there be?"

The crowd in the inn was on its feet, clamoring in excitement, calling out directions and advice and laying wagers on whether or not the adventurers would return. Earwig, tied fast, screamed and pleaded and begged and nearly yanked his hair out by the roots trying to free himself.

It was only the barmaid who saw Raistlin's frail hand very gently ruffle the sleeping child's hair in passing.

* * * *

Half the patrons of the inn accompanied them down an old, disused path to the fringes of a thick forest. Here, beneath ancient trees that seemed ill-disposed to have their rest disturbed, the crowd bid them good fortune.

"Do you need torches?" one of the men shouted.

"No," answered Raistlin. "*Shirak*," he said softly, and the crystal ball on top of his staff burst into bright, beaming light.

The crowd gasped in appreciative awe. The knight glanced at the glowing staff askance.

"I will take a torch. I will not walk in any light that has darkness as its source."

The crowd bid them farewell, then turned back to the inn to await the outcome. Odds were running high in favor of Death's Keep living up to its name. The wager seemed such a sure thing, in fact, that Raistlin had some difficulty in persuading Caramon not to bet against themselves.

Torch in hand, the knight started down the path. Raistlin and his brother walked some paces behind, for the young knight walked so swiftly, the frail mage could not keep up.

"So much," said Raistlin, leaning on his staff, "for the courtesy of the knights."

Gawain instantly halted and waited, stony-faced, for them to catch up.

"Not only courtesy but just plain good sense to keep together in a forest as dark and gloomy as this one," stated Caramon. "Did you hear something?"

The three listened, holding their breaths. Tree leaves rustled, a twig snapped. Knight and warrior put hand to weapon. Raistlin slid his hand inside his pouch, grasping a handful of sand and calling to mind words of a sleep spell.

"Here I am!" said a shrill voice cheerfully. A small, green and orange figure burst into the light. "Sorry I'm late," said Earwig. "My hair got caught in the booth." He exhibited half of what had once been a long tassel. "I had to cut myself loose!"

"With *my* dagger!" said Caramon, snatching it away.

"Is that one yours? Isn't that odd? I could have sworn I had one just like it!"

Sir Gawain came to a halt, scowling. "It is bad enough I must travel in the company of a magic-user—"

"I know," said Earwig, nodding sympathetically. "We'll just have to make the best of it, won't we?"

"Ah, let the little fellow come along," said Caramon, feeling remorseful when he looked at what had once been the kender's jaunty top-knot. "He might come in handy if we're attacked."

Gawain hesitated, but it was obvious that the only way to get rid of the kender would be to slice him in two, and though the Oath and the Measure didn't specifically ban a knight from murdering kender, it didn't exactly encourage it, either.

"Attack!" he snorted. The knight resumed his pace, Earwig skipping along beside him. "We are in no danger until we reach the keep. At least so His Lordship told me."

"And what else did His Lordship tell you?" Raistlin asked, coughing.

Gawain glared at him dourly, obviously wondering of what use this sickly mage would be to him.

"He told me the tale of the Maiden's Curse. A long time ago, before the Cataclysm, a wizard of the red robes—such as yourself—stole away a young woman from her father's castle and carried her to this keep. A knight, the young woman's betrothed, discovered the abduction and followed after to rescue her. He caught up with the mage and his victim in the keep in this forest.

"The wizard, furious at having his evil plans thwarted, called upon the Queen of Darkness to destroy the knight. The knight, in his turn, called for Paladine to come to his aid. The forces unleashed in the ensuing battle were so powerful that they not only destroyed the wizard and the knight, but they have, even after death, continued to drag others into their conflict."

"And you wouldn't let me make that bet!" said Caramon reproachfully to his brother.

Raistlin did not appear to hear him. He was, seemingly, lost in thought.

"Well," said Gawain abruptly, "and what do you think of that tale?"

"I think that, like most legends, it has outgrown the truth," answered Raistlin. "A wizard of the red robes, for example, would not call upon the Queen of Darkness for aid. That is something only wizards of the black robes do."

"It seems to me," said Gawain grimly, "that your kind dabbles in darkness no matter what color robes they wear—the fox cloaking himself in sheep's wool, so the saying goes."

"Yeah," retorted Caramon angrily. "And I've heard a few sayings myself about *your* kind, Sir Kettle-head. One goes—"

"That will do, my brother," remonstrated Raistlin, his thin fingers closing firmly over Caramon's arm. "Save your breath for what lies ahead."

The group continued on in a silence that was tense and smoldering.

"What happened to the maiden?" Earwig asked suddenly. All three started, having forgotten, in their preoccupation, the kender's presence.

"What?" growled Gawain.

"The maiden. What happened to her? After all, it's called the Maiden's Curse."

"Yes, it is," said Raistlin. "An interesting point."

"Is it?" Earwig jumped up and down gleefully, scattering the contents of his pouches across the path and nearly tripping Caramon. "I came up with an interesting point!"

"I don't see why it's called the Maiden's Curse, except that she was the innocent victim," answered the knight as an afterthought.

"Ah," said Earwig with a gusty sigh. "An innocent victim. I know what *that* feels like!"

* * * *

The three continued on their way. The walking was easy, the path through the forest was smooth and straight. Too smooth and too straight, according to Caramon, who maintained that it seemed bound and determined to deliver them to their doom as swiftly as possible. Several hours after midnight, they arrived at the fortress known as Death's Keep.

Dark and empty, its stone facade glimmered grayish white in the lambent light of the stars and a pale, thin silver moon. Massive and stalwart, the keep had been designed for function, not beauty. It was square, with a tower at each corner for the lookouts. A wall connecting the towers surrounded a structure whose main purpose had probably been to house troops. Large wooden doors, banded with steel, permitted entrance and egress.

But no soldiers had come here in a long, long time. The battlements were crumbling and in some places had completely fallen down. The walls were split by gigantic cracks, perhaps caused by the Cataclysm, perhaps by the supposedly magical battle that had been fought within. One of the towers had collapsed in upon itself, as had the roof of the central building, for they could see the skeletal outline of broken beams show up black against the myriad glistening stars.

"The keep is deserted," said Caramon, staring at it in disgust. "There's no one here, magical or otherwise. I'm surprised those jokers back at the inn didn't send us out here with a bag and tell us to stand in the middle of the path yelling, 'here, snipe!'"

"That will be the task I set for you, my bumbling brother!" Raistlin began to cough, but stifled the sound in his sleeve. "Death's Keep is *not* deserted! I hear voices plainly— or I could if you would silence yours!"

"I, too, hear someone calling out," said Gawain, awed. "A knight of my order is trapped in there, and he shouts for help!" The knight, sword in hand, bolted forward. "I'm coming!" he shouted.

"Me, too!" cried Earwig, leaping in a circle around Raistlin. "I hear voices! I'm positive I hear voices! What are they saying to you? Do you want to know what they're saying to me? 'Another round of ale!' That's what I hear them calling out."

"Wait!" Raistlin reached to grasp the knight, but Gawain was running swiftly toward huge double wooden doors. Once this gate would have been closed, locked fast against any foe. Now it stood ominously open. "He's an imbecile! Go after him, Caramon! Don't let him do anything until I get there!"

"Another round of ale?" Caramon gazed blankly at his brother.

"You blithering dunderhead!" Raistlin hissed through clenched teeth. He pointed a trembling finger at the keep. "I hear a voice calling to *me*, and I recognize it as coming from one of my own kind! It is the voice of a mage! I think I am beginning to understand what is going on. Go after him, Caramon! Knock him down, sit on him if that is all you can do to hold him, but you must prevent Gawain from offering his sword to the knight!"

"Knight? What? Oh, all right, Raist! I'm going. No need to look at me like that. C'mon, Nosepicker."

Earwig's topknot bobbed indignantly. "That's Lock—. Oh, never mind! Hey, wait up!"

Caramon, followed by the jubilant kender, dashed off after the knight, but he was late in starting and Gawain had already rushed headlong into the keep. Reaching the wooden doors, Caramon hesitated before entering and cast an uneasy glance back at his brother.

Raistlin, leaning on his staff, was walking as fast as he could, coughing with nearly every step until it seemed he must drop. Still, he kept going, and he even managed to lift his staff and angrily gesture with it to Caramon, commanding him to enter the keep without delay.

Earwig had already darted inside. Discovering he was alone, he turned around and dashed back. "Aren't you coming? It's wonderfully dark and spooky in here. And you know what?" The kender sighed in ecstasy. "I really am beginning to hear voices. They want me to come and help them fight! Just think of that. Can I borrow your dagger?"

"No!" Caramon snarled. He, too, could hear the voices now. Ghostly voices.

"My cause is just! All know wizards are foul creatures, spawned of darkness. For the pride and honor of our Order of the Sword, join with me!"

"My cause is just! All know the knights hide behind their armor, using their might to bully and threaten those weaker than themselves. For the pride and honor of our Order of the Red Robes, join with me!"

Caramon was beginning to get the uncomfortable feeling that the keep wasn't as deserted as he'd first thought. Reluctantly, wishing his brother were at his side, he entered the keep. The big warrior wasn't afraid of anything in this world that was made of flesh and blood. These eerie voices had a cold, hollow sound that unnerved him. It was as if they were shouting to him from the bottom of a grave.

He and the kender stood in a long passage leading from the outer wall to the inner hall. The corridor was adorned with various defensive mechanisms for dealing with an invading enemy. He could see starlight through arrow slits lining the cracked stone walls. Bereft of his brother's lighted staff and the knight's torch, Caramon was forced to grope his way through the darkness, following the flickering flame shining ahead of him, and he nearly bashed his head on an iron portcullis that had been partially lowered from the ceiling.

"Which side do you want to be on?" Earwig asked eagerly, tugging at Caramon's hand to drag him forward. "I think I'd like to be a knight, but then I've wanted to be a mage, too. I don't suppose your brother would let me borrow his staff—"

"Hush!" ordered Caramon harshly, his voice cracking in his dry throat.

The corridor was coming to an end, opened into a great, wide hall. Sir Gawain was standing right in front of him, holding the torch high and shouting out words in a language the big warrior didn't understand but guessed to be Solamnic.

The clamoring of the voices was louder. Caramon felt them tugging him in both directions. But another voice, a voice within him, was stronger. This voice was his brother's, a voice he loved and trusted, and he remembered what it had said.

You must prevent Gawain from offering his sword to the knight!

"Stay here," he told Earwig firmly, placing his hand on the kender's shoulder. "You promise?"

"I promise," said Earwig, impressed by Caramon's pale and solemn face.

"Good." Turning, Caramon continued down the corridor and came up in back of the knight.

"What's happening?" Earwig writhed with frustration. "I can't see a thing from here. But I promised. I know! He didn't mean me to say *here*, in this one spot. He just meant me to stay here—in the keep!" Happily, the kender crept forward, Caramon's dagger (which he had appropriated) in his hand.

"Oh, my!" breathed Earwig. "Caramon, can you see what I see?"

Caramon could. On one side of the hall, their bodies encased in shining armor, their hands grasping swords, stood a troop of knights. On the other side stood an army of wizards, their robes fluttering around them as if stirred by a hot wind. The knights and the wizards had turned their faces toward the strangers who had entered, and Caramon saw in horror that each one of them was a rotting corpse.

A knight materialized in front of his troops. This knight, too, was dead. The marks of his numerous wounds could be seen plainly on his body. Fear swept over Caramon, and he shrank back against the wall, but the knight paid no attention either to him or the transfixed kender standing by his side. The fixed and staring eyes of the corpse looked straight at Gawain.

"Fellow knight, I call upon you, by the Oath and the Measure, to come to my aid against my enemy."

The dead knight gestured and there appeared, standing some distance from him, a wizard clad in red robes that were torn and stained black with blood. The wizard, too, was dead and had, it seemed from his wounds, died most horribly.

Earwig started forward. "I'll fight on your side if you'll teach me how to cast spells!"

Caramon, catching hold of the kender by the scruff of his neck, lifted him off his feet and tossed him backward. Slamming into the wall, the kender slid down to the floor where he spent an entertaining few moments attempting to breathe. Caramon reached out a shaking hand.

"Gawain, let's get out of—"

The knight thrust Caramon's hand aside and, kneeling on one knee, started to lay his sword at the knight's feet. "I will come to your aid, Sir Knight!"

"Caramon, stop him!" The hissing whisper slid over stone and through shadow. "Stop him or we ourselves are doomed!"

"No!" said the dead knight, his fiery eyes seeming to see Caramon for the first time. "Join my fight! Or are you a coward?"

"Coward!" Caramon glowered. "No man dares call me—"

"Listen to me, my brother!" Raistlin commanded. "For my sake, if for no other or I will be lost, too!"

Caramon cast a fearful look at the dead wizard, saw the mage's empty eyes fixed on Raistlin. The dead knight was leaning down to lift Gawain's sword. Lurching forward on stiff legs, Caramon kicked the weapon with his foot and sent it spinning across the stone floor.

The dead knight howled in rage. Gawain jumped up and ran to retrieve his weapon. Caramon, with a desperate lunge, managed to grab hold of the knight by the shoulders. Gawain whirled around and struck at him with his bare hands. The legion of dead knights clattered their swords against their shields, the wizards raised their hollow voices in a cheer that grew louder when Raistlin entered the room.

"What an interesting experience," said Earwig, feeling to see if any ribs were cracked. Finding himself in one piece, he rose to his feet and looked to see what was going on. "My goodness, someone's lost a sword. I'll just go pick it up."

"Wizard of the Red Robes!" The dead were shouting at Raistlin. "Join us in our fight!"

Caramon caught a glimpse of his brother's face from the corner of his eye. Tense and excited, Raistlin was staring at the wizards, a fierce, eager light in his golden eyes.

"Raist! No!" Caramon lost his hold on Gawain.

The knight clouted him on the jaw, sending the big warrior to the floor, and bounded after the sword, only to find Earwig clutching it tightly, a look of radiant joy on his face that began to fade as the knight approached.

"Oh, no," said the kender firmly, clutching the sword to his bosom. "Finders keepers. You obviously didn't want this anymore."

"Raist! Don't listen to them!" Caramon staggered to his feet. *Too late*, he thought. His brother was walking toward the dead wizard, who was extending a bony hand for the glowing staff.

The chill fingers were nearly touching it when Raistlin suddenly turned the staff horizontally and held it out before him. The crystal's light flared, the dead wizard sprang back from the frail barrier as though it had scalded him.

"I will not join your fight, for it is an eternal fight!" Raistlin raised his voice above the clamoring. "A fight that can never be won."

At this, the dead ceased their calling. A brooding silence descended in the hall. Gawain ceased to threaten the kender and turned around. Earwig, suddenly losing interest in the sword, let it fall to the floor and hopped forward to see what was going on. Caramon rubbed his aching jaw and watched warily, ready to leap to his brother's defense.

Leaning on his staff, whose crystal seemed to shine more brightly in the chill darkness, Raistlin walked forward until he stood in the center of the hall. He looked first at the knight—the rotting, decaying face beneath a battered helm, a bony hand clutching a rusting sword. The young mage turned his golden-eyed gaze to the wizard—red robes, torn and slashed by sword thrusts, covering a body that had for centuries been denied the peace of death.

Then Raistlin, lifting his head, stared up into the darkness. "I would talk with the maiden," he called.

The figure of a young woman materialized out of the night and came to stand before the mage. She was fair-haired and pretty, with an oval face, rich brown hair, and blue eyes that were bright and spirited. So lovely was she, and so warm and seemingly alive, that it took some moments before Caramon realized she was long-since dead.

"*You* are the one who called down the curse, are you not?" asked Raistlin.

"Yes," the maiden answered in a voice cold as the end of the world. "Which side do you choose, mage? Here stands pride"—she gestured toward the knight—"and here stands pride"—she gestured toward the mage. "Which will you choose? Not that it much matters."

"I fight for neither," said Raistlin. "I do not choose pride. I choose," he paused, then said gently, "I choose love."

Darkness crashed down upon them with the weight and force of an avalanche, quenching even the magical light of the staff.

"Wow!" came the awed voice of the kender.

Caramon blinked and peered around, trying to see through the blackness, which was thick and impenetrable as solid stone. The ghostly armies were gone.

"Raistlin?" he called, panicked.

"I am here, my brother. Hush. Keep silent."

Feeling a hand grasp his shoulder, Caramon reached out and touched a warm human arm.

"Gawain?" he whispered.

"Yes," said the knight in strained tones. "What is happening? I don't trust that mage! He'll get us killed."

"So far it seems to me he's done a good job of keeping us alive," said Caramon grimly. "Look!"

"*Shirak*," said Raistlin and the crystal's light beamed brightly. Standing in front of Raistlin, illuminated by his staff, was the young woman.

"You have broken the curse, young mage," said the spirit. "Is there anything you would ask of me before I go to my long-awaited rest?"

"Tell us your story," said Raistlin. "According to the legend, the mage carried you off by force."

"Of course, that is what they have said, who never bothered to seek the truth!" said the spirit scornfully. "And their words were fuel to the fire of my curse. The truth is that the mage and I loved each other. My father, a Knight of Solamnia, forbade me to marry a wizard. He betrothed me to another knight, one whom I did not love. The mage and I ran off together. I left of my own free will to be with the man I loved. The knight followed us and we fled to this place, knowing that it had long been abandoned. The mage and I could have escaped, but he said that, for his honor, he must turn and fight. For his honor," she repeated bitterly. Her blue eyes stared into the shadows of the hall as though she could still see what had transpired there so long before. "Within these walls, he challenged the knight to battle and they fought—one with his sword, the other with his magic. They fought, for their honor!

"And I came to realize as I watched, helpless to prevent their quarrel, that neither loved me nearly so much as each loved his own misbegotten pride.

"When they were dead, I stood over their bodies and prayed to the gods that all men bound up in their own pride should come here and be held enthralled. Then I left this place and went forth into the world. I found a man who loved me truly enough to live for me, not die for me. I was blessed with a rich, full life, surrounded by love. After my death, my spirit returned to this place and has been here since, waiting for one who loved enough to ignore the voices"—her gaze went to Caramon—"and for one wise enough to break the spell.

"And now, young mage, you have freed them and you have freed me. I will go to my rest at the side of my husband who has waited patiently for me throughout the years. But first I would ask one thing of you. How was it that you saw and understood the truth?"

"I could say that I had a shining example of false pride before my eyes," said Raistlin, with a sidelong glance at the knight. Sir Gawain flushed and bowed his head. The mage, smiling slightly, added, "But it would be more truthful to say that it was mostly due to the curiosity of a kender."

"Me!" gasped Earwig, struck by this revelation. "That's me he's talking about! I did it! I lifted the curse! I *told* you it had to be a knight, a mage, *and* a kender!"

The young woman's image began to fade.

"Farewell," said Raistlin. "May your rest be undisturbed."

"Fare you well, young mage. I leave you with a warning. Very nearly you succumbed. Your wits and your will saved you. But unless you change, I foresee a time when this doom you have now avoided will drag you down at last."

The blue eyes closed, and were seen no more.

"Don't go!" wailed Earwig, rushing around and grabbing at the empty air with his hands. "I've got so many questions! Have you been to the Abyss? What's it like being dead? Oh, please . . ."

Caramon came forward cautiously, his eyes on the place where the spirit had been, fearful that she might suddenly burst back to life. His big hand rested on his brother's shoulder.

"Raist," he said worriedly, "what did she mean by that?"

"How should I know?" Raistlin snapped, pulling himself free of his brother's touch. He began to cough violently. "Go find wood to build a fire! Can't you see I'm freezing to death!"

"Sure, Raist," said Caramon gently. "C'mon, Earmite."

"Earwig," said the kender automatically, trudging after the big warrior. "Wait until Cousin Tas hears about this! Not even Uncle Trapspringer—the most famous kender of all time—ever ended a curse!"

Gawain remained standing in silence until Caramon and the kender had left the keep. Then, slowly, sword in hand, he approached the mage.

"I owe you my life," he said grudgingly, awkwardly. "By the Oath and the Measure, I owe you my allegiance." He held the sword—hilt first—out to the mage. "What would you have me do?"

Raistlin drew a shuddering breath. He glanced at the sword and his thin lip twisted. "What would I have you do? Break your Oath. Burn your Measure. As the maiden said, live for those you love. A time of darkness is coming to the world, Sir Knight, and love could well be the only thing that will save us."

The knight's lips tightened, his face flushed. Raistlin stared at him, unmoving, and the expression on Gawain's face altered from anger to one of thoughtful consideration. Abruptly, he slid his sword back into its sheath.

"Oh, and Sir Knight," said Raistlin coolly, "don't forget to give us our share of the reward."

Gawain unbuckled his sword belt and removed it from around his waist. "Take it all," he said, tossing sword and belt at the mage's feet. "I've found something of far greater value." Bowing stiffly, he turned and walked from the keep.

The red moon rose in the sky. Its eerie glow filtered through the crumbling walls of the ancient fortress, lighting the path. The mage remained standing in the empty hall. He could still feel, soft and silky beneath his fingers, the child's hair.

"Yes, Sir Knight, you have," said Raistlin. He stood a moment, thinking of the spirit's words. Then, shrugging, he tightened his grip on the magical staff. "*Dulak*," he said, and the light went out, leaving him to stand in darkness lit only by the rays of the red moon.

Dead on Target

Roger E. Moore

There'd goes!" called a hobgoblin drunkenly in the last red light of evening. "There'd goes! S'goin' away!"

No cloud remained in the darkening sky. The wind picked up around me, the low roar almost drowning out the laughter of the hobgoblin sentries forty feet up the steep hillside at my back. From the sound of things, the two of them had long ago broken into one of the wine casks they'd taken from a farm near the outskirts of Twisting Creek, basking in the natural satisfaction hobgoblins get from killing unarmed farmers—like my cousins, Garayn and Klart.

I licked my lips and felt for the leather waterskin on my belt, preparing to untie it, but found the water was already low. I released it and leaned back against the rock face, keeping my arm close to my side so that the hobgoblins above wouldn't notice the movement in the dim light. My fingers closed over my sword hilt but stayed relaxed. The glow above the plain to the west was almost gone; Lunitari was a low, red crescent on the horizon, the only moon visible. Far overhead, the pantheon of gods was played out in the brightening stars. It was beautiful, but I could tell there'd be rain by tomorrow night. Scouts know these things.

"S'all gone!" called the hobgoblin again. "N'more sun!"

Several distant shouts came back, all curses in the coarse hobgoblins' tongue. "You basdards wanned me d'be a lookoud, and I'm looking oud!" the hobgoblin roared back

---

hotly, then laughed again. He sounded as if he had a broken nose. "Bedder look oud for th' sdars! They're coming da ged ya!"

I'd gotten here only an hour ago but had already heard enough. About a dozen hobgoblins were camped out on this hilltop, near Solanthus's eastern border. Twisting Creek was two days to the southwest. On the other side of the low hills to the east, beyond the Garetmar River, was unclaimed territory populated by bandits, deserters, and hobgoblin garbage.

A hobgoblin snickered, then drunkenly mumbled a phrase that the wind carried away. Soon, both sentries would be dead to the world. They had nothing to fear that they knew of. They had been clever enough to raid light and avoid attracting too much unfavorable attention from Twisting Creek's militia. Hit fast, grab loot, and run—the same old formula. The hobgoblins had burned a few barns, killed some horses, and stolen some odds and ends before scurrying off. They didn't want a fight. They just wanted to rub it in that they were around.

I was Evredd Kaan: dark hair, dark eyes, good physique, ex-scout. I'd been out of the army since Neraka fell and my unit was disbanded. After that, I'd gone home to the city of Solanthus to find it mostly in ruins. I worked for a year on labor crews, shoveling ashes, rubble, and bones, sometimes taking night shift as a militiaman in a city overrun with beggars who stole to survive. Finally, I just quit and headed east for Twisting Creek, where my parents had lived years ago before fever took them. I worked on my uncle's farm and maintained the wagons for his trading business, which suffered more than a bit with the obnoxious hobgoblins around.

Three nights ago, the hobgoblins killed their first humans. Laughing Garayn and brooding Klart had been walking back from an evening in town when they were shot dead with crossbows. A hobgoblin dagger was found in one of the bodies. I watched as my neighbors wrapped my cousins for burial, then I went to my uncle and said I would be leaving for a few days.

"Family business," I said.

"Don't do anything foolish, my boy," my uncle urged. He was a big man with a pouchy face, hook nose, and receding hairline. Twisting Creek had been lucky enough not to be sacked and burned during the War of the Lance, ended just two years ago, and my uncle's business had survived. But now his two sons had been taken away from him, his life permanently scarred by the bad elements still roaming the land. "You're all I got left, Evredd."

"What I do," I said tersely, "won't be foolish."

His eyes glazed over. His hands moved around the valuables on his desk, touching them reassuringly. Tears squeezed from his eyes.

"There's been killing enough," my uncle pleaded. "Let it go."

Needless to say, I didn't listen to him. My uncle had been absorbed in his business lately, locking himself in his study with his ledgers and cursing the hobgoblins' effect on trade, and now this. He seemed like a destroyed man.

I left town at dawn, taking food, my sword, and little else. I knew where part of the hobgoblins' old trails usually went, so I followed that course until a regular path appeared, six miles outside of town. The tracks stood out as if they had been laid down by a small army instead of a few raiders loaded down with loot. Two days later, I was here.

One of the hobgoblins above me belched like a giant frog croaking, then dropped a metallic cup and cursed. "S'my damn drink!" he moaned. "S'all spilled!"

The other sentry cleared his throat and spat. "There's yer drink," he said, sniggering. "Put it in yer cup."

"I'll give ya somethin' for *yer* cup," muttered the first, and a rock sailed off the top of the hill, over my head and about sixty feet past me. I kept quiet in case one went to look off the cliff. Hobgoblins are a fun-loving race when it comes to humans. They would have lots of fun with me, good hobgoblin fun, with whips, knives, hot irons— the works.

Another rock flew overhead, landing in the grass beyond.

"Throw one more, and ol' Garith'll set yer dumb ass on fire," said a hobgoblin testily.

"Ya godda find 'im, firs'," retorted the other. "S'nod comin' back. Gonna live like a huuu-man now. Thinks 'e's so good."

"He's comin' back," snapped the first. "Didn't I tell him we wouldn't wait long 'fore we began to tear things up? He knows we'll cause trouble. Little toad-belly knows we want action. We got to keep movin', not sittin' on ass-bruises. And you put that rock down or I'll give you a face that would scare a blind dwarf."

After several more minutes of arguing, the hobgoblins settled down in wine-sodden silence. I decided to move out again in a bit when the sentries were either dozing or too groggy from drink and lack of sleep to notice. Then I'd take them, one by one, the way I'd learned to during the war. Only the crickets could be heard in the darkness. I sighed, waiting, fingers on my sword hilt.

Something punched my chest. Pain shot through my left lung, hurting far worse than anything that had ever happened to me at Neraka. I looked down, my hands involuntarily going for the source of the pain, and saw a short, feathered shaft sticking out of my leather surcoat, next to my heart. I could tell the arrow had gone right through me. I was never more surprised to see anything in my life.

Son of a bitch, I thought, desperately trying not to breathe or scream. They'd found me; the hobgoblins had found me. But how in the Abyss did they do that? I never heard them coming. I stood there like an idiot, looking down at the arrow shaft and wondering why the hobgoblins weren't now calling out in alarm. The shock and pain of being hit was too much to take. I couldn't think.

Something prickly and cold spread through my bloodstream from the wound. The pain ceased and became a cloud of nothingness, as if my chest had disappeared. My will broke then and I tried to scream, but I couldn't inhale. It seemed like a huge weight pressed against my rib cage, keeping out the air. I slumped back against the rock face, my vision swimming, my hands clutching the wound.

It came to me then that I was going to die. There was nothing I could do. I didn't want to die, not then, not ever. I wanted to go home. I wanted to breathe. I wanted to live. For a moment I thought of Garayn and Klart. I could almost see their faces before me.

The numbness reached my head. Everything became very light and airy. I felt a rushing sensation, as if I were falling.

This wasn't right, came a mad thought. The hobgoblins killed me. They'd killed my cousins, and now they'd killed me. It wasn't right, and I wanted them to pay for it in the worst way.

That was my last mortal thought.

*   *   *   *   *

I was having the worst of all nightmares, worse than the red dreams I'd once had of Neraka. I dreamed I was dead and buried. Ice-cold rain fell without end on me, trickling down on lifeless flesh. My body was dead-numb, my limbs chained down. I was hollow, a shell of nothing in the earth. I fought to wake up or even move a muscle. I begged the great gods of Krynn to let me wake up.

No one heard me.

I begged them for mercy. I pleaded for justice.

No voice spoke in the darkness.

Then I cursed them, I cursed the gods, and I cried for revenge.

I became aware of a colorless light. Without thinking, I opened my eyes, my lips still moving.

Gray clouds rolled swiftly above me, ragged-edged. Cold droplets slapped my face and fell into my unblinking eyes. I couldn't move my limbs. I felt nothing, nothing at all but the cold, and I listened to the drumming of the rain against and around me.

The gray clouds rolled on for ages. The rain fell. Then a weight seemed to fall away, and I knew I could sit up.

Very slowly, I rolled onto my side and pushed myself upright. Every movement was unbalanced, and I swayed dizzily until I braced myself with my arms. The tilting scenery settled in my vision, and I looked around.

The landscape appeared odd in the rain-washed light, but I was still at the foot of the rocky cliff. It was late in the evening now. I didn't know the day. The long grass of the plain had been beaten down by rain some time ago. A light wind blew across the field, rippling the bent and broken stalks.

I sat there stupidly for a long time, then looked down at myself.

The butt of an arrow was projecting from my chest. After a few moments, I remembered how it got there, and thought I was lucky that it hadn't killed me.

Then, of course, I knew the truth.

I stared at the arrow for a long time. The rain eventually slowed. All was quiet except for the cawing of distant crows. I wasn't afraid, only dully surprised. No heartbeat sounded within me, no blood ran from my wound. I felt surprised, but nothing more.

I hated looking at the arrow in me. It wasn't right. It ought to come out. Carefully, I reached up and touched it, then tapped it hard. There was no pain, only a sense of its presence. I reached up and carefully tugged on the shaft. It didn't budge. Then I took it in both hands and broke off the arrow at the point where it entered my chest, having it in mind not to open the wound any further. I felt a need to keep my body looking as good as possible. Self-respect, maybe.

That done, I reached behind me with one hand to find that the arrow point stuck out of my back by an inch or two, between two ribs. After some difficulty in getting a proper grip, I slowly pulled the arrow out, then held both pieces of it before me.

The arrow was shorter than I'd expected; the arrowhead was small and grooved. It was actually a crossbow bolt, not a longbow arrow—a well-made bolt, too; dwarven-make. Doubtless the hobgoblins had been picking up good weaponry on their raids.

I rolled to my knees, then staggered to my feet and looked myself over. I was filthy with mud. My sword scabbard was empty, my boots were gone, my food pouch was untied, and my waterskin had been cut loose. I knew that my pouch had been tied before I had been killed. My murderer must have checked me for loot. I had done it myself at Neraka, searching dead hobgoblins after the battles. I hadn't brought anything with me but a few odds and ends. I opened the pouch flap and found it was empty now. I looked down at my feet and saw my food in the mud and water. None of the food had been eaten; all was ruined. The boots and waterskin lay further away, slashed open. The sword was nowhere around, but the killer had undoubtedly taken it, probably discarded it later. It was cheaply made. My murderer was thorough.

I tossed the pieces of the bolt to the ground. I looked at my arms as I did so and realized that, for a dead person, I didn't look half bad. My skin was very pale, almost dull white. My hands and arms looked thinner than I'd remembered, more bony and less puffy and full. My trousers, boots, and surcoat were muddy and soaking wet, and my surcoat was also badly stained with what had to be blood. I must not have been dead for very long, maybe only a day or two.

I couldn't see my own face, of course. For that small blessing I felt curiously grateful. I touched my short beard and mustache, wiped them as free of dirt as I could, then adjusted my leather surcoat and brushed at the small hole in the front as if I had just spilled food there. My long, thin fingers were like icicles, but the cold was almost comfortable.

A stick snapped, the sound coming from somewhere beyond the edge of the cliff above me. I looked up, saw no faces, only clouds and rain.

Damn hobgoblins had probably forgotten about me, left me here for animals to feed on. Maybe they were still drunk.

Maybe I should find out.

I examined the cliff face. It was weathered and old, full of cracks and plant roots. It was worth a try. Wedging my bone-thin fingers into a vertical split in the rock, I found a foothold and began the ascent.

It took time to go up the cliff, but I didn't mind the climb. I felt no pain at all. I wondered what the hobgoblins would do when they saw me. I couldn't wait to find out. I had no sword, but I had my bare hands, and I was already dead.

Just below the top, I hesitated listening. Someone was

moving around up there; metal clinked, maybe chain armor. I had no fear of their weapons now, but I wanted surprise. I rocked slightly, then pulled myself up swiftly and quietly over the ledge.

At my feet in the tall wet grass lay a heavy-bodied figure, his misshapen head buried face-down in mud and brown water. A thick wolf pelt covered his shoulders and back. One gray-green hand was thrust forward, fingers digging into the wet ground. The hobgoblin looked as if he'd tripped over something while walking toward the cliff but had never gotten up. He wasn't going to get up, either. The crossbow bolt projecting from the back of his thick neck tipped me off. So did the hungry aura of black flies whirling around him.

He certainly hadn't been the one who snapped that stick I'd heard. Then, I saw who did. About twenty-five feet from me was a dwarf in an oilskin cloak. His back was to me. He bent over another fallen hobgoblin, his chain mail links clinked under the cloak. The dwarf straightened. He carried a bright, spike-backed war axe clutched in a leather-gloved fist. Then, looking around warily, he turned in my direction, revealing a wet and tangled brown beard, thick dark eyebrows, and small black eyes that widened violently when he saw me.

"Reorx!" the dwarf gasped. He swung the spike-backed axe in his right hand, his left arm coming up to block me if I rushed him. He took a half-crouch, feet set in a stance that could shift him in any direction. Another veteran of the war.

I raised my hands—palms out, fingers spread—and shook my head slowly. The dwarf didn't take the hint, still readied for an attack. The sight of him clutching that polished axe struck me as amusing, but I didn't smile.

I moved sideways to get away from the ledge, having none of the unsteadiness I'd felt earlier. The dwarf rotated to keep facing me.

I moved my lips to say something to him, but nothing came out. It took a moment to figure out why; then I drew a breath to fill my lungs. Part of my rib cage expanded, but there was an unpleasant sucking sound from my sternum

and the sensation that the left side of my chest was not filling. I quickly reached up and placed my right hand inside
the neckline of my surcoat to cover the bolt wound. I tried
again.

"Don't worry," I said—and was startled to hear my own
voice. It was burned hoarse, as if I had swallowed acid. I
forced another breath in. "I won't hurt you," I finished with
a gasp.

The dwarf gulped, never taking his eyes off me. A muscle
twitched in his left cheek. "'Preciate the thought," he muttered. "I'll keep it in mind."

I was curious about the dead hobgoblins. I gave the
dwarf an unconcerned shrug before kneeling to examine
one of the fly-covered bodies. As I'd suspected, the bolt
head projecting from the hobgoblin's neck was exactly the
same type as the one that had hit me. I let my right hand
drop from inside my shirt and reached out to examine the
dirtied tip.

I quickly pulled my hand back. A strand of black tar
clung to the bolt head, worked into some of the grooves. I
had seen that stuff before, at Neraka. Black wax, my commander had called it. Deadly poison. A handful of the
Nerakan humans had used it on their weapons, their idea of
a special welcome for us. The gods only knew where they
had gotten it; the Nerakans themselves hadn't known how
to handle it. We would regularly find their bodies, snuggled
into ambush points, with little spots of black wax on their
careless lips or fingers.

I remembered the sensation of nothingness spreading inside me as I died, the bolt through my chest. I'd been the
first that night to feel the poison's kiss. I figured my cousins
must have felt it earlier still. Too bad I hadn't thought to
examine their bodies.

I leaned over to continue checking the hobgoblin, who
had probably outweighed me by a hundred pounds in life.
He was a thick-necked brute; his clothes and armor were as
dirty as his skin. Knife slashes had opened up his belt
pouch, now empty, and the sides of his armor and boots.
He was also missing his left ear. It appeared to have been cut
cleanly away, below his helmet line.

I looked up at the dwarf, who hadn't moved, remembering to put my hand inside my shirt before I spoke. "What about him?" I asked hoarsely, pointing a clawlike finger at the dead hobgoblin behind him. I sounded like an animal learning to talk.

The dwarf eased up, but only by a hair. He stepped away from the body behind him, clearing my view. This hobgoblin lay face up, an arm flopped down beside an empty wine cask in the grass beside him. He'd been stabbed through the darkened leather armor over his abdomen. A second stab wound, blue-black now, was visible in his throat. His left ear was missing, too, cleanly cut away. He had not even gotten up; he had died sitting, then had fallen back.

I reached up and felt my own ears. Both were still intact.

"Maybe you could tell me a bit about what you want." The dwarf's voice was steady and low, his axe arm still raised for a strike or a throw.

I looked beyond the dwarf at the half-forested hilltop. No one else was around. "Looking for someone," I said finally.

This didn't answer everything, but the dwarf let it go for now. "Got a name?" he asked.

"Evredd," I said, the word sounding like a mumble. I covered the wound and said it again, more clearly.

The dwarf's flint-black gaze went to my chest. "You a dead boy, ain't you?" he said.

I found it hard to answer that. It wasn't something I wanted to face.

"You a rev'nant, I bet," the dwarf went on, knowingly. "Been dead a bit, I can tell. I seen dead boys before, but not walkin' ones like you. You a rev'nant, come back to get your killer man. That right?"

He was talkative for a dwarf. "Who did this?" I asked him, indicating the bodies.

The dwarf looked at me a while longer, then glanced around, one eye still on me. The sky was darkening with the coming sunset, but the rain had stopped. Behind the dwarf by a couple hundred feet, in a tree line, was an irregular outcropping of rock, overgrown with vines. A wide gully or eroded road ran out of the woods and undergrowth, then off along the top of the cliff toward the south.

"Can't say," said the dwarf, looking back at me, then down at the bodies. "Just got here myself." Rainwater dripped from the axe blade.

I stood up. The dwarf fell back, his face tight, and raised his axe arm.

"No," I said, but it came out as a gasp. I put my hand inside my shirt. "No," I repeated. "How long . . . What day is this?"

"Sixteenth," he said, his eyes narrowing again.

I'd been dead for a day, then. The hobgoblins had hit on the twelfth, and I'd left on the next day. "Are more . . . people with you?" It was hard to get the words out in one breath. I'd need lots of practice at this.

The dwarf hesitated. "Just me," he said. The dwarf grinned nervously and adjusted the grip on his axe. "I didn't make you a dead boy, and if you a rev'nant, you ain't gonna attack me, I reckon. You save that for your killer."

I had no urge to bother the dwarf if he didn't bother me, so I guess he had a point. I scanned the ground for any clues to the identity of my murderer. The dwarf stayed back, but soon got up the nerve to examine the stabbed hobgoblin again, checking for valuables with one eye locked tight on me.

The heavy rain had destroyed virtually all the clues there were—tracks, crushed grass, everything. For all that, I could still put together a few things about my killer. He had used a crossbow, probably a dwarven one. He knew about weapon poison. He could probably climb cliffs; he must have gone right up this one after killing me, then hit the hobgoblins. They'd been drunk and tired, but the lack of other bodies indicated that he'd moved with considerable speed, killing them before they could shout warnings, even to each other.

But if he'd killed hobgoblins, why had he also killed me? He must have known I was after them, myself. And if he could see well enough to shoot me this accurately, he couldn't have mistaken me for hobgoblin scum. I pondered for a minute, then looked off the cliff. I could still see a man-shaped impression in the muddy ground below, where

I had fallen. I scanned the field out to the horizon. About fifty feet to the west, away from the cliff base where I'd been shot, was a small dead tree with a briar bush cloaking the base of its trunk. I'd had my back to the cliff, facing west. The killer could well have been hiding out there somewhere in the darkness when he caught sight of me.

Yes, my killer was a damn good shot.

Maybe he could see in the dark, too.

"You know," said the dwarf casually, "hobs don't go in twos. Must be more dead 'uns somewhere here. Otherwise, we'd be covered in arrow stings 'bout now. Maybe we better look around."

The dwarf got to his feet. I'd almost forgotten he was there. Dwarves, I remembered, could see heat sources in the dark. So could elves and maybe wizards. Wizards couldn't use crossbows, though, and the elves I'd known in the war had universally despised them. Dwarves liked them.

"Hey," said the dwarf, waving his free hand, the other clenching the thick axe handle. "You deaf as well as dead?"

I shook my head, not wanting to talk much. "More of them?" I asked with one breath, indicating the nearest body.

The dwarf glanced back at the tree line. "Fort's back there," he said. "Old one. Bet we find 'em there."

I nodded, seeing now that the "outcropping" was really a half-collapsed wall. The distant shouts I'd heard the other hobgoblins give last night must have come from there.

The dwarf gave me a final look over. "Name's Orun," he said. He didn't put out his hand to clench my arm, as was the custom of most dwarves I'd known from these parts.

I nodded in return, then pointed in the direction of the fort. We left the bodies and started off. Orun made sure to keep a good two dozen feet between us. He was cautious, but he seemed to take to my presence. Either he had nothing against a walking corpse or else he was crazy.

But then I was dead, so I was no one to talk.

*   *   *   *   *

The fort in the trees was probably a relic from the times of the Cataclysm. Rough stone walls, the wooden double gate, a short stone-based tower to the left—all fallen into rot and ruin.

This place came with a third hobgoblin, lying facedown in the open gateway. The butt and fletching of yet another crossbow bolt was visible just under his leather armor; he'd fallen on it and broken the shaft after it had struck him. Humming flies circled over him, many feeding where his left ear had been. His arms were caught under him. He'd grabbed at the shaft, just as I had done. His sword was still nestled in its scabbard at his side. Another surprised customer.

Through the open gateway, we could see the fort's overgrown main yard, small when it was new but more so now with the bushes and trees thick in it. On the other side of the roughly square yard was the barracks building, its stone walls and part of its roof still standing. To the right, against a wall, was a low building that had probably been the stables. The tower to the left was mostly rubble. All was quiet except for the flies.

Orun glanced at me, then carefully leaned over the fallen hobgoblin and took hold of its rigid face with his free hand. Thick fingers poked at a gray cheek, then tugged down an eyelid to reveal a white eyeball.

"Dead 'bout a day," he muttered. He squinted up at me, then glanced around the fort's yard. "Think we're alone here," he added, matter-of-factly.

I nodded and went on through the gateway, the dwarf coming behind me.

The yard was largely covered with tall grass and thorn bushes. Trees stretched skyward by the stone walls. Someone, probably the hobgoblins, had partially covered the damaged barracks roof with animal hides. Pathways had been recently beaten through the tall grass, linking the barracks with the main gate. The stables to the right had their original roof and appeared more habitable than the other structures. The hobgoblins could stay safe and dry within the stables, firing through arrow slits at all intruders.

Intruders like us.

A squirrel ran lightly over the stable roof, stopped when it saw us, and watched with curiosity. It fled when I stared at it for too long.

"Bet you a steel," Orun said, pointing his axe at the barracks, "the rest of 'em's in there. Maybe your killer whatever's in there, too. Better go look."

We moved closer, Orun generously letting me lead. Dark shapes lay on the floor beyond the open barracks doorway. The dwarf stopped about thirty feet back from the single stone step, axe ready, watching both me and the doorway. He was no fool.

I hesitated only a moment before I mounted the step and went inside. The buzzing of insects filled my ears in the darkness. Weak light filtered in from the doorway and through holes in the makeshift roof. Water dripped constantly from above, splashing across the room.

As I looked around, I was glad to be dead. Not that the sight of bloated bodies affected me any longer as it once had on the bloody plains of Neraka. It was mere scenery now, shadows that held no terror. No one screamed, no one cried, nothing hurt. Everywhere I looked inside were bodies, and everywhere were black flies and crawling things at a morbid feast, carpeting the discolored, twisted bodies of the hobgoblin dead.

I counted eight bodies. Five clutched at their throats or faces. The rest gaped at the ceiling with bulging eyes and open, soundless mouths, their rigid arms grabbing at their chests or locked open in grasping gestures. It was hard to tell what they had been doing, but not one had made a move for his weapon. All swords were sheathed or leaning against the walls.

I looked around the room. There was a door to the right, apparently leading to the stables. The wood was gray with age and appeared ready to fall apart. It opened with ease.

Beyond the doorway it was very dark. I walked carefully to avoid stumbling over bodies that might be in the way. I didn't find any until I got into the stables themselves.

The hobgoblins had apparently cleaned up the stables and made them into a tidy home. Gray light leaked in from small holes in the ceiling and outer walls. The interior walls had long ago rotted away, but the hobgoblins had shoveled the debris with great efficiency. An ash-filled circle of stones served as a seat by a fire pit. A large mass of rotting cloth, half covering a pile of dry leaves, appeared to make up a bed. It was sufficient, if not cozy.

The body near the fire pit was the room's only occupant. I knelt down by it and took a long look. In life, it would have been the biggest hobgoblin I could have ever imagined—a head and a half taller than me. Even in the near darkness, I could still see a massive burned spot across the front of his hide armor. I'd seen its like only once before, when storm lightning had killed one of my uncle's horses in its pasture.

I looked up. The stables' roof was solid.

On impulse, I got up and walked over to the bed, searching the rags until I found a suitably long strip of cloth. This I wrapped around my chest with a bunched-up rag covering the bolt wound, then tied it off. I tried a few words and discovered that I could speak almost normally now, though I still sounded as if I had rocks in my throat instead of vocal cords.

"Thought I heard you talkin' to yourself," Orun muttered when I came outside. He'd moved closer to the barracks doorway, but the stench was obviously getting to him. He held his nose until he was away from it. "Any ideas what happened to our hob buddies?" He indicated the doorway with the axe.

I shook my head. The dwarf frowned and looked around. "What did for 'em?" he asked absently, then turned back to me. "There anyone else in there 'sides hobs?"

I shook my head no.

"No sign o' another dwarf, maybe? Kinda white-lookin' one, real ugly?"

Again, I shook my head, but more slowly. "Why?"

Orun looked away at the fort and mumbled something that I didn't catch.

"Sewer?" I repeated.

"No," he said in disgust, setting his axe down to rub his hands together. "Damn that runt. Theiwar."

The name was familiar. It had to do with a race of dwarves, I recalled. "Theiwar?"

"Jackals," he said thickly. "All of 'em are. Call 'emselves

true dwarves, but no relation I ever heard of. Some of 'em throw spells, the tougher ones do. Never let a Theiwar get behind you 'less he's already dead, and then you'd still better think about it. Born for evil, all of 'em."

A dwarf that threw spells? I'd never heard of such a thing, but I was beyond the point of disbelieving almost anything now that I was dead. "What kind of spells?" I asked.

"Oh," he said, "all sorts. Some of 'em's killer-type spells. Poison-gas spell's one of 'em. Could be what did for our hob buddies in there." He indicated the barracks. "Don't know what all they can do."

"You're hunting a Theiwar?"

Orun grinned self-consciously. "Funny you ask. Am at that." He looked up at me. "Bounty hunter. Come from Kaolyn. You know Kaolyn? Nice place."

Kaolyn was a respectable dwarven mountain kingdom, about eighty miles southwest of Twisting Creek. "Why hunt a Theiwar?"

He stroked his damp beard. "Traitor to Kaolyn. Supposed to've been spyin' on the draconians and hobs for us, chiselin' out a few when he could. Some Theiwar'll help you for the love of steel in their hands; some'll help you for the love of killin'. We put 'em to use." He sighed. "Gotta be done. War is war."

"What happened?"

Orun snorted. "Loved the killin' part too much, that one. Wanted more for 'imself. Sold out to the Blue Dragonarmy, east of here, and got to spyin' on us instead. We caught on and went after 'im. Got away with a band of hobs, and I bet these are them. Same armor, same tribal markin's." He reached up and rubbed his eyes with his broad fingers. "Don't know if he was the one who did for his own band, or why. Been the Dark Queen's own spawn to catch, that's for sure. Got real good with them 'lusions, changing his looks and all." He glanced down at his spike-backed axe, lying against his leg, then picked it up and hefted it, feeling its weight. "Sure was lookin' forward to meetin' 'im."

"What was his name?"

"The Theiwar? Garith. No last name."

My curiosity was aflame. Could it have been the same Garith I'd heard the hobgoblins talking about? I was on the verge of asking more when everything inside my head changed.

The sun had just set. The darkness had diminished perceptibly within the last few moments, but I knew on an even deeper level that the sun had gone. Something inside me woke up. It was like seeing and hearing after being born without eyes or ears. It was as if I knew everything now, everything that really mattered.

"Evredd?" Orun called as I left the fort. "Evredd!" I heard him swear loudly, then hurry after me with a hard-thumping gait.

I went to the edge of the cliff overlooking the place where I had been killed. There, past the bodies of the two hobgoblins, I stopped and gazed out to the southwest. Strength gathered in my limbs. My hands began to itch, and my fingers curled and uncurled uncontrollably.

All of a sudden I knew: I needed to head southwest as quickly as I could.

"Damn, you move fast for a dead boy," huffed Orun as he stopped behind me about twenty feet back. "You on to somethin', ain't you? I hear if you a rev'nant, you can smell your killer in the dark. You smell your boy out there?"

I turned and looked back at the dwarf. Another hand or two might be useful for what was coming.

"Follow me," I said, and started for the trail. I kept my stride slow so that Orun could keep up, but even then he had to jog. He followed and peppered me with questions that I ignored, then swore outrageously in frustration.

Ahead of me, miles away in the falling darkness, I sensed a presence moving. It wasn't really smell, and my night-awakened senses couldn't tell me who my killer was, but I knew *where* he was, exactly where.

If I hurried, maybe he and I could chat.

*　　*　　*　　*　　*

We walked for the entire night over lightly forested plains and across shallow streams. Orun kept up the pace beside me until he puffed like a horse, his chain-mail armor jingling rapidly as he moved. "Tired yet?" he asked once, but I never responded. The killer was ahead of us by a long distance.

"Doing okay myself," Orun said, sometime later. "Did this durin' the war. Marched two days once and never stopped." His words were almost lost as his breath gave out for a moment. "Fought an army o' hobs with my brothers right after that. Whipped 'em in one hour. Ran 'em right off into a canyon. Good day, you bet."

I said nothing. I was straining to see what else I could detect about my killer. I let my mind be open to everything.

"Like I said, I'm from Kaolyn," Orun went on, between his panting. "You know Kaolyn—up in the Garnets, nice place. I tell you that? Came out to see the world and fight in the war, been here and there ever since. You been to Kaolyn? Gotta see it sometime." I heard Orun pull free of a briar that caught his cloak. His armor clinked like a background song. "Real pretty in the spring."

The dwarf was silent before he asked, in a different tone, "Smell your killer man?"

I said nothing.

"Too damn nosy, that's me," he said with a sigh as he trotted along. "That's what they always said back at Kaolyn. Too damn nosy. I—"

"Yes," I told him, watching the dark fields ahead.

"Oh," Orun said, now haughty. "Well, now, I'm hardly as nosy as some people."

"Yes," I repeated, louder and more distinctly, "I can *see* my killer."

"Oh," Orun grunted, then said, "was told you smelled 'im." We traveled in silence for hours after that.

As the horizon in the east grew brighter, something began to slip out of my head. The clarity of mind I'd felt before ebbed away, and my sense of my killer's whereabouts grew elusive, foggy.

"Gettin' tired?" Orun asked, shortly before dawn. The sky was still overcast, and no rain had fallen.

"Tired?" Orun repeated a little later. I turned and saw rivers of sweat dripping from his face and beard.

"No," I said, not stopping. I could continue at this pace forever, but I'd noticed that my prey was slowing down. Was he tired already? He'd soon regret every pause for breath. "You?" I asked, wondering if Orun would make it.

"Haven't died yet," he said, then coughed and grew quiet for several minutes in embarrassment. He had eased the distance between us down to six feet during the night; he didn't increase it again. He seemed to be getting quite used to me.

The killer I was tracking continued to slow down as the cloud-hidden dawn approached. When the sun arose behind the thick morning clouds, my inner sense of the killer's location faded within moments. Some of my supernatural energy seemed to dissipate as well, but I was able to keep moving at a steady walking pace. Maybe the energy loss at dawn was part of being a revenant. Maybe I drew some of my sustenance from darkness. Since this was my first morning as a dead man, perhaps my ignorance could be forgiven.

By now I knew where the killer was headed. I knew the way to Twisting Creek blindfolded, having hunted across these plains only months before. It was nearly noon when we crossed an abandoned cart road and entered a small forest, beyond which lay the ruins of a pre-Cataclysm farmhouse. Only the stone foundation remained of the structure, and young trees lifted their branches where ground-floor rooms had once been. A brook ran through the trees nearby.

"Whoa," Orun huffed. "Hold there. Stop for a bit." He slowed down, dropping behind me. "Lemme rest."

I stopped, though I felt a powerful urge to continue on and catch up with my killer. I raised a thin hand and waved at the forest and ruins. "Rest," I croaked.

Orun grunted his thanks and wandered down to some trees for privacy, then went to the stream bank and placed his polished axe with care on a fallen log. Dust covered his face and clothing, and he was streaked and splattered with his own sweat. He set his helmet aside as he knelt at the stream, then bent over and splashed water on his head. After taking a long drink and rinsing off, he settled back on the bank, rubbing his knees.

Only the brook spoke for a long time. I thought about the

dead hobgoblins, my cousins, and myself. I wondered who had killed us all, and why.

I studied Orun then. He had leaned back against the fallen log on which his precious axe rested, his stumpy legs stretched out. His dark wet beard was as tangled and chaotic as a mop.

"Tell me about Theiwar," I said.

Orun glanced over in surprise. "Like what?"

"Everything," I said.

Orun shrugged. "Know anything at all 'bout 'em?"

"No."

"Mmm," he said. He looked down, chewing his lips. "Theiwar. They're sorta like dwarves, but not normal. Not at all like true dwarves. They're uglier, o' course. You heard me say they throw spells, and they do that. But they're weaker. Sunlight makes 'em puke; can't stand it at all. Have to hide in the day or else wrap 'emselves up in black. Inbreedin' does it."

He paused for thought. "Not ugly only on the outside, either. They're cowards, thieves, murderers. Those're their good points." He smiled only briefly. "They're like a bad relative. You got a distant cousin you hate. He cheats, lies, steals, thinks he owns the world. He's still family, 'long as he obeys the rules o' the house. Follow me so far?"

I nodded and thought about the hobgoblins. "They collect trophies?"

"Sure do. Ears they like—easier to cut off than fingers. Save 'em up, show 'em to their friends. Use 'em to prove their kills. Eat 'em later, maybe. Don't know, don't want to know." He stroked his shaggy beard.

"Theiwar use crossbows?" It was a long-overdue question.

"Sure," he said. He got to his feet, dusting off his trousers and cloak. "Got all sorts o' funny weapons, but they do like them crossbows."

It made sense that a Theiwar might have been my murderer. I knew a dwarf could see enough well in darkness. The Theiwar could have gone right up the cliff after killing me to do in the hobgoblin lookouts, then the rest of them. But why would a Theiwar kill me? Did he or the hobgoblins kill my cousins? Why would he kill his own allies? It made no sense.

Orun stomped his feet, then looked at the forest and ruins. He glanced back at his axe, still on the log, then shrugged and spat.

"Never thought I'd see a rev'nant, or talk to one," he stated, adjusting his cloak. "One of my old kin, great uncle, he was one. Lemishite killed 'im out in a field, took his steel. Broan came back, blood still on 'im, and called for aid. Two of my kin went with 'im. Found the Lemishite halfway back to his home. My kin came back, but not Broan. Kin never spoke of it much. Hundred, hundred ten years ago."

He rubbed at his throat. "Seen others who came back, but not like you. Walkin' dead, mindless. Black Robe wizards like 'em. Had one pass through Kaolyn once. Didn't let 'im stop. Had a bunch of dead helpers." Orun's face twisted with disgust at the memory. "Wizards," he sighed.

"Did you know this Garith?" I asked.

A muscle twitched in Orun's left cheek, pulling on the side of his mouth. He looked toward the road, remembering. "Was his contact with Kaolyn, kind o' to keep an eye on 'im. Supposed to have known what he was doing when he was killin' our people off, but he got by me." The dwarf grunted, pulling the cloak tightly around his shoulders. "Almost did for me, too, but I was lucky. Damn lucky."

I eyed him for a few moments. "You want him."

Orun was silent for a moment more, then slowly turned around and grinned at me in a dark way, almost shyly. "Sure do," he said, eyes like arrow slits in a fortress. "Want 'im bad. He killed some good friends o' mine. My fault, really. I know how y'feel. You want to get your claws 'round his scrawny neck and squeeze his life out, make 'im feel what you felt. That right?"

I said nothing.

He grinned more broadly. "Well, you miss 'im, and I'll finish it for you. Lookin' forward to it. Our boy's been a busy little runt, killin' everything he can find. Got it in for everyone, like the rest o' 'is folk. Thinks he's a bad boy. But he won't like seein' you and me together."

"Why aren't *you* afraid of me?" I asked.

The dwarf looked me over in silence, then snorted as if he'd heard a bad joke. "You want me to be afraid there, dead boy? I'll tell you somethin'. In the war, my commander got 'imself killed by a draconian, sivak type. They're the big silver ones what change their shapes when they kill someone, so they look like what they just killed. You heard 'bout 'em?"

I remembered sivaks very well from the war. "Yes."

"I saw the killin', but I wasn't in a way to do anythin' 'bout it right then and there. Had to travel with 'im for two days, pretendin' he was my friend, all the time knowin' he was gonna turn on me and my buddies and kill us off or take us to an ambush. Got some help in time, though, and we cut that reptile boy down to gully dwarf meat. You may be a dead boy, but after that sivak, nothin' much ever gets to me."

The dwarf clapped his hands together, then went to get his axe. "'Sides, like I said, you probably leadin' me right to Garith. Gonna be like a family reunion." He lifted the axe to gaze down the blade. "I been dyin' to see the boy. Like as not, he'll be dyin' too—after he sees me."

*　*　*　*　*

Evening came at last. We stopped once more for Orun to rest, then moved on as the sun went down. I told Orun about my cousins, my uncle, my life, and my death. He walked silently as he listened, asking few questions. I talked until I knew of nothing more to say.

At dusk, my awareness of my murderer's location arose in my consciousness as comfortably as if it had never left. He was still heading for Twisting Creek, but we were much closer to him now. He'd make it to town before morning, but we'd not be far behind him. His speed picked up as the evening deepened, and so did mine—and I was faster, even with Orun.

By noon the next day, we were just two hours outside of Twisting Creek. There we stopped at an abandoned farmhouse, one I knew had belonged to a couple who had moved away during the war. The log-and-stone home was overgrown with vines and had been boarded up, but it still appeared to be in good shape. It took only moments to break inside. There Orun slept until early evening. I knew we could afford the break. I wanted Orun in good shape when we found the Theiwar. Orun awoke "ready to do business."

"Wish I knew what spells he's been collectin'," Orun said for the third time later that evening. The whetstone in his hand made a soft grinding sound as he touched up the blade of his axe. "Garith could turn invisible, hypnotize folks with colors, and make light shine. And make poison gas, which he probably used on them hobs. But he knew lots more than that." He held up his axe and examined it in the dim light coming through the cracks in the shuttered windows. "Damn, I'm lookin' forward to seein' him."

Orun ransacked the house while I waited for my supernatural senses to focus. He found a moth-eaten gray cloak and dropped it on my lap, as well as a stained pair of trousers and a shirt. I needed something besides my old clothes to wear in town. It wouldn't do to have everyone know who I was—including the Theiwar, right at first. By the way his big nose wrinkled up, I knew the clothes had to stink of mold and mildew. I probably stank worse, but I couldn't tell, since I never breathed.

It grew darker outside. Energy poured into me like a cold river. When I faced in the direction of town, I could tell that my murderer was just a short walk away.

"I see him," I said.

Orun nodded, wrapping up his feet with a dry cloth strip. "Like I said," he replied, tugging on his boots next, "Theiwar hate sunlight. Probably stayed at an inn or in a cellar, hidin' from that sun and heavin' 'is guts out, waitin' for the night. Reorx Almighty, they hate that sun."

We left at nightfall. Orun had wrapped an extra layer of moldy cloth under his armor to add a little protection from the daggers he said Garith was fond of using. He knew it wouldn't stop a crossbow bolt, though, and I'd earlier told him about the poison I'd seen. Black wax was difficult to use, so it wasn't likely that Garith would have his bolts already poisoned. Still, we couldn't count on anything. He'd slain a dozen hobgoblins in one evening, probably without breaking into a sweat.

It was a clear night. The stars were out early. A warm wind rolled through town ahead of us. I remembered the last night I had known like that, how peaceful it had been, how everything had gone along fine right up to the end.

"Gonna miss you in a way," said Orun. His axe was tied to his belt. He walked with a broad, quick stride, matching my pace.

The comment caught me off guard. "How is that?"

"Well, you know all you are here for is for findin' your killer man. When it's over, you go, too."

I had suspected as much, but it didn't bother me. Dying a second time seemed like such a small trade for seeing my killer go first.

"Just lemme know when you see 'im," Orun added.

I wanted to laugh, but it wasn't in me. "You'll know."

As we entered the broad dirt streets of Twisting Creek, several people walked by us, giving me looks of disgust at the condition of my clothing and probably my smell. None of them even glanced at Orun. Dwarven merchants came here all the time from Kaolyn.

We passed rows of families sitting on the sides of the road, children chasing each other or fighting. Almost as many people in town had no home as those who did, thanks to the war. I recognized many of them, but none of them seemed to know me in the darkness.

"You followin' your man?" Orun asked quietly.

"He's not far."

Orun sniffed and smiled.

My senses led me on through town toward the other side. I had a strange feeling of dread when I realized I was walking in the direction of my uncle's farm.

We rounded the blacksmith's shop and stable. I looked up and saw a small manor house on a low hill, only a few hundred yards away. It was lit by yellow globes of glass set along the sides of the house and up the front walkway. The long rail fence I remembered repairing in life surrounded it and the farm buildings behind.

"There," I said, stopping. "He's in there."

Orun stopped, too, and squinted. "Nice place."

I nodded slowly as I started off again. "My uncle's."

Orun glanced at me, face hard. "He's in there with your kin?"

I said nothing. My uncle was a good man. He had his flaws, but if he was hurt, it would be one more thing I would owe the Theiwar when we met.

We turned at the half-circle wagon path that led up to the doors of the manor. Balls of yellow crystal set on posts lit the way. My uncle had imported them from the city of Solanthus—glass spheres with magical light in them that never went out. Always the best, he liked to say. Always get the best.

No one was outdoors as we approached. The place hadn't changed a bit since I was here last.

Orun pushed back his oilskin cloak and undid the strap on his axe.

I needed nothing but my hands.

We mounted the steps, slowing down, and reached the door. I hesitated, sensing my prey so strongly I felt I could touch him.

He was inside on the right. That would be my uncle's private study, to the side of the entry hall. Maybe he was holding everyone hostage, or he'd broken in and was borrowing a few things for his own use.

I wondered if, when I met him, I'd ask him why he'd killed me before I killed him.

I raised my hand and knocked hard, three times, and listened to the echo. Then we waited.

The lock clicked. The front door heaved, then pulled open. It was our elderly manservant, Roggis. His face went white when he saw me, his eyes growing big and round.

"Evredd!" he gasped. "Blessed gods, what happened?"

"I'm home," I said softly as I pushed past the old man and went in, Orun at my heels. The entry hall was brightly lit. The great curved stairs to the second-floor bedrooms ascended from either side of the room.

Something inside me tore free. I wanted to see my killer's face, *now*. The study door was closed, but I was there in a moment, with the door handle in my hand, pulling it open.

The cabinet- and bookshelf-lined study was before me. Yellow light fell from the globes hanging from the ceiling. Only one person was in the room, sitting at the center table's far end with a pile of ledgers in front of him. He was big, fleshy-faced, with a hooked nose and a receding hairline. He looked up with irritation as the door swung open.

My murderer, sang the cold in my blood.

My uncle, said my eyes.

"Can't you—" he began, before he actually saw me. He leaped back from his chair, knocking it over. His face went slack with terror. He grabbed for something on a stool beside him.

"Uncle," I said. I couldn't believe it, but I knew it. *He* had killed me. "What—"

My uncle swung around. He held a heavy wooden device in his hands. He pulled the trigger. A dwarven-made crossbow. The bowstring snapped.

The crossbow bolt slammed into my chest with the force of a mule's kick, tearing through my right lung and breaking a rib. The impact knocked me back several steps, almost into Orun, before I caught myself.

The bolt didn't hurt a bit.

I ran and lunged across the table for my uncle, my fingers out like claws.

He flung the crossbow at me, missing, and dodged back. My fingers locked on his clothes, ripping them. I tried to get to his throat.

There was faint popping noise in the air, a flash of light. My uncle was gone.

In his place stood a waist-high dwarf, clad in filthy black clothing. I held his torn shirt in my hands. His mushroom-white face showed only a dirty blond beard, watery blue eyes that bulged out like goose eggs, and a black-toothed mouth that was open like a wound. He was the ugliest dwarf I'd ever seen, and he gave out a shriek that would have sent me to my grave if I hadn't already been there.

My uncle . . . a destroyed man . . .

The Theiwar had used an illusion spell to disguise himself. I knew then what must have happened to my uncle, and why he had seemed to have changed lately. And who had really killed my cousins. Likely, they'd begun to suspect something.

Garith's gonna live like a huuu-man now, the hobgoblin had said.

"Garith!" shouted Orun from the door. The dwarf shut it behind him, cutting off Roggis's cries in the hall outside.

Panicked, the Theiwar ran under the table to escape me. I shoved myself off the table and snatched at a heavy wooden chair, swinging it up and over and down into the tabletop. The chair shattered; the table split in half and collapsed. Books and papers poured across the floor—and a bag full of rotting gray ears spilled with them. Some of the ears were gnawed.

I stepped back. The Theiwar had vanished.

"Garith!" roared Orun, his axe high. "You a dead boy, too, now! You a dead little white rat, you hear me!"

I caught something from the corner of my eye. The Theiwar had reappeared in a corner of the room, far from Orun and me. His hands leaped out of hidden pockets in his black clothing.

"*Orkiska shakatan sekis!*" he called out in a hoarse, high voice, holding something like a cloth and a glass rod and rubbing them together. He was aiming them at me.

"Reorx damn us!" shouted Orun, as I leaped for the Theiwar. "Evredd, he's—"

There was more light then than I'd ever seen in my life or afterwards. My body was suspended in the air, buoyed up by a writhing white ribbon of power that poured from the Theiwar's hands. For the first time since I'd died, I felt true pain. It was unearthly, burning into every muscle, every nerve, every inch of skin, and I couldn't even scream.

Then it was gone. I crashed to the floor. Smoke billowed from the smoldering rags I wore. My soot-stained limbs jerked madly as if I were the marionette of a bad puppeteer.

I flopped over on my stomach. The Theiwar was climbing a free-standing wall cabinet like a spider. Orun threw his axe. The weapon struck something in the air just before it reached the Theiwar and bounced away with a clanging noise, falling next to my head.

"Damn you, Garith!" Orun cried, snatching his axe up.

"Damn you and your magic! You a *dead* boy!"

My limbs began to move the way I wanted them to go, and I staggered to my feet. The Theiwar was on top of the cabinet. He pointed a short white finger down at us. "*N'zkool akrek grafkun—miwarsh!*" he shrieked, in triumph.

Greenish yellow fog blasted from his finger. A windstorm filled the room. The overhead lights were dimmed by the thick mist.

Orun started to shout, but his voice ended abruptly with a shocked gasp, then a loud, hacking cough. I could barely see him through the green fog. He clutched at his throat with both hands, the axe thumping into the floor. He gave a strangled cry, teeth clenched shut, his lungs filling with poisoned air.

I went for the cabinet. My hands gripped a shelf at the height of my head, and I pulled back hard. The dish-filled cabinet rocked; plates clattered flat. The Theiwar cursed and dropped to his knees, fingers grabbing for purchase on the top. I heaved against the shelf again and saw the cabinet lean toward me, then continue coming. I shoved it aside. It slammed into the floor away from the choking dwarf.

As suddenly as it had appeared, the greenish fog blew away as if caught by a high wind. Orun's hacking cough and hoarse cries echoed in the now silent room.

The Theiwar fell to the floor across the room. Rolling, he came up on his feet. He saw me coming around the fallen cabinet, and he tried to flee for the closed door. He jerked a long crystal vial from his belt. His bulging eyes were as big as moons when I tackled him.

My dead hands locked around his little body. You could hear him for miles, screaming like a spitted rodent with a giant's lung power. He punched and kicked in hysteria. I jabbed one hand through the hail of blows and got my long, cold fingers into the flesh at his throat, sinking in the grip. Gasping, he stabbed at my arm with the vial, shattering it with the first blow and opening up bloodless gashes that went down to the dull white bone.

Abruptly, he stiffened. I grabbed his arm with my free one and held it steady for an instant. I had seen it coming.

A red stream, mixed with strands of oozing black, was running down his arm. His huge, watery eyes focused on his hand with an expression of complete terror such as I had never seen on a living face before. His eyes rolled up then, and his body shuddered and went still.

Garith had just learned what the Nerakans had learned about black wax, with the same results.

I released his body and fell to the floor. I tried to keep myself up on my hands and knees, but my strength poured out of me now like water through a collapsed dam. In the background, I could hear Roggis wailing and Orun coughing. The door to the study burst open, and everyone in the manor surged in to shout and point. But they all kept away from me. They knew.

"The boys warned me that he wasn't the same!" Roggis was saying, in tears. "I didn't believe them. When they were killed, he acted as if he didn't care a whit. I thought he was mad, but I didn't dare speak to him about it. I was afraid he'd become violent. He hardly seemed himself!"

The racket was fading away, far away. I struggled to get up. It was no use. I'd done what I'd come back to do. I was more tired than I'd ever been before in my life.

"Evredd," wheezed a hoarse voice near my ear. "You still there?"

I managed to nod, but that was all.

"Good work for a dead boy," Orun said. "Right on target."

High praise. I wondered if I'd see Garayn and Klart soon, and my uncle, and what they would say about it. Family business.

I fell forward into the darkness. Everything was right again, and there would be no coming back.

WAR MACHINES

Nick O'Donohoe

———

THERE WAS A GREAT BLAST OF STEAM IN THE passage through the mountain. Gnomes came sliding down the rock sides, a few dropping from above and caught, heart-stoppingly, by nets; two popped out of compressed-air tubes in the ground and tumbled in the air before plummeting toward a landing-pad near the steam source. One landed on the pad, the other in a bush. The assembled gnomes pulled levers, rang bells, turned cranks, and shouted directions at each other without listening to the directions shouted back.

Mara dashed from rock to rock like a child playing hide-and-seek, each sprint taking her closer to her objective. In her whole life in Arnisson she had never heard this much whistling, clanking, and general noise. She resisted putting both hands over her ears and edged quietly and quickly through the assembled gnomes until she arrived at a narrow ledge at the point where the passageway met the inner crater wall of the mountain. She slid onto it, staring down in fascination at the array of gantries and cranes and at the almost continual rain of equipment and gnomes. Far below, she could see a trap door.

A loose cable drifted toward her.

Mara leapt nimbly out of the shadows, catching a hanging cable with her cloth-wrapped hand. She slid down, touching the mountainside lightly with her feet, then sailing back into open air. She vanished into a pit in the ground.

———

She saw above her, in a brief flash, layer on layer of gnome houses and workshops, cranes, nets, and the occasional flying (or falling) gnome. She congratulated herself on passing unseen and unheard, but part of her grudgingly admitted that any gnome who saw her would have assumed she was just testing a new invention, unless the gnome was also close enough to notice that she was human. And no one could have heard her over the clanking, whirring, grinding, and intermittent steam whistles.

The cable swung against the edge of the pit, which was now a skylight, above her. She climbed up with the rope, pumped with her legs to accelerate its swinging, tucked, sprang, rolled over in midair and landed noiselessly on the stone floor next to a gnomeflinger.

"Perfect, of course," she said with satisfaction. Mara unwrapped her hand from the rope, took three swaggering steps forward, and accidentally knocked down a gnome who was looking the other way. Mara sprawled backward, legs in the air and arms flailing.

The gnome scrambled up and offered her a hand. "Awfully sorry; it was my fault, after all I was busy thinking, there must be a defect in the—"

"It was my fault really," she began. "I'm sorry—" Then she realized that he hadn't stopped talking.

"—a little borrowed hydraulic gear would make it more efficient yet, if it didn't make it top-heavy—and a spring with a trigger-catch might store the energy—"

"Stop."

He did.

"Now," Mara said, "what are you talking about?"

"I was just telling you," the gnome said impatiently, "about the idea I had when I watched you trying to sneak down here—"

"You saw me coming?" She sagged slightly.

"—and I thought, if people are going to jump through the air, which I hadn't considered—until I saw you; you were obvious—we need precautions because of the gnomeflingers." His eyes, a light violet, all but glowed. "We all need bumpers. Yes. Being-bumpers, employing my sensors. Large, high-tension fenders suspended from our

---

74

shoulders to absorb the shock. They'd have metal frames, cloth padding on the outside—"

"They sound awfully heavy," Mara objected. She was quite young, and slightly built, compared to the gnome.

"Then we'd add wheels to it," he continued without pausing, "And a spring-loaded axle for each wheel, and a governor to keep the axles balanced—"

"Who could move with all that on?"

"—and a motor to move the whole thing," the gnome finished firmly. "How do you expect to walk anywhere, if you don't use a motor? Youngsters these days." He rolled his eyes, but smiled at her. "Excuse me." Pulling a bulky pen from a loop on his belt, he tucked his chin and began drawing frantic, jagged lines across his shirt—a shirt that was already covered with sketches of wooden frames, toothed and worm gears, and interlocking systems of pulleys. One design started on his belly and moved through conduits and guy ropes all down his left sleeve.

The gnome looked up and saw Mara staring at him. "Well, I can't always find a sheet of paper when a thought strikes," he said with some asperity.

"Is each shirt a different project?"

"Of course not. In fact, some designs are on five or six different shirts. I keep hoping," he said wistfully, "that some day I'll be able to cross-index them, but every time I even get close, I need to do laundry. And here you are." He peered at her. "Speaking of you, are you someone I should know?"

"Everyone should," Mara said proudly, standing very straight.

"Everyone doesn't," the gnome said thoughtfully, "because I don't. Who are you?"

"I am known," she said with a bow and flourish, "as Mara the Wild." She did a standing flip. "Also Mara the Clever." She tapped the gnome's pockets significantly. "Also," she said in a loud whisper, "Mara the Queen of Thieves."

The gnome blinked. "Goodness," he said disapprovingly, "have you stolen much?"

"Not—much," the Queen of Thieves admitted. She scuffed her toe on the tunnel floor. "Not anything, in fact."

This was why, after announcing her current planned heist to her family, she was also known as Mara the Dangerously Stupid.

She looked defiantly at the gnome. "But I'm sure that I could steal something if it was really important. I am also," she said demurely, "a woman of dazzling beauty, whom all men worship and crave." She coyly brushed at her short-cropped dark hair.

The gnome only looked at her.

"Okay," Mara said grudgingly, "so I won't be a woman of dazzling beauty for a couple of years. It's going to happen, I promise."

"I hope," he said seriously, "that you can accept all that worship and craving without becoming overly vain."

Mara smiled and, in the absence of a mirror, admired her slender shadow against the rock wall. "I'm sure I'll manage perfectly. Anyway, what's your name?"

The gnome immediately went on at some length, pausing for breath in what were clearly accustomed places.

"I only asked your name," Mara broke in finally.

The gnome looked disconcerted. "I'm not even halfway through it."

"Maybe I asked the wrong question. What does your name mean to humans?"

He nodded. "It's very descriptive, even for my people, and surprisingly apropos. I'm known among humans as He Who Will Not Stand Upon Accepted Science, But Will Research Back Into Dangerous and Even Unworkable Ideas, Nor Will He Stand on Conventional Testing, But Will Fall Back on Hazardous and Injurious Techniques, and Will Stand up for Belief in Technology, Which, Back Before the Great Cataclysm—"

"What," Mara said desperately, "do humans call you for short?"

The gnome said simply, "Standback."

Mara leaped back.

"No, no," said the gnome. "That's my name. Standback."

"Are you an inventor? Where's your workshop? Do you do all your work down here? You're not going to tell anyone you've seen me, are you?"

Poor Standback had no idea how to answer four questions thoroughly without taking a month off. "Would it upset you terribly if I answered in brief?" he said diffidently.

Mara, realizing with a shudder how narrowly she had avoided dying of old age during a participial phrase, put a hand on the gnome's arm. "Please, take as little of your research time as possible."

Standback was flattered and grateful. He concentrated. "Yes, I'm an inventor. These tunnels are my work area; I know they don't look like much, but they're roomy. I do all my work here. And no, I won't tell anyone I've seen you," he finished with slight melancholy, "because there's no one else to tell. I'm the only one—down here. It's nice to talk to somebody. Where are you from?"

Mara assumed an heroic stance, arms folded across her thin chest. "I am from Arnisson, a village under siege, desperate to keep itself free from the cruel talons of the draconian army. We are under the command of a lone Knight of Solamnia, a former townsman named Kalend. He's a friend of my older brother's," she sighed and her voice softened. "Kalend's nice, and he thinks *I'm* wonderful, but that's really not that surprising, because I'm ravishingly beautiful." She sighed again, this time in dejection. "Though I do wish he'd stop calling me 'little girl' all the time. Anyway, when I met him on the rampart walls a few nights ago, I asked him if we were likely to survive, and he said not really, but if the draconians attacked too early or while they thought we were unprepared, we still might win. And he said that if he had even one working gnome weapon, we'd stand a chance. And I think he meant it," she added sincerely.

She went on and on—some about the draconians, some about how dire the situation was, but mostly about Kalend, who grew taller and better looking as her story progressed. Standback nodded frequently.

"And so," she said, resuming the heroic stance, "I left Arnisson that very night. I left unseen," she added, pausing and staring at Standback earnestly.

"Unseen," he echoed dutifully.

"Exactly." She stared into space. "Stealthily creeping out

under the cover of darkness, I, alone, crawling through the enemy camp . . .

She went on again for quite some time, not bothering much about the truth, which was actually pretty boring and she was sure no one wanted to hear anyway.

Standback listened patiently, feeling only a little put out that she had been going on like that after making him be brief. When she finished, he said, "But why did you come?"

"What?" Mara brought herself back to being Queen of Thieves. "I came here," she began boldly, then faltered as she realized how it would sound, "to—borrow, or—get, or somehow—take—okay, *steal* some gnome weaponry for the war with the draconians." She was blushing.

Standback decided that he liked her, but he wasn't sure how sensible she was.

"Gnome technology is famous throughout Krynn," Mara added wheedlingly, with some truth. *Famous* and *infamous* were fairly close. "There are legends of past great weapons. The Knights of Solamnia still speak of your poison gas—"

"Yes, well," Standback said uncomfortably, "it was supposed to make us invisible, you know. Still, not a total loss; it does wonders for pest control down here. Mostly." He glanced from side to side.

"Mostly?" Mara jumped as a loud chittering sound flew by her ear. She whirled, but saw nothing.

"We ran out of the original batch lately, so we made a new one. It doesn't seem to kill them any more." Standback ducked as a flapping sound passed near his head. "Lately it just makes them invisible."

Mara looked around nervously. The tunnel, at the bottom of the crater that formed Mount Nevermind, was rough-hewn rock scored by some huge excavating blade and riddled with drill holes and iron bolts. Ropes and cables hung every which way, with pulleys, blocks and tackles, and crane tracks running the length of the ceiling.

Though there were no torches, the tunnel was quite bright. Mara gingerly felt the walls; they were warm to the touch, but nowhere near hot enough to give off light. "How are these tunnels lit?"

Standback pointed to the glowing fungi on the wall. "We

cultivated them for food. Fortunately, the ones we cultivated for light are quite tasty." He mused, "You know, we'd
like to do more with biological engineering. It's the technology of the future."

"Or the end of the world," Mara muttered. She was beginning to worry, marginally, about the wisdom of stealing
gnome inventions. However, if the wise and wonderful Kalend, Knight of Solamnia, believed in gnome technology . . . "Could you show me some of your weapons?"

"I would love to," Standback said unhesitatingly and formally. "This way, please."

They moved down the junk-strewn tunnel. "You seem
awfully at ease with women, even startlingly beautiful
ones," Mara told him.

Standback was silent—a rare condition for a gnome. Finally he said, "Perhaps that is because I love someone."

"Really?" Mara was fascinated. "What's she like?"

Standback went on at length about the exquisite curve of
her left little finger.

"Okay, we'll take it that she's pretty. What's her name?
Her human name," Mara added hastily.

"It's very beautiful." Standback stared upward dreamily.
"She's called Watch As Her Machines Move In and Out,
Like a Night Watchman Blowing Out A Candle to Light a
Lamp of Such Incredible—"

"The short form."

"Watchout." He sighed.

Mara nodded. "Standback and Watchout. You were
made for each other."

"I think so," he said sadly, "and she thinks so. But unless
things change, it can never be."

"Why?" Mara asked sympathetically.

Standback glowered and said suddenly, gnome-to-
gnome, "Thatisabsolutelytheworstpart—"

"What?"

He took a shuddering breath and said in slower human
fashion, "That is absolutely the worst part of this whole
business. I have not as yet received approval for my Life
Quest."

"Your what?"

"My Life Quest. My one achievement, my one goal. It is to be the sensors that go into the burglar alarms. I've already designed them and put them in place throughout Mount Nevermind."

Mara, remembering how she had slipped in without setting any off, murmured, "Still in the development stage, I guess."

"Oh, no; they're highly functional. By the way, how did you pass them?"

"I made an elaborate and clever plan to drop from the top of the crater by rope on a winch . . ." Mara hesitated.

Standback shook his head. "Impossible. I have every passage, every window, every cranny and cut of the outer mountain covered by a sensor. How did your plan work?"

Mara fidgeted. "I didn't use it," she said finally. "I was standing at the steel entrance doors, trying to figure out how to climb up the mountain, while the doors were sliding shut. But the triple-lock fell off and jammed them open so I was able to slip through—"

"The doors." Standback slapped his forehead, leaving a pen mark. "Of course. I knew I'd forgotten something. Sensors on the doors. Still," he said quickly, "it was very clever, making a plan with a lot of rope and a winch. You're almost thinking like a gnome."

Mara chose to take that as a compliment. "Have you shown the committee the evidence of your research?"

"I can't." Standback looked uncomfortable. "I was cleaning them—with a perfectly fine solvent invented by a friend of mine—when they dissolved. Also, the table under them. Wonderful stain remover, though." Standback's shaggy eyebrows dropped low as he brooded. "I can't re-apply until I've proven that I have a semi-working prototype." He added sadly, "If only you had been caught or killed."

Mara sighed in her turn. "If only *you* were the master of the Weapons Guild."

Standback shook his head. "If I were, Watchout and I would be married by now. And I would be far above." He looked upward wistfully, as though he could see through the ceiling. "Up where there is honor, glory, and matching funding. Where draftsmen constantly draft bigger drafting

---

boards for bigger projects with larger cost overruns . . ."

Mara, disheartened, listened as he described the Schedule Rescheduling Department, the Management Oversight Overseers, and the apparently all-powerful Expanding Contractors. "Tell me," she broke in finally, "have any of these projects ever been finished?"

Standback, shocked to the depth of his stubby little being, stared at her. "Young woman, any project worthy of state funding should be perfected, never finished."

"Well, if you're not the master of the Weapons Guild, then what *are* you?" she asked.

He lowered his eyes. "I'm a lower-level inventor whose future life work must be scrounged from the debris left by the failures of others—"

"Have you invented *anything*?"

"I've done more varied work than most gnomes you have met."

Since Mara had met no other gnomes, she simply nodded.

"My Life Quest—" Standback stopped, looked pained, and said with careful stress, "my primary work just now is still sensor-related, since that was my Life Quest. I invent security and safety equipment for home or fort, for the detection and prevention of unwanted forcible spies, intruders, or weapons—"

"Paladine's panties," Mara said irreverently. "You make burglar alarms and traps."

Standback said happily, "That's why I was so happy when you appeared. What luck, really—a burglar, coming straight through the burglar alarms and lockouts. It will be a boon to my data."

"Not luck." Mara was having trouble understanding. "I mean, Kalend ordered that I take this dangerous mission."

Standback looked dubious. "No offense and don't take this the wrong way, but you *are* rather young and did he really order you?"

Mara nodded emphatically. "It was when I was walking with him on the ramparts, which I try to do a lot—not that he minds or anything, even though I'm younger than he is, since I'm remarkably mature, responsible, and exceptionally good-looking for my age—and we were talking about the war. He said, 'If only there were one working gnome weapon, and we had it . . .'" Mara stopped and chewed her lip thoughtfully. "Or maybe he said, 'If there was only one gnome weapon that worked and we had it . . .'

"Anyway," Mara went on, "I remember thinking that he'd better not talk like that where the draconians could hear him, or they'd go get a weapon first, and then I thought about how happy he'd be if I went first instead and found him a weapon and saved the village, and—well, I left." She folded her arms over her chest. "Under cover of darkness, like I said. Through the draconian camps—"

The gnome raised a bushy eyebrow. He was coming to know Mara. "*Through* their camps?"

"Well, around. Under their very scaly noses."

"So you saw them?"

"Not actually saw them," she admitted, but added quickly, "*but* I knew they were there, and was too clever to be caught by them. Alone and courageous, I came—"

"To find weapons." Standback frowned, thinking. "To fight these draconians, whom you haven't really seen. Um."

He reached a conclusion and rubbed his stained and callused hands together. "Well, as long as you're here, I don't see why we shouldn't strike a deal. Do you still want some gnome weapons?"

"What?" It took Mara, caught up in dreams of her own heroism, a moment to remember what she was doing here. Her thin young mouth set firmly. "More than ever."

"I'll let you take one," he said. "Any one you want. If you'll test my security device."

She swallowed. Anti-burglar devices? "Do I have a choice?"

Standback was ecstatic. "And right afterward," Standback burbled happily, "I'll write up my test results and submit them to the Committee. And then if they approve my work—and I have no doubt they will—I'll marry Watchout."

They strode down the tunnel together, their footsteps setting off an uneasy rustling and flapping in the invisible colony clinging to the walls and roof above them.

"They're only bats," Standback said reassuringly. "I hope," he added, less so.

They walked past a number of side tunnels, their entrances half hidden by debris and hanging ropes and cables. Mara, like a good thief, took note of the turns and the fork back to the exit. "Where does the money come from for weapons research?"

"I use only junk, spare parts. The main projects were started on a grant from the Knights of Solamnia."

"The knights?" Mara looked serious. "I hope you're not counting on them for support. They aren't as rich as they used to be, you know—"

"This was a while back. They aren't as frequent visitors as they used to be, either," Standback pointed out. He screwed up his forehead. "In fact," he said thoughtfully, "I haven't seen them since the last In-House Weapons Test, several years ago. No, make that several decades ago."

"And you kept the project going?"

"It never lapsed, even before I took it over. A project," Standback said stiffly, "is a commitment. It's as important as a vow."

"They paid in advance, didn't they?" Mara asked dryly.

"Well, yes. Quite a lot, in fact. Here we are."

He pulled an elaborate key (four notches and a combination lock) from a ring at his waist. He inserted the key with some difficulty in a lock attached to a thick beam door in the tunnel wall. After three tries, it opened easily. "After you," he said. "This room has my first anti-spy device."

Mara stepped in cautiously. "Shouldn't your alarms have sensed me?"

"It's a proximity alarm," the gnome said. "Once testing is complete, I'll put hundreds of them in any place that needs monitoring. You can't have too much redundancy, you know." He was scribbling another note on his shirt. "Would you mind standing on that large black X on the floor?" The X had a small bump at the cross-point.

A gnome-size test dummy on wheels stood next to the X. Mara rolled it almost onto the X and stood well off to one side. "Let's try it this way first."

"I've done this many times," Standback objected, "with

that very dummy."

Mara said firmly, "Well, I haven't seen it work yet." She noted that the dummy hadn't a mark on it, though the walls and floor of the room were dented and scraped.

Standback complained, with some justification, "You promised. Is there no honor among thieves?"

"There was once," Mara said. "Someone stole it." Then she sighed and moved the dummy off the X. "I warn you, I'm leaving at the first sign of danger. What is it we're testing?"

"It's called the Room Security Spybanger," Standback said impatiently. "Now will you step on the X?"

Mara tapped the X with her toe, leapt, tucked, and rolled easily away, preparing to watch from a safe distance.

She heard a *twang*. A stone mallet—its head the size of her own—whistled above her close enough to ruffle her hair. Mara ducked, heard a second *twang* and felt a sudden sharp sting on her cheek as an elastic cord attached to the mallet handle snapped taut against her skin.

The mallet struck the far wall. A trap door popped open beside it. The mallet whizzed back. Mara's back flip carried her just out of range. She dropped flat as a second mallet spun out of the trap door and careened past her, setting off a third mallet.

Soon six stone hammers were ricocheting and thudding around the room. Mara rolled, leapt, ducked, twisted, and at one point slid down a thrumming elastic cord to keep out of the way.

Eventually, in desperation, she crawled back to a section of floor that every last mallet had failed to pass over. She glanced in all directions, poised to spring, until the mallets gradually lost momentum and dangled limply from the tangled elastics.

In the far corner, Standback applauded. "A perfect test." He wrote furiously on his stomach. "Absolutely perfect, with the exception of a few trajectory defects."

Mara looked down. She was crouched over the X. "You tried to kill me."

Standback shook his head violently. "Never. The Spybanger is designed only for self-protection; killing is purely accidental. Can you help me rig these back up?"

From a corner cabinet, Standback produced a large wooden crank. He inserted the crank into a spring and ratchet arrangement in the first trap and turned it until the mechanism was tight enough to leave room for the hammer in front of it. He lifted the mallet laboriously, then stood back, panting.

"And so amazingly easy to reload," he said, struggling to shut the trap before the hammer flew out.

Mara helped crank and lift the other five. "What else have you been working on?"

In answer, he led her through a second door—which led through a short tunnel to another room.

"This isn't for spies, and it's not an offensive weapon. It's a shock-lessening device, a preventive measure for high-impact disasters. A pneumatically seismosensitive counter-measure for offsetting combat-related upheavals."

"What does it do?"

"I just told you," Standback snapped. "When we get there, would you stand in the center of the room, right on the X?"

Mara started to agree readily, then stopped. "Is it sup-posed to be the safest place?"

Standback nodded.

"In that case," Mara said politely, "why don't *you* stand on it, and I'll observe?"

The gnome's shaggy eyebrows shot up. "That's kind of you." He stepped onto the X. "You don't mind taking the extra risk?"

"Never." Mara folded her arms. "Danger and I are well acquainted."

"All right. Watch, then. The Thudbagger is designed to protect against impact." He paused. "You've seen the gnomeflingers in use, above?"

Mara shuddered. She had flitted down from level to level in the shadows, watching as gnomes sailed from level to level (and, usually, down again) from the bulky catapults that were equipped with everything except accuracy and control.

"Well," Standback continued, "this may surprise you, but

several visiting knights thought that the gnomeflingers might also be dangerous."

"No!"

"Truly. They thought—now, to my mind, it takes a twisted mind to think this in the first place—that someone could use the gnomeflingers to throw dead weight projectiles instead of passengers. Well, we performed some experiments, but we never got reliable enough results to suggest that this would work."

"Why not?" Mara asked.

Standback sighed. "Mostly because the note-takers kept getting crushed by thrown rocks. At any rate, the knights asked us to come up with a defense to protect getting hurt by flying rocks. They talked about shields, and barriers, but our Hazard Analysis Committee interviewed the gnomeflinger Impact Test Survivors and concluded that the problem went beyond shields and walls. I brought their results down here with me." He led her into the next room.

The furniture, Mara noted with relief, did not look banged up at all. How dangerous could this room be?

A closer look revealed the furniture to be brand new. The corners of the room contained large piles of splinters.

"Are you sure you want *me* to stand on the X?" Standback asked. "After all, I guarantee it to be the safest place in the room."

Mara bowed to him. "All the more reason to give it to you."

He was flattered. "How kind you are, and how brave."

"I am also called Mara the Courageous," she said.

Standback was not surprised.

He stepped onto the X and folded his arms confidently. "This room has a broad-band sensor." He pointed to a small round bump in the floor. "Stamp anywhere. You don't need to do it very hard."

The floor looked to be some kind of parquet, broken at regular intervals with circular lids each the size of a melon.

Mara eyed Standback narrowly and slammed her foot against the bare floor. Nothing happened. She stamped again, harder. Still nothing. She took a running start and stamped with both feet, hard enough to hurt her ankles.

Nothing. She gave up and leaned on the wall.

Huge leather balloons popped out of the floor. Filling instantly with compressed air, the balloons smashed the new furniture to kindling.

Mara sidled around the edge of the room, squeezing between the wall and the balloons. "That's pretty impressive, Standback—hello?" She squeaked a balloon with her thumb. "Standback?"

Mara heard an answering squeak. She leapt onto one of the balloons, poised there like a cat, and saw a hand struggling upward in the crack where all the balloons met.

Mara rolled down to the hand and planted her feet against balloon, her right shoulder against another. Gradually, the two moved apart. She heard a gasping inhale below her, then a thump as something hit the floor.

"Thank you so very much," Standback said feebly. "The Thudbaggers are nearly perfect—I don't have a bruise on me—but I couldn't really breathe in there."

"You could make a snorkel," Mara said sarcastically. She had grown up near the sea, "—a short breathing tube."

There was a hiss, then another. The balloons were deflating. Standback appeared among them, stuffing them back below floor level. He said dubiously, "That's an awfully simplistic answer. You should leave design questions to the specialists. On the other hand," he added thoughtfully, "if it had reserve tanks—and an air pump—and free-swinging gimbals to keep it upright . . ." He sketched it all out on the only clear portion of his shirt.

Mara, who needed a rest, sat beside him, her chin in her hand. "I see why you're having problems getting promoted. Do you have to get these all working to win approval?"

"Oh, my goodness, no." Standback caught himself and added, almost defensively, "Besides, they all work wonderfully!" He stared out at the smashed furniture wistfully. "No, it's simply a matter of getting the Committee's stamp of approval. Unfortunately, I can't even get their attention. They completely ignore me."

"Do you do everything by committee?"

"Some humans think we invented the committee."

"And until you get their approval, poor Watchout can't

be betrothed to you?"

"Nor should she be," Standback said glumly. "After all, would you agree to marry a gnome with no credentials?"

Mara didn't think she would marry a gnome at all, but decided it wouldn't be polite to point that out. "You're very nice just for yourself, credentials or no. And now," she said firmly, "what about the weapons?"

"A bargain's a bargain." Standback, making a final note on his shirt, opened the rear door of the Thudbagger room, and Mara found herself in a branch of the main tunnel again. They walked back toward the place where the tunnel split in two. Mara looked interestedly at the piles of debris and the bulky inventions half hidden under canvas or in shadow. Several of them were labeled, but life's too short to spend reading gnome labels.

"Wait." Mara had noticed a device carelessly tossed to one side on the tunnel floor.

It had a shiny black hand-grip butt and stock that supported a shining tube-and-yoke arrangement of blue steel and black wire, which was topped by a small sighting tube and a tiny ring with crossed hairs in it. The whole effect was remarkably menacing.

"What is it?" she asked, staring at it in awe.

"What? Oh, that." Standback nudged it with his foot disdainfully. "A co-worker made it."

"You disapprove of him?" Mara hazarded.

Standback nodded, his beard whipping up and down rapidly. "It was to be his Life Quest, and he abandoned it. Can you imagine, abandoning your Life Quest? He's always sworn that he'd fix it some day, but I doubt if he can; it has too few parts, it's far too small, and it can't even carry itself." He finished indignantly, "It doesn't even have a place for the operator to sit!"

Mara bent over it. "It fits in your hand."

"You see what I mean?"

She didn't, but only asked, "What's it for?"

The gnome snorted. "It's supposed to dowse for water, but it's hopeless. I can tolerate a few false starts, or a near miss, or the occasional explosion or dismemberment, but this—"

"It doesn't find any water, then?"

Standback said disgustedly, "Just diamonds, emeralds, rubies, other rocks . . ." He shoved it aside with a kick.

Mara looked back at it longingly, but kept walking.

Leaning alongside a hanging drop cloth on the tunnel wall was a human-size mannequin with some sort of backpack on it.

"This," Standback said as impressively as a gnome can be, in brief, "is the Mighty Thunderpack."

Mara examined the three nozzles connected to two tanks and what looked like a fire-starting flint. Near the top of the unit was also the now-familiar bulge of one of Standback's sensors. She gingerly touched the directional fin, like a fish's, on the Thunderpack. "How do you aim it?"

Standback laughed tolerantly. "It's not a weapon; it's personal troop transport."

Mara put it on her shoulders. For metal work, particularly for gnome metalwork, it was surprisingly light. "Very impressive," she said. She pictured an army (led by herself, naturally) swooping through squadrons of draconians and cutting them into small, non-combative strips. "How does it start up?"

"From the mere touch of an iron weapon," Standback said proudly. "I used a special kind of rock in it. Do you have a dagger?"

Mara hesitated.

"Come, come," the gnome said impatiently. "All thieves have daggers."

Embarrassed, Mara handed him the paring knife she had brought with her from her mother's kitchen.

Standback took it and said, "When I wave this near the sensor, the Mighty Thunderpack will burst into action." He tensed his arms and said in a melancholy voice, "Well, good-bye."

Mara, seeing the knife wave and noticing belatedly Standback's emphasis on "burst," lurched forward out of the way as Standback's arm moved near. To her relief, the Thunderpack did not activate. "What do you mean, 'good-bye?' Has this thing been tested before?" she demanded.

"Of course, extensively. Just look in the side room." The

gnome gestured to the left, behind the drop cloth that Mara had assumed was hanging against the tunnel wall.

Mara lifted the cloth. Stacked floor to ceiling were the charred arms and legs of test dummies. Not one torso remained. "Has it ever been tested by a living person?"

"Of course not; why do you think—Oh, you mean, 'by someone living at the time he tested it.' Yes, once." Standback looked solemn. "Poor fellow. And so young."

Mara took off the Thunderpack, and, to her credit, she was barely shaking. "What else do you have?"

"I have other transport devices." He escorted her to what he called, "a variation on the gnomeflinger. I named it the Portapult."

It looked more like *them*. The Portapult consisted of two gnomeflingers, ingeniously and intricately linked by cable, chain, and several pieces of fine wire, for which Mara could imagine no purpose.

Each gnomeflinger rested on six wheels on three axles. The front axle had a built-in pivot and the pivot axle of each gnomeflinger was connected to the other by chain.

Standback followed Mara's confused glance. "Oh, they're inseparable," he said proudly. "Linked in frame, function, and trigger. The Portapult breaks apart for transport"—it looked as though it might break apart as he spoke—"but it re-assembles for synchronized action. The Portapult can deliver six soldiers simultaneously, send them hundreds of feet through the air. . . .

"Isn't it wonderful?" he finished huskily, and patted one of the delivery platforms affectionately. The platform shot upward and the Portapult spun sideways. An identical platform on the second gnomeflinger shot upward and that unit turned sideways as well—sideways toward the first—and the two platforms met with a *smack* that blew Standback's hair straight behind him and made Mara's ears pop.

"I should check that trigger again," he said thoughtfully. "Also, perhaps, the targeting ratchets."

He sat in a narrow seat beyond one of the platforms and pedaled strenuously. A chain on a toothed gear cranked down one platform; the other inched down in time with it. Mara heard the faintest of clicks as the minuscule triggers hooked over the platforms to hold the bent, straining beams and cablework in place.

She helped the gnome as, very gently, he put the two units side by side again. "They look dangerous," she said.

Standback misunderstood. "Oh, yes," he said happily. "Someday they'll have great strategic importance."

"But not yet." Mara sighed. "Is there anything useful down here?"

The gnome considered. "There is," he said slowly for a gnome, "a powerful defensive weapon, designed to break through any surrounding force. I'm not sure that I should let you see it—"

"Please." Mara had little faith left in gnome technology, but she wanted very badly to leave with something.

"Very well." Standback walked her down several bends in the corridor to a side tunnel. In the middle of it was a tarpaulin covering something the size of a crouching man.

"Why isn't this one in a room?" Mara asked.

Standback shuddered. "In a room, with this? That would be far too dangerous." He pointed to the long horizontal gashes in the tunnel walls, and parallel marks on the floor, chiseled into the rock. Some of them were bright and new.

Mara perked up. "Is it really so dangerous as all that?"

"Absolutely," the gnome replied. "You can parry a sword. You can beat back a spear." Standback paused for effect, not an easy thing for a gnome. "But there is no way for your adversary to fight off the astonishing Floating Deathaxe."

He pulled a cloth off the axe.

In spite of her disappointment, Mara felt like laughing at the sight of a pendulum-shaped axe, swinging from a framework of three strange oar-shaped wooden fans. The fans were attached to a gear arrangement of spools of thongs and elastics.

"Good design," she said finally. "If it's deadly, it hides its function well."

"You think so?" Standback peered at it. "It looks like any other weapon's design to me."

"How does it work? No offense, but it looks as though it is designed to mix bread in some demented kitchen. What do these little oars do?"

The gnome reached a stubby finger out and spun them fondly. "They're called propellers. When they're in balance, they propel it."

Mara stared confusedly at the propellers, which weren't attached to any wheels or rollers. "How?"

"In a straight line, if it's properly adjusted."

"No, I mean, how can they move it?"

"It flies."

Now Mara did laugh. "And what makes it fly?" She saw a pull-cord hanging from one of the spindles. "This?"

"Yes, but only after it's properly adjusted. If you—"

"Oh, leave it alone," Mara said tiredly.

Standback looked crushed.

"I'm sorry." Mara sighed. "I didn't mean that. It's just—I was going to bring back such wonderful things, and save my people and make Kalend notice me—" She choked back her tears. Queens of Thieves don't cry.

Standback patted her sympathetically and they walked together in silence, two people with little in common but the fact that life was not going well for either of them.

They returned to the skylight where Mara had first entered. She stood in the smoke and steam-filtered daylight of the square hole above them and slumped against the rock wall, looking at the hall of useless inventions.

From somewhere far overhead came a muffled *boom*. The entire tunnel shook, dropping dust and cobwebs. A huge bell carillon somewhere far above them clanged frantically, followed by some kind of trumpet, several clappers, a siren, and numerous whistles.

Invisible creatures shook themselves free of the ceiling and flapped to and fro in panic. Mara clapped her hands over her ears. Standback shouted in delight, "It works!"

"What?" Mara could read his lips, though that was hard because of the gnome's beard.

"The perimeter alarm. I set it up around the top of the mountain." Standback was actually dancing. "It notifies bystanders—"

"I'll say."

"—locates the point of entry, and even seals off rooms and levels." He pointed to the stone trap door sliding slowly over the skylight to the crater floor.

Then he looked concerned. "They'll need me up there to shut it off. They're probably completely deaf right now."

"*Whaaat?*"

"*Nothing.*" Standback dashed over to the Gnomeflinger, leapt on the payload pad several times and (amazingly enough) sailed easily through the half-shut skylight. "Illbebacktheleverletsyouout—"

The trap door slid shut and fell in place with a thud. The bells, whistles, clappers and sirens above grew muffled.

Mara stared upward, her mouth hanging open. A gnome device had actually worked as it was supposed to. But now how was she going to get out?

She examined the lever on the wall and tried to trace its relationship to the trap door. She could see a slack rope that disappeared into a hole in the tunnel ceiling, and she noted a rod leading from the lever up to a cantilever, but she couldn't understand how it would work.

The alarm noises stopped abruptly. Standback or someone else had found a way to shut them off or, more likely, had accidentally silenced them. Mara had seen enough of the gnomes to hope that there were no casualties.

Her ears adjusted to the sudden near-silence; she heard the soft hum (and drip) of ventilation devices somewhere, and the restless motion of invisible flying pests, and something else: a rustling, back in the side tunnels.

Feet moving—a scraping sound, not quite boots and not quite barefoot. The clink of metal on metal. It sounded definitely ungnomelike. At that point, it occurred to Mara that *something* had set off Standback's alarms. A *real* thief . . . Mara hid in a niche in the wall.

A shadowy figure came into view, wearing a helmet with a dragon crest.

"These must be the weapons the knights spoke of. Quick!" he hissed, "While the gnome is gone. Take what looks useful and leave."

It was a draconian! Two draconians! "What about the girl we followed here?" The other draconian asked.

Mara's heart sank. She heard again in her mind Kalend saying, *They'll camp around us and wait for something to break—reinforcements, or better weapons . . .*

The captain shrugged. "She's served her purpose. If you see her, kill her, and don't waste time."

Mara pressed against the tunnel wall, hidden by the shadows of cable and hanging hardware.

Four other draconians marched out of the narrow side tunnel into the hall. They were all carrying huge, cruel weapons. Their wings filled the tunnel. They had clawed hands and horrid sharp fangs. One of them started right for her. Mara the Brave couldn't help herself. She whimpered.

The draconians heard her. One lashed forward with a spear. Panicked, Mara dropped flat. The spear nearly parted her hair. Another draconian hissed and slashed sideways with his sword. She leapt up, dodged the sword, backing farther away. A mace raked her shoulder.

She began running, heading for escape out the skylight. I should stop them! she thought frantically, but a cold voice in her mind said, "Face it. You're not a warrior, not even a thief. You're only a very stupid little girl."

She bounced from wall to wall randomly to dodge more thrown weapons, stumbling over a pile of canisters. She paused. The top one had a label; in the middle of the polysyllables, Mara recognized the common word for *pest*. She picked the canister up and tucked it under her arm. If it was the new batch of pesticide, she could dump it over herself and it would make her invisible. She began opening it, then stopped.

If it was the old batch, it might kill her.

But then, she could throw it back at the approaching draconians and kill them. She tugged at the top again.

Or she might make them invisible. She had a brief vision of herself surrounded by invisible draconians. She tossed the canister aside and kept running.

The draconians were close behind her when she reached the skylight. She leapt for the opening lever, pulling it down with her full weight. It groaned as it moved . . . and lowered a cantilevered weight, which tugged a guy rope, which spun a flywheel, which rotated an axis, which turned a worm gear, which wound up the pull rope . . .

Which broke. The whole system coasted to a stop, the

end of the rope flapping uselessly.

"It would be nice," Mara muttered between clenched teeth, "if just once, a gnome invention worked reliably." And that gave Mara the idea.

She grabbed the dangling rope, swung up on it, pumping her legs vigorously. Kicking off the ceiling, she spun around and swung back over the heads of the astonished draconians. One of them raised a spear, but not quickly enough; it barely scratched her.

Mara let go of the rope, landing well behind the confused draconians, and dashed back the way she had come. But she had to make certain they followed her. At the bend in the tunnel, she scooped up a handful of decaying spare parts from old mechanisms and skimmed them off the tunnel walls and ceiling into the draconians. A rusted bolt caught the captain on his reptilian snout.

The captain howled. "After her! Kill her!"

"Quickly, or slowly?" A subordinate asked.

"Quickly," he hissed. A hex nut clanged off his helmet. "But not too quickly."

They dashed after her again, weapons ready, their terrible jaws open. Mara fled, but made sure that they saw which way she turned. They chased her confidently; after all, what did they have to fear from a single unarmed human child?

The draconians came on her suddenly, around a corner. She was apparently helpless with fear.

The draconian captain leered at her and barked unnecessarily, "Now you die."

"If you must!" she said more coolly than she felt. "But be quick."

The draconian eyed her with resentment, tinged with admiration. "Don't we frighten you?"

"You? Never." Mara pointed to the floor. "That thing frightens me. I can bear anything," she said earnestly, "but the Flying Deathaxe."

At a gesture from his captain, the lead draconian picked it up. "This thing?" he said, laughing, incredulously.

Mara shrank away. "Don't pull that cord. Please. Put it down—"

The captain smiled at her, revealing an amazing quantity of pointed teeth. "Of course, I'll put it down." He set it on the ground in front of her with a low bow. As he straightened up, with one swift motion he pulled the starting cord, setting the propellers in motion. He watched, chuckling evilly.

The propellers spun and, unbelievably, the Deathaxe rose into the air. As it cleared the floor, the razor-sharp axe blade swung back and forth with a loud shearing noise. It hovered, hesitated, then began slowly spinning in a circle. Mara watched, open-mouthed, as the axe blade sliced through a boom extending from the tunnel wall. Now the axe was moving faster, and the circle was widening as well. Mara took a nervous step backward.

The Deathaxe hit the roof and bounced off. The blade sliced through the helmet and head of a draconian soldier without slowing down. The soldier turned to stone and toppled.

The captain uttered a command, succinct even for draconian field orders: "Run!"

Mara obeyed. So did the other draconians. The axe gashed the wall where she had been standing a moment before, spun back on itself, and cut one of the draconian soldiers in the chest before careening upward to strike the ceiling and spin back down.

The wounded draconian, shouting in panic, crashed head-on into one of his companions. Both sank to the tunnel floor, unconscious but not dead. The remaining two sprinted after Mara, just ahead of the whining, humming Deathaxe.

Mara wouldn't have thought that the heavy draconians could run that fast, but then she surprised herself with her own speed. Once, in a crazy rebound off a hanging pulley, the Deathaxe spun into the floor in front of her and shot straight up at her. She fell backward, rolled between the legs of the startled draconian soldier behind her, and leapt to one side. The Deathaxe cut off his head. Turning to stone, it thudded to the floor where she had been. The draconian captain behind her screeched with frustration. The Deathaxe, now behind him, spun back toward both of them, and they were off again.

Perversely, the axe continued after them, instead of back-tracking or taking wrong tunnels. Mara wondered if that was a side-function of Standback's sensors. She also wondered how long she and the draconian captain could keep up their pace; she was naturally faster, but he had more endurance. If she should tire or fall . . . She grit her teeth and kept dodging and running.

After what seemed like days, Mara thought that the axe might be slowing down. A minute more and she was positive; it was losing forward momentum and spinning more slowly. Finally, with a creak from its handle and a flutter of propellers, the Deathaxe crashed to the tunnel floor. Mara and the draconian, wheezing, collapsed—a spear's length apart—just beyond it.

The draconian recovered first. He rose unsteadily and searched for the sword. He had dropped it when he fell. The weapon was now lying within Mara's reach.

Mara staggered to her feet, picked up the heavy sword and nearly overbalanced. The draconian laughed at her and moved forward to recover it and kill her.

Mara heard an uneasy rustling on the tunnel ceiling above her, though she could see nothing. She swung the sword against the tunnel wall and banged it, shouting.

The air was suddenly filled with a terrible chittering and the sound of hundreds of wings. The draconian, disconcerted, waved his arms in the air. Mara steadied the sword, gathering her strength.

The draconian opened his mouth and snapped at the noises in the empty air; there was a tiny shriek, which cut off abruptly. Mara, feeling sick, took a deep breath and lunged with the sword.

It was far too heavy for her, but she managed to catch the draconian captain just below the kneecap. He roared, driving away all the flyers. Mara let go of the sword and backed off.

Grimacing, he looked down at his leg. Green blood oozed from the wound. He opened his mouth to shout at her; nothing but snarling and flecks of foam came out.

Mara dashed away, thinking to herself, "I'll need a new name. Mara the Warlike . . . Mara, Queen of Battle . . . " A thrown dagger flashed between her arm and her side. Mara, Queen of Battle, legged it like Mara the Rabbit down the left fork of the tunnel. The draconian lumbered after her, limping painfully.

Mara dashed into a room. The draconian found her, crouched against the far wall. She stood holding the leg of a splintered chair as a weapon. As the captain came forward, she dropped it and shrank against the wall, her face a mask of terror.

"I have you," he said slowly, with satisfaction. He limped into the center of the room, smiling—

Mara tapped the wall lightly with one finger.

The Thudbaggers activated. The draconian lost his footing. Both his arms were pinned in place by the bags; he couldn't reach the sword he had dropped when the first bag inflated in his face. He poked his head up out of the balloons, and glared helplessly at Mara, who had clambered onto the bags. "You!" he said bitterly, beside himself with rage. "You—"

"Shut up," said Mara and, pulling off his helmet, knocked him cold.

She heard the sound of running feet, and then Standback appeared in the door.

"Are you all right?" He was panting.

Mara slid off the balloon. "Mara the Bold is always all right."

"That's good. When I arrived at the top level, I thought that it was a false alarm, and I came back down, and then I saw the dead and knocked-out draconians—" He paused. "You're bleeding."

She looked at her shoulder in surprise. "Not too badly." She grinned. "I gave better than I got."

Standback looked at the unconscious captain. "I see that," he said, impressed. "Were they after my weapons?"

Mara nodded. Standback, looking again at the pinned and unconscious captain, said thoughtfully, "Mount Nevermind isn't at war with draconians. We don't dare kill them, and they're too dangerous to take prisoner. What are we going to do with them?"

"I've thought about that." Mara paused for effect. "Let

them escape."

Standback goggled at her. "But if they escape, they'll take our weapons or plans for our weapons away with them—"

"You want them to," she said simply.

Standback was now a complete rarity in Mount Nevermind or anywhere else: a speechless gnome.

"Think about it," she went on. "The draconians want the weapons. You need the weapons tested. They're soldiers. Who could better test them?"

As he still hesitated, she added, "And isn't the theft by real warriors a kind of validation that your weapons are worth testing? You'll be able to tell that to the committee and then ask for the hand of Watchout."

Standback blinked. "But you're not afraid to let them use these . . . terrible weapons against your people?"

Mara thought about draconian troops setting off the Portapults in the field. "They are indeed terrible weapons," she said, "but letting the draconians have them will only make it a more even battle. It's a matter of honor—something the knights are big on."

Standback took her hand, pumping it up and down. "Never have I met a warrior of so much integrity—"

"Oh, I wouldn't say that."

"—and modest too." He looked back at the unconscious draconian captain. "I'll let them escape with the Portapult, the Flying Deathaxe—"

"Um, I don't know that they'll want the Deathaxe. Why don't you let them have the Thunderpack, instead?"

Standback protested. "This is too much. Won't you take anything for yourself?"

"Sometimes," Mara said nobly, "there's a greater joy in giving." She had a sudden thought. "If you don't mind, I'll just take the little failed dowser." She picked it up.

"The one that can't even find water? You want it?"

"Just as a souvenir."

Standback, tears in his eyes, said, "You're amazing. Nothing but a trinket for yourself, while you give full-scale gnome weapons to your worst enemies."

Mara, pocketing the jewel-finder, beamed. "Well," she said modestly, "I'm like that."

The Promised Place

Dan Parkinson

ONCE, VERY RECENTLY, THIS HAD BEEN A CITY. ONLY days before, there had been a tiered castle on the highest point of the hill. Studded battlements overlooked the lands for miles around. In a walled courtyard, throngs gathered.

Below the battlements, spreading down toward the fields, had been a raucous, bustling city—inns and dwellings, shops and markets, public houses, smithies, barns and lofts, weavers' stalls and tanneries, music and noise and life.

Chaldis had been a city. But the dragonarmies of the Dark Queen had come and the city was a city no more. Where battlements had stood was smashed and blackened rubble, and all beneath was scorched, twisted ruin. Of Chaldis, nothing was left. Only the road it had defended was yet intact, and its surface showed the tracks and treads of armies just passed. The people who had been here were gone now—some fleeing, some dead, some led off as slaves. Where there had been herds now were only scorched pastures, and where crops had grown now were ruined fields.

Stillness lived here now. A somber stillness—shadows and silence, broken only by the weeping of the wind.

Yet in the stillness, something lurked. And in the shadows, small shadows moved.

Muffled voices, among the rubble: "What kind place this? Ever'thing a real mess." "Talls been here. Somebody clobber 'em, I guess." "This all fresh scorch." "Forget scorch!

Look for somethin' to eat."

And another sound, from somewhere in the lead, "Sh!"

A thump and a clatter.

"Sh!"

"Somebody fall down."

"SH!"

"Somebody say, 'Sh.' Better hush up."

Another thump and several clatters.

"Wha' happen?"

"Somebody bump into somebody else. All fall down."

"SSSH!!"

"What?"

"Shut up an' keep quiet!"

"Oh. Okay."

Abruptly hushed, the shadows moved on, small figures in a ragged line, wending among fallen stone and burned timbers, making their cautious way through the rubble that once had been a city. For several minutes, they proceeded in silence, then the whispers and muted chatter began again as the effect of exercised authority wore off.

"Wanna stop an' dig? Might be nice stuff under these gravels."

"Forget dig. Need food first. Look for somethin' make stew."

"Like what?"

"Who knows. Mos' anything make stew."

"Hey! Here somethin' . . . nope, never mind. Just a dead Tall."

"Rats."

"What?"

"Oughtta be rats here. Rats okay for stew."

"Keep lookin'."

"Ow! Get offa my foot!"

Thump. Clatter.

"Sh!"

"Somebody fall down again."

"Sh!"

They were travelers. They had been travelers since long before any of them could remember, which was not very long unless the thing to remember was truly worth remembering: traveling generally was not. It was just something they did, something they had always done, something their parents and their ancestors had done. Few of them had any idea why they traveled, or why their travels—more often than not—tended to be westward.

For the few among them who might occasionally wonder about such things, the answer was simple and extremely vague. They traveled because they were in search of the Promised Place.

Where was the Promised Place? Nobody had the slightest idea.

Why did they seek the Promised Place? No one really knew that, either. Someone, a long time ago—some Highbulp, probably, since it was usually the Highbulp who initiated unfathomable ventures—had gotten the notion that there was a Promised Place, to the west, and it was their destiny to find it. That had been generations back—an unthinkable time to people who usually recognized only two days other than today: yesterday and tomorrow. But once the pilgrimage was begun, it just kept going.

That was the nature of the Aghar—the people most others called gully dwarves. One of their strongest driving forces was simple inertia.

The size and shape of the group changed constantly as they made their way through the ruins of the city, tending upward toward its center. Here and there, now and then, by ones and threes and fives, various among them lost interest in following along and took off on side expeditions, searching and gawking, usually rejoining the main group somewhere farther along.

There was no way to know whether all of them came back. None among them had any real idea of how many of them there were, except that there were more than two—a lot more than two. Maybe fifty times two, though such concepts were beyond even the wisest of them. Numbers greater than two were seldom considered worth worrying about.

Gradually, the stragglers converged upon the higher levels of the ruined city. Here the fallen building stones were more massive—huge, smoke-darkened blocks that lay aslant against one another, creating tunnels and gullies roofed by shattered rubble. Here they found more dead things—humans and animals, corpses mutilated, stripped and burned, the brutal residue of battle. They crept around these at a distance, their eyes wide with dread. Something fearful had happened here, and the pall of it hung in the silent air of the place like a tangible fear.

At a place where a flanking wall had fallen, some of them paused to stare at a tumble of great, iron-bound timbers that might once have been some piece of giant furniture but now was a shattered ruin. The thing lay as though it had fallen from high above, its members and parts in disarray. Having not the faintest idea of what it might be, most of them crept past and went on. One, though, remained, walking around the huge thing, frowning in thought.

His name was Tagg, and an odd bit of memory tugged at him as his eyes traced the dimensions of the fallen thing. He had seen something like it before . . . somewhere. Tugging at his lip, Tagg circled entirely around the thing. A few others were with him now. They had seen his curiosity and returned, curious themselves.

"Got a arm," he muttered, squatting to reason out the placement of a great timber jutting outward from the device. Within the twisted structure itself, the timber was bound to a sort of big, wooden drum, with heavy rope wrapped around it and a set of massive gears at its hub.

"Fling-thing," he said, beginning to remember. It was like something he had seen from a distance, atop some human structure his people had skirted long ago in their travels. He remembered it because he had seen the Talls operate it, and had been impressed. It was a wooden tower atop a tower, and a lot of the humans—the Talls—had gathered around it and slowly cranked the extended arm around and back, then abruptly had released it. It had made a noise like distant thunder, and the thing that flew from it had been very large and had knocked down a tree.

"That it," he decided. "One a' them. Fling-thing."

Several other gully dwarves were gathered around him now. One asked, "What Tagg talkin' 'bout?"

"This thing," Tagg pointed. "This a fling-thing. Throws

stuff."

"Why?" another wanted to know.

"Dunno. Does, though. Throws big thing, knock a tree down."

"I know. Cat'pult."

"Nope. That some other kind. This called a . . . uh . . . dis . . . disca . . . somethin'."

"Okay." Losing interest, some of them wandered away again, though Tagg and two others lingered, creeping through the wreckage in wonder. One was a white-bearded ancient named Gandy, who was given to occasional bursts of lucid thought and served as Grand Notioner to the combined clans of Bulp. The other was a young female named Minna.

Tagg was vaguely glad that Minna was interested in the same thing that interested him. He found her presence pleasant. His eyes lighting on a glistening bauble among the rubble, he picked it up and held it out to her. "Here," he said, shyly. "Pretty thing for Minna."

Climbing among the twisted members of the fallen discobel, Tagg helped Minna across a shattered timber, then turned and stumbled over old Gandy. The Grand Notioner was on his knees, staring at something, and Tagg tripped over him and thudded facedown in the sooty dust.

Barely noticing him, Gandy brushed his hand over a vague shape on the floor and said, "Here somethin'. What this?"

Tagg crawled over to look, and Minna peered over his shoulder. The object was a big, iron disk with sharpened serrations all around its edge, except for one area where it had been blunted and bent.

"That disk," Tagg said. "It what th' fling-thing fling. Knock down trees with these."

"Knock down somethin'," Gandy decided, looking at the blunted edge. The disk had hit something very solid, very hard. He rubbed it again and looked at the dark stains on its surface. There were other stains on the cracked floor nearby, as though blood had congealed there. He scraped the stain with his finger, then tasted his finger. He frowned and spat. It was not any kind of blood he knew about.

It reminded him, though, of the primary goal of the moment. He stood, tapping the ground with the battered old mop handle he always carried. "'Nough look at stuff," he proclaimed. "Look for food first. Come 'long."

Obediently, they followed him out of the wreckage of the war engine, then paused and looked around.

"Where ever'body go?" Tagg wondered.

Gandy shrugged. "Aroun' someplace. Can't get far, followin' Highbulp. Glitch don' move that fast."

From where they were, a dozen tunnels and breaks in the rubble led away. Choosing one at random, old Gandy led off, with Tagg and Minna following. "Now watch good," he ordered.

"Watch what?"

"What?"

"You gonna do trick or somethin'?"

"No! Watch for food. Need to find stuff for make stew."

The tunnel they were in was a long, winding way created by the spaces between building stones that had fallen on one another. After a few minutes, Tagg asked, "What kind food Grand Notioner expect find here?"

"He didn' say," Minna said.

Just ahead of them, Gandy turned, frowning in the shadows. "Any kind food," he snapped. "Keep lookin'. If it moves, it prob'ly good for stew."

"Okay." Moving on, Tagg stepped into the lead.

They had gone only a few steps when Tagg, his alert young eyes scanning everywhere, saw something move.

It was something that protruded, curving downward, from a crack between fallen stones. It was a tapered thing, about as long as his arm. Dark and greenish, it was almost invisible against the muted, mottled colors of the rubble around it. But as his eyes passed over it, it twitched.

Tagg stopped, and the others bumped into him from behind. Old Gandy tottered for a moment, then regained his balance. Minna clung to Tagg, her pressure against him totally distracting him. He decided at that moment that any time Minna wanted to bump into him, it was all right as far as he was concerned.

"Why Tagg stop?" Gandy snapped. "I nearly fall down."

"Okay," Tagg murmured, paying no attention at all to the elder. "That fine."

"Not fine!" Gandy pointed out. "S'posed to be lookin' for food, not foolin' aroun'. You!" He nudged Minna with his mop handle. "Leggo Tagg. Stop th' foolishness!"

"Oh." Minna backed away, shrugging. "Okay."

With a sigh, Tagg turned to go on, then saw the thing he had seen before. The thing that twitched. He pointed at it. "What that? Maybe food?"

They gathered close, and Gandy bent for a better look. The thing was sticking out of a small crevice in the rubble. It was hard to tell in the subdued light, but it seemed to be round and tapered, with a sort of sharp ridge running along the top of it. Its color was dark green. And as they stared at it, it twitched again.

They stumbled back, wary.

"What it is?" Tagg asked.

Gandy peered again. "Dunno. Maybe half a snake?"

"Might be." Tagg approached it carefully, thrust out his arm and prodded the thing with his finger, then jerked away. When he touched it, it writhed with a motion that was more than a twitch. Like the tail of a huge rat, it swayed this way and that. But it seemed otherwise harmless. Whatever might be at the other end of it, this end had no teeth or claws.

"This food?" Tagg asked the Grand Notioner.

"Might be," Gandy decided. "Snake okay for stew sometimes, if not bitter. Check it out."

"What?"

"*Taste* it. See if it bitter."

Reluctantly, Tagg approached the thing again, grasping it with both hands. It writhed and struggled in his grip. Whatever it was, it was very strong. But he held on, and when it seemed a bit subdued, he lowered his head, opened his mouth and bit it as hard as he could.

Abruptly, the thing flicked and surged, flipping Tagg across the jagged tunnel into the far wall. And all around them, seeming to come from the stone itself, a huge roar of outrage rang through the air.

Tagg got his feet under him just as the Grand Notioner

surged toward him, running for his life, with Minna right behind. Both of them collided with Tagg, and all three went down, rolling along the cracked floor, a tumble of arms, legs and muffled curses.

They had barely come to a halt when others—a lot of others—piled into them, over them, and onto them. The main party, led by the Highbulp Glitch I himself, had been emerging from a connecting way when they heard the roar and panicked. In an instant, there were gully dwarves tumbling all along the tunnel, and a great pile of gully dwarves at the convergence where Glitch I—and everyone behind him—had stumbled over the flailing trio.

It took several minutes to get everyone untangled from everyone else, and Tagg—at the bottom of the heap—was thoroughly enjoying being tangled up with Minna again until he looked up and gazed into the thunderous face of his lord and leader, Glitch I, Highbulp by Persuasion and Lord Protector of This Place and Anyplace Else He Could Think Of.

Glitch glared at the three just getting to their feet. "Gandy! What goin' on here?"

"Dunno," Gandy grumbled. "Ever'body pile up on me. How I know what goin' on? Couldn' see a thing."

"Heard big noise," the Highbulp pressed. "You do that?"

"Not me," Gandy shook his head. He pointed an accusing mop handle at Tagg. "His fault. He do it."

"Do what?"

"Snakebite."

Feeling that he should explain, Tagg pointed up the corridor. "Somethin' stickin' out over there. Like half a snake. Tasted it to see if it bitter."

The Highbulp squinted at the twitching thing. "Is it?"

The earlier roar had faded into echoes, leaving an angry, hissing sound that seemed to come from nowhere in particular.

"Is now, sounds like." Tagg nodded.

Cautiously, the clans of Bulp gathered around the green thing protruding from the rubble. Glitch scrutinized it carefully, first from one side, then from the other, then beckoned. "Clout, come here. Bring bashin' tool."

A squat, broad-shouldered gully dwarf stepped forward uncertainly. On his shoulder he carried a heavy stick about three feet long.

Glitch pointed at the twitching thing. "Clout, bash snake."

Clout looked doubtful, but he did as he was told. Raising his stick over his head, he brought it down against the twitching thing with all his might. This time the roar that erupted, somewhere beyond the rockfall, was a shriek of sheer indignation. Stones trembled and grated, dust spewed from crevices, and the entire wall of fallen rock began to shift. The twitching green thing disappeared, withdrawn into the rubble, and massive movements beyond sent fragments flying from the rocks there. All around, the debris shifted and settled, closing crevices and escape tunnels.

As gully dwarves scampered back, falling and sprawling over one another, the entire wall of rubble parted, and in the settling dust a huge, scaled face glared out. Slitted green eyes as bright as emeralds shone with anger, and a mouth the size of a salt mine opened to reveal rows of dripping, glistening fangs. The scale crest atop the head flared forward, and the head was raised to strike. Then the emerald eyes widened slightly and the mouth closed to a grimace.

"Gully dwarves," Verden Leafglow hissed, her voice laced with pain and contempt. "Nothing but gully dwarves."

*   *   *   *   *

For a time, she simply ignored them. Their pleas for mercy, the smell of their fear, the cowering huddles of them here and there in the shadows, were dimly pleasant to her, an undertone like music, soothing in its way.

A gaggle of gully dwarves. They could do her—a powerful green dragon—no harm. They could not get away—all the exits they might reach were sealed by rockfall—and at the moment, she decided, they were not worth the effort it would take to crush them. So she ignored them, concentrating instead on her wounds. The indignities of a bitten and thumped tail rankled her, but she could deal with the perpetrators later, when she was stronger. They were trapped here in the rubble with her. They had nowhere to go.

The saw-edged disk had ripped into her body, bringing her down in the rubble. In the darkness of the fallen castle, almost buried by debris, she had lain bleeding as the armies of the Dragon Queen passed by—passing, she thought bitterly, and leaving her behind. For that, she would not forgive Flame Searclaw. The huge, arrogant red dragon with his preoccupied human rider, had known she was there. In her mind, clearly, had been his dragon-voice, chiding and taunting her.

Her left wing hung useless beside her, her left foreclaw was terribly maimed and it had been all she could do—through spells and sheer concentration—to close the gaping slash at the base of her neck. That wound alone could have killed her, had her powers been less.

Still, the healing was slow, painful, and incomplete. In ripping through the armored scales at her breast, the disk had cut her potion flask—hidden beneath the scales—and carried away the precious self-stone concealed there. It was gone, somewhere among the rubble, and without it the powerful green dragon lacked the magic to reshape her maimed parts. The ultimate healing power was beyond her, without her self-stone.

Focusing all of her concentration upon the damaged parts of her, she drew what strength she had and applied it to healing. And when the effort tired her, she slept.

* * * * *

When their initial blind panic began to fade, replaced by simple dread and awe, the subjects of Glitch I—Highbulp by Persuasion and Lord Protector of This Place, Etc.—turned to their leader for advice. They had to find him first, though. At first sight of the apparition that had appeared in the shifting rubble, Glitch had darted through the first several ranks of his subjects, crawled over, around and under several more layers of panicked personnel, and finally wedged himself into a crack behind all of them. Getting him out was a task made more difficult by the fact that he did not want to come out.

Finally, though, he stood among them, gawking at the huge, green, sleeping head of the thing in the hole only a few feet away. "Wha . . ." He choked, coughed and tried again. "Wha . . . what that thing?"

Most of them looked at him blankly. Some shrugged and some shook their heads.

"That not snake," Tagg informed his leader. "Not stew stuff, either."

Emboldened by the Highbulp's restored presence, old Gandy, the Grand Notioner, crept a step or two closer to the sleeping thing and raised his mop handle as though to prod it. He changed his mind, lowered his stick and leaned on it, squinting. "Dragon?" he wondered. "Might be. Anybody here ever see dragons?"

No one recalled ever seeing a dragon, and most were sure that they would remember, if they had.

Then Tagg had a bright idea. "Dragons got wings," he said, adding, doubtfully, "don't they?"

"Right," Gandy agreed. "Dragons got wings. This thing got wings?"

Some of them crept about, trying to see around the huge head in the hole, to see what was beyond it. But the dim light filtering in from above did not reach into the hole. There was only darkness there. They couldn't see whether the creature had wings or not.

"Somebody bring candle," Glitch I ordered. "Highbulp find out."

With glances of surprise and admiration at such unexpected courage, several of them produced stubby and broken candles, and someone managed to light one. He handed it to Glitch. The Highbulp held it high, stood on tiptoes and peered into the darkness of the hole. Then he shook his head and handed the candle to Tagg, who happened to be nearby. "Can't see," he said. "Tagg go look."

Taken by surprise, Tagg looked from the candle thrust into his hand to the fierce, sleeping features of the thing in the hole. He turned pale, gulped and started to shake his head, then saw Minna in the crowd. She was gazing at him with something in her eyes that might have been more than the candle's reflection.

Tagg gulped a shuddering breath, steeling himself. "Rats," he said. "Okay."

The huge, green head almost filled the hole in the wall of rubble. As Tagg eased alongside it, his back to the stones at one side, he could have reached out and touched the nearest nostril, the exposed dagger-points of the great fangs, the glistening eyelid. The spiked fan of the creature's graceful crest stood above him as he crept deeper, edging alongside a long, tapered neck that was nearly as wide as he was tall and seemed to go on and on, into the darkness.

"Tagg pretty brave," Minna whispered as they watched him go. Instinctively, her hand went into her belt pouch and clutched the pretty bauble Tagg had found for her. Her fingers caressed it, and the great, sleeping creature stirred slightly, then relaxed again in sleep.

"Not brave," Gandy corrected. "Just dumb. Highbulp gonna get Tagg killed, sure."

Tagg crept through sundered rubble, just inches away from the big green neck that almost filled the tunnel. Then he was past the rubble, and raised the candle. The place where he found himself was some kind of cavern, beneath a rise in the sundered hill above. It was dim and smelled musty, and was nearly filled by the huge body of the green creature.

Where the thing's neck joined an enormous, rising body, Tagg spotted ugly, gaping wounds in the scales. He stared at them in awe, then beyond them, and his eyes widened even more. The green thing was huge. Arms like scaly pillars rested below massive shoulders, and ended in taloned "hands" as big as he was—or bigger. The nearest shoulder had another ugly wound, and the hand below it was mangled as though it had been sliced apart.

He raised his eyes, squinting in the dim candlelight. Above the thing, on its far side, stood a great, folded wing. Nearer, a second wing sprawled back at an angle, exposing yet another gaping wound.

"This thing in bad shape," Tagg whispered to himself. "Pretty beat up."

The huge body towered over him and its crest was lost in shadows above. Farther along, the body widened abruptly, and he realized that what he was seeing was a leg— a huge leg, folded in rest. Beneath it was a toed foot with claws as long as his arms. Beyond, curled around from behind, was the tip of a long tail. He recognized that appendage now. It was what he had bitten, when he thought it might be half a snake. The recollection set his knees aquiver and he almost fell down.

Tagg's nerves had taken all they could stand. He had seen enough. He headed back.

Just as he was edging past it, the nearest eye opened an inch, and its slitted pupil looked at him. With a howl, Tagg erupted from the hole, bowling over a half-dozen curious gully dwarves in the process. Behind him, the great eyelid flickered contemptuously, and closed again.

As Tagg got to his feet, Glitch stepped forward. "Well?"

"Well, what?"

"Well . . ." Glitch hesitated in confusion, trying to recall what he had sent Tagg to do.

"That thing got wings?" Gandy rasped.

"It got wings, all right. Got claws an' tail an' gashes, too." Recovering his candle, Tagg handed it back to Glitch. "Highbulp want any more look, Highbulp go look. I've seen enough."

"Gashes?" Gandy blinked. "What kind gashes?"

"That dragon all sliced up," Tagg told him. "Somebody hurt it pretty bad."

Minna eased up beside him, gazing with sympathy at the hideous face of the green dragon asleep a few feet away. "Poor thing," she said.

As she spoke, the dragon's eyes opened to slits, then closed again. It shifted slightly, sighed, and seemed to relax, as though the pain of its wounds had somehow eased a bit.

For an hour, then, they searched for a way out of the rubble trap. They found nothing—at least, nothing they could reach without going past the dragon. The shifting of the beast in its lair had resettled the fallen stone, blocking every exit. One after another, the searchers gave up, shrugging and gathering into a tight little group as far from the dragon as they could get.

When it was obvious that they were truly trapped, Clout

asked—of no one in particular—"So, now what?"

Gandy scratched his head and leaned on his mop handle. "Dunno," he said. "Better ask what's-'is- name."

"Who?"

"*What's*-'is-name. Th' Highbulp." He turned. "Highbulp, what we do now?" He peered around in the dimness. "Highbulp? Where th' Highbulp?"

It took a few minutes to find him. With nothing better to do, Glitch I had curled up beside a rock. He was sound asleep.

* * * * *

They were all asleep when Verden Leafglow awakened— gully dwarves everywhere, scattered in clumps and clusters about the dim recess, most of them snoring. At a glance, she counted more than sixty of the little creatures in plain sight, and knew there were more of them behind rocks, in the shadows, and beneath or beyond the sleeping heaps. One of them, she knew, had even crept past her into her lair, thinking that in sleep she might not notice. But it had only looked around and returned to the others.

Her first inclination was to simply exterminate them. But she had a better idea. They might be useful to her, if she kept them alive for a time—and if she could make them serve her.

Gully dwarves. Her contempt for them was even greater than the contempt most other races felt for the Aghar. As a dragon, she loathed *all* other races, and these were certainly the most contemptible of the contemptible. Even compared to the intelligence of humans, full dwarves, and others of the kind, the mentality of gully dwarves was so incredibly simple that it bordered on imbecility. And compared to dragon intelligence, it was nothing at all.

Still, the pathetic creatures had certain instincts that might be useful. They were excellent foragers, adept at getting into and searching out places that others might not even know existed. And they were good at finding things, provided they managed to concentrate their attention on the effort for any length of time.

Somewhere here, among the rubble of the destroyed city of Chaldis, was her self-stone. In her sleep she had sensed its presence. With her self-stone, she could heal herself completely. Properly motivated, the gully dwarves might find and deliver the self-stone.

Closing her eyes, she thought a spell, and her dragonsenses heard the beginnings of tiny movements among the rubble beyond the rock-fall cavern where the gully dwarves were trapped. Tiny, scurrying sounds, hints of movement carried more by vibration in the stones than by any real noise. She concentrated on the spell, and the hints of movement increased in number and volume. She added a dimension of difference to the spell, and other movements could be sensed; slithering, scuffing movements seeming to come from the soil above her lair.

The vibrations became true sound, and things scuttled in the deepest shadows within the chamber. From cracks and crevices everywhere, small things emerged, coming toward her. Rats and mice, here and there a squirrel, a rabbit or a hare—they emerged by the dozens, answering the call of her spell.

For a moment it seemed the place was filled with rodents, darting around and over the tumbles of sleeping gully dwarves, then they were all directly in front of her. Moving carefully, ignoring the pain of her injuries, she thrust out her right paw, and its talons sliced downward, slaughtering great numbers of the rodents. Using her tail, she scraped the ceiling of her lair, and brought forth the herbs and roots that hung there, drawn downward from above by her magic. These she pushed from tail to foot to forepaw, and deposited them in front of her hole, beside the dead rodents there. A final twist to the spell, and rocks moved, somewhere above. Seconds later, water began to drip from the roof of rubble, a small spring diverted to flow through the chamber. And a small, crackling fire appeared in mid-chamber.

"Wake up, you detestable creatures," Verden Leafglow rumbled. "Wake up and make stew. You are no good to me if you starve."

* * * * *

"Sure. We find thing for you. No problem. What thing is?" Glitch I stifled a belch and grinned a reassuring grin at the monstrous face looking at him from its hole.

After the first shock of sharing a closed cave of rubble with a dragon had worn off, and when it became obvious that the dragon didn't intend to kill them and eat them—at least not right away—the Clans of Bulp had gotten down to business. First things first. They were hungry, and there was food.

Within minutes, savory stew was bubbling in their best pot over what—to some of the ladies especially—was the most remarkable cooking fire they had ever encountered. The fire seemed to have no fuel, nor to need any, and none of them had ever seen stew become stew so quickly.

Then, when their bellies were full, the dragon explained to them what she needed. She seemed, despite her great size and horrendous appearance, to be a pleasant enough dragon. Her voice was low and comforting, her words simple enough for most of them to understand and she even managed to seem to smile now and then. Quite a few of them discovered—without ever considering that there might be a touch of magic involved here—that they were really quite fond of the unfortunate Verden Leafglow.

"The thing I need is a small thing," she told the Highbulp. "It is a sort of stone, about this big. . . ." A huge, three-fingered "hand" with needle-sharp talons a foot long appeared beside the green face, two talons indicating a size. About an inch and a half.

"Lotta stones 'round here," Glitch said dubiously, looking around the cavern. "Whole lot more outside, though. Oughtta look outside of here."

"By all means," Verden agreed. "Outside, of course. And I am sure that, once you are outside, you wouldn't for a minute consider just going off and leaving me, would you?"

"Nope," Glitch shook his head, speaking just a bit too loudly. "Nope, wouldn' do that. Sure wouldn'."

"Of course you wouldn't," Verden said softly. "Because that would be very unwise."

"Sure would," Glitch agreed emphatically. Then his face twisted in confusion. "How come not wise?"

"Because only a few of you will go out to search," the dragon hissed. Suddenly, as subtly as the narrowing of her eyes, all hints of the "friendly" dragon were gone and the gully dwarves saw Verden Leafglow as she really was. "All the rest will remain here," she said, "with me."

As they cowered away from her, she pointed with a huge talon. "You," she said, pointing at old Gandy. "You will search. And you." This time she pointed at Tagg. "You two, and three more. The rest stay. The way out is here"—a talon turned, pointing—"just behind my head."

Some of them crept closer to look. Just behind the "hole," on her right side, was a crevice in the rubble. Tagg grabbed Minna's hand and headed for the opening. Abruptly, the dragon moved over her head, blocking the way. "Not the female," Verden hissed. "She stays."

Verden knew her choices were right. The old gully dwarf with the mop handle staff was, within the limits of Aghar intelligence, the smartest of them all. He would search well, and he was the least likely to wander off. The young male was the same one who had slid past her to look into her lair. For his kind, he had a certain courage and a degree of curiosity. And it was unlikely that he would flee, as long as the dragon had the female he favored.

She would also keep the one they called Highbulp. The rest had a certain dim loyalty to him, she sensed— probably more than he had to any of them.

She moved her head again. "Go. Now! Find the disk that cut me. The stone should be nearby."

Tagg and Gandy darted past the dragon's jaws and through the opening, Tagg glancing back at Minna with frightened eyes. As soon as they were out, others hurried to follow them. Verden let three others pass, then blocked the way again.

Verden relaxed. There was a chance the gully dwarves would find the self-stone. It was somewhere nearby. She could sense its presence, dimly. There was a chance they would recover it for her. If not . . . well, then she would just have to kill them and try to find it, herself.

As her eyes closed, the hostages began to chatter among themselves. She ignored them, then opened one eye in mild curiosity. "Promised place?" she murmured. "What promised place?"

From his refuge behind a rank of his subjects, Glitch peeked out at her. "P . . . Promised Place," he said. "Where we s'posed to go. Our de . . . density."

"Density? You mean, destiny?"

"Right. Dest'ny."

"And where is the Promised Place?"

"Dunno," Glitch admitted. "Nobody know."

She closed her eye again, bored with the "density" of gully dwarves. Within seconds she was asleep.

* * * * *

With Clout and two others—Gogy and Plit—following them, Gandy and Tagg made their way back to where they had found the dented disk. The dragon had said to look there, and they were in no mood to argue with a dragon.

More than a day had passed. Maybe two or three days, for all they knew. The smoke that had lingered above the ruined city was gone now, blown away, and only bleak rubble remained. But otherwise, things were as they had been . . . almost. Rounding a turn in a ravine among rubble, the five heard voices ahead. Clinging to shadow, they crept forward to see who was there. Tagg was the first to see, and he almost bowled the others over, backpedaling. "Talls," he whispered. "Sh!"

From the shadowed mouth of a "tunnel" where great stones had fallen across the gaps between other stones, they peered out.

The humans ahead of them were ragged and scarred. There were two of them, and they were working frantically at the great, tumbled skeleton of the fallen discobel, turning its huge crank inch by inch as the long throwing arm rose above them. Lying on its side, the sidearm thing became a slanted pole, its outward end creeping toward the sky above the sheer walls of rubble around them.

"No business . . . comin' this way . . . in the first place," one of them grunted, heaving at the windlass of the crank. "Nothin' here . . . just ruins."

"Shut up!" the other hissed. "Your fault we . . . fell in this—canyon . . . now pull . . . harder . . . only way to . . . get out of here."

In the shadows, Clout whispered, "What Talls doin'?"

"Dunno," Gandy shrugged. "Tall stuff don' make sense. Hush."

Slowly, out in the little clear area (which was, indeed, like a deep canyon among sheer walls, if one looked at it as a human would, not seeing the many avenues of exit that were like highways to gully dwarves), the two men labored at the discobel's windlass and the sling arm rose inch by inch. Several times they had to stop and rest, but finally the arm stood straight up, its tip only a few feet from the nearest wall of stone.

The men looked up. "That'll do," one of them panted. "Let's tie it off. I'd hate to have that thing trigger itself while we're climbing up there."

The other paled at the thought, and trembled. "Gods," he muttered. "Splat!"

"Shut up and tie this thing off with something. Here, what's this? The set-pin?" He picked up a sturdy cylinder of worked hardwood, about three feet long, and glanced from it to the barrel of the discobel. "Yeah, there's its slot. Hold that windlass 'til I get this in place."

With the other bracing the windlass, he set the pin in its slot and tapped it with a rock to firm it. The other eased off on the crank, eased a bit more, then stood back, sighing in relief. The pin held. The machine remained motionless.

"Let's get out of here," one of them said. Gingerly, he stepped to the base of the cranked-up arm and grasped it. Using its guy-bars as hand- and foot-holds, he began to climb. The other followed. From below, they looked like a pair of squirrels climbing a huge tree trunk, except that instead of branches, the trunk had triangles of cable bracings, held outward by heavy wooden guy-bars. They climbed higher and higher. At the top they hesitated, then swung from the tip of the arm to the top of the jagged wall, and disappeared from sight. Their voices faded, and were gone.

"Wonder what that all about," Tagg muttered. He scratched his head and looked around, puzzled. There was something he was supposed to do, but he had become so engrossed in watching the Talls that he had forgotten what it was. The others had, too, but after a moment old Gandy snapped his fingers. "Find stone for dragon," he reminded them. "Stone 'bout this big."

They stepped out from the "tunnel" and peered around. "Lotta stones 'bout that big, all over," Tagg pointed out. "Which one?"

"Dunno," Gandy admitted. "Better take 'em all."

They set to work gathering small stones—all except Clout, who had lost his bashing tool somewhere and felt uncomfortable without it. He set about finding a new bashing tool.

With Gandy selecting rocks, and Tagg, Plit, and Gogy collecting them, they had a nice pile of stones going by the time Clout found what he was looking for. It was a sturdy cylinder of polished hardwood, resting among the inexplicable vagaries of the great wooden device lying in the rubble.

It was exactly what he wanted, but it seemed to be stuck. He pulled at it, heaved at it, and it budged slightly but would not come free. Frowning with determination, he clambered out of the maze of timbers, found a good, heavy stone, and went back in.

Clout had a philosophy of life—only one, but it had always served him well. His philosophy was: if a thing won't move when you want it to move, bash it.

From outside, they heard him hammering in there—among the maze of timbers—and looked up. "What Clout doin'?" Plit asked.

"Dunno," Gandy shrugged, frowning. "Not gettin' stones, though."

The hammering went on, and then its ringing took on a new sound. After each thud, something creaked, and far above—though those below didn't notice it—the great braced arm began to tremble.

"Almos' got it," Clout's voice came from the timbers.

He banged again, and again, and abruptly the whole

world went crazy. The entire maze of timbers groaned, crackled and heaved upward, seeming to dance. And the tall, heavy arm above shot downward, with such force that the air sang around it. It arched toward the ground, impelled by the released windlass, and smashed into the soil only yards from where the other gully dwarves were stacking their rocks.

The impact was enormous. Gully dwarves, rocks and surrounding rubble flew upward. Partial walls that still stood among the rubble teetered and fell, and a cloud of dust rose to blank out everything from sight. Below the dancing rubble, a deep, cavernous rumble sounded, and in its echoes came a muted roar of surprise and outrage. The very ground seemed to fall, resettling several feet lower than it had been.

For a time there was silence, then the dust blanketing the ground shifted and a small head came up. "Wha' happen?" Tagg asked.

Around him, others arose from the dust, wide-eyed and shaken. Plit and Gogy appeared first, then old Gandy, coughing and spitting dust.

"Wha' happen?" someone echoed Tagg's question.

Gandy looked around, bewildered. Then he looked up and blinked. "Fling-thing fall down," he said.

Not far away, the maze of timbers that had been a discobel was now an entirely different maze. It had rolled over, its timbers realigning in the process. At first the gully dwarves could see no movement there, then there were scuffing sounds and Clout appeared, crawling from a gap between broken spars. He got out, dusted himself off and blinked at the rest of them.

"Where Clout been?" Gandy demanded.

Clout held up a sturdy cylinder of polished wood. "Got new bashin' tool," he explained. "Wha' happen out here?"

The carefully-collected pile of rocks was gone—scattered all over the clearing. Gandy sighed and began again to pick up stones. The others watched for a moment, then joined him. And as other gully dwarves appeared, chattering, Gandy silenced them with a glare. "No talk," he snapped. "Get rocks."

Soon there were dozens of them there, all busily picking up stones. And then more, and then still more.

Suddenly, Tagg glanced around and saw Minna beside him, gathering rocks. He blinked, frowned and remembered. "What Minna doin' out here?" he asked.

"Gettin' little rocks," she explained. "Somebody say to."

"Where dragon? Let everybody go?"

"Hole fall down," she said. "Dragon can't move. Foun' new gully, though, for come out."

"Oh." He looked around. There were gully dwarves everywhere, all collecting stones. But to Tagg, that didn't seem quite as important as it had before. He went and found Gandy, and explained the situation to him. "Dragon don' got everybody anymore." he said. "Look."

It took a lot longer for Gandy to get everyone to stop collecting rocks than it had taken to get them to start. Inertia is a powerful force among gully dwarves. But finally they were all gathered around Gandy and someone asked, "What we do now?"

"Dunno," he said. "Ask Highbulp." He turned full circle, searching. "Where what's-'is-name?"

"Who?"

"Th' Highbulp! Ol' Glitch. Where th' Highbulp?"

None of them knew, so they went looking for Glitch I. They found him, eventually, right where they had left him.

Glitch had slept through the "earthquake," only to wake up and find everyone gone. He sat up, rubbed his eyes and noticed that the stones had shifted and a new tunnel had opened. So he headed that way, grumbling. It was just like his subjects to wander off and leave their leader to catch up when he got around to it.

He was just ducking to step through the opening when a voice behind him said, "Oh, all right! Let's make a deal!"

At first he couldn't see who had spoken. Sometime during his nap, a whole new rockfall seemed to have filled about half of the cavern. Huge slabs of stone had crashed down from above, and torrents of gravel with them. He peered here and there, then found the speaker: a big, angry green eye stared back at him from the depths of a crevice among the stone.

"Who that?" Glitch asked, backing hastily away.

"Verden Leafglow, you little imbecile!" The crackling voice subsided into a rasp of resignation. "I'm ready to make a deal."

"What kin' deal?" He hugged the cavern wall, ready to flee at an instant.

"I'm trapped here," the dragon voice admitted. "The hill fell in on me, and I can't move." The statement wasn't entirely true. She knew she could fight free if she had to, but the effort it would take to get loose—in her condition— might kill her. "I need help," she said.

The Highbulp relaxed slightly. "What kin' help?"

"The same thing I needed before!" the answer was almost a roar of aggravation. Then the dragon sighed and lowered her voice. "My self-stone. I told you about my self-stone. Remember?"

It took a bit of head-scratching, but then the Highbulp remembered. "Little stone? 'Bout this big? Special stone?"

"That's the one. I need it, and I need you and your . . . your people to find it for me."

The Highbulp scowled in deep thought, scuffing the ground with his toe. Then his eyes lighted with a shrewd look. "What in it for me?" he asked.

The deep growl that seeped through the fallen stone mixed irritation and controlled rage, but Verden held herself in check. She was trapped, but not helpless. It would be the work of a moment to free a claw and rend the arrogant little nuisance to shreds. But that wouldn't solve her problem. "What do you want?" she asked.

* * * * *

When the rest of his tribe found him—right where they had left him—Glitch I, Highbulp Etc., was sitting on a rock in the rockfall cavern, his chin resting on his knuckles. At first, he seemed to be deep in thought; then the other dwarves noticed that he was asleep.

They gathered around him, curious. Old Gandy walked around him, then prodded him with his mop handle staff to get his attention. "What Highbulp doin'?" he asked.

Glitch blinked, raised his head and looked around. "What?"

"Why Highbulp sittin' here?"

"Thinkin'," Glitch said, irritated at being awakened. "Highbulp doin' big think."

"Soun' 'sleep, thinkin'? Think 'bout what?"

Glitch scratched his head, trying to remember what he had been thinking about. From the shadowed rockfall beyond, a voice thin with exasperation said, "He's trying to decide what he wants from me."

The voice so startled the gully dwarves that several of them tripped over others, and for a moment the place was a tumble of confusion. Then Gandy stooped to look under the rocks. "Dragon? That still you?"

"It's still me," Verden Leafglow assured him. "I can't believe that little oaf went to sleep. I thought he was thinking."

"Highbulp always go to sleep, when try to think," Gandy explained. "Think about what?"

"I am prepared to offer you stinking little . . . you people . . . something that you want, in return for delivery of my self-stone. *So what in the name of the gods is it that you want*?"

Gully dwarves tumbled about again, some diving for cover, some running for the exit. With a hiss, Verden exhaled a jet of noxious vapor—just a small stream, but aimed directly at the exit tunnel. Gully dwarves darting into the mist recoiled, gasping and coughing, tumbling backward as the green fumes assailed them. "No running away!" Verden commanded. "We are going to settle this, here and now! Tell me what you idiots want."

The Grand Notioner looked around him, puzzled. "Want? Dunno. Anybody know what we want?"

"Stew," several offered. "Out," a few others said. "Rats?" someone wondered.

"Make up your minds," the dragon hissed.

"We find self-stone, give to you, you give us somethin'?" Gandy pressed, trying to get it clear.

"Yes."

"What you give us?"

"*I don't know! I'm trying to get you to . . . !*"

Gully dwarves were diving, tumbling and rolling everywhere. The Highbulp tried to hide behind the stew pot, then sniffed at its aroma and realized that he was hungry.

With an effort, Verden lowered her voice again, speaking very slowly.

"I . . . am . . . trying . . . to . . . find . . . out . . . what . . . you . . . want," she said.

Gandy peeped out from behind a rock. "Oh," he said. "Okay. Highbulp, what we want?"

Glitch didn't respond. He was busy eating stew.

Something akin to inspiration tugged at Tagg's mind, possibly stirred up by realizing that Minna was beside him, holding his hand. "Maybe what we always lookin' for is what we want," he suggested.

Gandy glanced around. "What that?"

"Promised Place. Seem like we always lookin' for Promised Place."

"Mebbe so," Gandy nodded. To the dragon, he said, "We get you stone, you lead us to Promised Place?"

"Yes," she agreed, sighing. "Where is it?"

"Dunno," he said. "Hopin' you'd know."

"Rats," the dragon muttered.

"Rats, too," Gandy pressed. "Throw in some rats."

"All right! It's a deal."

Gandy crept nearer to the rockfall and leaned down to peer into the depths. A big, green eye looked back at him. "You say true?" Gandy asked.

The dragon glared at him, then sighed. "I say true. Have I ever lied to you?"

"Okay," Gandy decided. "When Highbulp finish eatin', somebody tell him he decided what we want. We get little rock for this dragon, we go to Promised Place."

Within moments, there were gully dwarves filing through the exit, all telling one another, "Find little rock, 'bout this big."

Tagg started to follow them, but Minna pulled him back. Still holding his hand, she crept toward the rockfall and looked beneath. "How come dragon make deal with us?" she asked.

"My lair collapsed," Verden said.

"Oh," Minna breathed. Again she looked into the depths of the fallen rock, at the great, green eye looking back at her. "Oh. Poor thing." Sympathetic and truly concerned, she reached into her belt pouch and brought out her finest treasure, the little bauble given to her by Tagg. "Poor dragon," she said. "Here. Here a pretty thing for you."

She reached the bauble toward the hole, and the green eye brightened. The dragon voice hissed, "That's it! It's mine!" A talon shot upward, spraying rock fragments into the cavern.

Tagg tumbled back, pulling Minna with him. She lost her hold on the self-stone, and it arced upward, then down.

There was a splash, and Glitch snapped, "Watch it! Highbulp eatin'!" Glaring, he swigged another mouthful of stew, gulped it down and grumped, "How come stew got rocks in it?"

"My self-stone!" Verden Leafglow shrieked. "You . . . you *swallowed* my self-stone!" Rocks erupted again, and a gigantic clawed arm emerged. For a second, huge talons flexed above the horrified Highbulp, then Verden hissed with frustration and pulled back her claws. The little nuisance might be nothing but a gully dwarf, but he was a living thing. And her self-stone was inside him. The self-stone, with its affinity for life.

If he died with the self-stone inside him, the crystal would be destroyed.

*   *   *   *   *

Under smoky skies, across a war-ravaged land, the combined clans of Bulp made their way out from Chaldis and into the vast reaches of the Kharolis Mountains, ever onward and ever upward, led by a thirty-six-foot-long green dragon who carried a Highbulp at her breast.

Verden Leafglow was not happy about the situation. As a guide for the puny creatures she so despised, she felt humiliated and degraded. She longed to simply splash their blood all over the nearest mountainside. She dreamed of doing that, but she did not do it. She was stuck with them. By holding Glitch I—and the self-stone within him—close to her breast, she had managed a temporary healing of her wounds. But it was only temporary, until she had her self-stone back, intact and uningested.

She needed the detestable little imbecile, and he knew it. At first, the sheer terror of being gripped in dragon claws and pressed against a dragon's breast had almost killed him. A more complex individual probably would have died from compounded fright and shock. Glitch had only screamed and passed out.

Since then, though, he had decided that he enjoyed being carried around by a dragon, and seemed to be doing everything in his power to maintain the status quo. Whether by his own doing or by simple luck, Glitch had kept Verden's self-stone lodged somewhere inside him for nearly a week. Through sheer stubborn perversity, it seemed, Glitch I had become constipated, and seemed determined to remain that way until Verden delivered him and his subjects to their Promised Place. She couldn't kill him, she couldn't dispose of him—each time she let go of him for more than an hour, her wounds began to open again—and she couldn't separate him from the rest without chancing that he would somehow disgorge the stone and lose it.

The self-stone in his belly was the Highbulp's guarantee, and the arrogant little pest knew it. Somehow, through all the days and all the stews, the self-stone remained inside Glitch as though it were glued there.

Their Promised Place. They didn't know where it was, or even what it was, but Glitch I was basking in his new-found glory as a dragon owner, and would settle for nothing less than the perfect spot. He had become downright obnoxious about it. Into the region of Itzan Nul she led them, and there—as the Aghar slept under bright moons—a familiar dragon-voice came again to Verden, speaking within her mind. "You have survived," it said. "I wondered if you would."

"No thanks to you, Flame Searclaw," she responded in kind, hatred riding on the thoughts. "You left me back there. You knew I was there, and you left me to die."

"You were injured and useless." The red dragon's mind-voice seemed almost to yawn with disinterest. "There are uses for you, now, though. The armies are . . ."

"Don't speak to me of uses," Verden shot, hot rage edging the thoughts. "You and I have much to settle . . . as soon as I am free to come for you."

"You have a duty. . . ." Searclaw's thoughts were scathing.

"Begone!" Verden thought, blanking out the mind-talk.

She would not forget her "duty." But first she must retrieve her self-stone. She must deliver these useless gully dwarves to their Promised Place. Visions of slaughter danced in her mind as she thought of the moment when her precious talisman was safe once more. The Highbulp and all the rest . . . how she would make them suffer when they were no longer needed. But first . . .

Where might it be—the place they would accept as their Promised Place? There were many places—abandoned places, devastated places, places where no one now lived or might ever want to live again. Such, logic said, was a fair definition of a Promised Place for gully dwarves. So Verden led them, on and on, as the days passed. Past the fortress realm of Thorbardin, through wilderness and uncharted lands, beyond Pax Tharkas they journeyed, skirting the beleaguered realms of elf and man.

As she scouted aloft, carrying Glitch I at her breast, the voice of Flame Searclaw again sought her out. Cruel and impatient, its tones as fiery as the ruby scales that flashed when he flew, the red dragon penetrated her mind with his distant voice. "What are you doing?" he demanded. "You were told to come, but you are not here. Report!"

"You should be glad I have not come to you, Flame Searclaw," she shot back, fiercely. "We have a score to settle, you and I."

"Any time you like, green snake," his voice was contemptuous. "But first, you have a duty. Why are you not here?"

"I can't come," she admitted. "Not just yet. There are these . . . these creatures. They have a hold on me, and insist that I lead them . . . somewhere."

"Creatures?"

In her mind she felt the red dragon's presence, sensing beyond what she had said. Then it recoiled in disbelief. "*Gully dwarves?* You, the great Verden Leafglow, a hostage to . . .

to gully dwarves?" Cruel laughter echoed in the mind-talk. "What is it they want of you?"

"To take them to their Promised Place. But they don't know where that is!"

"Gully dwarves." Again the cruel, shadowy laughter. "Hurry and deal with your . . . with your new masters, Verden Leafglow. Your presence here is commanded."

The mind-voice faded and Verden trembled with rage.

"Ouch!"

She glanced down at the struggling Highbulp. "What?"

"You squishin' me! Don' squeeze so hard!"

You little twit, she thought. I could squeeze the very life out of you with no effort at all. Still, she sensed the self-stone lodged inside the little creature, responding to his discomfort. *Her* self-stone. It must be protected. Reluctantly, she eased her grip.

Everywhere, the dragonarmies were on the move, and Verden Leafglow ached to join them—to join in the death and destruction they brought. She itched for the sport of it.

A dozen times, holding the smelly, irritating little Highbulp to her breast, she led them to dismal, deserted, unwanted places—splendid places for gully dwarves. But each time, Glitch I, the Highbulp, took a slow, arrogant look around and said, "Nope, this not it. Try again."

Verden thought longingly of how pleasant it would be to slice the strutting little twit into a thousand bloody chunks and scatter him all over Ansalon. But for the self-stone lodged within him . . .

"Not Promised Place," he insisted, time and again. "Nope, this place okay for This Place, but not Promised Place. Dragon promise Promised Place. Try again."

Beyond the Kharolis', while her unwanted charges slept beneath the visible moons, a thoroughly exasperated Verden Leafglow took Glitch and went scouting. On great wings, fully healed if only temporarily, she soared high in the night sky. All her senses at full pitch, she searched, and where ancient scars creased the shattered land, the mind-talk came again.

Like a taunting, contemptuous message, hanging in the air, waiting for her to hear it, it was there. Flame Searclaw's voice, from far away. A chuckle of evil mirth, and words.

"So they still possess you," it said. "The least among the least, they search for their heritage. And Verden Leafglow is their slave. How marvelous. There is an answer to your riddle, though."

"Continue." Verden Leafglow sneered mentally. "You have my attention."

"Destiny," the non-voice snickered. "A Highbulp of destiny. And one such as you to guide him. How exquisite."

Verden growled in fury, but listened.

"Xak Tsaroth," the dragon voice said. "Xak Tsaroth is a suitable Promised Place. Xak Tsaroth. The Pitt. They belong there. Let the Pitt be their destiny. And delivering them to such a place, at such a time, is your reward."

With a final chuckle of deep, taunting amusement, the voice of Flame Searclaw repeated, "Xak Tsaroth . . . the Pitt . . ." and faded.

Xak Tsaroth. Soaring on wide wings, Verden looked down at the Highbulp Glitch I, pressed to her breast. The little twit had, of course, heard none of it. He was sound asleep. Xak Tsaroth. Despite her hatred of Flame Searclaw and the murderous rage she felt toward him, an evil delight grew in Verden. Her reward, indeed. She knew what was in Xak Tsaroth. There could be no finer revenge on the gully dwarves than to deliver them there. Others of their kind were there . . . enslaved, abused and at the mercy of draconians. These should join them.

The idea was very sweet to her.

Verden Leafglow had returned to the combined clans by the time they awakened. Like a great, serpentine pillar of brilliant emerald, she towered above them. Her vast wings were radiant in the morning sun and her formidable fangs alight in her dragon mouth. Little Highbulp seemed a ragged doll clenched at her breast. Huge and malevolent, Verden Leafglow loomed over the puny creatures—and shuddered with revulsion when one of them tripped sleepily over her toe.

Without ceremony, she rousted them out and told them, "I have found your Promised Place. Get a move on, and I'll take you there."

"No hurry," Glitch squirmed in her grasp. "This place not bad This Place. Maybe stay here a while, then go."

"We go now," she hissed.

Gandy squinted up at her. "Where is Promised Place?"

"Xak Tsaroth."

"Bless dragon," Minna said.

"What?"

"Dragon sneeze."

"I did not sneeze! I never sneeze. I said, 'Xak Tsaroth'."

"Bless dragon," Minna repeated. "Where Promised Place?"

Verden shook her head as though insects were tormenting her. "The Pitt," she said.

All around her, gully dwarves glanced at one another with real interest. "That sound pretty good," several decided.

"Sound all right," Glitch conceded. "Maybe think 'bout that, day or so, then . . ."

"*Shut up!*" Verden roared. "*We go now!*"

Never before—as far as anyone who might have cared knew—had gully dwarves traveled as fast or as purposefully as the combined clans of Bulp traveled during the following two days. It was a nearly exhausted band that gathered by evening's light to gaze on Xak Tsaroth. They stood at the top of a high, sheared slope above shadowed depths, and looked out at distant crags beyond which were the waters of Newsea.

"The Promised Place," Verden Leafglow told them. "I have brought you here, as I promised. I have kept my word."

"Promised Place?" The Highbulp squinted around. "Where?"

"Down there," Verden pointed downward with a deadly, eloquent talon. "The Pitt." Not gently, she set Glitch down and said, "This is it. Now cough up my stone."

Tagg crept to the edge and looked down. It was a slope of sheer rock, a vertiginous incline that dropped away into shadows far below. "Wow," he said.

The Highbulp only glanced into the depths, then turned away, an arrogant, scheming grin on his face. "Prob'ly not it," he decided. "Nope, prob'ly not Promised Place. Better try again." With a casual wave of his hand, he added, "Dragon dis—dismiss for now. Highbulp send for you when need you."

It was just too much for Verden Leafglow. She had taken more than she could stand. "Dismissed? You imbecilic little twit, you dismiss *me*? Rats!"

Gully dwarves backpedaled all around her, tumbling over one another. Some went over the edge, sliding and rolling away toward the shadowed depths. Others turned to watch them go. "They really movin'," someone said. "That steep." "Smooth, though," another noted. "Good slide."

"*Rats!*" Verden roared again, exasperated beyond reason and reverting to the vernacular of her charges. "*Rats!*" Annoyed beyond control, she aimed a swat at Glitch. The Highbulp dodged aside, ducked . . . and belched. Something shot from his mouth, to bounce to a stop at Verden's foot. She scooped it up. It was her self-stone. She had it back, intact.

"Rats," Gandy said, realizing that the good times were over.

"That right," the Highbulp remembered, snapping his fingers. "Rats, too. Dragon promise us rats."

"You . . . want . . . *rats*?" The huge, dragon face lowered itself, nose to nose with the little Highbulp. "You want rats? Very well. You shall have rats."

Closing her eyes, she murmured a spell, and her dragon-senses heard the scurrying of tiny things in the distance—sounds below sound that grew in volume as they came closer.

The gully dwarves heard it then, too, and stared about in wonder. The sounds grew, seeming to come from everywhere. Then there were little, dark shadows arrowing toward them, emerging from crevices, coming over rises and up gullies—dozens, then hundreds, then thousands of small, scurrying things, homing in on them. Rats. A leaping, bounding, flowing tide of rats.

"Wow," Tagg murmured.

"Lotta rats," Minna concurred. "Gonna make lotta stew,

for sure."

Clout, never one to be concerned with details, brandished his bashing tool and prepared to deal with dinner.

Gandy, though, took a different view of the matter, "Too much rats," he started. "Way too much rats for . . ."

The tidal wave of rats swept around them, under them, over them—and carried them with it. A second later, Verden Leafglow stood alone on the ledge, looking down at a slope awash with rats and gully dwarves, all gathering momentum on their way to Xak Tsaroth, buried city within the Pitt.

As they disappeared into shadows, her dragon eyes picked out details: Tagg and Minna hand in hand, their hair blowing around them; old Gandy flailing his mop handle as he tried to maintain his balance at great speed; Clout busily swatting rats and gathering up their corpses; and the Highbulp—Glitch I was rolling, tumbling downward, a flailing tangle of arms, legs and whipping beard, and his panicked voice rose above the others.

"Make way!" he shouted. "Get outta way! Highbulp on a roll!"

Somehow, even disappearing into the depths and the shadows—and the unsuspected horrors—of the ancient, lost city that was his destination and his destiny, Glitch I, Highbulp by Persuasion and Lord Protector of Lots of Places—including, now, the Promised Place—still managed to sound arrogant.

Clockwork Hero

Jeff Grubb

This is a Gnome Story. Such stories turn up now and again, around hearths and over cups of mulled wine. The talespinner of a proper Gnome Story should always state at the outset that his is a story of the gnomish type, so that the listeners are not surprised by that which follows. The Lower Planes hold no fury compared to that of an intent and dutiful audience that suddenly discovers they are trapped in a Gnome Story, with no escape other than the bodily expulsion of the talespinner. Heads have been broken, families split asunder, empires uprooted, and all because of an unannounced Gnome Story.

This is a Gnome Story then, and that in itself is considered fair and proper warning. And it is a Gnome Story because it deals with, to a great degree, gnomes.

Gnomes, you see, have the boundless curiosity of men, but lack the limitation of sense, the directness of thought, or the wisdom to control this curiosity. This disposition makes gnomes a vital part of talespinning, as much as the country fool who proves to be the wisest person of the party, or the holy man who arrives at the last minute to resolve all the characters' problems. In a similar fashion, gnomes—with their insatiable curiosity, their gleeful cleverness, and their perseverance through frequent (and dramatic) failure—serve as a guiding light, a beacon for other races. In holding up their failings, their ramshackle inventions and plots, we see more than a little of ourselves, and consider ourselves cautioned against their excesses. So gnomes have an important place in the universe (at least fictionally), such that if gnomes did not exist, they would demand to be invented, and nothing short of another gnome could invent such a concept.

Fortunately for all, they do exist.

This, then, is a Gnome Story, with all of its vantages, *ad* and *dis*. It is an odd tale, in that it tells the story of a gnome who succeeds, a gnome who creates a most wondrous thing. But that is getting ahead of the tale.

Gnome Stories usually begin with the talespinner speaking of some outsider stumbling onto the hidden land of the gnomes. The idea of a hidden land of the gnomes is usually an artistic "cheat," a stretching of the imagination, since there are very few places more noisy, smoky, smelly, and downright noticeable than a gnome community. Incontinent volcanos or a week-long reunion of gully dwarves would run a close second or third, and, like a cluster of volcanoes or gaggle of gully dwarves, a gnome community is generally well-noted by its neighbors and left alone. It is, therefore, remote from the rest of civilization, but at civilization's behest.

This particular gnome community—this talespinner must assure you—was an extremely noisy place, resounding with the clang of hammers, the hiss of escaping steam, and the occasional explosion. The louder the gnomes, the more remote their home, and this was a most remote location indeed. So remote that the events of the outside world—the return of dragons, the coming of the Highlords and heroes, the war and all manner of destruction—passed this place by. In short, it was the perfect place to be an outsider, since there was much more outside than inside.

The outsider in question was not the standard singular found in most Gnome Stories, but rather two, a doubleton of strangers, a windfall in terms of Gnome Stories. These strangers had two things in common: they were from outside this village of gnomes—yes, that's true—but more important, they were first found sprawled in awkward but comfortable-looking positions on the ground, next to a large, formerly leather-winged form. Said form had earlier been a dragon, but was now little more than an open buffet for the local scavengers.

The outsiders were both alive, however. One was a warrior wrapped head to toe in dark armor, while the other was softer, plumper, unarmored, dressed in tattered finery and bound firmly at the wrists and ankles. The warrior was a woman, though this was not immediately apparent from her armor; the one in ragged finery was a man. For gnomes, gender is as unimportant as eye color or taste in music, but since these are *human* outsiders, it will become important. More on that later, because the gnome had finally arrived on the scene to survey the damage. And this is a Gnome Story.

It was a gnome named Kalifirkinshibirin who discovered the comfortably sprawled outsiders outside (of course) his village. Kalifirkinshibirin (or Kali, shortening further a name already truncated due to space) was a smallish gnome, whose hobbies included spoon-collecting and putting dried flowers under glass. He also had what passed for healing skill, being versed in some natural poultices and potions that had the unique advantage (among gnomes) of not killing his patients outright.

Kali was gathering ingredients for said potions and poultices in that particular field on that particular morning, and so, it fell to him to discover those particular remains of that particular dragon, and the outsiders resting comfortably nearby. He was definitely not in the field because he was looking for new discoveries to be made, new revelations to be revealed, or new objects to muck about with. Kali was, to put it delicately, different from his fellows.

No, better to strip away the kindness of language and face this straight out. Kali was a queer duck among his people. Most gnomes live to invent. They have fives, even tens of projects in the works at the same time, one often spilling into another at random. Gnomes see the world as inherently wrong (not an unpopular sentiment), but gnomes differ from the rest of the universe in that they believe it is their job to set matters right. That's why they invent—continually, relentlessly, and explosively—all manner of gimcracks and snapperdoodles and thingamabobs.

It's the thing that gnomes just naturally do, like breathing or taking tea.

But Kali didn't have that same sort of drive as his fellows. He was pretty content in doing what he was doing with potions and plants and poultices to relieve the occasional outbreak of flu or bad colds. He had his spoons, of course; inscribed with wildflowers, legendary heroes, and mythical animals (which was how he recognized the dragon, by the by), but none of them were mechanical in the least. He kept plans for a solar-powered lighthouse about his parlor—for appearances—but he hadn't added to them in years.

In short, Kali was an underachiever. (This was not a criminal offense to Kali's fellow gnomes—they tended to be understanding about it. Indeed, the fact that Kali's healing methods would not vary from week to week did something for his reputation as a healer).

In any event, it was Kali who found the outsiders. He determined they were within the bounds of "still breathing," and dragged the armored and unarmored forms back to his house in the village. (This is important, for it would make these outsiders—by custom—Kali's salvage and Kali's responsibility.) By the time he brought the second one (the unarmored, plumper, male one) back, a small crowd of his fellow gnomes had gathered about his front porch. They were armed with all manner of fearful-looking devices, and a sharp gleam shone in each and every eye.

To an outsider (particularly a human outsider), these gnomes would appear to be a horde of evil torturers prepared to initiate a cruel inquisition, but Kali recognized that these were merely his fellow inventors. The devices were hastily-assembled inventions that would straighten a leg, lance an infection, or immobilize a thrashing patient (the last invention was a necessity for experimental surgery). The gleam that seemed so evil was only the heartfelt and honest lust that every gnome feels when one of his inventions might prove useful.

To an outsider, though, the gleam would look undoubtedly and understandably malicious, and the size and number of sharp edges on the devices would tend to intensify said doubt. Were the two outsiders healthy, they would not walk into this apparently dangerous realm without at least a dozen more of their kind, and with a healthy reward promised on the other side.

Kali was dragging the large, plumper figure onto his porch when he found his way blocked. The first outsider, the armored one, had awakened and now stood tottering in the doorway. She looked dangerous and tall, and while the last word could be attributed to all humans by all gnomes, this one looked taller still, swaying in her blood-colored leather boots like an improperly planted pine in the first windstorm of spring. The impressive nature of this outsider was further enhanced by the mass of her armor, and the great horns that rose from her helm like the misplaced pincers of some irate beetle.

The gathered gnomes set up a sigh of disappointment. Apparently, her injuries were not serious.

The woman unlatched the toggles on her helmet and removed it, revealing a sharp, angry face cradled in a scarf of blood-red hair. Swaying as though the ground were on unsteady terms with her, she scowled, then bellowed in a wavering voice, "You are all to surrender or—"

She did not provide another option, for the weight of her words unbalanced her and she crumbled neatly in the doorway. It was obvious to all that she had suffered greater damage than initially thought. She needed help.

The gathered gnomes were ecstatic.

The pair of humans—armored and unarmored, female and male, soldier and well . . . the male was dressed like a merchant, mage, or alchemist—rested in Kali's house for five feverish days. Neither was strong enough to wake, take food, or make demands. The man-merchant slept the dreamless sleep of the dead, while the woman-warrior shuddered with fits that brought her half-waking into the pain of this world. During this time, Kali was forced to convince more than one of his gnomish compatriots that a newly invented device—such as the one to bore a small hole in the forehead to witness their dreams—was unnecessary, and proceeded to work his own craft upon them. Kali's craft was healing, and he was quite good at it . . . as gnomes go.

On the morning of the sixth day, Kali awoke to find the tip of a sword at his throat. This was a surprise because he normally kept such things as swords in a large glass case marked "SWORDS" in the other room. Not surprisingly, given the location of the sword, the woman-warrior was at the opposite end. Kali had restrained the pair in their sleep, so they would not hurt themselves in a violent dream, but he had made their shackles of loose cloth.

Too loose.

"Surrender or die," she hissed.

Kali gave careful (and rapid) thought to his options, and asked her what she wanted for breakfast.

The news of Kali's surrender to the awakened outsider moved through the village like the fiery results of a failed chemical experiment.

(In Gnome Stories the outsider always declares [him- or] herself master of the land, and the gnomes always agree. Some uncharitable souls say this is because the gnomes are stalling while they gleefully plan their revenge. In reality, gnome tribes are truly interested in learning as much as possible from newcomers, and will try to make them happy. If surrendering is what the outsider wants, it is a small price to pay as long as the outsider remains. So it was in this case.)

Soon, a horde of short but passionate individuals queued up outside Kali's house, each seeking to surrender to the awakened woman-warrior, who was breakfasting within on blueberry muffins and sausage. Some gnomes wrote long poems, others recited longer declarations of allegiance, while still others attempted to surrender by mime, juggling sparklers so they would not be ignored in favor of those declaring and rhyming. Some few brought swords to beat into plowshares, though these arrived last, since they had to beat the plowshares into swords in the first place (and indeed, many of the swords had a distinct plowsharish look to them).

Rather than being pleased, the woman-warrior (the gnomes were already calling her Outsider A and her companion Outsider B in their journals) seemed threatened by this outpouring of mass poetry, oratory, and mime. Indeed, a huge collection of small people shouting and waving, with others coming up behind bearing large plowsharish-looking swords would unnerve any stern general unschooled in gnomecraft. Unfortunately the woman-warrior reacted like a typical human, and charged into a disaster of her own making.

She strode out onto the porch to order the gnomes to scatter. The sight of her was enough to inspire a mass shout from the crowd. She, in turn—thinking that an attack was imminent—brandished her sword. The gnomes surged forward, each intent on surrendering first. The startled outsider backed into the doorway, feinted at the crowd with her sword, then rapidly backed up again . . .

. . . And toppled backward over a cast iron boot-holder Kali kept by the door (for cast iron boots). Woman and sword went boots over boots with a resounding crash. She was soon resting comfortably on the floor again, with a small bruise on the top of her head.

Kali shooed his friends, family, and fellow inventors out of the entranceway and, with a sigh, returned to his healing craft (which he was quite good at . . . as gnomes go). Her weapons and armor he hid in a back room, since twice now the warrior had become most unwell after using them.

The warrior-woman would awake two days later, but in the meantime the other outsider, Outsider B, awoke, though with less spectacular effects. He merely wondered what was for breakfast, and, though it was noon, Kali set his clock back six hours in order to be accommodating.

Outsider B, who astounded the surrendering gnomes by informing them his name was Oster, seemed a bit befuddled, but less violent, when the herd of half-sized humans humbugged and mimed their absolute fealty to him. Then the assembled gnomes ran home to cross out "Outsider B" and write "Oster" in their journals. Oster went inside to have breakfast and dined pleasantly as the sound of erasers ripping through thin paper resounded through the village.

After breakfast, Kali shooed away the last few neighbors who had stopped by to surrender (and to see if any blueberry muffins were left). He returned to ask Oster about his travels and how he and the woman came to this place, but found his ambulatory charge missing from the main room. A sudden panic gripped Kali. He feared that this stranger had wandered off and, knowing humans, gotten himself into trouble.

A quick search revealed Oster in the second spare guest room, at the foot of the bed where the warrior-woman was resting. The human had an odd look on his face, that look that gnomes get when they realize an invention requires no more modification. Rapture would be a good word for it. So would golly-woggled-knocked-off-the-pins-in-love, but rapture is shorter and as such will be used henceforth.

Kali moved quietly into the room and stood there for several heartbeats, shifting his weight from foot to foot and not knowing if he should leave.

Finally the man sighed. A deep, room-filling sigh that would have driven the atmospheric pressure indicator in the bedroom up a few notches, had Kali thought well enough to install such a device. It was a human, rapture-filled sigh.

"She is beautiful," he said. "Healer, who is she?"

Kali was thunderstruck. He had assumed the two outsiders knew each other, since they were found near the same wreckage. Kali wondered if the man's mind had been damaged by the fall, as the woman's apparently had.

"She, ah . . ." began the gnome, "she was not with you?"

Oster snorted like he had inhaled a fish. "With me? Nay, Healer. I am a simple merchant, too bull-headed to live quietly under tyranny, but too old and fat to fight it well. My wagons were confiscated and I joined a small party that raided and ambushed the invaders, burning their supplies and freeing their slaves. For that crime we were hunted through hills and valleys by a greater force than we could have imagined. My comrades were soon dead and scattered, and I was left to face the fury of the Dragon Highlord on my own."

The human shook his head, but his eyes never left the slumbering form of the woman. "Damned fool that I was, I did not run, nor beg for mercy, nor even think to draw my weapon. By the time I had even conceived of such things, the hell-spawn commander of that force—the Dragon

Highlord himself—was upon me, and knocked me out. Why the Highlord did not kill me there I do not know, Morgion rot his bones. Instead he trussed me and slung me dragonback like a sack of flour. When I awakened to my fate, we were in the air. Then a massive blow struck the beast in its flight, and we crashed. I awoke to find myself in your parlor, with all these odd, pleasant little people, and with this"—he leaned toward the woman—"vision of loveliness."

The woman-warrior was lean and stringy, her battle-hardened muscles honed by war. But she was fair of face and, with her auburn hair spread out on the down pillows, looked almost angelic. It was easy for a human to think of her as beautiful when she was unconscious.

Kali, being a gnome, was thinking along other lines.

"This Highlord," he asked, "did you know him?"

"No," answered Oster, staring rapturously at the woman. "I never saw him without his mask."

It was then apparent to Kali that the "foul hell-spawn" and the radiant creature with whom the man was smitten (for even gnomes can recognize someone who is smitten) were one and the same. But more important at the time was the news that a massive blow hit the dragon they were riding and forced it to crash. Weapons that could deliver massive blows out of the sky and force dragons to crash sounded suspiciously gnomish to the gnome.

Of course, the outsider Oster would be disappointed to find out that his vision of loveliness and his Morgion-cursed captor were one and the same. Were Kali a less honorable and more honest individual, he would have burst Oster's bubble at once. But Kali was a gentlegnome, and there were some things you just don't do in polite society: disappointing someone to whom you have surrendered was one of them.

Oster broke in on the gnome's reverie with another room-filling sigh. "Does she have a name?"

"Er . . . ummm," stuttered the gnome, thinking on his feet. "Did she give me a name when . . . ah . . . she brought you in? Something about fighting a dragon. Yes, that's it, something about a fight with a dragon. She hit it with some great magic, that must have . . . ah . . . been the massive blow you felt. And you fell off of it and . . . ah . ." He scanned the room for inspiration, his eyes settling on his collection of ornamental spoons painted with wildflowers. He tried to think of a flower name. "She brought you here, but was . . . drained by the battle, and took ill herself soon after . . . something about the battle that wore her out. Columbine. Yes, *that* was the name. Columbine."

"Columbine," said Oster, sighing again, a deep sigh that made Kali think of a bellows in need of repair. "I owe my life to her. I feared that I would be held prisoner or slain by the Highlord, but now I have made good an escape to a magical land. Rescued by a beautiful and magical woman."

He turned to the gnome, transfixing Kali in an intense gaze. "I must help her recover, little healer. What can I do to help?"

Kali stammered and stuttered, but at last instructed the man Oster in some simple methods of healing, little more than the applying of cold compresses and the like. Then he left his two charges alone and fled the house. He needed to think about what had just transpired and, more importantly, to confirm his immediate fears concerning the dragon's demise.

Kali went from house to house, a long, tedious business that took most of the rest of the day. This is not because the gnomish community was large—it was not—but at every house, a visiting gnome must make pleasant conversation, have tea, report on any recent findings, have some more tea, look at the host's latest researches, make more pleasant conversations, and so forth, before pressing on. Kali hoped he was not offending others by refusing a third helping of tea, but after the sixth house he was beginning to slosh as he walked.

At the seventh house, the one belonging to Archimedorastimor the Lesser, son of Archimedorastimor the Greater (and the Later), Kali found the answer he feared. The Archimedorastimors (father and son) had both been involved with astronomy and had long been wondering what to do with their time when it was overcast or daylight. While most gnomes in the field simply attempted to build large towers to get above the clouds and beyond the sun, the Archimedorastimors (Archies for short) instead came up with the novel idea of firing their telescopes from large catapults to get above the clouds and the sun. Other gnomes scoffed at the foolishness of the theory and went back to building towers. But Archie father and son went on experimenting until the time, three years ago, when Archie father built an explosive catapult and launched his entire laboratory into the air, from whence it never came down. Archie, son of Archie, had since continued his father's research, but (save for creating a combination parachute and pillow) had added little to the science. Occasionally, however, he managed to launch a large rock that would fall down on a building or three.

In any event, it was at the seventh house that Kali found the answer he was dreading. Yes, five days back Archie had been out in the field experimenting with a new astronomical catapult, and from that testing he had just returned. The experiment had been a failure because something large and lumbering had gotten in the way at the last moment. The large and lumbering something sounded to Kali suspiciously dragonlike. When he proposed this theory, Archie did admit that the lumbering something was more than a little reptilian in appearance. Further, it made a sudden and steep dive after it flew into his rock. Kali took tea and made small conversation for the rest of the afternoon, adjuring Archie not to mention the details of this experiment to the new outsiders—Oster and the warrior-woman. Archie promised and also said he would be by later to surrender when he had finished his journal.

Kali, having resolved the first problem, now turned to the second. The warrior-woman was a Dragon Highlord (whatever that was), and had taken Oster as a prisoner—in a mean fashion at that. The Highlord's armor, which Kali had hidden in a back room, apparently had concealed the fact that she was a woman. Oster was now smitten (as only humans can be smitten) with her in her true appearance. When the woman awakened again, Kali figured, she would probably be mean to Oster again. Oster would be hurt that this radiant creature was not only not named Columbine, but was also the individual that was so mean to him before.

That would make *two* people that the gnomes had surrendered to unhappy.

That would not do at all.

When Kali returned to his house, he found that the man Oster had gathered some wildflowers and placed them in a vase by the woman's sickbed. Kali decided the man had not been addled by the fall after all. From the Human Stories he'd heard beside hearths and over cups of mulled wine, Kali knew such behavior was typical. Humans were always engaging in activity that seemed fruitless, pointless, and overly emotional, making use of grand gestures and mighty oaths.

The first step, thought Kali, is to make sure the man Oster is not around when the warrior-woman comes to. Her last two outings among the living had proved to be less than peaceful, and based on that sort of previous behavior, the next occasion boded no better. At least he should get the man away and talk to the woman, explain the situation, and calm her down. If she were half as reasonable as Oster, all would work out for the best. Perhaps she had imprisoned him because she liked his appearance as well as he liked hers, Kali reasoned. Human Stories made much of the fact that humans were very poor at expressing themselves, particularly to those they liked.

When Kali walked into the room, he noticed Oster holding the woman's wrist, as though that would indicate anything more than that the body in question had a pulse. Steeling himself for deception, the gnome walked up to the foot of the bed and grabbed the woman's exposed big toe. Scowling as he imagined wise humans would scowl, Kali gave a grumbling sigh.

Oster looked up at the gnome at the foot of the bed.

"Not good," said Kali.

"Not good?" said Oster

"Complications," said Kali. "Straining of the impervious maximus. Omar's syndrome. Liberal contusions. It may be a while."

Oster rose to his full height and stamped his foot. "Then I shall remain and help!"

Kali was prepared for the human to issue a mighty oath

on the matter, but when none was forthcoming, he scowled deeper and thought quickly. "I'm . . . ah . . . going to need some supplies. You may help best—if you are up to it—by going to fetch them."

"Anything to aid, little healer."

Kali went to his desk and drew out a parchment and pen. He listed five things at random: hen's teeth, black roses, rubbing alcohol, toad eyes, and feldspar chips. He gave the list to Oster. "These will aid," said the gnome. "You can gather some gear from the storage area and set off. You may need several days to gather the items, but take your time."

"Can I have a guide to help?"

Kali thought of Archie. "I can arrange something. Now come. The woman . . . er, Columbine . . . needs peace and quiet as well as those items."

The man went back to rummage in the storage area and Kali wrote a note to Archie, explaining the situation and the need to take the man on the longest possible course to get these items. He was going to post it normally, but checked himself, noting that the gnomish postal service would just as likely deliver it to Oster or back to himself, since their names were mentioned. He ended up delivering it himself.

Archie and Oster left the next morning, and the woman-warrior awoke that evening, feverish and angry. Kali was entertaining another colleague, Etonamemdosari (Eton), a weaponsmith, who was working on a sword that could be used directly as a plowshare, when the woman stumbled into the room. The pair of gnomes looked up from their mulled wine. (They were trading Human Stories).

Awake, the woman was less lovely than asleep, for her waking thoughts and memories pinched her face into a tightly-muscled scowl that would scare the cat, had Kali had any cats. (He did not, for they made him sneeze, but *had* he a cat, said cat would be considering changing his lodgings after looking at the woman).

"My weapons," she said in a voice that would frighten a watchdog. (See the above note on cats, for they apply in this case to dogs as well).

"Er . . . Have some wine?" asked Kali.

"Roast the wine!" bellowed the woman, crossing the

room in a single stride and thumping the table with both fists. "Where are my weapons? Where is my armor? Where is my dragon?"

"Dragon?" said Kali, hoping to sound much more innocent than he felt.

The woman made a noise like a machine caught between gears and pitched the table over, mulled wine and all. Kali could see this was not going to work out as well as he had hoped.

"Try again," she said, an evil glint in her eye, "or I'll twist your head off."

"Ahem . . . Well. Ah. . ." Kali's mind raced for a moment, trying to remember how much of the tale he told Oster applied here. "We, ah, I, ah . . . that is . . . You were brought here by a hero who slew the beast you were riding. He thought it a wild creature, but, when he found you and realized it was yours, he . . . ah . . . brought you here to recover and, ah . . . left to gather some healing herbs to aid you. He says he's terribly sorry."

Kali's words struck the angry woman like a blow. She visibly sagged for a moment, her shoulders drooping. Kali could see that the deceased dragon meant as much to her as a cat or dog would to him, except it would probably not make her sneeze. She slumped into a chair, and after taking a few breaths to steady herself, said in a wavering voice. "The prisoner?"

"He, ammm"—Kali's mind jumped its track for a moment—"didn't make it, I'm afraid." Perhaps she would show sympathy, and that would let him comfort her by revealing that Oster was alive and well. Or maybe even returned to life by a passing holy man.

"And his body?" she continued. Something in her tone, her tight smile, the way her fingers dug into the wood of the table told Kali that sympathy was not a current priority for the woman.

"Well," Kali said, "We ah, tend to burn such things. Had we known you wanted it, we would have kept it for you. I didn't know he meant that much to you."

The woman laughed—a throaty, deep-seated laugh that started in orbit around her stony heart and, by the time it escaped her lips, held the cruelty of a creature who would throttle birds before breakfast. (See above notes on cats and dogs. Kali's case: no birds were endangered by the laugh.)

"Meant much? I wanted to take him apart in pieces, cracking each bone, and hang him by his living entrails on a hook in the village to show how I deal with traitors and rebels. His kind cost me a treasure train, and now he has cost me my dragon as well. May Morgion rot his body and Chemosh stir his bones!"

Kali was struck by the coldness of her oaths, which carried none of the nobility and passion of Oster's oaths, though they invoked the same beings. This human did not seem to have much difficulty in expressing herself at all. It now dawned on him that if he brought her together with Oster, she would be irate—not only at Oster, but at Kali as well. Best to backtrack, he thought, and try to make the situation turn out right.

"Well, he seemed a nice sort before he, ah . . . well . . ." Kali looked at Eton for support in the conversation. His fellow gnome had backed up next to the hearth and was trying to blend in with the fireplace furnishings.

"Did he suffer?" asked the woman. "Were his bones snapped?

Kali said yes and answered in the affirmative to a long list of horrible things that she described, just about filling the dance card with all the things that can happen to an individual who has fallen from a high place to a low one. Snapped bones, shattered skull, inner workings scattered over sharp rocks, just enough breath left in the crushed body to plead for mercy and deliver a parting rattle. Kali wondered if this passed for polite conversation where the woman came from. His answers seemed to get the woman more agitated and excited, until he would swear her eyes became like twin pilot lights, glowing and sparking in a malevolent fashion.

Having exhausted that interesting subject, the woman demanded, "My weapons? My helm? My armor?"

"The hero, ah, the one who brought you in . . . ah . . . hid them," said the gnome.

"Hid them?" she shrieked, rising from the table.

"Ah, yes. To keep away burglars, you know. He said he

would return them when he got back . . ."

Kali intended to say that the hero would not return for more than a few days and why didn't the woman rest, but things started to happen very quickly then. Making that gear-grinding noise again, the warrior pushed both hands up under the gnome's beard and, taking a firm hold of his neck, lifted him off the ground. Kali found that the grip closed off his breathing pipes. Small sparks danced between the woman's face and his. She enlivened this by screaming at him that he and his rat-faced friends would find her weapons if they had to eat their way through the mountains with their teeth, punctuating her remarks by banging Kali's head and shoulders against the back wall. The impact with the wall caused Kali to miss some of her words, but he caught the gist.

How long this fit went on Kali did not know. He was aware, finally, that he could breathe again, and save for a sore neck and a ringing headache, was still alive. He saw before him the form of the warrior-woman, resting less than comfortably in a heap of broken furniture, facedown. Across from him, Eton was holding a wide-mouthed shovel used to clean the hearth.

Kali gave a breathy, hoarse thanks, but he could see how Eton was already trying to figure out how to turn the hearth shovel into a combination sword/plowshare.

Kali put the woman back to bed and arranged for the delivery of new furniture by the time Oster and Archie returned with the material the next day. In that time, Kali had a long time to rub his sore head and think things through.

Now, despite a lot of stories, gnomes are not by nature violent. Nor, despite similar stories, are they stupid. Kali could see that this warrior was going to become enraged every time she awoke, and that telling her the truth would result in a rampage that would end up destroying a goodly amount of gnomish property and perhaps gnomish bodies. This would not be a good occurrence, given the fact that gnomes had surrendered to the woman and everything. Further, she would likely harm Oster if she knew he was alive. In the brief time Kali had known Oster, the gnome had decided that the man was one of the good humans, even given his terrible choice in creatures to fall smitten with. It would crush his heart if he found out she so cruel and mean. It would also likely crush his windpipe if the two were left in the same room together.

The problem was, Kali decided, that he was trying to work in an area he was unfamiliar with. He knew humans only from stories and wild tales, and his current personal encounters indicated something was lacking from his store of knowledge. Human emotions were even farther removed. Like most gnomes, Kali was most familiar with things he could touch, grip, twist, break, and repair. If only this situation had such a simple, physical solution.

Looking at the blanket-covered woman, peaceful as the dead and lovely as the morning, Kali realized that perhaps there *was* a simple, physical solution.

By the time Oster and Archie had returned, Kali had not only laid out a plan, but he had made a list of materials: a closed wagon with oxen, two hundred pounds of plaster, a similar amount of wax, a stone mausoleum with an iron fence around it, seven tins of pastels and other shades of paint, the aid of Organathoran the painter, and sufficient medication to keep a horse in slumberland for a week.

He was just drawing up the last of it and was about to check on the woman (to make sure she had not woken up again), when Oster and Archie returned. A crowd of other gnomes clustered around them as Archie described something in glowing detail, making swing-of-a-sword gestures with his hands.

Kali met the pair at the door and Oster presented the gnome with a small package containing the herbs and other items they had gathered from the wild. At his side he had another, larger bundle. The human gave Kali a small, almost embarrassed smile, but all eyes were on Archie, who was gesticulating wildly.

"It was wonderful," cried Archie, noticing Kali for the first time. "The lad, er, the human Oster was magnificent! We were in the Smoking Vale two miles from here when suddenly we startled a wyrm of some type. A true monster, straight from the pits, with the legs of a pill-bug and the hunger of a bear and fangs twice as long as my arm."

"It was a behir," Oster said softly, his ears tinged with red, "and a small one at that."

Archie hurtled on without stopping to note the interruption. "I would have been dinner on a plate, but Oster—Oster the Brave—mind you, threw me out of the way of certain death."

"I, ah, knocked him over when I turned to run," Oster corrected, the glow spreading to his cheeks and increasing in intensity with each moment.

"Then brave Oster, armed with only with a sharpened rock, caught the beast's attention. It lunged at him." And here Archie did his best imitation of a serpent lunging forward, such that some of the gathered gnomes backed up a few paces. "And he pulled the side of the mountain down on the beast, killing it!"

"I tried to scramble up the cliff out of its path, and brought down an avalanche. Nearly buried us all." Oster's voice had grown quiet now as he saw that most of the gnomes liked Archie's recollection of events better than his.

Archie rolled on like a perpetual motion machine. "The beast was mortally wounded, and tried to turn on us. Oster took a mighty boulder and smashed it until it was no more."

"Well, I . . . It wasn't that big of a . . . well . . . I guess . . ." Oster shrugged his shoulders. Had he known that in gnomish discussions silence meant agreement, he would probably have protested his innocence of heroism a while longer. But he did not know, so he did not protest—which was as good as admitting it.

Archie motioned for the sack. "And we found all manner of gems and magic in the creature's lair."

The gnomes naturally demanded to see the treasure, and so Oster pulled from the larger bag one item after another. Fistfuls of gems, long strings of pearls, and a set of plate mail of a golden hue, topped by a wondrous helm of similar color, ringed with gems. Finally he drew forth a scabbard and a copper-colored blade from the bag.

News of Oster's prowess (and his treasure) spread about the community quickly, and a number of gnomes came to surrender all over again to Oster (or rather, the Hero Oster, as he was now known). Archie had to tell his tale a second and a third time, and the hero's mighty attacks became mightier with every telling. Oster soon gave up trying to correct all the minor differences between Archie's version and his, and seemed to enjoy the attention.

Oster gave the bulk of the jewels to Archie, and the gemstones to Kali. The mail, copper sword, and helm he kept for himself, as they were all man-size, and Oster was the only being currently awake in the community who matched the description.

At the insistence of the gnomes, he put on the armor, though he had to let out the chains on the side plates to their maximum length. With the helm down over his face, he looked like a clockwork figure or automaton, and the name Oster the Clockwork Hero went down in many journals that night.

It was only when Oster had finished displaying and giving away his booty and Archie had finished describing (for the fifth time) the masterful strokes that the Clockwork Hero has delivered against the hordes of serpent creatures that the trio went back into the house. Oster let out a gasp of shock when he saw the drawing room in shambles.

"What happened?" he demanded, looking at the broken table, the shattered chairs, and the crushed crockery.

"Well, that is . . ." Kali stammered, thinking that he had best use this time to tell Oster the truth—that his lady fair had woken and destroyed the room, all the while gleefully describing the tortures she would heap upon him, Oster.

"It looks like a fiend hit this place," continued Oster.

"Ah . . . yes. A fiend." Kali shoved the truth to the back of his mind. Oster had been a hero only moments before, and the truth would only hurt him.

Kali had no fiends illustrated on his spoon collection and wondered what one truly looked like, but taking a deep breath he plunged on. "Ah . . . A fiend was here. Tall he was, so that his horns scraped the ceiling, and with plates of red, hardened chitin jutting from his shoulders, and a weave of black wires where his mouth was."

"Was he large? Did he carry a sword in a mailed glove? And armor?" asked Oster, his brow furrowed.

"Yes, yes, he was, and armored all over." Suddenly Kali

clamped a hand over his own mouth. In seeking to describe the "fiend" who had leveled the place, he had described the Highlord's dragonarmor.

"So," said Oster sternly, drawing himself up to his full height. "He lived through the death of his dragon. Why would he come here . . . unless . . . the Lady Columbine? Is she safe?"

"She . . . ah . . . rests comfortably in her room. The fiend made no attempt to get to her." Kali hoped that when Oster checked on her condition, he was not knowledgeable enough to spot an additional bump where Eton had clobbered her with a shovel.

"He was looking for me, wasn't he?" asked Oster grimly.

"No. I mean yes. I mean . . ." Kali said, trying to avoid tripping over his own tongue. Other gnomes, such as Archie, could spin tall tales until morning, but Kali always feared that one word would fall against another and leave him revealed as a liar. "He was here, and looking for you, and was most angry when I told him you were dead. He wanted your body, but I said we had burned it. I didn't mean to lie, but it seemed to be a good idea at the time." And I mean that in all possible ways, he added to himself.

"You did well, little healer," said Oster. "But you risked much to deceive one such as that. He will probably be back. When he does return, we must be ready for him. Tell me, what is the condition of the lady?"

"She . . . rests," said Kali, still choosing his words carefully. "I have given much thought to her injuries, and fear she might not recover." He was going to add that it would be in everyone's best interest if she *not* recover, but he made the error of looking into Oster's face, and saw the pain in his eyes. The human had stopped being a hero and became once more a middle-aged merchant. So Kali said instead, "I have a list of further medications that may cure her illness. But it will take time."

Oster immediately volunteered to go fetch them, and Archie chimed in his aid as well. Only Eton and Kali would know that the lady was no lady, and the ingredients the Clockwork Hero gathered were mixed to form a smoky concoction, the fumes of which would keep the woman in her blissful sleep until Kali could work his own solution.

The next few weeks—the time through high summer—passed with as few incidents as could be expected for a community of gnomes. Oster the Clockwork Hero's prestige in the community increased as he slew a few of the creatures that had plagued the area, including a large hydra that ruled the Steaming Stream and a beholder that had set up shop in an ancient dwarven mine.

The fact that in the former case he was accompanied by a party of gnomes armed with Eton's automatic lasso-projectors and in the latter the sword he found had been forged specifically to slay beholders did nothing to diminish his prestige. Oster was well-loved by the gnomes, never more so than when he rescued the Kastonopolintar sisters when their alchemy shop decided to blow up on Solstice Eve.

Yet most of the time when he was not out adventuring or attending this dinner or that fest in his honor, Oster sat by the bedside of the lady, now known in the community as Oster's Lady, waiting for her to recover, watching her passive, quiet face in the moonlight as her coverlets rose and fell with each breath. The gnomes respected Oster, and in turn respected his sleeping lady, so none of them mentioned her erratic behavior when she had first arrived, or that Kali seemed less effective than normal in working a cure. They did not want to worry the human needlessly.

Kali was miserable, of course. He knew the truth, more than any of his comrades, and it hurt him to see that he himself was responsible for Oster's heartache. It was clear that the human had built up an imagined image for his lady, a lady who, once awake, would undoubtedly shred Oster limb from limb. On more than one occasion, Kali screwed up his courage to the point where he decided to confront Oster with the truth. The gnome mentally rehearsed his lines and thought of every reason or argument why he should tell the human the truth. And each time he attempted the truth, the following would happen:

Kali would say, "Oster, we must talk."

Oster would sigh, clutching the hand of his beloved, and say, "Yes, I know I spend all my time here when I am not elsewhere. You think it unhealthy."

Kali would say, "Well yes, but . . ."

And Oster would break in with, "I just worry that some time when I am not here, the thrice-damned Highlord will return and hurt you and my friends and my lady." And here would be another room-filling sigh as he would add, "Is she not beautiful?"

At this point, Kali, hating himself every step of the way, would always remember a project that was half finished and leave the sighing Oster with his lady. The plate mail of the Clockwork Hero fit better as he got more exercise, and old skills he thought long-forgotten returned to him. He gathered many weapons and strange items in his travels around the valley, keeping for himself a clutch of silver daggers worn at the belt and a magical cape, but giving the rest to friends. Kali sent the hero out on none-such missions for unneeded materials, while he and Organathoran the painter—whom Kali had bonded to silence—set about their craft.

Each day, when Oster was gone, they would mix plaster and make a mold of some part of the lady—her hand or her arm or foot. The molds would then be filled with hot wax. It took several weeks of work to finally get adequate casts of the hands, and longer for the legs, torso, and face. The poor castings were melted in the hearth, as were a few good molds that had to be jettisoned when Oster returned in triumph too early.

Once, when taking the mold of the woman's head, Kali thought for a moment of covering her fully with plaster, of letting her perish. It would solve the problem, and make everything so much easier. Even if it did break Oster's heart.

But as the thoughts crossed his mind, Kali's hands began to shake, and he had to step outside to compose himself. They were unworthy thoughts, for both a healer and a gnome. Humans may take the easy route, but a little complexity never stopped a gnome. He would proceed as he had planned.

When the model was finished, Kali stored it in a hidden back room next to the Highlord armor. Using the hair of a long-haired fox, Kali fashioned a suitable wig, and Organathoran worked on duplicating the looks of a sick but living human being.

As the work completed, Kali placed an order with his fellow gnomes for a stonework mausoleum and a sepulchre. In true gnome fashion, the work took several tries, and resulted in a building whose design would drive mad the best human architects, complete with a long span of glossy black stone leading up to its foot-thick doors. The sepulchre itself was carved of crystal.

Kali's final plan was simple (for a gnome). The mannequin would be placed beneath the crystal in the tomb. Oster would be told that the crystal sepulchre would keep his lady alive in sleep for the rest of her days, for there was no way even Kali could cure her. Oster would be hurt, but it would be a hurt with hope for the future, a lesser hurt than losing one you love (at least, this was Kali's reasoning). The hellspawn who wanted to throttle him would, at the same time, be placed in the ox-cart, unconscious, and set out without a driver on the road. By the time she awoke, she would be miles from the gnomes' remote home, with a few months missing from her life, and Kali would not be a murderer.

That was the plan, at least, and the leaves were just being to turn their fall colors when all was ready. Kali and Eton lugged the finished mannequin from its secret hiding place one day when Oster had been sent on some quest for Archie. They laid the figure to rest in the tomb and closed the fasteners. Beneath its glass now lay a beautiful princess suitable for use in a Human Story. Her lips were cold and red, and her eyes coated with bluish-tinged blush, never to open.

The entire task took them about two hours. When they returned, they were shocked to discover Oster there waiting for them.

Oster the Clockwork Hero was still in his plate armor, helmet tucked under his arm, pacing in the drawing room. He warmly welcomed Kali and Eton with a broad grin.

Kali coughed and launched into what he hoped was to be his last lie. "Oster, I must tell you terrible news. The condition of Lady Columbine has not remained constant while you were gone. Rather, it has worsened, such that we found it necessary to place her in a magical bier in a stone building on the hill. I'm sorry, but I'd . . ." His voice trailed off as he looked into Oster's puzzled eyes.

"What are you talking about?" asked Oster. "She is still resting within." He motioned toward the bedroom door and Kali, for the first time, realized they left the secret closet open in that room. "I have glorious news. While traveling through the hill looking for ingredients, I chanced to rescue a priest—a true priest—one with the skills to heal the sick and cure the diseased. I brought him here to cure Lady Columbine. No slur on your abilities, Kali, my dear friend, but all your potions have been for nought. He's been in there for half an hour, ever since—"

Oster's words were cut short. The door to the bedroom snapped off its gnome-built, reinforced hinges. Through it came hurtling the broken body of the priest. The Dragon Highlord, dressed in full armor, strode into the room. Even with her features masked, Kali could sense that she was smiling. A dog-frightening, bird-throttling, cat-killing smile.

Kali's heart sank. The figurative jig was up, and Kali realized for the first time that he had built his invention of fiction without tightening the smallest bolt, building one lie upon another until he created an edifice of falsehoods, a structure that now swayed in the harsh wind of truth. He thought of the old Human Stories, and wished fervently for an easy fix—a wise old holy man to wander onto the scene and provide the solution to all problems.

And with another start, he realized that this was precisely what *had* almost happened. The holy man lay in a pool of his own blood, paying the price for wandering into the wrong tale.

But, while Kali's mind was stopping and starting, rushing from one revelation to another like a frightened child in an old house, the humans thundered on in the manner that all humans do. The Highlord laughed and leapt forward, lunging with a straight sword blow toward Oster's chest. The Clockwork Hero brought his own blade up quickly and parried the lunge, tossing his helmet at the Highlord. She dodged, but the bronze helm grazed her head, disorienting her for a moment. Oster used the moment to draw back into the room, waving to Kali and Eton to move away.

Kali and Eton scurried to the fireplace, which was graced by a number of Eton's new plow-share-shovels. These fireplace tools had a graceful sweep of metal welded to the base, making them useless for scooping ashes, but excellent for small gardening tasks and fair for bashing. The pair edged around the perimeter of the battle. Kali had heard that kender could merge into the stone itself and move without leaving a shadow. He desperately wished for that ability now.

Oster's attention was riveted on the dark-armored form before him. Kali expected the Highlord to taunt, laugh, snarl, and behave in the way of all good bad people when confronted with virtue, but the Highlord kept her input to a few growls of the mid-gear type. She lunged forward in a flurry of blows, lunges, and backswings. Oster parried them easily, and drove her back with a swing to the midsection, a swipe to the head. What he lacked in form, he made up in force, and the Highlord was staggered when one of Oster's strong lunges caught her in the left arm.

They fought for a minute, two minutes, an eternity of three. The Highlord never lost track of the two gnomes (learning from her experience), and avoided all their attempts to get behind her. The two main combatants made quick work of most of Kali's living room furniture—every breakable was introduced to the dangers of being inadvertently close to clashing steel. The Highlord would charge, locking steel with Oster. The pair would stagger against each other in a few deadly dance steps, then one or the other would be flung backward, usually just far enough to reduce some other furnishing to its component parts. Lunge, the clash of locked blades, the stagger, the destruction of a chair. Lunge, lock, stagger, writing desk. Lunge, lock, stagger, spoon collection.

Sweat was now running down Oster's face in rivulets, but his eyes burned with fury. The battle had run long now, and Kali knew that all their deaths were long overdue. A bud of insight blossomed within his skull, and he suddenly understood why the Highlord had not made quick work of all of them. While Oster had been in training as the local hero of the gnomes, the Highlord had been under an enforced and extended rest for six months. While the Highlord was sufficiently powerful to make short work of a pair of gnomes, or a surprised cleric expecting a demure young lady, she was having more trouble with someone trained for combat.

The length of the battle was telling on the Highlord. Blood leaked between the epaulets of her wounded upper arm, forming a deadly calligraphy on her armor. Even Kali could see she was favoring that arm, and Oster pressed his advantage, driving her back, step by step, to the bedroom door.

Kali's eyes took in the battle, but his mind whirled with options, all of them bad. At first it seemed to him that Oster would surely perish under the attack, which was good in that at least he would die without finding out his ladylove was his murderer, but bad considering that said murderer would probably avenge herself on the rest of the community. Now it looked like Oster would be victorious, which would be equally disastrous, for once he discovered the Highlord was his Columbine, he would perish just as surely of a broken heart, if not busted ribs.

Kali chewed on his beard, fidgeted, raised his weapon, fidgeted again. Eton was a statue next to him, working out his own thoughts, or perhaps preparing himself for the afterlife. The pair were enraptured by the deadly ballet played out before them.

Oster was now beating the Highlord's attacks easily, reducing her to weak parries and dodges. The two locked blades again (Kali made a mental check to see if there was any surviving furniture). This time, when they broke, the Highlord's sword separated from its owner, burying its point in the china cabinet (shattering the last of the unbroken teapots). Oster brought his sword around in a mighty blow, aimed at his opponents' throat, as smooth and as level as carpenter's beam.

Kali stepped forward and, in a loud voice, shouted, "Oster, don't do it! It's your Columbine!" Or rather, he fully intended to. A great, soft explosion blossomed at the base of his own skull and he toppled forward. The room pitched and the floor rose up to meet the gnome. He was dimly aware of two other forms striking the floor before he reached it, one the shape of a full human helmet, the other resembling a human sans both helmet and head. A part of Kali's mind paused to calculate how long it would take a plummeting gnome, a falling severed head, and a crumbled body to all hit the ground at the same time. Then the void closed up over him.

Kali awoke to find himself in his own bed, looking up at a grim Oster and a worried-looking Eton. The expression on his fellow gnome's face told the story—that shamed-dog look of gnomish responsibility when an invention goes slightly awry, combined with a mild sense of pride that the idea proved feasible. He still had his combination plowshare-shovel in his hands.

Oster's face was human and therefore unreadable. Gray. It looked like that of a gnome who has realized his invention is unworkable, and nothing could change that fact. A look of defeat, tinged with worry.

"She's dead," Kali croaked. Not a question, but a notation, a footnote.

"They both are," said Oster, putting a hand on the reclining gnome's shoulder. "And the priest, too, I'm afraid."

"Both?" Kali's brow clouded.

"The Highlord, and . . . and . . ." Oster shook his head. "Eton showed me the tomb you made for her. It is very sweet. Almost as if she were alive. When I pointed the priest toward the bedroom, the Highlord was waiting. If you hadn't come home, he would have caught us both."

Kali looked hard at Eton, hoping to elicit from his fellow gnome an explanation that would at least bring him up to date.

Eton avoided his eyes, and instead grabbed Kali's big toe and looked at his wrist. "Hmmm, confused from a lateral conclusion. He'll need his rest. If you don't mind, Oster?"

The human nodded and saw himself out. The bedroom door had been replaced with a roughly-hung carpet, and Kali could hear the human busying himself outside.

Eton leaned over to check the dressing wrapped at the

base of Kali's skull. The small healer grabbed his caretaker's beard and pulled him close, hissing so Oster could not hear.

"How did you keep him from finding out?"

"Quick presence of mind," whispered Eton. "Before he could examine the body, I told him that if the Highlord was near, other enemies may be around as well. Oster scouted. I gathered up the pieces. By the time he had returned, I had placed the body, still in its armor, on the pyre."

"And Columbine?"

"Still in her crypt. The Clockwork Hero made up his own story, and did a better job than we did. He's broken up about it, but he'll get over it. I think. Humans are so difficult to figure out."

"Why the . . .?" Kali glowered at the destructive weapon Eton held.

The other gnome sighed and said, "Because you created something that worked, and I did not want you to throw it away."

Kali's head hurt, perhaps just from the shovel blow, but he wasn't sure. He frowned, but remained silent. And silence for gnomes means agreement.

"You created a hero, Kali," Eton said quietly, gently. "Oster arrived as a prisoner, a failure as a merchant and a rebel. But because of all the lies you spun—the tale of Columbine, the errands to fetch useless items—he found a purpose in life. I knew you had decided to tell him the truth, and I had to stop you. If you had told him, he might have pulled his blow, and she would have killed us all."

"But he believes a lie!" groaned Kali, still keeping his voice down.

Eton shrugged. "From what I know of humans, that is a standard state of affairs. They excel at self-deception. Sometimes the lie is the unity of a nation, or the perfection of a cause. Or the love of a good woman—"

"—who doesn't really exist," muttered Kali.

"Exactly." Eton nodded. "It might even be preferred that way. Less fuss and bother. I might create one for myself . . ."

Kali hrumphed weakly and drifted off to sleep. After a few days he came around to seeing things as Eton did. And Oster did heal over time and come to conquer the wound in his heart made by Columbine's death at the hands of the Highlord. And after a time it became less and less important for Kali to tell Oster the truth of the matter. Even so, he himself pledged to tell no more lies. No more dangerous ones, at least.

And so it has been from that day to this. There still is a gnome village so remote that other gnomes refer to it when talking about remote villages, a noisy place of clanging hammers and the occasional explosion. And it has as its protector a champion in bronze armor, a human in clockwork attire. And its healer is a gnome who has an air of satisfaction because he made something that works, though, even if pressed, he won't reveal the nature of his discovery.

Now, if you ever encounter this Clockwork Hero, you can ask him the tale, and he will tell, as best he is able with his human tongue and direct manner, of the story of his reluctant heroism, of finding himself entrusted to protect a group of small, foolish gnomes. He will speak of encountering a beauty wrapped in slumber, a fair maiden who never spoke to him, yet captured his heart. And he will tell of the fell creature who killed her and threatened his newfound people, such that they called upon him for salvation. And he will speak of sacrifices made and mighty oaths sworn and horrible battles fought and how justice and valor prevailed at the end, though at terrible cost.

But that, of course, is a Human Story, and as such we shall not worry about it.

The Night Wolf

Nancy Varian Berberick

———

The village of Dimmin lay snugly in a fold of the Kharolis Mountains, tucked between the elves' Qualinesti and Thorbardin of the dwarves. On the outskirts of that little village, beyond the bend of the brook where willows overhung the water on both sides, stood a small stone house. It was the mage's house, and Thorne had lived there for twenty years. To the eye, he was a man just come into his prime, but he'd been looking like that for all these twenty years past, never a hair turned gray, and so folk reckoned that he had an elf lurking in his ancestry somewhere.

Mages enjoyed no good reputation in those days just after the Cataclysm, but the villagers liked Thorne. From the headman to the lowliest dairy maid, they knew him as "our mage." Even Guarinn Hammerfell—the dwarf who did the blacksmithing—couldn't hide a grudging fondness for Thorne, and that was saying something. Until the mage's arrival, Guarinn could name only one friend—Tam the potter. But for Tam the potter, Guarinn had always kept to himself, a grim fellow, without much warmth of feeling. Yet, when Thorne arrived, Guarinn made room in his lean heart for another friend. Long-lived dwarf and long-lived mage . . . the villagers joked that Guarinn must have reckoned Thorne would be around for a while, so he might as well get used to him.

The people in Dimmin didn't know the half of what was

———

to be known about Guarinn and Tam and Thorne, though they did consider it natural that Roulant Potter, grown to manhood tagging at the heels of Tam and his friends, stepped into his father's place after the potter's death—and became just as friendly with Guarinn and Thorne.

Likely, they predicted, when young Roulant married Una the miller's girl they'd get themselves a son who'd inherit his grand-da's friends. No one thought it would be a bad inheritance, mage and all. People had gotten used to Guarinn the blacksmith. And Thorne was helpful in the way mages can be, for he was able to charm a fretful child to sleep or bring water springing up from a dry well—always willing to turn his mysterious skills to good use.

No one blamed Thorne that he was never able to do anything about the Night of the Wolf.

Anyone with eyes in Dimmin could see that it was a great source of frustration and sorrow to their mage that he could offer them no protection against the wolf that terrorized the countryside one night each year. For thirty years it had avoided traps and hunters, and that was enough to make people understand that this was no ordinary wolf. What natural beast could live so long?

Yet Thorne could offer no better wisdom than that everyone keep within-doors; for life's sake, never venture out into the dark when the two moons rose full on the first night of autumn. And so, on this one day each year, all around Dimmin, small children were shooed early into cottages, cached behind bolted doors. And if a child's bed should be near a window, this night the little one would sleep in the loft with his parents.

Most often a stray sheep or roaming dog, sometimes a luckless traveler benighted in the forest, satisfied the hunger of the great beast. But only three years ago on the Night of the Wolf, a farmer who lived but a morning's walk from Dimmin had wakened at moonset to hear one of his children wailing. Fast as he ran to the youngster's bed, he'd found only an empty pallet, and the broad, deep tracks of a large wolf outside the window. No one questioned Thorne's advice to keep close to home on the Night.

It must be a curse, they muttered as they bolted their

doors. What else could it be?

It was exactly that. Thorne had always known how to end the curse, and no one wanted that ending more than he.

* * * * *

On the first day of autumn, Thorne sat before a banked hearth-fire. Outside the stone house, cold wind hissed around the eaves, but he didn't hear it. Eyes wide, he dreamed as though he were deep asleep. In his dreams the two moons, the red and the silver, filled up the sky, showered their light upon the jagged back teeth of a ruin's broken walls while cold, hungry howling ran down the sky. In his dreams Thorne cried out for mercy, and got none.

He sat so all morning, sat unmoving all afternoon. When the light deepened toward the day's end, he heard his name urgently whispered, and he came away from his dreaming slowly, like a man swimming up from dark, deep waters. Guarinn Hammerfell stood at his shoulder, waiting. The dwarf's face was white, drawn in haggard lines; his dark, blue-flecked eyes were sunk into deep hollows carved by weariness. Thorne hadn't stirred even once during the long day, but he knew that Guarinn had kept watch beside him and never took a step away.

"It's time, my friend," Thorne said.

Guarinn nodded, wordlessly agreeing that it was. He said nothing as he and the mage dressed warmly in thick woolen cloaks and stout climbing boots, spoke no word as he slung a coil of heavy rope over his shoulder and thrust a short-hafted throwing axe into his belt.

They crossed the brook by the old footbridge and entered the darkening forest. At the top of the first low hill, Thorne stopped to look down upon Dimmin as lights sprang up in the windows of the cottages, little gleams of gold to console in the coming night. He watched the last cottage, the one that stood alone at the far end of the village where the street became a narrow footpath winding down toward the potter's kiln at the edge of the brook. When that light sighed to life he knew that Roulant Potter was taking up his bow and quiver, making ready to leave.

"And so the Night comes," Thorne whispered. "And we'll try again to kill the wolf, to end the curse."

His words fell heavily into silence. Guarinn turned his back on the lights of Dimmin and began the climb to the tall hill in the forest, the bald place where the ruin lay. Thorne followed, and didn't trespass into the dwarf's silence.

Their friendship was older than people in Dimmin realized. Guarinn knew that the mage was once called Thorne Shape-shifter. And he knew that Thorne Shape-shifter was the wolf. With Tam Potter, Guarinn had been present twenty years ago when Thorne had bared his wrists and taken up a keen-edged dagger, blindly seeking to end the curse by killing himself.

"There *is* no hope but this blade," Thorne had cried that day, sickened by the taste of what the wolf had killed. "I will change every year, unless one of you kills the wolf. Neither of you has been able to do that."

He'd meant no reproof, for he knew why his friends had failed each year. That, too, was part of the curse. Still, they reproached themselves, and he knew that, as well.

He found no hope anywhere, not even among the wise at the Tower of Wayreth. He'd fled there, after the curse had been spoken, but he'd been driven from that haven by the dark magic of the curse itself, compelled to return to the broken ruin in the mountains at the rising of the full autumn moons. Ten years he'd hidden there. The efforts of the most skillful mages at Wayreth had not been able to blunt that compulsion. The wisest had sadly counselled Thorne that he must accept that there was only one way to end the curse. The wolf must die, and only Guarinn or Tam Potter could kill it. So said the curse. But they had failed him.

It was twenty years ago that Thorne decided there might be another way to end the curse. And so, with careful precision, he'd set a dagger's glinting edge against the blue veins in his wrist. In the end, whether by some agency of the curse itself, or an innate will to survive that was stronger than he'd guessed, he'd not been able to draw the steel across his wrist.

Guarinn had wept for both joy and rue over his friend's inability to end his life. And Tam Potter, taking the dagger gently from the mage's hand, said: "Thorne, come back and live in Dimmin with Guarinn and me. We'll find a way to kill the wolf. We'll keep trying."

In the summer when Tam died, Roulant Potter learned that he'd inherited his father's part in a curse that was older than he. Thorne had told Roulant just what he knew his father had believed—what Guarinn yet believed: when the wolf was dead, the curse would end. "What will happen to you?" young Roulant had asked. "I will not be hurt," Thorne had replied. "I will be free."

Some of that was true, and some of it wasn't. Thorne never told his friends all he'd learned during the time at Wayreth.

*   *   *   *   *

Shrouded in shadow, hidden beneath a stone outcropping at the forest's edge, Una wrapped her arms around her drawn-up knees, hugged herself to muffle the drumming of her heart. She was outside after sunset on the Night of the Wolf. Una had not lived in Dimmin but five years, come to stay with her cousin, the miller's wife, after her parents died. She'd been thirteen then, and it hadn't taken her very long to learn that no one in the village ventured outdoors on the first night of autumn.

No one, that is, except—lately—Roulant Potter. He would stealthily enter the forest here soon. Una had seen him do this each year on the Night for two years, and there had never been a question in her mind that she'd keep Roulant's secret faithfully. She'd loved him as long as she'd known him, and he'd never been shy about letting her know that he felt the same way. They would marry soon. Maybe.

And maybe not. Una's faithful silence on the subject of Roulant's Night-walk extended to Roulant himself, for she didn't know how to ask the question that would sound like an accusation: *What do you know about the Night of the Wolf that even our mage doesn't?*

And so the secret cast a shadow between them. Day by day, a little at a time, the shadow was changing them, as if by a malicious magic, into uneasy strangers.

As darkness gathered beneath the forest's thin eaves, old dead leaves ran scrabbling before the wind. In the luminous sky, one early, eager star shone out. A dark shape stood atop the hill, a young man with a great breadth of shoulder and a long, loping stride. Roulant stopped at the crest and stood silhouetted against the sky, the last light shining on his brown-gold hair. Still as stone, he hung there, between the village and the wildwood—stood a long time before he at last vanished into the twilight beneath the trees.

The wind moaned round the rocks, and Una shivered as she checked the draw of the dagger at her belt. She was afraid: of the Night, and of what she might discover, and of what she might lose. But she hugged her courage close. She would follow Roulant tonight, and she wouldn't turn back. She had to know what part he played in this yearly night of dread.

* * * * *

Soft on the cold air, Roulant heard a whisper, the dry rattling of brush behind him. He turned quickly, saw a flash of red in the tangled thickets on the slope below: some padding fox or vixen on the trail of prey. Roulant went on climbing. He must reach the ruin before moonrise.

The tumbled stone walls atop the bald hill in the forest had been his destination each Night for the past two, as it had been his father's every year since Roulant could remember. When he was a boy, after his mother's death, Roulant used to think he knew why his father went out into the forest on the Night of the Wolf. He believed that Tam was a brave champion upon a secret quest to help save the people of Dimmin. Roulant'd never told anyone what he believed, nor did he mention it to his father. A secret is a secret, and Tam need not carry the burden of knowing his had been discovered.

The year the wolf had killed the farmer's child was the last Tam went up to the ruin. The summer after, he died. Roulant was seventeen then, and that was when he learned that Thorne was the wolf.

It was a hard thing to learn. Roulant had known Thorne since childhood, had felt for him the magical awe and affection that is hero-worship. Even knowing that the mage became the wolf, once every annum, could not break their bond. From that year to this, enmeshed in the web of an old curse, Roulant had been drawn out into the forest on the Night to stand with Guarinn Hammerfell and promise Thorne they would kill the wolf, swear they would free their friend from the curse.

This, on the face of it, was a difficult promise to keep, for wolves are hard to hunt and kill. But Roulant, in youthful zeal, had never truly thought it would be impossible. He was a good hunter. His father had taught him to be a faultless shot with bow and arrow. Guarinn had taught him to track, and made the lessons easy, companionable rambles in the forest. As he'd stood faithfully with Tam, Guarinn was always with Roulant. Yet, just as Tam had failed his own promise, Roulant had, too—so far.

There were reasons for that, the kind Roulant dared not think about here and alone in the dark forest.

Wind soughed low, herding fallen leaves. All around, the night drew in close, dark and sighing. Roulant stopped for breath before he began to climb the last stony path, the barely seen trace that would lead him to the ruin. Watching his breath plume in the frosty air, he thought that the pale mist was just like the promises he'd made to Thorne—easily blown away.

And Roulant knew that if he failed again tonight, he'd be forced to break a different promise, one that had nothing to do with wolves and curses. If he didn't kill the wolf tonight, in the morning he would go to Una and tell her that he couldn't marry her. He would do that, though both their hearts would break.

A dear and pretty girl, his Una, with her earnest green eyes and her red-gold hair. He was no poet, but late at night Roulant liked to watch the fire in the hearth and think that the rosy flames, so lovely and generous with their warmth, reminded him of Una. Whatever joy would come on their wedding day would be swiftly overshadowed by his terrible obligation to go up to the ruin year after year, trying, as his father had tried, to bring an end to the Night of the Wolf. How could Roulant come back to Una every year, with blood on his hands as surely as it was on Thorne's?

And yet . . . how could he bear to look down the long years of a life without her?

Roulant put his back into the last climb and soon left the dark fastness of the forest to see Thorne and Guarinn waiting in the paler light of the clearing. The moons were rising, mere suggestions of light above the mountain. Soon they would spill red and silver light on the bald hill crowned by frost-whitened, shattered walls. Roulant left the forest, trying to shut out the grim sense that the events of this Night were fated.

From the obscuring dark at the forest's edge, Una watched him join his friends. Once Roulant and Thorne and Guarinn climbed the hill to the ruin, Una went noiselessly around the base, up the slope as silently as a shadow, and entered at the opposite side to hide in the small shelter of blackened beams and piled stone that once had shaped a bridal chamber.

* * * * *

Thorne stood in the center of the ruin, surrounded by the broken stone, his back to the rising moons. He lifted his head, sniffed the air. Guarinn tied a slipknot around one end of the rope he'd carried. Roulant strung his bow and placed three arrows in easy reach on the flat of a broken stone.

"Time, my friend," the dwarf said, his forge-scarred hands shaking a little, though he gripped the rope hard. They'd tried to hold Thorne with rope before, five years ago. It was Tam who had stood readying bow and bolt then, not Roulant. Guarinn thought it might be different this time with a younger eye, a steadier hand to take a well-timed shot at the instant of changing. Thorne closed his eyes, shut out the sight of the rope that would hold him, of Roulant readying a long, steel-headed shaft for flight, and nodded to Guarinn.

"Do it, and hurry."

When the noose passed over his head and settled on his neck, Thorne heard himself panting hoarsely, like an anxious beast mindlessly straining for release. The rope stank of hemp and tar and the dark scent of smoke, fire's ghost. In moments, like the return of an unhealed malady, he'd feel the bonds of humanity fall away from him: compassion replaced by hunger, an imperative that knew no mercy. Reason and skill changed by fast, fevered degrees to instinct, which existed only to serve the needs of survival. Even now, his senses filled with the complex richness of scent only an animal knows. Even now the scents aroused hunger.

The man knew the fear he smelled on Guarinn as well-justified, not to be scorned. The wolf would only smell the fear and know instinctively that this was a victim to feed hunger. Thorne wished that Guarinn would hurry, for very soon Thorne Shape-shifter, once known for his mastery of this most difficult of the magic arts, would not be able to hold back the changing.

* * * * *

Crouched in her cold dark shelter, Una stared in amazed alarm to see Guarinn place the noose round Thorne's neck. Like most people in Dimmin, she felt like an intruder in Guarinn's company, his glum silences made her a stranger to be kept at arm's length, mistrusted. But she knew that Roulant loved Guarinn as truly as he loved Thorne and had loved his own father. Though she'd heard Thorne invite the binding, saw Roulant standing by in silence, Una watched the dwarf with narrowed eyes.

Each knot he tied was strong, and as he worked, Guarinn's face was like a stark, bleak landscape, scoured by sorrow, forsaken of all but the thinnest hope. Yet he did the rough work carefully and, were it anyone else, Una would have said tenderly. He took great care to cause no hurt, and watching, unable to find any reason for what she was seeing, Una swallowed hard against an ache of tears. Tears for Thorne, bound; for Roulant, who stood as still as the mage, watching. And for Guarinn Hammerfell who, of them all, looked as if he alone hated what was being done.

And she wondered, what *was* being done? And why?

From the forest Una heard the clap of an owl's wings; hard on that, the faint, dying scream of a small creature caught in dagger-sharp talons. The wind stirred, cold from behind her as a long, low moaning slid across the night. An uncanny sound, a grievous pleading.

Trembling, with cold fear, she saw Roulant pick up an arrow, nock it to the bowstring, his stance the broad one of a man preparing to put an arrow right through a straw-butt at the bull's-eye. Guarinn moved to the side, moonlight running on the bitter edge of the throwing axe in his hand.

The mage, alone, wearing the light of the moons like a shimmering cloak of red and silver, sank to his knees. Guarinn took two more quick paces to the side, careful not to get between the mage and the wall. Roulant stood where he was, and, after he'd marked Guarinn's position, he never looked away from Thorne.

The night began to shimmer around Thorne, waver like the air above a banked fire. Una, who'd been still as stock, made a sound then, a whisper of boot-heel against stone as she crept closer to the opening of her small shelter to see.

Faint though the sound had been, it was heard.

Thorne jerked his head up, looked directly at her.

Cold fear skittered along Una's skin, cramped her belly painfully. She wanted to reach for her dagger, but she could only sit motionless, caught and stilled by Thorne's eyes—the eyes of an animal lurking beyond the campfire's pale. And the shape of him, she thought, the shape of him is somehow *wrong*. Something about his face, the length of his arms. But surely that was a trick of moonlight and shimmering air? And crouching there, he didn't hold himself like a man, on his knees. He had hands and feet flat to the ground, as an animal would.

Una pressed her hands hard to her mouth, trying to muffle her cry of horror and pity when she saw Thorne look away, turn all his attention to a feverish gnawing at the rope that bound him.

The rope wasn't doing a good job of holding him now, for his shape was changing rapidly, and in some places the coil was slipping away from what had once been a man's wrist or ankle . . . and were now the smaller joints of an animal, a broad-chested wolf, its gray pelt silver in the light of two moons, its dripping fangs glistening.

Guarinn cried "Now, Roulant! *Do it!*" and instinctively Una shoved herself far back against the broken wall behind her, flinching as rubble slithered down the hill, the clatter of stone loud in the night.

The sound did not distract Guarinn, his axe hit the wolf in the shoulder, biting hard, though not lodging in either muscle or bone. But Roulant hesitated, if only the space of a heart's beat, and so when the wolf leaped at him, it was well beneath the arrow's flight. Roaring, the wolf hit him hard, sent him crashing to the stony ground, pinned him there with its weight.

And then Una bolted out of her shelter, ran across the moon-lighted ruin, her own dagger in hand, before she knew exactly what she meant to do.

* * * * *

They were upon him, the smaller male and the young female, with daggers that would bite deeper than his fangs could. The wolf, who knew nothing about rage or vengeance or any purpose other than survival, heaved up from the one sprawled helpless beneath him, abandoned the enticing scent of blood and meat for immediate survival.

On the wings of pain, like wings of fire, the wolf won its freedom at the price of another agonizing bound over the broken wall. It left blood on the stones of the hillside, all along the path into the forest, and it carried away with it the noose still clinging round its neck.

* * * * *

Guarinn had made a bright, high campfire in the center of the ruin, but Roulant didn't think it was doing much to warm or comfort Una. Nor did it seem to help Una that Roulant held her tightly in his arms—he wondered if she would ever stop weeping. Somewhere to the north the wolf howled, a long and lonely cry. Una shuddered, and Roulant

---

175

held her closer.

"Una," he said, turning away from the reminder of failure. "Why did you follow me here?"

She sat straighter, her fists clenched on her knees, her eyes still wet but no longer pouring tears. "I've known for two years that you went out into the forest on the Night. And I've known . . ."

She looked at Guarinn sitting hunched over the fire. The dwarf turned a little away, seemingly disinterested in whatever they discussed. Roulant, who knew him, understood that he was offering privacy.

"You've known what?" he asked, gently.

"That something's come between us. Something—a secret. Roulant, I've been afraid, and I had to know why you went into the forest on the Night, when no one else—"

"Someone else," Guarinn amended. "Thorne and me. And now that you're here, I suppose you think you should know the secret you've spied out?"

Una bristled, and Roulant shook his head. "Guarinn, she's here and that gives her a right to know what she saw."

"Not as far as I'm concerned."

"Maybe not," Roulant said. "But she has rights where I'm concerned. I should have honored them before now."

Guarinn eyed them both, quietly judging. "All right, then. Listen well, Una, and I'll give you the answer you've come looking for.

"This ruin you see around us used to be Thorne's house," he said. "A quiet place and peaceful. No more though. It's only a pile of stone now, a cairn to mark the place where three dooms were doled out this night thirty years ago. Three dooms, twined one round the other to make a single fate."

The wind blew, tangling the smoke and flame of the small campfire. Roulant wrapped his arms around Una again and held her close for warmth.

"Girl," the dwarf said. "Your hiding place tonight was once a bridal chamber. It never saw the joy it was fitted out for . . ."

* * * * *

"Thorne asked but two guests to come witness and celebrate his marriage. One of them was me, and I was glad to stand with him as he pledged his wedding vows. The other was Tam Potter, and his was a double joy that night, for he was Thorne's friend and the bride's cousin. She was from away south, and I don't think her closest kin liked the idea of her wedding a mage. But Tam was fair pleased, and so he was the kinsman who bestowed her hand.

"Mariel, the girl's name; and she was pretty enough, but no rare beauty. Yet that night she glowed brightly, put the stars to shame; for so girls will do when they are soon to have what they want and need. She needed Thorne Shapeshifter and had flouted most of her kin to have him. No less did Thorne need her.

"The first night of autumn, it was, and the bright stars shone down on us as we stood outside the cottage. Old legends have it that wedding vows taken in the twined light of the red moon and the silver will make a marriage strong in love and faith. Perhaps those legends would have been proven that night. Perhaps. We did never learn that, for another guest came to the wedding—uninvited, unwelcome, and the first we knew of his coming was when he stood in our midst, dark and cold as death.

"A mage, that uninvited guest, black-robed and with a heart like hoar-frost—and you must remember that this is no tale of rival suitors, one come in the very nick of time to rapt away the maiden he loves. This is a tale of two young men, one so poisonously jealous of the other that he must—for hate—spoil whatever his rival in power had.

"The name of the Spoiler? I will not speak it. Let it never be remembered. This is how dwarves reward murderers, and I know no other way as good.

"He laid hands on the girl, that dark mage, in a way no man should touch another's wife; magicked her from sight before any one of us could move to prevent. Aye, but he didn't take her far, in hatred and arrogance took her only within the cottage. In the very instant we knew her gone, we heard her voice raised in terror and rage. Close as she was, the evil mage's wizard ways kept us from coming to her aid until it was too late. The spell lifted. Thorne found her quickly in the bridal chamber. And he saw the mage defile her . . . and worse.

"Mariel lay cold and still on the ground, like a fragile pretty doll flung aside and broken, Thorne's dear love stricken for spite by the Spoiler.

"Seeing her dead, Thorne Shape-shifter showed the Spoiler how he'd earned his name.

"You have seen the wolf, and so you know what the Spoiler saw in the moments before his death. But you have never heard such screaming as I heard that night: never heard such piteous pleading, nor heard anyone wail for mercy as the Spoiler did, him torn by the fangs of the great gray wolf.

"Tam Potter and I could have tried to stop Thorne, but we did not. We stood by, watched the wolf at his ravening work. We should have granted mercy."

* * * * *

Despite the hot, high fire, Una sat shivering, her hand a small fist in Roulant's.

"Tam died wishing we'd granted that mercy," Guarinn said softly. "And I sit here now wishing no less, for the Spoiler died with a curse on his lips. It was a hard one, as the curses of dying mages tend to be, and it marked us all with the fate of hunter and hunted."

Stiff and cold from sitting, Una got to her feet; she did not answer when Roulant called to her. She needed a place to be private with what she'd learned. The night was crisp and bright, as lovely as it must have been this time thirty years ago. As she walked, Una discovered the shape of the ruin, saw that it was very like the little stone house near the bend of the brook in Dimmin. It lacked only one room to be exactly the same. In the Dimmin house, Thorne kept only a stark sleeping loft under the eaves.

Una stood for a long time before the dark mouth of the little cave of fire-blacked beam and broken stone that had sheltered her tonight; all that was left of a fouled bridal chamber.

She returned to stand by the fire. "Tell me," she said.

"Thorne must surrender his very self one night each year and hope that Roulant or I will end the curse by killing the wolf. This," Guarinn said, "is an inherited obligation."

Una stood quietly, her eyes on the fire, the flames and the embers. "If you kill the wolf, what will happen to Thorne?"

It was Roulant—silent till then—who answered.

"The curse will be over. He'll begin to age, grow old again, like the rest of us. Thorne hasn't got any elven blood, Una, though everyone thinks so. It's the curse that's held him in time."

"Guarinn," she said softly. "Why haven't you killed the wolf in all these thirty years?"

"You'd think it would be easy, aye? Take the first shot as he was changing and end the matter. It isn't so easy. Once before, binding him slowed the change, and we tried that again tonight. But sometimes . . . " The dwarf shuddered. "Sometimes he's changed between one breath and the next. Sometimes faster than that, and the wolf is gone before either one of us can pick up a weapon. He doesn't just *look* like a wolf. He *is* one! He'll tear at you, running, and he's too canny to stay around fighting losing battles."

"So," she said. "You have to go out and hunt the wolf?"

Neither answered. A glance passed between them and Roulant got to his feet. He took her hand, his own very cold as he led her into the shadow of a low broken wall.

"Una," he said. "We can kill the wolf if we can find it—"

"That won't be hard tonight. You could track him by the blood."

"We could. Except . . . " His face shone white in the moonlight, his eyes dark with dread. "Except that we dare not set foot out there!"

She frowned, leaned on the wall to look out. All she saw was night and stars and the moons hanging over the clearing. She heard night noise, owls wondering and hares scampering, a stream laughing over stones.

"I know," Roulant said. "I see everything that you see, just as you see it. When I'm standing here." He turned his back on the forest. "When I set foot outside the ruin—even hold my hand out beyond the wall . . . It's terrible out there. The Spoiler laid a curse on us too, one we've never found a way past. In here, we're safe. Out there . . . they'll kill us."

Una heard this, but she was staring out at the forest and the night, thinking about what he'd said about things being very different beyond the wall. She looked down and saw her loosely clasped hands just beyond the wall. Unlike the others, she neither saw nor felt any curse in the forest or the night.

Una turned away from the wall and walked past Roulant and Guarinn without a word. She picked up Roulant's bow and quiver on the way. She'd not gotten but a few yards when she heard Roulant shout something, heard Guarinn scrambling to his feet, echoing the warning cry. Una ran, heeding no warning. She vaulted the wall where the wolf had fled.

As she bounded down the hill, Una hoped that whatever kept Roulant and Guarinn helpless in the ruin would not affect her. It was frightening enough to go hunting a wounded wolf in the night, and her only a middling shot with a bow. Still, the beast was wounded, and if she could once get a good aim, she'd be able to kill it.

*　*　*　*　*

Roulant jumped the wall, chased heedlessly after Una. And he thought: Idiot girl! Guarinn was a long reach behind. He prayed that Roulant would be able to snatch her back to safety in time, that he wouldn't have to follow.

Una was too fast. She vanished into the shadows at the foot of the hill. Roulant stood where he'd landed.

Guarinn eyed the darkness, and Roulant standing outside the wall, straining like a leashed hound. The night would spring alive at any moment, suddenly boiling with horror. The wall would be on them.

Guarinn nervously fingered the haft of his axe. "Roulant, what do you think?"

"I'm going to fetch Una back, that's what I think!"

Guarinn heard Roulant's answer only faintly, for the young man was already at the foot of the hill. Alone in the ruin, Guarinn shifted from foot to foot, indecisively. "This is insane," he muttered. "I *know* what's going to happen to me if I leave here . . . "

He took a breath, fueling courage and a suddenly rising hope. Maybe nothing would happen.

Roulant can chase after his girl if that's what he wants to do, Guarinn thought. But I still have my axe and good strong arm, and I'm going for the wolf.

Guarinn hopped the wall. But when his feet hit the ground he found himself on the wrong side of the border between reason and nightmare, caught in the trap the Spoiler had laid for any wolfhunter who ventured out of the ruin.

*   *   *   *   *

The wall walked. And the dead with him.

They crawled, and shambled, and dragged themselves staggering through a foul and freezing fog, each trying desperately to reach Guarinn as the damned would grasp at one last hope. He could not move, stood rooted like an oak in the ice-toothed mist, helpless as decaying hands plucked at him, clung to him, shoulder and wrist and arm. And this was no silent place, this nightmare-realm. It was filled up with the mad shrieking and frenzied grieving of people he'd known in life, and some he'd never seen until they were dead.

A hunter who'd died to feed the wolf's hunger.

An old peddler night-caught in the forest, hardly recognizable as human when he'd been found.

A child, a little boy screaming now as it had when, three years ago, the wolf had torn him from his bed. Or was that Guarinn's own voice screaming, his own throat torn with the violence of terror as the child's had been by the wolf's fangs?

Then came a howling, a long, aching sound of abandonment. The wolf. Or a friend forsaken. Or an innocent dying.

Guarinn, you've failed me, failed them all!

Hands clawed at his face, dug and tore at his throat, leaving bits of their own flesh and grave-mold behind to foul his beard and hair.

Faithless friend! You stink of their blood, Guarinn Hammerfell!

Guarinn cried out in terror, couldn't tell his own voice from theirs, no longer knew who accused—they or him. The ice-mist filled up his lungs, stopped his breath, suffocating him.

Murderer! Guarinn Child-killer! Guarinn—

*   *   *   *   *

"Guarinn! Breathe! Come on, breathe!"

Roulant shook his friend till his teeth rattled, shook him harder still, but to no effect. Roulant'd heard but one choking gasp of terror, just as he was entering the forest, and he'd known that whatever chance-found charm was keeping him safe and sane outside the ruin wasn't working for Guarinn. The dwarf was trapped, unable to move, even to breathe, while mind and soul were adrift in the cold country of nightmare.

"Guarinn," Roulant shouted, fearful. Perhaps Una was safe because the Spoiler's trap was meant to harm no one but those who bound by the curse. Perhaps Roulant was safe because he left the ruin to find Una, not to end the curse. But Guarinn must have left the ruin with plans to kill the wolf. That's what sprung the Spoiler's trap, Roulant thought.

"Guarinn!" he cried again, gathering his friend close, holding him. "We've got to find Una! I need you to help me. Please, Guarinn! Come back and help me . . ."

A breath, just a small one.

"Guarinn—help me find Una. We must find Una!"

The dwarf drew another breath, no steadier, but deeper. Roulant held him hard, forced him to look nowhere but into his eyes. "Listen—*listen!* Don't think about anything else but this: We have to find Una. Don't even think about why. We're here for no reason but to find Una. Do you understand?"

Guarinn swallowed hard.

"*Do you understand?*"

"Yes," Guarinn said hoarsely. "What next?"

Roulant thought as he helped his friend to his feet.

*   *   *   *   *

The wolf woke to pain and hunger. He was not frightened by the pain, knowing he could transcend it. He was afraid of hunger. Wolves worship only one god, and the god's name is Hunger.

He'd found shelter quickly after he'd fled his attackers, a soft nest of old leaves beneath a rock outcropping. There, downwind of his enemies so he could smell them if they pursued, he'd licked clean the shallow cuts on his belly and legs, the deeper one on his shoulder. He'd gnawed off the trailing end of the rope, for that frightened him nearly as much as hunger. It had more than once snagged in bushes to choke him as he'd fled. He'd gotten most of it, wearing only the noose now, a foul-smelling collar. Free and safe, he'd curled tight against the cold—sleeping lightly, dreaming of thirst and hunger as a thin veil of clouds came from the east to hide the stars.

Now the shadows had softer edges and the darkness was deeper. The wind told him that water was no great distance away—clean and cold by the smell; by the sound, no more than a streamlet. It would be enough to provide thirst's ease. And there was another scent, not close yet, only faintly woven into night, but the wolf knew it—human-scent, burnt meat and smoke and old skins; sweat and the light, sweet odor of flesh; running beneath that, the warm smell of blood; over it all, the tang of fear, sharp and enticing on the cold night air. He'd seen this young female not long ago, and he had the mark of her steel fang on him. Hers was the least of his wounds, for she'd been distracted by fear and not very strong.

With his lean god for company, the wolf rose stiffly from his warm nest.

*   *   *   *   *

Una knelt to examine the dark blot marking the faded earth of the deer trail, and by the thin light of the moons

saw that it was no more than shadow. Cold wind blew
steadily from the east, carried the smell of a morning snow.
Una shivered and got to her feet. She'd not seen a blood-
mark or the imprints of the wolf's limping passage for some
time now, but the last real sign had been along this game-
trail, a path no more than a faint, wandering line to show
where deer passed between high-reaching trees in their for-
aging. Lacking a better choice, Una continued along the
path.

The wolf had not proven as easy to track as she'd
thought, and now she wondered whether she'd ever find
him. She wondered, too, whether it would turn out that the
beast found her, or was even now stalking behind. She tried
not to think about that. All she needed was a clear shot.
She'd put plenty of arrows through the straw-butt, she
could put an arrow through a wolf. She could free Thorne.
She could free them all. But she had little confidence ruling
her thoughts, and so, her attention was focused behind her
rather than in front when the deer trail ended abruptly at
the muddy verge of a shallow stream.

Una and the wolf saw each other at the same moment,
and she knew—as prey knows in its bones—that she might
have time to nock an arrow to string, but she wasn't going
to have time to let the bolt fly.

* * * * *

Guarinn tried to maintain a narrow focus, to shut down
all thinking and track like an animal, using only sight and
scent and hearing. He measured his success by the nearness
of dead voices. At best, the haunting dead were never
wholly gone, only banished to a distance he could endure.
The protection Roulant had shown him was working, but
only just. How fast would the Spoiler's trap catch them if
they came upon the wolf?

Soft—a whisper shivering across the night—Guarinn
heard the rattle of brush. He stopped, keeping his hands
fisted and well away from the axe in his belt while he waited
to hear the sound again.

"The wind," Roulant said, low.

Guarinn didn't think so. That one soft rattle had been a discordant note. When the sound came again, Guarinn knew it wasn't wind-crafted. Nor was it soft now. Something was running through the brush.

"It's Una!" Roulant cried and bolted past Guarinn.

She wasn't alone. Like a dark echo, something else came crashing through the brush behind her.

Fleet, eyes huge as a hunted doe's, Una burst through the brush, frantically trying to nock arrow to bow as she ran. She was having little luck, and even at a distance Guarinn saw her hands shaking, fumbling uselessly at shaft and string.

"Una," Roulant shouted. "Here!"

Seeing them for the first time, she redoubled her speed. Relief and joy and—last—panic marked her face when her foot turned on a stone and she fell hard to the ground, the breath blasted from her, and the bow flung from her hand.

Guarinn saw the wolf first. The sight of it—eyes redly blazing, fangs gleaming—triggered instinct. In the very moment the wolf leaped, the dwarf snatched his throwing axe from his belt—and tumbled over the edge of nightmare.

* * * * *

The wolf smelled fear and loved it—the scent of easy prey. He sensed no threat in the smaller male, standing motionless; nor was the young female—struggling for breath, fighting to rise from the ground—any danger. These he could ignore for now. But the third, the bigger male . . . from him came the fiery scent of a pack-defender. He was the danger and the threat.

* * * * *

The wolf hurtled past Una. Choking on the sudden, cold rush of air, she heard the impact of bodies—the wolf snarling and Roulant's grunt of shock and pain.

And she saw Guarinn standing still as stone, his throwing axe gripped in a nerveless hand.

"Guarinn!" she cried, clawing at the ground in desperate

search of the bow. "Help him!"

Guarinn never moved . . . and she found the bow, string-broken, useless. Roulant screamed, a raging curse turned to pain as the wolf's fangs tore at his shoulder. The cry of pain became a chant—her name, gasped over and over in the staggering rhythm of his ragged breathing as he struggled with the beast.

Una gained her feet, running. She flung herself at the wolf's back, dagger in hand. Clinging to the writhing beast's neck, choking on the smell of blood, she struck wildly. Poorly. Hurting, but not killing.

The wolf heaved up.

"Guarinn! Help me! The wolf is killing him!"

The beast twisted sharply, and threw her off. Its fangs dripped frothy red, and behind it, Roulant lurched to his feet, gasping his terrible chant. The wolf turned, leaped at him. Una didn't know which of them screamed, man or wolf. The sound of it tore through the night, a wild howling.

* * * * *

Guarinn Hammerfell stood at the center of a maelstrom of wild moaning and screaming. *Guarinn! Help him!* Hands clawed at him, shreds of livid flesh falling away to expose bones as white and brittle as ice. *The wolf is killing him!* Hollow voices accused him, and the foul names—child-killer! murderer! faithless friend!—turned the ice-mist filling his lungs to poison.

A wind rose to pound at him, tear at him, with such violence that even the dead hands, shedding tattered flesh, rattling bones, fell away before it. Howling, screaming, deafening wind.

Roulant! Familiar with everyone who haunted this nightmare realm, Guarinn knew that name had no business being spoken here. He snatched at it, clutched it tight for a lifeline. He was choking, fighting for air, falling . . . and staggering on the deer trail, his axe clenched tight in his fist.

The wolf lunged again at Roulant, leaping for his throat. In the only instant of sanity he might get before the dead snatched him back into the Spoiler's trap, Guarinn sighted, threw, and didn't miss.

The wolf fell to the ground, its spine severed.

Hard and dark, the beast's eyes held Guarinn for a long moment. Then they softened, and the night filled up with silence.

The dying wolf became man. A moment, the man had, and he used it to speak. Only whispered words, barely heard.

"Roulant . . . are you hurt?"

Roulant ignored the question. "Thorne! You're . . . dying! No, Thorne. This isn't how it's supposed to be! You said . . ."

Thorne smiled, shifting his gaze to Guarinn.

"You," Thorne said. "Old friend, you knew I wouldn't survive, didn't you?"

Guarinn heard grieving, Una and Roulant, one sobbing softly in shock and the aftermath of terror, the other offering comfort in the face of his own astonished grief.

"And you killed the wolf. Knowing." Thorne closed his eyes. "Thank you."

Guarinn lifted his friend's hand and held it, very gently, close against his heart until he felt the last pulse, and some time longer after that.

* * * * *

Limping, leaning on Una for support, Roulant knelt beside his friends, the living and the dead.

He and Guarinn and Una knelt together as snow began to fall, listened to dawn-wind singing. It held no echo of wolfish howling. The Night of the Wolf was over, and Roulant saw the peace of it in Guarinn's smile.

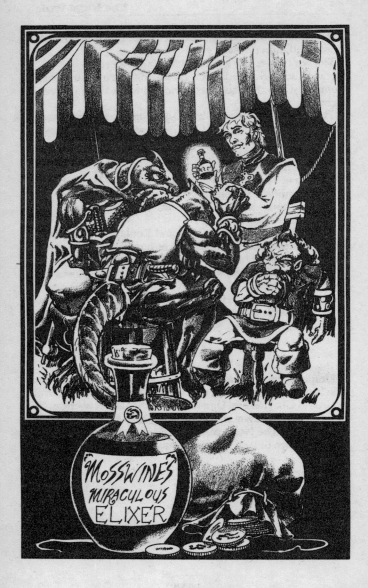

The Potion Sellers

Mark Anthony

———

It was just after Midsummer's, on a fine, golden morning, when the seller of potions came to the town of Faxfail.

Perched precariously upon the high bench of a peculiar-looking wagon, he drove through the borough's narrow, twisting streets. The wagon, pulled by a pair of perfectly matched dappled ponies, was a tall, boxlike craft all varnished in black and richly decorated with carved scrollwork of gilded wood. On the wagon's side panel, painted in a fantastically brilliant hue of purple, was the picture of a bottle above which was scribed, in flowing letters of serpentine green, three strange words: MOSSWINE'S MIRACULOUS ELIXIRS. It was a mysterious message indeed, and startled the townsfolk who looked up from their morning tasks and chores in curiosity as the wagon rattled by.

The seller of potions himself was a young-looking man, with hair the color of new straw and eyes as blue as the summer sky. He was clad in finery fit for a noble—albeit in hues a bit brighter than most nobles would choose—and his dark, crimson-lined cape billowed out behind him in the morning breeze. He waved to the townsfolk as he passed by, his broad grin rivalling the sun for sheer brilliance.

On the hard wooden bench next to the seller of potions bounced a short, swarthy-looking fellow. His look was not nearly so cheerful as his companion's, but then this was only typical. He was a dwarf, and it has often been said that dwarvenkind is every bit as hard and unyielding as the metals dwarves are so fond of forging deep in their dim mountain smithies. This particular dwarf wore a dour expression, his heavy eyebrows drawn down over his iron-gray eyes in a scowl. His coarse black beard was so long he wore it tucked into his broad leather belt, and his shaggy hair was bound with a leather thong into a braid behind his neck.

"You know, you're going to scare the townsfolk out of what little wits they have with that sour look you're wearing," the seller of potions said quietly to the dwarf through clenched teeth, all the while grinning and waving. "It won't do us a great deal of good if they all take one look at you and go scurrying inside to bolt their doors. At least, not until after we have their money. I don't suppose you could smile for a change, could you?"

"I am smiling," the dwarf answered in a gruff voice. His craggy visage was not quite as warm and friendly as a chunk of wind-hewn granite, but almost.

The seller of potions eyed the dwarf critically. "Maybe you shouldn't try so hard," he suggested lightly, but the joke was completely lost on the dour-faced dwarf. The seller of potions sighed and shook his head. His name was Jastom, and he had traveled with this particular dwarf long enough to know when argument and teasing were pointless. The dwarf's name was Algrimmbeldebar, but over the years Jastom had taken to simply calling him Grimm. Not only did the name slip more readily from the tongue, it also suited the dwarf's disposition far better.

Rumors sped faster than sparrows through the town's narrow streets, and by the time the wagon rolled into Faxfail's central square, a sizeable crowd of curious townsfolk had gathered expectantly. It wouldn't be the largest audience Jastom had ever hawked potions to, but it wouldn't be the smallest either. Faxfail was a town deep in the Garnet mountains of southern Solamnia. The nearest city of consequence—that would be Kaolyn—was a good three day's journey to the north and west. These were country folk. And country folk tended to be far more trusting than city folk. Or gullible, depending upon one's choice of words.

"I suppose this means I'll have to mix more elixirs," Grimm grumbled, eyeing the growing throng. The dwarf opened a small panel behind the bench and nimbly disappeared inside the wagon.

Concocting potions was Grimm's task; selling them was Jastom's. It was an arrangement that had proven quite profitable on their journeys from one end of Ansalon to the other. The two had first met some years before, in the markets of Kalaman. At the time, neither had been making a terribly good living for himself. Even Jastom's brilliant smile and ingenuous visage had not been enough to interest folk in the crude baubles he was attempting to foist off as good luck charms. And as for the dwarf, his gloomy, glowering looks tended to keep potential customers well away from the booth where he was trying to sell his elixirs. One night, the two had found themselves sharing a table in a tavern, each lamenting his particular misfortune over a mug of ale. Both had realized that each had what the other lacked, and so their unlikely but lucrative partnership was born.

The wagon rolled to a halt in the center of the town's square, and Jastom leapt acrobatically to the cobbles. He bowed deeply, flourishing his heavy cape as grandly as a court magician, and then spread his arms wide.

"Gather 'round, good folk of Faxfail, gather 'round!" he called out. His voice was clear as a trumpet, honed by years of hawking wares until it was as precise as the finest musical instrument. "Wonders await you this day, so gather 'round and behold!"

From out of nowhere (or, in fact, from out of his sleeve) a small purple bottle appeared in Jastom's upturned palm. A gasp of amazement passed through the crowd as folk young and old alike leaned forward to peer at the odd little bottle. The morning sunlight sparkled through the purple glass, illuminating a thick, mysterious-looking liquid within.

"Wonders indeed," Jastom went on, lowering his voice to a theatrical whisper that was nonetheless audible to even the most distant onlookers. "After just one sip of this precious potion, all your aches and ailments, all your

---

malingering maladies and ponderous pains, will vanish as though they had never been. For a mere ten coins of steel"— a dismissing gesture of his hand made this particular detail seem of the barest significance—"this bottle of Mosswine's Miraculous Elixir will heal all!"

This last, of course, was not precisely true, and Jastom knew it. He and Grimm were charlatans. Fakes. Swindlers. The potion in the purple bottle couldn't so much as heal a rabbit of the sniffles let alone any of the dire ills he was claiming. Mosswine wasn't even Jastom's real name. It was Jastom Mosswallow. However, by the time folk in any one place realized the truth of things, Jastom and Grimm would always be long gone, headed for the next town or city to ply their trade.

It wasn't at all a bad business as Jastom reckoned things. He and Grimm got a purse full of coins for their efforts, and in return the folk they duped got something to believe in, at least for a little while. And these days even a brief hope was a rare thing of worth.

It was just six short months ago, in the dead of winter, that all of Krynn had suffered under the cold, hard claws of the dragonarmies. The War of the Lance had ended with the coming of spring, but the scars it had left upon the land— and the people—had not faded so easily as the winter snows. The folk of Ansalon were desperate for anything that might help them believe they could leave the dark days of the war behind, that they could heal themselves and make their lives whole once again. That was exactly what Jastom and Grimm gave them.

Of course, there were true clerics in the land now, since the War. Some were disciples of the goddess Mishakal— called Light Bringer—and they could heal with the touch of a hand. Or at least so Jastom had heard, for true clerics were still a rarity. However, he and Grimm did their best to avoid towns and cities where there were rumored to be clerics. Folk wouldn't be so willing to buy false healing potions when there was one among them with the power of true healing.

Abruptly, there was a loud, surprising clunk! as the wagon's side panel flipped downward, revealing a polished wooden counter and, behind it, a row of shelves lined with glimmering purple bottles. Grimm's glowering eyes barely managed to peer over the countertop, but the crowd hardly noticed the taciturn dwarf. All were gazing at the display of sparkling elixirs.

Jastom gestured expansively to the wagon. "Indeed, my good gentlefolk, just one of these elixirs, and all that troubles you will be cured. And all it costs is a mere ten coins of steel. A small price to pay for a miracle, wouldn't you say?"

There was a single moment of silence, and then as one the crowd gave a cry of excitement as they rushed forward, jingling purses in hand.

* * * * *

All morning and all afternoon the townsfolk crowded about the black varnished wagon, listening to Jastom extol the wondrous properties of the potions and then setting down their cold steel on the counter in trade for the small purple bottles.

There was only one minor crisis, this around midday, when the supply of potions ran out. Grimm was busily scurrying about inside the cramped wagon, measuring this and pouring that as he hurriedly tried to mix a new batch of elixirs. However, a few burly, red-necked farmers grew impatient and began shaking the wagon. Jars and bottles and pots went flying wildly inside, spilling their contents and covering Grimm with a sticky, medicinal-smelling mess. Luckily, the dwarf had managed to finish a handful of potions by then, and Jastom used these to placate the belligerent farmers, selling them the bottles for half price. Losing steel was not something Jastom much cared for, but losing the wagon—and Grimm—would have been disastrous.

After that interruption, Grimm was able to finish filling empty bottles with the thick, pungent elixir, and business proceeded more smoothly. However, the dwarf's eyes were still smoldering like hot iron.

"Fine way to make a living," he grumbled to himself as he tried to pick sticky clumps of herbs from his thick black beard. "I suppose we'll swindle ourselves right out of our own necks one of these days."

"What did that glum-looking little fellow say?" a black-smith demanded, hesitating as he started to lay down his ten coins of steel on the wooden counter. "Something about swindle?"

Jastom shot a murderous look at Grimm and then turned his most radiant smile to the smith. "You'll have to forgive my friend's mumblings," he said in a conspiratorial whisper. "He hasn't been quite the same ever since one of the ponies kicked him in the head."

The blacksmith nodded in sympathetic understanding. He left the wagon, small purple bottle in hand. Jastom's bulging purse was ten coins heavier. And Grimm kept his mouth shut.

*　*　*　*　*

It was midafternoon when Jastom sold the last of the potions. The corpulent merchant who bought it gripped the purple bottle tightly in his chubby fingers and scurried off through the streets, a gleam in his eye. The fellow hadn't seemed to want to discuss the exact nature of his malady, but Jastom suspected it had something to do with the equally corpulent young maiden who was waiting for him in the door of a nearby inn, smiling and batting her eyelids in a dreadful imitation of demureness. Jastom shook his head, chuckling.

Abruptly there was a loud *whoop!* Jastom turned to see an old woman throw down her crooked cane and begin dancing a spry jig to a piper's merry tune. Other folk quickly joined the dance, heedless of the aches and cares that had burdened them only a short while ago. One shabbily-dressed fellow, finding himself without a partner, settled for a spotted pig that had the misfortune to be wandering through the town square. The pig squealed in surprise as the man whirled it about, and Jastom couldn't help but laugh aloud at the spectacle.

This was the work of the elixirs, of course. Jastom wasn't altogether certain what Grimm put in the small purple bottles, but he knew the important ingredient was something called dwarf spirits. And while dwarf spirits were not known to possess any curative powers, they did have certain potent and intoxicating effects.

Jastom had no idea how the dwarves brewed the stuff. From what little he had managed to get out of Grimm, it was all terribly secret, the recipe passed down from generation to generation with ancient ceremony and solemn oaths to guard the formula. But whatever was in it, it certainly worked. Laborers threw down their shovels, goodwives their brooms, and all joined what was rapidly becoming an impromptu festival. Respected city elders turned cartwheels about the square, and parents leapt into piles of straw hand-in-hand with their laughing children. For now, all thoughts of the war, of worry and of sickness, were altogether missing from the town of Faxfail.

But it couldn't last.

"They won't feel so terribly well tomorrow, once the dwarf spirits wear off," Grimm observed dourly.

"But today they do, and by tomorrow we'll be somewhere else," Jastom said, patting the nearly-bursting purse at his belt.

He slammed shut the wagon's side panel and leapt up onto the high bench. Grimm clambered up after him. At a flick of the reins, the ponies started forward, and the wagon rattled slowly out of the rollicking town square.

Jastom did not notice as three men—one with a sword at his hip and the other two clad in heavy black robes despite the day's warmth—stepped from a dim alleyway and began to thread their way through the spontaneous celebration, following in the wagon's wake.

* * * * *

Jastom whistled a cheerful, tuneless melody as the wagon jounced down the red dirt road, leaving the town of Faxfail far behind.

The road wound its way across a broad vale. To the north and south hulked two slate-gray peaks that looked like ancient fortresses built by long-vanished giants. The sky above was clear as a sapphire, and a fair wind, clean with the hint of mountain heights, hissed through the rippling fields of green-gold grass. Sunflowers nodded like old good-wives to each other, and larks darted by upon the air, trilling their glad melodies.

"You seem to be in an awfully fine mood, considering," Grimm noted in his rumbling voice.

"Considering what, Grimm?" Jastom asked gaily, resuming his whistling.

"Considering that cloud of dust that's following on the road behind us," the dwarf replied.

Jastom's whistling died.

"What?"

He cast a hurried look over his shoulder. Sure enough, a thick plume of ruddy dust was rising from the road perhaps a half mile back. Even as Jastom watched, he saw the shapes of three dark horsemen appear amidst the blood-colored cloud. No . . . one horseman and two figures running along on either side. The sound of pounding hoofbeats rumbled faintly on the air like the sound of a distant storm.

Jastom swore loudly. "This is impossible," he said incredulously. "The townsfolk couldn't have sobered up this soon. They can't have figured out that we've swindled them. Not yet."

"Is that so?" Grimm grunted. "Well, they're riding mighty fast and hard for drunken men."

"Maybe they're not after us," Jastom snapped. But an uncomfortable image of a noose slipping over his neck went through his mind. Swearing again, he slapped the reins, urging the ponies into a canter. The box-shaped wagon was heavy, and they had just begun to ascend a low hill. The ponies couldn't go much faster. Jastom glanced wildly over his shoulder again. The horseman had closed the gap to half of what it had been only a few moments before. He saw now that two of them—the ones running— wore heavy black robes. Sunlight glinted dully from the sword that the third rider had drawn.

Jastom considered jumping from the wagon but promptly discarded the idea. If the fall didn't kill them, the strangers would simply cut him and the dwarf down like a mismatched pair of weeds. Besides, everything Jastom and Grimm owned was in the wagon. Their entire livelihood depended upon it. Jastom couldn't abandon it, no matter the consequences. He flicked the reins harder. The ponies strained valiantly against their harnesses, their nostrils flaring with effort.

It wasn't enough.

With a sound like a breaking storm, the horseman rode up alongside the wagon. One of the dark-robed men dashed up close to the ponies. With incredible strength, he grabbed the bridle of the nearest and then pulled back hard, his feet digging into the gravel of the road. The dapples reared, whinnying in fear as the wagon shuddered to a sudden stop.

"Away with you, dogs!" Grimm growled fiercely, reaching under the seat for the heavy axe he kept there. The dwarf never managed to get a hand on the weapon. With almost comic ease, the second dark-robed man grabbed the dwarf by the collar of his tunic and lifted him from the bench. The dwarf kicked his feet and waved his arms futilely, suspended in midair, his face red with rage and lack of air.

Jastom could pay scant attention to the spluttering dwarf. He had worries of his own. A glittering steel sword was leveled directly at his heart.

Whoever these three were, Jastom was quite certain that they weren't townsfolk from Faxfail, but this did little to comfort him. The man before him looked to be a soldier of some sort. He was clad in black leather armor sewn with plates of bronze, and a cloak of lightning blue was thrown back over his stiff, square shoulders.

Suddenly, Jastom was painfully aware of the fat leather purse at his belt. He cursed himself inwardly. He should have known better than to go riding off, boldly flaunting his newly-gained wealth. The roads were thick with bandits and brigands these days, now that the war was over. Most likely these men were deserters from the Solamnic army, desperate and looking for foolish travelers like himself to waylay.

Jastom forced his best grin across his face. "Good day, friend," he said to the man who held the sword at his chest.

The man was tall and stern-faced, his blond, close-cropped hair and hawklike nose enhancing the granite severity of his visage. Most disturbing about him, however, were his eyes. They were pale and colorless, like his hair, but as hard as stones. They were eyes that had watched men die and not cared a whit one way or another.

The man inclined his head politely, as though he wasn't also holding a sword in his hand. "I am Lieutenant Durm, of the Blue Dragonarmy," he said in a voice that was steel-made—polished and smooth, yet cold and so very hard. "My master, the Lord Commander Shaahzak, is in need of one with healing skills." He gestured with the sword to the picture of the bottle painted on the side of the wagon. "I see that you are a healer." The sword point swung once again in Jastom's direction. "You will accompany me to attend my commander."

The Blue Dragonarmy? Jastom thought in disbelief. But the war was over! The dragonarmies had been defeated by the Whitestone forces. At least, that was what the stories said. Jastom shot a quick look at Grimm, but the dwarf was still dangling in midair from the dark-robed man's fist, cursing in a tight, squeaky voice. Jastom turned his attention back to the man who called himself Durm.

"I fear that I have an appointment elsewhere," Jastom said pleasantly, his grin growing broader yet. He reached for his heavy leather purse. "I am certain, lieutenant, that you can easily find another who is not so pressed for—" —time, Jastom was going to finish, but before he could, Durm reached out in a fluid, almost casual gesture and struck him.

Jastom's head erupted into a burst of white-hot fire. He tumbled from the wagon's bench to the hard ground, a rushing noise filling his ears. For a dizzying moment he thought he was going to be sick. After a few seconds the flashing pain subsided to a low throbbing. He blinked his eyes and looked up. Durm had dismounted and stood over him now, his visage as emotionless as before.

"I recommend that you not speak falsehood to me again," Durm said in a polite, chilling voice, his tone that of a host admonishing a guest for spilling wine on an expensive carpet. "Do you understand, healer?"

Jastom nodded jerkily. *This man could kill me with his bare hands and not even blink,* Jastom thought with a shudder.

"Excellent," Durm said. He reached down and helped Jastom to his feet—the same hand that had struck him a moment before. Durm gestured sharply, and the dark-robed man who had been holding Grimm let the dwarf fall heavily back to the wagon's bench, gasping for air.

"If you lie to me again, healer," Durm went on smoothly, "I will instruct my servants to deal with you. And I fear you will not find them so lenient as myself."

Durm's dark-robed followers pushed back the heavy cowls of their robes.

They were not human.

The two looked more akin to lizards than men, but they were not truly either. The two of them gazed at Jastom and Grimm with unblinking yellow eyes. Dull, green-black scales—not skin or fur—covered the monsters' faces. They had doglike snouts. Short, jagged spikes sprouted from their low, flat brows, and where each should have had ears there were only small indentations in their scaly hides. The monster nearest Jastom grinned evilly, revealing row upon row of jagged, yellow teeth, as if it enjoyed the idea of having Jastom to do with as it wished. A thin forked tongue flickered in and out of the thing's mouth.

Draconian. Jastom had never seen such a beast in his life, but he had heard enough tales of the War of the Lance to put a name to it. The draconians were the servants of the Dragon Highlords, and they had marched across the land to lay scourge to the face of Krynn even as the evil dragons themselves had descended from the skies.

"You might as well save everyone the trouble and let the lizards have us now," Grimm shouted hotly. "We're only—"

Jastom elbowed the dwarf hard in the ribs.

"Apprentice healers. New at this. Very new." Grimm mumbled, saying something about "necks," but fortunately only Jastom heard him.

Jastom drew upon all his theatrical skills to pull his facade back together. "Very well, my good lieutenant, we shall journey with you," he said, tipping his cap. As if we had a choice in the matter, he added inwardly.

"That is well," Durm said simply.

The lieutenant mounted and spurred his horse viciously

into a canter. Jastom realized there was nothing to do but follow. He climbed back onto the wagon and flicked the ponies' reins. The craft lurched into motion. The two draconians ran along either side, hands on the hilts of their wicked-looking sabres. Jastom cast a quick look at Grimm. The dwarf eyed his friend, then shook his head gloomily.

For the first time he could ever remember, Jastom found himself wishing his elixirs could truly work the wonders he claimed.

*   *   *   *   *

Dawn was blossoming on the horizon, like a pale rose unfurling its petals, when the wagon rattled into the dragonarmy encampment.

They had traveled all through the night, making their way down treacherous mountain roads guided only by the dim light of the crimson moon, Lunitari. More than once Jastom had thought that wagon, ponies, and all were going to plummet off the side of a precipice into the deep shadows far below. Yet he had not dared to slow the wagon's hurtling pace as they careened down the twisting passes. Jastom feared tumbling over a cliff a good bit less than he did facing Durm's displeasure.

Now, in the pale silvery light of dawn, they had left the mountains behind them somewhere in the gloom of night. The dragonarmy encampment sat in a hollow at the edge of the rolling foothills. Stretching into the distance eastward was a vast gray-green plain, its flowing lines broken only here and there by the silhouette of a cottonwood tree, sinking its roots deep for water.

The encampment was not large—perhaps fifty tents in all, clustered on the banks of a small river. But Jastom had not realized that there were still any dragonarmy forces at all so close to Solamnia, or anywhere for that matter. From the stories, he thought they had all been driven clean off the face of Krynn. Obviously that was not so.

Most of the soldiers in the encampment were human, with deep-set eyes and cruel mouths. There were a number of draconians as well, dressed in leather armor similar to that of the human soldiers. Short, stubby wings sprouted from the draconians' backs, as leathery as a bat's, but they seemed to flutter uselessly as the draconians stalked across the ground on clawed, unbooted feet.

"This doesn't look like one of the friendlier audiences you've ever had to hawk potions to," Grimm noted as the wagon rolled into the center of the encampment.

Jastom had played to dangerous audiences before, unruly crowds of ruffians who were more interested in breaking bones than in buying magical potions. But he had won even these over in the end.

A gleam touched Jastom's blue eyes. "No, but they *are* an audience all the same, aren't they?" he said softly, glad for the dwarf's reminder. "Let's not forget that, Grimm. They think we're healers. And as long as they keep thinking that, we'll keep our heads attached to our necks." There was only one rule to remember when hawking to a nasty crowd: never show fear.

Jastom shook the wrinkles out of his cape and cocked his feathered cap at an outrageous angle. "You there," he called out to a man in the crowd, donning a charming smile as easily as another man might don a hat. "Might I ask you a question? How did—"

The lieutenant whirled his jet black mount sharply and rode beside the wagon. "If you have questions, healer, address them to me." Durm's voice was a sword's edge draped with a silken cloth.

"You—You have so many soldiers in this camp," Jastom gulped, doing his best to sound as if he were simply making casual conversation. "How did they come to be here?"

A faint smile touched Durm's lips, but it was not an expression of mirth. Jastom fought the urge to shiver. "What tales do the knights tell in Solamnia?" Durm asked. "That they swept the dragonarmies from the face of Krynn? Well, as you can see, they have not. I will grant the Whitestone armies this—they have won an important battle. But if the Knights of Solamnia believe this war is truly over, then they are as foolish as the tales tell them to be." Durm gestured to the camp about them as he rode. A line of soldiers, holding their swords at ready, marched by in formation, saluting

Durm as they passed.

"In truth, this is but a small outpost," Durm went on. "Far more of our forces lie to the east. All the lands between this place and the Khalkist Mountains belong to the Highlord of the Blue Dragonarmy. And the other dragonarmies hold still more lands, to the north and east. Already the Dark Lady—my Highlord and master—draws her plans for a counterstrike against the knights. It will be a glorious battle." For the first time Jastom thought he saw a flash of color in Durm's pale eyes.

"So do not despair, Jastom Mosswine, that the Dragon Highlord now owns you," Durm went on in his polite, chilling tone. "Soon she will own all of Ansalon."

Jastom started to ask another question, but Durm held up a hand, silencing him. They came to halt before a tent so large it might more properly be called a pavilion. A banner flew from its highest pole, a blue dragon rampant across a field of black. Two soldiers stood at the tent's entrance, hands on the hilts of their swords.

An ancient-looking cottonwood tree spread its heavy, gnarled limbs above the tent. A half-dozen queer-looking objects dangled from several of the branches. Some seemed to be no more than large, tattered backpacks, but a few of them had a shape that seemed vaguely familiar to Jastom. Suddenly a faint breeze ruffled through the tree's green leaves, and the dangling bundles began to spin on their ropes. Several pale, bloated circles came into view.

Faces.

Jastom quickly averted his eyes, slapping a hand to his mouth to keep from spilling his guts. Those weren't bundles hanging in the tree. They were people. Each seemed to stare mockingly down at Jastom with dark sockets left empty by the crows.

"Reorx!" muttered Grimm. "What've you gotten us into?"

"Those are the healers that have been here before you," the lieutenant said flatly. "The first among them was our cleric, Umbreck. It seemed his faith in the Dark Queen was not great enough. She closed her ears to his prayers. All of them failed to heal Commander Skaahzak."

Jastom swallowed hard, the sour taste of fear in his throat. But he forced his lips into a smile. "Fear not, lieutenant," he said boldly. "We will not fail. Remember, Mosswine's Miraculous Elixirs heal all."

Grimm choked at that but, thankfully, said nothing.

Jastom and the dwarf climbed down from the wagon's bench, and Durm led them into the dimness of the tent. A rotten, sickly-sweet odor hung thickly upon the air, almost making Jastom gag. Herbs burning on a sputtering bronze brazier did little to counter the foul reek.

The tent was sparsely furnished. There was a table scattered with maps and scrolls of parchment and a rack bearing weapons of various kinds—sabres, maces, spears—all dark and cruel-looking. A narrow cot stood in one corner of the tent, and upon it lay—not a man—but a draconian. Commander Skaahzak.

Jastom did not need to be a true healer to see that the commander was dying. His scaly flesh was gray and withered, clinging tightly to the bones of his skull. His yellow eyes flickered with a hazy, feverish light, and his clawed hands clutched feebly at the twisted bed covers. His left shoulder had been bound with a thick bandage, but the cloth was soaked with a black, oozing ichor.

"Commander Skaahzak was wounded a fortnight ago, in a skirmish with a roving patrol of Solamnic Knights," Durm explained. "At first the wound did not seem dire, but it has festered. You will work your craft upon him, healer. Or you will join the rest outside."

"We . . . uh . . . we have to prepare an elixir," Jastom said, doing his best to keep his voice from trembling.

Durm nodded stiffly. "Very well. If you require anything in your task, you have only to request it." With another faint smile, devoid of warmth, the lieutenant left them to their task.

* * * * *

When Jastom and Grimm were alone in the cluttered space inside their wagon, the dwarf shook his head.

"Have you gone completely mad, then, Jastom?" he whispered. "You know very well we sold our last potion in Fax-fail, and yet you go offering one up like we can conjure them out of thin air."

"Well, I couldn't think of anything else to say," Jastom returned defensively. After Faxfail, they had planned to head for Kaolyn to buy ingredients so Grimm could brew another batch of dwarf spirits.

"Besides," Jastom went on, "there must be something we can do. If we don't come out of here with an elixir, and soon, Durm's going to feed the crows with us." He began rummaging around the boxes, pots, and jars strewn about the inside of the wagon. "Wait a minute," he said excitedly, "there's still something left in the bottom of this cask." He tipped the cask over an empty purple bottle. A thick, brown, gritty-looking fluid oozed out.

"You can't give the commander that!" Grimm cried hoarsely, trying to snatch the purple bottle away.

"Why not?" Jastom asked, holding the bottle up out of the dwarf's reach.

Grimm glowered, stubby hands on his hips. "That's pure mash—goblin's gruel, my grandpappy always called it. The dregs left over after distilling the dwarf spirits. That stuff makes the rest of the batch seem like water. Oh, it'll make him happy—might say *quite* happy for a while—but in the end . . ." Grimm shook his head.

"*A while!* That's all the time we need to get away," Jastom said desperately, stoppering the bottle.

Grimm shook his head dubiously. "We're going to make a fine feast for the crows."

*   *   *   *   *

The draconian Commander Skaahzak moaned as he thrashed in his fevered sleep. Jastom held the small bottle filled with the goblin's gruel. Grimm stood beside him. Durm watched the two from across the commander's bed, his expression stony. With a flourish of his cape, Jastom lifted the purple bottle and unstoppered it. No sense in sparing the dramatics.

Jastom nodded to Grimm. The dwarf grabbed the draconian's twisting head and held it steady, forcing the monster's jaws open with strong fingers. Jastom tipped the bottle and poured the thick contents past the draconian's lolling forked tongue and down his gullet. Grimm let Skaahzak's jaws snap back shut. Jastom waved his hand, and the empty bottle seemed to vanish into thin air. Durm never even blinked an eye.

Jastom took a deep breath, searching for something suitably dramatic to say. But before he could, the fetid air of the tent was shattered by a blood-curdling shriek.

Skaahzak.

The draconian shrieked again, writhing upon the bed. Jastom and Grimm gaped at the creature. In a flash, Durm drew his sword and levelled it at Jastom's heart.

"It seems you have failed," Durm spoke softly, almost as a father might chide an erring son, except that his voice was so deathly cold.

Abruptly, the draconian commander leapt from the bed and knocked Durm's sword aside. The goblin's gruel was coursing through the creature's blood, lighting him aflame. The gray tinge had left Skaahzak's flesh, and if his wound was causing him any pain he did not show it. His yellow eyes glowed brightly now.

"Stop this foolishness, Durm," Skaahzak hissed. "I will have your head if you dare strike either of these most skillful healers."

Jastom's head was spinning. But he was not about to let this opportunity go to waste. He doffed his cap and bowed deeply. "It gladdens my heart to see milord in such excellent health," he proclaimed in a deeply-felt tone. He surreptitiously kicked Grimm's knee, and the dwarf toppled forward in clumsy imitation of Jastom's graceful bow.

"You have done me a great service, healer," Skaahzak said in his dry, reptilian voice, donning a crimson robe that an attendant soldier offered him.

"I am overjoyed that I could restore such a brilliant commander to health," Jastom said. Grimm muttered something inaudible under his beard.

"That you have," Skaahzak hissed. Suddenly he spun about wildly, a ferocious, toothy grin on his face. "I've never felt better in my life!" He lurched dizzily and would have fallen but for Durm's strong hands steadying him.

There was no doubt about it. The draconian was rip-roaring drunk.

"Take your filthy paws from me!" Skaahzak spat, shrugging off the lieutenant's grip. "You, who have brought me healer after healer, cleric after cleric, all who poked, prodded, and prayed to their foul gods over me, and all who failed. I should have you flailed for letting me suffer so long." Skaahzak's expression flickered between intoxicated ecstasy and livid rage. Little seemed to separate the two emotions in this creature.

Durm watched silently, impassively.

"However, you *did* bring these most excellent healers to me," Skaahzak said, his voice crooning now. "Thus I will be merciful. I will even grant you a reward to show you the depths of my kindness." He held out his left hand. "You may kiss the ring of your master, Lieutenant Durm."

On the draconian's clawed middle finger was a ring set with a ruby as big as a thumbnail. Jastom guessed that Skaahzak hadn't removed the ring in years. In fact, he doubted the draconian would be able to take it off at all. The monster's scaly flesh was puffy and swollen to either side of the ring. Durm did not hesitate. He knelt before Skaahzak's proffered hand.

Leaning forward, he pressed his lips to the glimmering ruby. As he did so, Skaahzak struck the lieutenant. Durm did not even flinch. Slowly, he rose to his feet. The ruby had cut his cheek, and a thin trickle of blood, as crimson as the gem, ran down his jaw. The draconian grinned.

"There, lieutenant," Skaahzak said, his reptilian voice slurred and indistinct. "Your reward is complete."

Durm bowed stiffly, giving Jastom a brief, indecipherable glance.

Jastom tried to swallow his heart, but it kept clawing its way up into his throat. He cast a meaningful look at Grimm. It was time to get out of this place. The dwarf nodded emphatic agreement.

"Well, I am delighted to see that all things appear to have been set aright," Jastom said pleasantly, placing his cap back on his head. "Thus I believe that we will be—"

Skaahzak interrupted him.

"I have a proclamation to make!" the draconian shouted. He sloshed some wine into a silver goblet—spilling the better portion of it on his robe—and began to weave drunkenly about the tent, stumbling over chests and pieces of furniture. One of his attendants followed behind him with a quill and parchment, taking down each word. "Be it known that, for their most excellent service, these two healers shall hereby become my personal physicians, from now until the end of all days!" He spread his arms wide in a gesture of triumph. The silver goblet he clutched struck the head of his attendant with a loud *clunk!* The soldier dropped to the floor like a stone, the parchment and quill slipping from his fingers. Skaahzak did not notice.

Jastom and Grimm exchanged glances of alarm. "Er, begging your pardon, milord," Jastom said hesitantly, "but what exactly do you mean by that?"

Skaahzak whirled about to face Jastom, his eyes burning with the consuming fire of the goblin's gruel. "I mean that Lieutenant Durm here will show you to your new quarters," the draconian said, displaying his countless jagged teeth in a terrible smile. "You will be remaining here in this camp with me. Permanently. You are my healers, now."

Jastom could only nod dumbly, feeling suddenly ill. Impossible as it seemed, it looked as if this time his elixir had worked too well for his own good.

* * * * *

"How many soldiers are standing guard out there?" Jastom whispered.

"Two," Grimm whispered back, peering through a narrow opening beside the canvas flap that covered the tent's entrance. "Both are draconians."

Jastom tugged at his hair as he paced the length of the cramped, stuffy tent. The air was musty with the smell of the sour, rotten hay strewn across the floor. The only light came from a wan, golden beam of sun spilling through a small hole in the tent's canvas roof.

"There must be a way to get past them," Jastom said in agitation, clenching his hands into fists.

"Too bad we can't get them drunk," Grimm noted dryly.

Jastom shot the dwarf an exasperated look. "There's always a way out, Grimm. We've been in enough dungeons before to know that. All we need is time to come up with the answer."

Grimm shook his head, his shaggy eyebrows drawn down in a scowl. "Even now, the goblin's gruel will be burning Skaahzak from the inside out, as sure as if it was liquid fire he'd drunk. He'll be dead by morning." The dwarf paused ominously. "And I suppose we will be, too, for that matter."

Jastom groaned, barely resisting the urge to throttle the glum-faced dwarf. His energy would be better directed toward finding a way to escape, he reminded himself. Once they were free, *then* he would have all the time he wanted to throttle the dwarf.

With a sigh of frustration, Jastom sat down hard on the musty straw, resting his chin in his hands. Grimm's doom-and-gloom was catching.

The tent's entrance flap was thrown back. The two draconian guards stood against the brilliant square of afternoon sunlight, their forked tongues flickering through their jagged yellow teeth.

"It's mealtime," one of the draconians hissed, glaring at Jastom with its disturbing yellow eyes.

For a startled moment Jastom didn't know whose mealtime the draconian meant: Jastom's or its own. With a rush of relief, he saw the bowls that the creature carried in its clawed hands. The draconian set the two clay bowls down, their foul-smelling contents slopping over the sides. The other draconian threw a greasy-looking wineskin down with them.

"The commander ordered that you be given the finest fare in the camp," the other draconian croaked, a note of envy in its voice. "Skaahzak must hold you in high esteem, indeed. Consider yourselves fortunate."

After the two draconians left them alone, Jastom eyed the bowls of food warily. The lumpy, colorless liquid in one of them began to stir. A big black beetle crawled out of the gray ooze and over the rim of the bowl. Jastom let out a strangled yelp. The insect scuttled away through the straw.

"Paugh!" Grimm spat, tossing down the rancid-smelling wineskin. "What do these beasts brew their wine out of? Stale onions?"

Jastom felt his gorge rising in his throat and barely managed to choke it back down. "If this is the finest fare the camp has to offer, I really don't want to think about what the common soldiers are eating." He began to push the clay bowls carefully away with the toe of his boot, but then he paused. A thought had suddenly struck him.

Quickly he rummaged about his cape until he found the secret pocket where he had slipped the empty potion bottle after pouring its contents down Skaahzak's gullet. He pulled out the cork and then knelt beside the bowl. Carefully, so as not to spill any of the putrid substance on himself, he tipped the bowl and filled the bottle partway with the slop. Then he took the wineskin and added a good measure of the acrid-smelling wine to the bottle. On an afterthought he scraped up a handful of dirt from the tent's floor and added that as well. He stoppered the bottle tightly and then shook it vigorously to mix the strange concoction within.

"What in the name of Reorx do you think you're doing, Jastom?" Grimm demanded, his gray eyes flashing. "Have you gone utterly mad? I suppose I should have known the strain of all this would be too much for you."

"No, Grimm, I haven't gone mad," Jastom said annoyedly, and then he grinned despite himself, tossing the bottle and deftly snatching it again from the air. "Get 'em drunk, you said."

"But you never listen to me," Grimm protested. "And I don't think now is a good time to start!"

"Just go along," said Jastom.

* * * * *

It was sunset when the two draconians threw back the tent's flap again and stepped inside to retrieve the dishes.

"Thank you, friends," Jastom said cheerily as the draconians picked up the empty bowls and wineskin. "It was truly a remarkable repast." In truth, he and Grimm had buried the revolting food in a shallow hole in the corner of the tent, but the draconians need not know that. The two creatures glared at Jastom, the envy glowing wickedly in their reptilian eyes.

"You're right, Jastom," the dwarf said thoughtfully, gazing at the two draconians. "They *do* look a little gray."

The first draconian's eyes narrowed suspiciously. "What does the nasty little dwarf mean?"

Jastom nodded, a serious look crossing his honest face. "I see it, too, Grimm," he said gravely. "There's only one thing it can be. Scale rot."

" 'Scale rot?' " The second draconian spat. "What is this foolishness you babble about?"

Jastom sighed, as if he were reluctant to speak. "I've seen it before," he said, shaking his head sadly. "It's a scourge that's wiped out whole legions of draconians to the far south, in Abanasinia. I didn't think it had traveled across the Newsea, but it seems I was wrong."

"Aye, I saw a draconian who had the scale rot once," Grimm said gloomily. "All we buried was a pile of black, spongy mold. He didn't die until the very end. I didn't think a creature could scream as loud as that."

"I've never heard of this!" the first draconian hissed.

Jastom donned his most utterly believable face. The gods themselves wouldn't know he was lying. "You don't have to believe me," he said with a shrug. "Judge for yourself. The first symptoms are so small you'd hardly notice them if you didn't know what to look for: a pouchy grayness around the eyes, a faint ache in the teeth and claws, and then . . ." Jastom let his last words fade into an unintelligible mumble.

"What did you say?" the second draconian barked.

"I said, 'and then the hearing begins to fade in and out,' " Jastom said blithely. The draconians' eyes widened. They exchanged fearful glances.

"What can we do?" the first demanded.

"You are a healer, you must help us!" the second rasped.

Jastom smiled reassuringly. "Of course, of course. Fear

not, friends. I have a potion right here." He waved a hand, and the small purple bottle filled with the noxious concoction appeared in his hand. The draconians stared at it greedily. "Mosswine's Miraculous Elixir cures all. Even scale rot."

"Aren't you forgetting something?" Grimm grumbled.

Jastom's face fell. "Oh, dear," he said worriedly.

"What is it?" The first draconian positively shrieked, clenching its talon-tipped fingers and beating its leathery wings in agitation.

"I'm afraid this is our very last potion," Jastom said, the picture of despair. "There isn't enough for both of you." He set the potion down on the floor, backing away. He spread his hands wide in a gesture of deep regret. "I'm terribly sorry, but you'll have to decide which of you gets it."

The two draconians glared at each other, tongues hissing and yellow eyes flashing.

They lunged for the bottle.

* * * * *

"Well, they seemed to have hit upon the only really fair solution to their dilemma," Jastom observed dryly.

The two draconians lay upon the floor of the tent, frozen in a fatal embrace. The remnants of the purple bottle lay next to them, crushed into tiny shards. The fight had been swift and violent. The two draconians had grappled over the elixir and in the process each had driven a cruelly barbed dagger into the other's heart. Instantly the pair of them had turned a dull gray and toppled heavily to the floor. Such was the magical nature of the creatures that, once dead, they changed to stone.

"Reorx's Beard, will you look at that!" Grimm whispered. Even as the two watched, the bodies of the draconians began to crumble. In moments nothing remained but their armor, the daggers, and a pile of dust.

Jastom reached down and brushed the gray powder from one of the barbed daggers. He grinned nervously. "I think we've just found our way out of here, Grimm."

Moments later, Jastom crawled through a slit in the back wall of the tent and peered into the deepening purple shadows of twilight. He motioned for Grimm to follow. The dwarf stumbled clumsily through the opening, falling on his face with a curse. Jastom hauled the dwarf to his feet by the belt and shot him a warning look to be quiet.

The two made their way through the darkened camp. Jastom froze each time he heard the approach of booted feet, but they faded before a soldier came within sight. A silvery glow was beginning to touch the eastern horizon. The moon Solinari would be rising soon, casting its bright, gauzy light over the land. They had to hurry. They couldn't hope to avoid the eyes of the soldiers once the moon lifted into the sky.

They rounded the corner of a long tent and then quickly ducked back behind cover. Carefully, Jastom peered around the corner. Beyond was a wide circle lit by the ruddy light of a dozen flickering torches thrust into the ground. Jastom's eyes widened at the spectacle he saw before him.

"I can fly! I can fly!" a slurred, rasping voice shrieked excitedly. It was Commander Skaahzak.

He careened wildly through midair, suspended from a tree branch by a rope looped under his arms. Two draconians grunted as they pulled on the rope, heaving the commander higher yet. Skaahzak whooped with glee, his small, useless wings flapping feebly. His eyes burned hotly with the fire of madness.

"It's the goblin's gruel," Grimm muttered softly. "It's addled his brains. But he'll stop laughing soon, when it catches his blood on fire."

A score of soldiers watched Skaahzak spin wildly on the end of the rope, none of them daring to laugh at the peculiar sight. Suddenly Jastom saw Lieutenant Durm standing at the edge of the torchlight, apart from the others, his eyes glittering like hard, colorless gems. Once again, his lips wore a faint, mirthless smile, but what exactly it portended was beyond Jastom's ken.

Quickly Jastom ducked behind the tent. "Durm is there," he whispered hoarsely. "I don't think he saw me."

"Then let's not give him another chance," Grimm growled. Jastom nodded in hearty agreement. The two slipped off in the other direction, deep into the night.

* * * * *

The tall wagon clattered along the narrow mountain road in the morning sunlight. Groves of graceful aspens and soaring fir slipped by to either side as the dappled ponies trotted briskly on.

Jastom and Grimm had ridden hard all night, making their way up the treacherous passes deep into the Garnet Mountains, guided only by the pale, gossamer light of Solinari. But now dawn had broken over the distant, mist-green peaks, and Jastom slowed the ponies to a walk. The dragonarmy camp lay a good ten leagues behind them.

"Ah, it's good to be alive and free, Grimm," Jastom said, taking a deep breath of the clean mountain air.

"Well, I wouldn't get too used to it," the dwarf said with a scowl. "Look behind us."

Jastom did as the dwarf instructed, and then his heart nearly leapt from his chest. A cloud of dust rose from the dirt road less than a mile behind them.

"Lieutenant Durm," he murmured, his mouth dry. "I *knew* this was too easy!"

Grimm nodded. Jastom let out a sharp whistle and slapped the reins fiercely. The ponies leapt into a canter.

The narrow, rocky road began to wind its way down a steep descent. The wind whipped Jastom's cape wildly out behind him. Grimm hung on for dear life. Jastom barely managed to steer around a sharp turn in the road. They were going too fast. He leaned hard on the wagon's brake. Sparks flew. Suddenly there was a sharp cracking sound— the brake lever came off in Jastom's hand.

"The wagon's out of control!" Jastom shouted.

"I can see that for myself," Grimm shouted back.

The wagon hit a deep rut and lurched wildly. The ponies shouted in terror and lunged forward. With a rending sound, their harnesses tore free, and the horses scrambled wildly up the mountain slope to one side. The wagon careened in the other direction, directly for the edge of the precipice.

All Jastom had time to do was scream, "Jump!"

He and the dwarf dived wildly from the wagon as it sailed

over the edge. Jastom hit the dirt hard. He scrambled to his feet just in time to see the wagon disappear over the edge. After a long moment of pure and perfect silence came a thunderous crashing sound, and then silence again. The wagon—and everything Jastom and Grimm owned—was gone. In despair, he turned away from the cliff . . .

. . . and saw Durm, mounted on horseback, before him. A half-dozen soldiers sat astride their mounts behind the lieutenant, the sunlight glittering off the hilts of their swords. Jastom shook his head in disbelief. He was too stunned to do anything but stand there, motionless in defeat. Grimm, unhurt, came to stand beside him.

"Commander Skaahzak is dead," Durm said in his chilling voice. "This morning there was nothing left of him save a heap of ashes." A strange light flickered in the lieutenant's pale eyes. "Unfortunately you, his personal healers, were not by his side to give him any comfort in his final moments. I had to ride hard in order to catch up with you. I couldn't let you go without giving you your due for this failure, Mosswine."

Jastom fell to his knees. When all else failed, he knew there was but one option: grovel. He jerked the dwarf down beside him. "Please, milord, have mercy on us," Jastom said pleadingly, making his expression as pitiful as possible. Given their circumstances, this wasn't a difficult task. "There wasn't anything we could have done. Please, I beg you. Spare us. You see, milord, we aren't heal—"

"Shut up!" Durm ordered sharply. Jastom's babbling trailed off feebly. His heart froze in his chest. Durm's visage was as impassive as the mountain granite he stood upon.

"The punishment for failure to heal Skaahzak is death," Durm continued. He paused for what seemed an interminable moment. "But then, it is the commander's right to choose what punishments will be dealt out." Durm held out his hand, conspicuously displaying the ring—Shaahzak's ring—he now wore on his left hand. The ring's thumbnail-sized ruby glimmered in the sunlight like blood. "Because of you and your elixir, Mosswine, *I* am commander now." Absently Durm brushed a finger across the cheek where Skaahzak had struck him. "I will be the one, then, who will choose your punishment."

Durm's black-gloved hand drifted down to his belt, toward the hilt of his sword. Jastom made a small choking sound, but for the first—and last—time in his life, he found himself utterly at a loss for words.

Durm pulled something from his belt and tossed it toward Jastom. Jastom flinched as it struck him in the chest. But it was simply a leather purse.

"I believe ten coins of steel is what you charge for one of your elixirs," Durm said.

Jastom stared at the lieutenant in shock. For once Jastom thought he recognized the odd note in Durm's voice. Could it possibly be amusement?

"Job well done, *healer*," Durm said, that barely perceptible smile touching his lips once again. Then, without another word, the new commander whirled his dark mount about and galloped down the road, his soldiers following close behind. In moments all of them disappeared around a bend. Jastom and Grimm were alone.

"He knew all along," Jastom said in wonderment. "He knew we were charlatans."

"And that's why he wanted us," Grimm said, his beard wagging in amazement. "Letting his commander die outright would have been traitorous. But this way it looks like he did everything he could to save Skaahzak. No one could fault him for his actions."

"And I thought *we* were such skillful swindlers," Jastom said wryly. He looked wistfully over the edge of the cliff where the wagon had disappeared.

"Well, at least we have this," Grimm said gruffly, picking up the leather purse.

Jastom stared at the dwarf for a long moment, and then slowly a grin spread across his face. He took the purse from Grimm and hefted it thoughtfully in his hands. "Grimm, how much dwarf spirits do you suppose you could brew with ten pieces of steel?"

A wicked gleam touched the dwarf's iron-gray eyes. "Oh, ten steel will buy enough," Grimm said as the two started down the twisting mountain road, back toward inhabited lands. "Enough to get us started, that is . . ."

The Hand That Feeds

Richard A. Knaak

VANDOR GRIZT USED TO THINK THAT THE WORST SMELL in the world was wet dog. Now, however, he knew that there was a worse one.

Wet, *dead* dog.

Helplessly bound to the ship's mast, Vandor could only stare into the baleful, pupil-less eyes of the undead monstrosity that guarded him. The combination of rot and damp mist made the pale, hairless beast so offensive to smell that even the two draconians did their best to stay upwind of the creature. Vandor, however, had no such choice.

Vandor was forced to admit that he probably didn't smell much better. Bound head and foot, he'd been dragged over rough roads for four days to the shores of the Blood Sea, then taken aboard ship. He was not his usual, immaculate self. He hoped none of his customers had seen him; the degrading spectacle would be bad for business . . . providing he survived to *do* business.

Tall and lean, Vandor Grizt was usually either quick enough or slippery enough to evade capture—be it by local authorities or the occasional, unsatisfied customer. When speed failed him, his patrician, almost regal features, coupled with his silver tongue, enabled him to talk his way out. Vandor never truly got rich selling his "used" wares, but neither did he ever go hungry. No, he'd never regretted the course his life had taken.

Not until now.

Vandor shifted. The undead wolf-thing bared its rotted fangs—a warning.

"Nice puppy," Vandor snarled back. "Go bury a bone, preferably one of your own."

"Be silent, human," hissed one of the two draconians, a sivak. The draconians appeared to be a pair of scaly, near-identical twins, but Vandor had learned from painful experience that they were quite different. The sivak had a special talent—having killed a person, the sivak could alter its features and shape to resemble those of its victims. In the guise of one of Vandor's trustworthy friends, the sivak draconian had led Vandor into an alley. There, he had been ambushed. He realized his mistake when he watched the sivak change back to its scaly self . . . and inform him that his friend was dead.

Given a chance, Vandor Grizt would cut the lizard's throat. He had few enough friends to let them get murdered. Why the draconians had gone to the trouble, Vandor still did not know. Perhaps, the black-robed cleric who led the party would tell him. It would at least be nice to know why he was going to die.

"We give thanks to you, Zeboim, mistress of the sea!" intoned the cleric.

Vandor—self-styled procurer of "lost" artifacts and "mislaid" merchandise—could not identify what god or goddess the cleric worshipped on a regular basis, but doubted that it was the tempestuous sea siren who called Takhisis, Queen of Darkness, her mother. Zeboim did not seem the type who would favor the hideous, white, skull mask that covered the front half of the cleric's face. Some other deity fancied skulls and dead things, but the name escaped Vandor. Gods were not his forte. He himself gave some slight service to Shinare, who watched over merchants, including (he liked to think) enterprising ones such as himself. Since Shinare was one of the neutral gods, Vandor had always concluded she did not mind that he prayed only when in dire need. Now, however, he wondered if this were his reward for taking her for granted. Gods were peculiar about that sometimes.

The ship rocked as another wild wave struck it. The

Blood Sea was a terror to sail at the best of times, but sailing it in the dark of night, during a storm, was suicidal folly as far as Grizt was concerned.

His opinion had been ignored by both crew and passengers.

Skullface turned around and summoned his two draconian companions. Magical torches, which never went out despite the constant spray, gave the cleric's mask a ghoulish look. Only the mouth and a thin, pointed chin were visible beneath the mask.

"You two draconians—set up the altar for the summoning!" the cleric commanded.

Vandor shivered, guessing that the summoning could only mean dire things for him.

A kapak draconian looked at its master questioningly. "So soon, Prefect Stel?" Saliva dripped as the creature talked. The minotaur crew was not enamored of the venomous kapak. Every time it spoke, it burned holes in the deck.

Prefect Stel pulled sleek, black gloves over his bony hands. He dresses very well, Vandor Grizt thought. Not my style of clothes, of course, but beautiful fabric. Under other circumstances, Stel would have been a client of potential. Vandor heaved a sigh.

Stel was talking. "I want the altar to be ready to be put to use the moment we are over the site." The dark cleric pulled out a tiny skull on a chain from around his neck. Vandor studied the jewel closely, first for possible value and then because he realized it was glowing.

"What about this human, prefect?" the sivak asked.

"The dreadwolf will guard him. He does not appear to be a stupid man." The cleric turned to Vandor. "Are you?"

"I would have to say I am still debating that issue, my good master," the independent merchandiser responded. "My current prospects do not bode well for hopes of profit."

Stel was amused. "I can see that." He leaned closer and, for the first time, his prisoner caught a glimpse of the dark pits that were his eyes. Vandor wondered if Stel *ever* removed the mask. In the days since falling into the trap, Vandor had yet to see the face hidden behind.

"If I were a priest of greasy Hiddukel rather than of my lord Chemosh, I would be tempted to offer you a place at my side," said Stel. "You are truly dedicated to the fine art of enriching yourself at the cost of others, aren't you?"

"*Never* at the expense of my good customers, Master Stel!" Vandor protested, insulted. But the protest was half-hearted.

Chemosh—lord of the undead. The mask should have been sufficient evidence, and the undead dog the ultimate proof, but the confused and frightened Vandor had not made the connection. Vandor was in the hands of a necromancer, a priest who raised the dead for vile purposes, vile purposes that usually required a *sacrifice*. But why specifically Vandor Grizt? The shape-shifting sivak had come for him and no one else.

The sailing ship rocked again in the turbulent waters. A wave splashed over the rail, soaking everything but the magical torches and—oddly enough—the cleric. Stel's tiny skull gleamed brighter now. His clothes were perfectly dry.

Thunder crashed. A series of heavy thuds continued on after; the noise caused Vandor to look up to the heavens to see what could create such a phenomenon. A massive form came up beside him and Vandor immediately realized that what he had taken for part of the storm had actually been footfalls.

"Prefect," the newcomer rumbled, his voice louder than the thunder.

"Yes, Captain Kruug?"

Kruug appeared ill-at-ease before the cleric. Odd, since the minotaur was over seven feet tall and likely weighed three times more than Prefect Stel. Vandor had no idea how long the beastman lived, but Captain Kruug looked to have been sailing the seas for all of Vandor's thirty years and more. Such experience made Vandor's chances of surviving the rough waters and threatening storm much better, but that didn't hearten the captive. It only meant that he would live long enough to confront whatever fate the cleric of Chemosh had in mind for him.

"Prefect," Kruug repeated. The minotaur's very stance expressed his dislike for the necromancer. "My ship is here

only because you and your Highlord ordered my coopera-
tion."

Vandor's hopes rose. Perhaps the minotaurs would refuse
to sail on, destroy whatever dread plan the necromancer
had in mind.

"My crew is growing anxious, cleric," the captain said.
Minotaurs did not like to admit anxiety. To them, it was a
sign of weakness. "The storm is bad enough and sailing
through it at night is only that much worse. Those two
things, though, I could handle at any other time, *prefect*."
Kruug hesitated, unable to stare directly at the mask for
more than a few moments.

"And so?" Stel prompted irritably.

"It's time you tell us why we are sailing to this location in
the middle of the deepest part of the Blood Sea. There are
rumors circulating among the crew and as each rumor
grows, they, in turn, become more uneasy." Kruug snorted,
wiping sea spray from his massive jaw. "We find it most
interesting that a priest of Chemosh has spent so much time
paying homage to the Sea Queen that it seems he has
forgotten his own god!"

The dreadwolf snarled, its pupil-less eyes narrowed. Stel
petted it.

"You are being paid well, captain. Too well for you to ask
questions. And I would think that you would approve of
my efforts to appease the Sea Queen. Is she not deserving of
respect, especially now? We are in her domain. I give her
tribute as she deserves."

Vandor Grizt's heart sank. *My luck has become like a
pouch filled with coin . . . all lead!*

Kruug apparently did not trust Stel's smooth words. He
snorted his disdain, but glanced around uneasily. A creature of the sea, the captain had to be more careful than most
in maintaining a respectful relationship with the tempestuous Sea Queen.

The storm worsened. The sea mist that drenched all save
the cleric was accompanied by a light sprinkle, a harbinger
of the torrential downpour to come. Lightning and thunder
broke overhead.

"You had better pray that Zeboim has listened to you,

prefect," the minotaur retorted. "Else I shall appease her by throwing you and your stinking mutt over the side. My ship and my crew come first." He grumbled at no one in particular. "It's easy for the Highlord to agree to mad plots when he's safe in his chambers back on shore! He isn't the one who'll suffer, just the one who'll reap the benefits!"

Stel smiled unpleasantly. "You were given a choice, Kruug. Sail with me or surrender the *Tauron* to a *braver* captain who would."

Kruug growled, but he backed down.

For one of Kruug's race, the choice was no choice at all. No minotaur dared let himself be thought a coward.

Stel looked past the captain, who turned to see what had the cleric's attention. Vandor—tied to one of the masts—was unable to turn around, but he knew from the clanking sounds that the draconians must be returning from their excursion below deck. The two draconians dragged forward a peculiar metal bowl on three legs. Captain Kruug glared at the kapak.

"And I'll throw those lizards over, too, especially the one who can't keep his mouth shut!" Kruug added. "If he burns one more hole through the deck . . ." But the minotaur was being ignored. Seeking a target on which to vent his frustration, Kruug glanced down at Vandor, who suddenly sought a way to shrink into the mast. The minotaur's smile vied with that of the dreadwolf for number of huge, sharp teeth. "And maybe I'll throw this piece of offal over right now!"

"Touch him, my horned friend, and your first mate finds himself promoted." Stel was deadly, coldly serious.

Kruug was taken aback. "What's so special about this thieving little fox?"

"Him?" Stel glanced at Vandor. "By himself, he is worthless."

Despite his predicament, Vandor was offended.

"It is his blood I find invaluable," Stel continued.

Vandor was no longer offended . . . he was too busy trying to recall the proper prayers for Shinare. If he'd had any doubt before as to his fate, that doubt was gone now.

"I do not understand," replied the captain.

Stel looked down at the skull on the chain. "In a few

minutes, Captain Kruug, you *and* Vandor Grizt will understand. We are nearing our destination. Please have your crew prepare to stop this vessel."

"In this deep water, our anchor won't hold!" Kruug protested.

"We do not need to be completely still. Just make certain we stay within the region. I think you can manage that, captain. I was *told* that you are an expert at your craft."

Kruug bridled. "I've been sailing these waters—"

A crackle of thunder drowned out whatever the minotaur said after that, but the fury on his face and the speed with which he departed the vicinity of Prefect Stel spoke plainly. Vandor Grizt was sorry to see the captain leave. Of all Vandor's unsavory companions, the minotaur captain was the only one who seemed to share his fear. Kruug was merely carrying out orders and with a lack of enthusiasm that Vandor dismally appreciated.

The draconians set up the altar quickly despite the constant rocking of the ship. They lashed the legs of the metal monstrosity to various areas of the deck, assuring that the huge bowl would remain in place regardless of how rough the sea. When the draconians were finished, the two stumbled back to Stel, who seemed to have no trouble moving about, unlike everyone else.

"The sea grows no calmer, prefect!" hissed the sivak. "Despite your prayers to the Sea Queen, the ropes may not hold!"

"She will listen!" Stel declared. "I have sought her good will for three days now. We dare not attempt this without the Sea Queen's favor. We dare not steal from her domain!" Stel paused, considering. He glanced at Vandor Grizt, then again at the draconians. "I will have to give an offering of greater value than I had supposed. Something that will prove to Zeboim my respect for her majesty! Something that will acknowledge her precedence over all else in this endeavor! It will have to be now!"

"Now?" snarled the kapak, surprised. "But now is the time for your evening devotions to Chemosh, prefect!"

"Chemosh will understand." Stel turned again to Vandor and pointed. "Unbind him!"

As the draconians undid his bonds, Vandor tried to slip free of them. For a brief moment, he escaped, but then the dreadwolf was in front of him, ready to spring. Vandor's terrified moment of hesitation was sufficient time to permit the draconians to reestablish their hold on him.

"Bring him to the altar!" Stel commanded.

The draconians dragged Vandor Grizt across the wet deck to the odd-looking bowl that Stel had identified as an altar.

"Master Stel, surely I am not a proper sacrifice!" Vandor protested. "Have you considered that I am hardly a worthwhile present to be given to one so illustrious as beautiful, wondrous Zeboim!"

"Silence the buffoon," the cleric muttered in a voice much less commanding than normal. Stel's dark eyes turned on the dreadwolf that had been guarding Vandor. At the silent command, the undead animal joined its master. Prefect Stel returned his attention to the prisoner.

"Hold out his arm. The left one."

Vandor struggled, but his strength was nothing compared to that of the draconians.

The servant of Chemosh removed a twisted, bejewelled dagger from within his robe. Vandor Grizt recognized it—a sacrificial knife. He had even sold a few. None had ever been so intricate in detail . . . or looked so deadly in purpose.

Stel brought the dagger down lightly on Grizt's outstretched arm. The tip of the blade pricked his skin and drew blood. Muttering under his breath, Stel cut a tiny slit in his captive's forearm. It was painful, to be sure, but Vandor had suffered far more pain at the hands of city guards. A tiny trail of blood dripped slowly down the side of his arm and into the round interior of the altar bowl. The blood struck the bottom and sizzled away with a hiss. The metal began to radiate heat. Vandor swallowed, fearing what would happen if his flesh touched the hot metal.

Removing the blood-covered blade, Stel looked down at the dreadwolf, which stared back with sightless, dead eyes.

The cleric turned to face the sea. "Zeboim, you who are also known as the Sea Queen, hear me! I give you something of great value, something that will prove my humble respect for your power! I give you a part of me!" The black cleric drove the dagger into the skull of his pet, not ceasing until the hilt was touching the bone.

The wolf howled in fierce pain and anger. Several of the minotaur crewmen looked their way. Vandor Grizt pulled his arm back from the hot metal. The two draconians had loosened their hold on him in their shock over the cleric's act.

The servant of Chemosh removed the dagger from the head of his dreadwolf. The monstrosity collapsed the moment the blade was no longer touching it. The dead creature crumbled, becoming ash in the space of a few breaths. Vandor Grizt, looking up at his captor, saw the cleric's hands shake. Prefect Stel gave all the appearances of a man who has just cut off his own hand.

A muttering rose among the minotaurs. The stomping of heavy feet warned Vandor and his captors that Captain Kruug was returning.

"Prefect Stel! What in the name of Sargonnas have you done now? I will not risk my ship in this venture any more, threats or no—"

Stel raised his free hand and silenced the captain. He looked out at the sea in expectation.

For a short time, Vandor Grizt, like the rest, saw nothing out of the ordinary. The sea was calm and the storm clouds near motionless. The Blood Sea was as calm as a sleeping child.

Then it struck Vandor that *this* was out of ordinary.

The sea had calmed, the storm had ceased . . . with a suddenness that could only be called *divine* in nature.

"Shinare . . ." Vandor whispered, once more wishing he had been just a little more consistent with his praying.

Moving a bit unsteadily, Prefect Stel turned on the sea captain. "You were about to say, Kruug?"

It is not often that a minotaur can be taken aback by events, but Kruug was. The beastman swallowed hard and stared at the cleric with awe and not a little fear.

"I thought as much." Stel said, evilly smiling. "We are almost over the exact location, captain. I suggest you and your crew bring us to as dead a stop as you can."

"Aye," Kruug replied, nodding all the while. He whirled about and started shouting at the other minotaurs, taking out his fear and shame on his crew.

Stel turned to Vandor. The cleric smiled. "It is as I hoped. Your blood is the key. She has heard us. She has given us her favor."

"My blood? Key?" Vandor babbled.

"Oh, *yes*, Vandor Grizt, petty thief and purveyor of purloined properties, your blood! Can't you hear the voices?" The deep, black eyes behind the mask widened in anticipation. "Can't you hear them calling you?"

"Who?" Vandor gasped.

"Your ancestors," Stel said, looking at the sea.

"Prefect!" The kapak was spluttering with fear. A tiny bit of acidic saliva splattered Vandor on the cheek. He flinched in pain, but there was nothing he could do with his arms pinned. "Prefect, you sacrificed the *dreadwolf!*"

"It was necessary. Chemosh will understand. Zeboim has to be placated. This venture is too important."

"But the dreadwolf . . . it was bound to you by your lord!"

Stel's destruction of his ungodly pet had evidently taken much out of him and the kapak's reminder was only stirring the pain. If what the draconian said was true, then the prefect had wantonly destroyed a gift from his god in order to gain the favor of the Sea Queen.

A costly venture this, Vandor thought fearfully.

The skull mask made its wearer look like the embodiment of death itself. Stel's voice was so steady, so toneless, that both Vandor and the draconians shrank back in alarm.

"We are in the Sea Queen's domain. Even my lord Chemosh must be respectful of that. It is by his power that this task will be done, but it is by *her* sufferance that we survive it!"

The skull necklace flared brighter, so bright that the two draconians and Vandor were forced to look away.

Stel shouted, "Captain Kruug! This is the position! No farther!"

The minotaur dropped anchor; the vessel slowed, but

continued to drift, giving Vandor a brief hope. But, the minotaurs turned the vessel about and slowly brought it back.

"Still a short time left," Stel whispered. In a louder, more confident voice, he asked, "Do you hear them, Vandor Grizt? Do you hear your ancestors calling you?"

Vandor, who could not trace his ancestors past his barely-remembered parents, heard nothing except bellowing minotaurs and the lightest breeze in the rigging. He refrained from responding however. The answer might mean life . . . or death. He needed to know a bit more to make the correct choice.

"You don't, do you?" Stel frowned. "But you will. Your blood is the true blood, child of *Kingpriests.*"

"*Kingpriests?* Me?" Vandor stared blankly at his captor.

"Yes, Kingpriests." Stel toyed with the dagger and stared off at the becalmed sea. "It took me quite some time to find you, thanks to your nomadic lifestyle. I knew that I would not fail at what I undertook. *I* was the one who found the ancient temple, who understood what *others* of my order did not."

"You have me completely at a loss, Master Stel," Vandor quavered. "You say I am a descendent of the Kingpriests?" As he asked, Vandor shivered uncontrollably. He remembered suddenly what legend said lay at the bottom of the Blood Sea.

Istar . . . the holy city brought down by the conceit of its lord, the Kingpriest. In the blackest depths of the Blood Sea lay the ruins of the holy city . . . and the rest of the ancient country for that matter.

"Of direct descent." Stel touched the blazing skull. "This charm marks you as such, as it marks where the great temples . . . and storehouses . . . of Istar sank. The spells I cast upon it make it drawn to all things—including people—that possess a strong affinity with Istar. The charm was carved out of a stone from the very temple where I found the records, duplicates preserved by the magic of the zealous acolytes of the Kingpriest. Preserved but forgotten, for those who had stored them there either perished with the city or abandoned the place after their homeland was no more."

"Please, Master Stel." Vandor hoped for more information, though he had no idea what good it could do him. "What great wonder did these records hold that would make you search for one as unworthy as myself?"

Stel chuckled—a raspy, grating sound. "During the last days of Istar, the Kingpriest persecuted and murdered many such as myself. The clerics of good stole many objects of evil from the bodies of clerics of Takhisis, Sargonnas, Morgion, Chemosh. The fools who followed the Kingpriest either could not destroy these powerful artifacts . . . or found them too tempting to destroy, just in case they could find uses for them."

Vandor Grizt almost laughed aloud. It was too absurd. He knew how easily such rumors got started. He'd created a few himself in order to sell his wares. The Knights of Solamnia were rumored to have once stored such evil clerical items, but no one had ever actually *seen* one. A *real* one, that is. Still, the cleric did not seem a man who would be chasing after . . . ghosts.

A thought occurred to Vandor Grizt. "I am certain, Master Stel, that you must have been pleased to find records of your stolen property. But if that property is at the bottom of the sea . . ."

The cleric looked knowingly at Vandor. "Of course, I knew that the treasures I sought—the talismans of my predecessors—were out of my reach. Even a necromancer such as myself could not summon the ancients of Istar. Their tomb lies buried deep beneath the sea; they do not dwell in my lord's domain. But, if I use the blood of kin— however many generations distant—I might be able to summon these dead."

Vandor Grizt was skeptical. "If I am related to the . . . um . . . Kingpriests, how did you find me?"

"I told you I will permit *nothing* to remain beyond my grasp. I followed the pull of the skull talisman, traveling through land after land until it led me to you in Takar. You are as great a charlatan—in your own way—as your ancestors. It was simple to trap you."

The sivak draconian laughed.

"Now," Stel continued, "we are almost at the end of my

quest. There is one item in particular—relic of Chemosh—
that I have sought ever since I discovered its existence. A
pendant on a chain, it may be the most powerful talisman
ever created, an artifact that can raise a legion of the undy-
ing to serve the wearer!"

The image of hundreds, perhaps thousands, of undead
warriors marching over the countryside was enough to sink
even Vandor's jaded heart.

Stel grimaced. "Do not think that I will neglect the other
treasures, though. I will be able to pick and choose! I will
wield power like no other!"

The familiar stomping that marked Captain Kruug's
coming sent a shiver through Vandor.

"We're as steady as we can be, Prefect Stel! If you're going to do anything, do it now!"

Stel looked up into the eerie night sky. "Yes, the time is
close enough, I think." To the draconians, he barked,
"Stretch the fool's arm over the altar!"

Shinare! Vandor tried praying again, but he kept forgetting the proper words and losing his place in the ritual.

"Blood calls blood, Vandor Grizt," murmured Stel.

"Surely, my blood is so tainted by lesser lines that it
would hardly be worth anything to you!" Vandor squirmed
desperately.

The draconians seemed to find this statement amusing.
Stel shook his masked head, touched the glowing skull.

"Your blood has already proven itself. For you, that
means a reward. When the time comes, I will kill you in as
swift and painless a fashion as I can."

Vandor did not thank him for his kindness.

Stel raised his dagger high and intoned, "Great Sea
Queen, you who guide us now, without whom this deed
could not be done, I humbly ask in the name of my lord
Chemosh for this boon . . ."

Vandor Grizt heard nothing else. His eyes could not leave
the dagger.

The blade came down.

Vandor flinched and cried out in pain, but in what
seemed a reenactment of the first ritual, the cleric of
Chemosh pricked the skin of Vandor's arm and reopened

the long wound. Vandor gasped in relief.

Blood dripped into the altar. Stel muttered something.

At first, Vandor neither felt nor heard anything out of the ordinary. Then, slowly, every hair on his head came to life. A deep, inexplicable sense of horror gripped him. Someone was speaking his name from beyond the minotaur ship!

"Come!" Stel hissed. "Blood calls!"

Vandor trembled. The draconians dug their claws into his arms. The minotaurs, who generally grumbled at everything, paused at what they were doing and watched and waited silently.

The waters around the *Tauron* stirred. Something was rising to the surface.

Shinare? Vandor Grizt prayed frantically.

"Answer them!" Prefect Stel hissed again, beckoning. "You cannot resist the blood!"

To Vandor's dismay, he saw a ghostly, helmed head rising above the rail. "B-blessed Shinare! I implore you! I will honor you twice . . . no! . . . four times a day!"

"Stop babbling, human!" snarled the nervous sivak. Then, it, too, saw the monstrosity trying to climb aboard. "Prefect Stel! Look to your right!"

Turning, Stel sighted the walking corpse. "Aaah! At last! At last!"

Much of the visage was hidden by the rusting helm, but two empty eye sockets glared out. The armor that it wore was loose and clanked together. The undead being floated onto the deck. From the waist down, its legs were obscured by a chill mist.

Stel eyed the breastplate. "The insignia of the house guard of the Kingpriest!" He looked up into the ungodly countenance. "A royal cousin, perhaps?"

Vandor Grizt's *ancestor* did not respond.

"Prefect Stel!" hissed the draconian again.

Another form, clad in what had probably been a shroud, rose almost next to Vandor Grizt. He thought he saw a crown beneath the shroud, but he could not be certain. He had no desire to take a closer look.

"Better and better . . ."

A third spectral figure joined the other two. The cleric

fairly rubbed his hands in glee. "I had hoped for one, perhaps *two* after so long, but thr—four!"

Four it was—for the space of a single breath. Then, two more rose from the water. They seemed less substantial than the others; Vandor wondered if that meant they had been dead longer.

Stel glanced heavenward, then at his captive. "There is the answer to your protests, Vandor Grizt. Your blood runs truer than you—than *I*—thought."

The dark cleric looked at the night sky. The clouds were thickening and the winds were rising. "Time is limited! We must not try the Sea Queen's admirable patience!"

Holding the dagger before him, Stel summoned forth the undead that had been first to appear. With his other hand, the cleric removed the tiny skull on the chain and handed it to Vandor's ancestor. "You are mine. You know what I desire, do you not?"

The helm rattled as the ghost slowly nodded.

Vandor Grizt found himself sympathetic to his ancestors. It was not right that they be used as menial servants. Perhaps, he thought desperately, if blood truly called to blood, he could send them back to their rest.

"Don't listen to him!" Vandor shouted. "Go! Go back." His cries were cut off as one draconian put a scaly hand over his mouth and the other twisted his arm painfully.

It all proved to be for nothing. His shambling ancestors paid no attention to him, but listened obediently to the masked cleric who had summoned them.

"Make haste, then," Stel continued, ignoring his prisoner's outburst. "The talisman will guide you. Bring what you can, but most important, bring the Pendant of Chemosh! Its image is burned into the device I gave you. You cannot help but be drawn to it, no matter how deep it be buried!"

The six spectral figures floated from the ship . . . and sank into the murky depths.

I'm finished! Vandor thought. There was nothing he could do but wait until Prefect Stel sacrificed him. He morbidly wondered which god was going to get him, Chemosh or the Sea Queen. Chemosh, surely, for Stel had already given up a great deal to the Sea Queen.

"Great Chemosh, magnificent Zeboim," Vandor muttered, "do either of you really want someone as insignificant and unworthy as I? Surely a nice draconian would do better!"

Captain Kruug had finally regained enough nerve to rejoin the priest. The minotaur even dared peer over the rail after the undead. "By the Mistress's Eyes! I've never seen such before!"

Stel smiled. "Yes, the spell worked quite well."

"As you say. How long will . . . will it be before they return?" The minotaur was clearly unnerved.

"You mean how long will it be until we can depart?"

Kruug glared at him, but finally nodded. "Yes . . . how long? The skies grow darker. The clouds are gathering and the sea is beginning to stir. It never pays to overtax the good nature of the Sea Queen. She's known to change her mind, prefect."

"It will not be long, captain. My servants do not face the barriers that stop the living. No matter how deeply sunken are the artifacts I seek, the undead will find them in short order. The talisman I gave them will further shorten their search. I, too, am trying to expedite things, you see."

"Good." Kruug straightened to his full height. "I never thought I'd be saying it, but I look forward to dry land this night." He thrust a thumb at Vandor Grizt. "And what about that one?"

Stel's hand stroked the dagger. "He is the last order of business. When we are about to depart, I will sacrifice him to Zeboim as a final gift."

The draconians looked at each other and muttered. Vandor took his cue from them. He did some fast calculating. The nearest Temple of Chemosh had to be at least twenty days' journey from here . . .

"You give me to Zeboim, Master Stel? Not Chemosh? You should really give this some lengthy consideration! If I were the wondrous Chemosh, I would be offended at such shabby treatment!"

"Chemosh will understand. Chemosh is wise. Now cease your prattle; I know what I do." But Stel looked uncertain.

"We invade her domain. We must make restitution." Was he trying to convince himself?

The minotaur growled. "It would not be good to retract a promise to the Sea Queen. She would be offended."

"I had no intention of doing so," Stel snapped. He pointed into the dark waters. "There! You see?"

The draconians, curious, dragged their captive to the side with them, enabling Vandor to see much more than he wanted.

First one helmed head, then another appeared from the murky water. Slowly, as if constrained to obey the one who wielded power over them against their wishes, the ragged shapes rose. Each carried within its skeletal arms encrusted artifacts. Stel's reluctant servants bowed before the cleric of Chemosh and piled the various jewels, scroll cases, staves, and weapons on the deck at his feet.

Everyone else backed away from the ghastly minions, but Stel stepped forward eagerly to inspect his treasure. He picked up first one object, then another. His excitement swiftly changed to frustration.

"These are useless! They are dead! There is little or no magic in most of them! Nothing!" The cleric froze. "The Pendant of Chemosh is not here!"

Vandor noticed then that there were only five undead. The last of his unfortunate ancestors had not returned; the one, in fact, who held the skull talisman. Had he somehow broken free?

Clouds were beginning to gather. The wind blew stronger. The *Tauron* rocked. Prefect Stel glared at his prisoner. "I see that I shall need more than a little blood. I think it is time for you to join your ancestors in my quest, thief!"

"I assure you that I would make a useless corpse, Master Stel!" Vandor blurted, struggling. The draconians dragged him to stand before the cleric. Vandor glanced briefly at his sea-soaked forebears, who remained steadfastly oblivious to all around them. He wondered what it would be like to exist so, figured he didn't have long before he found out.

"Your blood will strengthen my hold, Vandor Grizt, and you shall be my messenger to the Sea Queen. You should consider yourself honored; this will probably be the only thing of significance you've ever done in your paltry life!"

"Hurry! The storm is strengthening," Captain Kruug warned.

The draconians held Vandor over the altar. Recalling how his blood had sizzled upon touching the hot metal, he twisted and turned, trying desperately to avoid it. One of the guards finally used its claw to shove him down. Vandor yelped, then realized that he was not being scalded. His relief was momentary, though; a fate worse than being scalded awaited him.

One of the draconians leaned close and hissed, "If you say one more word, thief, I'll bite off your tongue and eat it! I'm sick of your chatter!"

Vandor clamped his mouth tight. Trapped, he searched frantically for some way out. His gaze lighted upon the eyeless visage of an armored ghost, rising above the rail.

In its brown, skeletal hands it held two chains. One was the skull talisman Stel had given it for the search. The other, much heavier, chain held a black crystal encased in an ivory clasp.

"Master Stel, look!" Vandor cried. "You don't need me. He has returned!"

Thanks to Shinare! Grizt added silently.

The cleric beckoned the ghost to him. His ungodly servant raised the pendants high. Stel snatched his talisman back, but seemed hesitant to touch the darkly glimmering creation in the undead's other hand.

"Magnificent! Perfection!" Stel danced back and forth. Then, recalling where he was and who was watching, the prefect quieted and carefully reached for his prize. All sound silenced, save for the wind and the waves beating against the sides of the minotaur ship.

Vandor Grizt's ancestor did not at first seem inclined to relinquish the prize, but a muttered word of power from the cleric forced it to release its hold. Skull mask eyed skull face for a breath or two, then Prefect Stel forgot the impudence of his unliving slave as he looked down at the pendant.

"The power has leeched away from most of the other prizes, but this still glows with life! It is all I hoped for and more! At last it shall serve its purpose! At last *I* will take my own rightful place as the greatest of my Lord Chemosh's loyal servants!"

Stel raised the thick chain over his head and lowered the pendant onto his chest. No crack of thunder or blare of horns marked the cleric's triumph, but a horrible, breathless stillness momentarily passed over the region.

Captain Kruug was the first who dared interrupt the cleric's worship. "Is that all, then? Are we soon to leave this place?"

"Leave?" Stel was surprised by the suggestion. "We can't leave now! If this artifact still survives, there *must* be others! I will send them down again! And, with this pendant, I can summon hundreds of blindly obedient searchers!"

"You push our luck, human! There are limits—"

"There are *no* limits! I will show you!" Raising his hands high, Prefect Stel cried strange words. The black crystal began to shine with an eerie, grayish light.

Now, thunder rolled and lightning crashed. An enormous swell of water shook the *Tauron*. Rain and hail poured down.

"Come to me!" roared the ghastly priest.

The water began to froth around them, as if the entire sea were coming to life. Captain Kruug was either swearing or praying beneath his breath. He began bellowing orders. The two draconians, absurdly obedient, fought to keep Vandor over the altar.

A huge wave broke over the deck, drenching Vandor and his guards. It became clear to Vandor that he might *drown* before he could be sacrificed.

Stel ignored the tempest, ignored the maddened sea. He stared at the water in expectation.

Up and down the *Tauron* rocked, tossed about like a toy in a rushing stream. Another wave knocked both Vandor and the draconians away from the altar. His two guards maintained their hold on him and saved him from being washed overboard. One of the draconians grabbed ahold of the rail and pulled Vandor and the other draconian closer. All three held on for their lives.

And then . . .

"Shinare!" Vandor gasped, spitting sea water from his

mouth. "Has he raised *Istar?*"

It seemed so, at first. In the darkness, all Vandor could see was an enormous, irregular landmass rising from the depths. The only feature he could make out for certain was a peculiar ridge of high hills lined up neatly by twos and running the length of the land. Then, as the mass rose still higher, two eyes gleamed bright in the darkness.

This was not an island.

"Shinare!" Vandor Grizt whispered. Beside him, the sivak hissed in fear.

"It's going to crush us!" a minotaur roared.

But as the head—a head resembling that of an enormous turtle—cleared the water, the leviathan paused. It might have been some huge stone colossus carved by the ancients of Istar, so still was it.

Stel shouted triumphantly. He was facing the monster, the pendant of Chemosh held tight in one hand.

Stel's ancient pendant might not have summoned up the legions of undead that the cleric had sought, but it had summoned up something far more impressive. The draconians left the rail, dragging Vandor back to the altar.

"Surely this is no longer necessary!" he protested. "Master Stel has no time for this now! We should not bother such a busy man!"

In response, the draconians threw Vandor over the blood-spattered bowl and waited for orders.

"See what I have done!" Stel cried. "I have the power to raise monsters from the depths!"

"*Dead ones, yes . . .*" muttered Vandor.

"Yet, this is not what I expected," Stel quieted, then gazed down at his prize. "I meant to summon the dead of Istar, not this . . . this beast. This is not how the spell is supposed to work. Time has wreaked havoc with the pendant. I shall have to do something about that."

Stel removed his gloves and began probing at the crystal. There was a *snap* and a tiny burst of light. Stel cried out in pain. The crystal fell from the ivory casing.

With a wordless cry, Stel tried to catch the magical gem in midair, but he missed. Vandor shut his eyes—prayed that the explosion of sorcery unleashed by the shattering crystal would make his end swift.

The ebony gem struck the deck with a disappointing clatter. It rolled a moment, then slid toward Vandor Grizt.

He reacted without thinking, seeing only a valuable jewel heading toward the sea. Vandor put his foot out, caught the crystal between the sole of his boot and the deck. Grizt, the draconians, and Prefect Stel exhaled in relief. Only then did Stel realize what Vandor was doing.

"Stop him, you fools!"

Vandor Grizt stomped his foot down as hard as he could, trying desperately to crush the damnable artifact. Something gave way and at first Vandor believed he had succeeded. But try as he might, he could not reduce the thing to powder.

One of the draconians hit Vandor, dragging him back, away from the pendant.

Quickly Stel bent over and snatched up his prize. He inspected it for damage, then, satisfied, tried to replace it in the clasp. The crystal would not stay. Stel studied the clasp closer and cursed.

"Broken!"

Vandor smiled ruefully, though he could not help but sigh over the precious loss. The pendant had survived the sinking of Istar and centuries of burial in the depths of the Blood Sea, only to come to such an ignominious end.

Stel shook his fist at Vandor.

"You did this! You could not crush the jewel, but you cracked the framework around it." He thrust the gem close, so that Vandor could see the tiny, intricate workings that wrapped around the ebony jewel, like skeletal fingers clutching a prized possession. One of them had clearly broken off.

Whatever his fate now—and it certainly could get no worse—Vandor Grizt could die in peace, knowing the monstrous pendant was destroyed.

"I see your look!" Stel hissed. "But I will build the pendant anew, thief! The framework is nothing! It can readily be replaced! As long as I have the jewel I will . . . I will . . ."

He stared at it. The jewel—Grizt realized—had ceased to glow.

The two draconians exchanged worried glances. "Prefect," asked the sivak, "is there something amiss?"

Stel did not answer. The dark cleric shook the gem, muttered some words under his breath, and touched the crystal with his index finger.

Grizt dared a fleeting, hopeful smile.

One of the draconians, glancing at him, snarled, "What do *you* find so funny, human?"

He did not get the opportunity to reply.

"It's . . . it's dead . . ." Stel gasped. He shook the jewel again for good measure. "I do not understand! It worked perfectly until it fell out of the clasp, but the lack of a frame should only make the power a little less focused, unless . . . of course!" He fumbled with the casing. "This is bone ivory! Part of the spell's matrix! The pendant must be whole to function or it loses all power!"

Stel tried pressing the gem back into the casing, but it would not hold.

A massive wave shook the *Tauron*. Stel almost lost his footing. Captain Kruug shouted a warning, but his words were overwhelmed by the violent surging of the Blood Sea and a crash of thunder.

"*Now* what?" Stel snapped.

"Prefect! The monster!" shouted the draconians.

Stel turned around and stared at the leviathan the pendant had helped him summon.

It was moving . . . and the *Tauron* lay directly in its path.

"Sargonnas take you, priest!" Kruug roared. "Listen to me! Send that thing away or it will kill us all!"

"Preposterous! It will do no such thing! I am the one who summoned it!"

The minotaur snorted.

Vandor Grizt, who was measuring the direction and speed of the undead leviathan, turned to his draconian guards. "Listen to him! The captain is right! Do something!"

"Be silent or I'll tear you in half!" the sivak hissed.

Undaunted, Vandor screamed at them. "Just look! Your master no longer controls it! It comes for us!"

Tentacles as thick as a man's body rose above the water, reaching for the ship as the creature neared.

"First rank! Axes!" Kruug roared. Several massive minotaurs abandoned what they were doing and rushed toward the steps leading into the vessel's interior.

Through all of this, Stel had remained standing still staring at the oncoming behemoth. He shook his head. "With the pendant, I could easily regain total control . . . but the pendant . . . is broken and I don't . . ." He eyed Vandor, who now regretted his attempts to pulverize the jewel. Death appeared to be his fate no matter *what* happened. "But I might be able to use it to enhance my *own* power . . . if I have a sufficient blood sacrifice to Chemosh to feed the spell."

Shinare! Why does everything involve my blood? "But I am promised to the Sea Queen!" Grizt protested. "If you use me for this, she might grow angry . . . angrier!"

"There will be enough blood to keep you alive . . . barely. She will understand."

Stel, it seemed, believed in very understanding gods. Vandor Grizt thought that if he were either Chemosh or the Sea Queen, he would be insulted by all of these shabby half-measures and broken vows.

The *Tauron* had begun to list. The minotaurs had apparently lost control of the ship. Of all those on board, only Vandor's ancestors—still in thrall to Stel—remained unaffected by the terror. They stared blindly in the direction of Stel and, it seemed, at their descendant who would soon be joining them in death.

Dagger in one hand and gem in the other, the cleric of Chemosh faced the undead leviathan surging toward them. Stel appeared to have confidence in himself, if no one else did. Raising the gem high, the black-robed cleric began to shout words of power. The hand with the dagger rose over the chest of Vandor Grizt.

It was then that the world turned about. Vandor Grizt was not certain of the order of events, but suddenly the storm burst into full fury, sending the ship keeling over in the opposite direction. At least one minotaur was washed overboard by a massive wave. A bolt of lightning struck one of the masts, cracking it in two. The burning wreckage crashed down on the hapless crew.

More than a dozen tentacles wrapped around the *Tauron*

and began to drag it under.

Stel stood frozen, disbelief registered in every bone of his body. He dropped the dagger, much to the captive's relief, and clawed at the tiny skull pendant. As he pulled it free, it *crumbled*.

The *Tauron* was beginning to break up, as the tentacles threatened to crunch it. Captain Kruug and several minotaurs rushed forward, attacking the creature with heavy axes. The rotting skin of the behemoth gave way. It took the minotaurs only a few blows to sever the one tentacle and only a couple more to cut a second in two.

Unfortunately, as Kruug and his men finished the second, a dozen more ensnared their ship.

"All hands to battle!" roared the captain. Minotaurs all over the *Tauron* abandoned their stations and joined the fight against the beast.

Another wave washed over the front of the ship. Vandor's left arm was nearly torn from its socket and something like an army of blades tore at his flesh. He was being flayed. In desperation, he lifted one foot and kicked. His boot struck something solid. He kicked again.

The blades pulled free of his flesh. Only when the first shock subsided did he realize that the sivak draconian—the cursed shapechanger—was no longer holding him. He looked around but saw no sign of the foul reptile. The draconian had been washed overboard. At least he had succeeded in avenging himself on the creature that had killed his friend and captured him.

A brief satisfaction was all he was allowed. Then, it was a matter of struggling for his own life. Another wave washed over the ship. The other draconian released Vandor and fled, slipping and sliding, for the *Tauron's* interior, choosing self-survival over the orders of the cleric.

Stel had moved to one side and was holding onto the rail, eyes wild. He was shouting something at the leviathan but his words were having no effect. Desperate, the gaunt priest whirled on the silent figures of the merchant's ancestors and made a sign.

The undead shuffled forward, forming a half-circle around the cleric.

Struggling to maintain his own hold on the rail, Vandor Grizt sought some sort of escape. To stay aboard the ship was folly in his opinion, but the Blood Sea offered the only other option.

"Shinare," he whispered, "is there *anything* I can offer you?"

Kruug, axe covered in a brown, thick muck, was trying to get his crew's attention.

"Prepare to abandon ship!" Kruug glanced around and spotted Vandor. Grimacing, the minotaur called, "I'll not leave even you to this, manling! Get over to the—"

A tentacle struck the captain. Kruug flew over the other side of the ship and, as Vandor watched helplessly, the beastman dropped into the water and vanished beneath.

The *Tauron* began to shudder and crack.

This is the end for all of us! Vandor thought.

His undead ancestors had formed a tighter ring around the cleric. No longer were they the blindly obedient slaves that Stel had summoned. They had the prefect pinned against the rail and were closing the circle around him.

Chemosh will understand . . . Stel had said that over and over. Chemosh—Lord of the Undead—had not been as understanding as his servant imagined.

One of the wraiths, the skeleton in armor, reached out and tore the mask from the cleric's face. The skeletal hand closed over Stel's throat. Stel screamed horribly. The other undead closed around him.

A gigantic wave swamped the *Tauron.*

Vandor Grizt lost his hold, falling overboard. The sea took him. He could no longer see the *Tauron* and for all he knew it had been pulled under after the last wave. Water was all there was in the world. It surrounded him; it filled him.

Then he saw a woman, a beautiful but fiery creature of the depths. She was reaching for him, but something . . . no *someone*—another woman . . . was pulling him away from her.

Vandor Grizt smiled vaguely at the first woman, regretting that their liaison was not possible.

Then, he was no more.

*   *   *   *   *

Vandor Grizt discovered he did not like the taste of sand.

Raising his head, an act that strained to the limit what few resources he had left, he spat out a grainy mouthful.

Vandor kept his eyes closed. He was not at all certain he wanted to know where he was. After all, if he were dead, he might be in the domain of Zeboim . . . or worse.

Curiosity got the better of him.

All he saw was a beach. Daytime. Brilliant light nearly blinded him. Closing his eyes, he restarted the process, allowing himself only a narrow gap of vision at first.

He allowed that gap to widen when he saw the feet in front of him. They were not human feet.

"So you survived," rumbled a horribly familiar voice. "Some god truly watches over you, human . . ."

Vandor Grizt rolled over, the best he could do at the moment, and stared at the looming bestial countenance of Captain Kruug. After a moment, Vandor became aware of the presence of three other minotaurs, one of whom leaned heavily on another.

Vandor tried to speak, coughed and spit up sea water.

Kruug snorted. He looked tired. Very tired. "Save your words, human. I've no interest in you. Anyone who survived that folly . . . and I'm amazed there are any of us . . . deserves some peace." The minotaurs started to turn away, but the captain held back long enough to add, "If you'll take my advice, you'll go inland. *Deep* inland. If I see your ugly face again, I might remember how I lost my ship because of you."

Although he had a somewhat different perspective on the recent events, Grizt did not think it wise to argue. He watched in silence as the battered foursome stumbled off.

"You're lucky, Vandor Grizt," he said as he lay there trying to regain enough strength to move on. "The bull-man must be right: some god does smile on me!" The thought comforted him. If that was true—and it certainly seemed so—then it might be a wise time to begin a new life.

Grizt started to rise, but felt something under his left hand. He dug the object out of the sand and stared long at it.

It was the upper portion of Stel's skull mask—an eyehole and part of the cheek. Vandor smiled. His ancestor had bequeathed him a present.

Vandor dropped the battered mask and, finding new strength, rose to his feet. He looked around and saw that the minotaurs were still within sight, their pace slowed by the injured member.

Vandor Grizt ran after them, calling out in order to get their attention. Kruug turned around, his fists balled tight. When he saw who it was, his anger was replaced by annoyance.

"What do you want? I thought I told you—"

"Please!" Vandor Grizt put up both hands in placation. "Just a question of directions. That is all I ask. You know this region much better than I."

"All right. Where is it you want to go?"

Trying not to sound too anxious, Vandor asked, "Would you happen to know the way to the nearest temple of Shinare?"

The Vingaard Campaign

Douglas Niles

---

*F*ROM THE RESEARCH OF FORYTH TEEL, SENIOR
Scribe in the service of Astinus, Master Lorekeeper of
Krynn.

Most Gracious Historian, you do me too much honor! To
think of this task—the study of the greatest military campaign in the post-Cataclysm history of Krynn—and to realize that you have selected *me* to prepare the documents! I
am honored, humbled. But, as always, I shall endeavor to
do my best, so that the truth can be recorded and saved.

Thank you too, Excellency, for your concern about my
health following my previous mission. My nerves have settled and the tremors have almost disappeared from my
hands. Also, I am able to sleep for several hours at a time
without suffering the recurrence of nightmares.

As always, a return to my work seems to promise the
most complete cure—and in this assignment, Your Grace,
you could not have provided a more perfect medicine. The
tale of the Vingaard Campaign! The very phrase strikes a
martial note in my soul! I hear the clash of steel, the thunder
of hooves and the strident call of the battle trumpet! I imagine the wings of dragons, good and evil, blotting out the
sky. I picture the blasts of powerful magicks, the gallant
charge of the knights!

But forgive me. I have not forgotten that the historian is a
dispassionate reporter of the truth. Such flights of fancy are
for poets, not scholars such as I. I shall try to control my

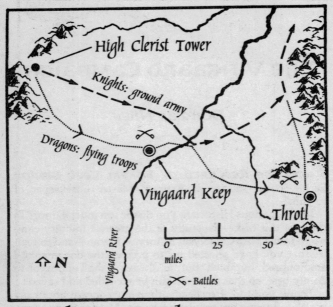

The Vingaard Campaign
Phase I—Laurana's Attack

emotions. Nevertheless, as I relate the exciting story of a young elven princess who changed the face of Krynn in a few short weeks—the sharp, dangerous attacks that baffled her foes, the fast marches across the plains placing her miles from her supposed location, and of course, her epic victory at Margaard Ford—I trust that Your Excellency will forgive an occasional exclamatory aside.

In studies, I will examine the topic primarily from the

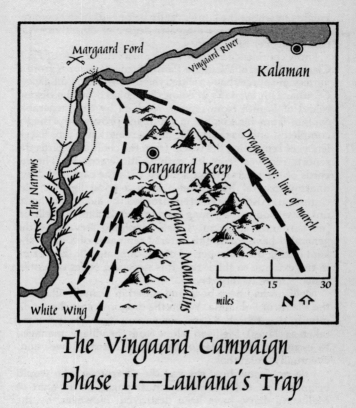

Margaard Ford

Vingaard River

Kalaman

Dragonarmy: line of march

Dargaard Keep

The Narrows

Dargaard Mountains

0   15   30

miles   N

White Wing

The Vingaard Campaign
Phase II—Laurana's Trap

viewpoint of the Army of Solamnia. The records of the dragonarmies were relatively well kept, and have been researched by many scribes. The campaigns from the Golden General's side, on the other hand, have only been discussed in the histories of the Knights of Solamnia. To read them, one might think that the contributions of the good dragons to these battles was merely to fan the battlefield with their wings, cooling the sweat from the brows of the hard-riding knights to whom the laurels really belonged! In my own reports, I shall strive for a greater degree of objectivity—as befits a proper historian.

I now commence my task in the musty library of the High Clerist's Tower at Westgate Pass. Extensive records from a variety of sources have yielded themselves to my diligence. Gunthar Uth Wistan's account, formulated on the distant island of Ergoth from reports received by that venerable captain from his knights in the field, proves surprisingly complete—and accurate. (He does a remarkable job, Excellency, of separating the wheat from the chaff as regards the reports received from his enthusiastic warriors!) The records of the interviews conducted with the captured dragonarmy general Bakaris also shed a good light on the campaign. Also, I have been afforded the aid of a hitherto unknown source: a young human female named Mellison (no surname, apparently), self-appointed servant of the general. I have found the tattered remnants of a diary she kept during the short period of the campaign (it is amazing in the extreme to think that this sweeping series of battles lasted a mere twenty days!).

Mellison had been born and raised in a small village on the Plains of Solamnia. When the dragons came, her community was scorched, and her parents slain (or, perhaps, taken as slaves). Mellison, alone from the village, managed to escape to the shelter of the High Clerist's Tower and, eventually, Palanthas.

I do not know how she met the elf woman who would become the Golden General—those pages, at the start of Mellison's diary, have been destroyed. However, by the time Laurana had been appointed by Gunthar Uth Wistan, Grand Master of Solamnia, to command the knights and the army of Palanthas, the human girl had attached herself to the elf woman.

Mellison proved very useful to the general, preparing Laurana's tent for those nights when the general was able to steal a few hours' sleep; and Mellison always fanned a blaze into light for her mistress's predawn awakenings. Though the young woman participated in none of the battles, her observations of Laurana's campfire councils have provided us with key insights into the development of the campaign.

The first of these discussions occurred on the field below this very tower, and it is here that Mellison gives us a picture of Laurana's council of war. Present were the elf woman, the two Knights of the Crown—Sirs Patrick and Markham—who served as her chief lieutenants, and two unnamed knights of the other orders. Mellison refers to them, in her childlike hand, as "Lord Sword" and "Sir Rose." Gilthanas—Laurana's brother and proud prince of the Qualinesti elves—also attended.

(Incidentally, Your Grace, the letters sent by Gilthanas to his brother Porthios provide us an additional primary source on this campaign, especially as it was seen from an elven point of view.)

Of course, the context of the meeting is well known: the dragonarmy known as the Blue Wing had been blunted (but not destroyed) in the Battle of the High Clerist's Tower. These troops, under the command of the Dark Lady—the Highlord Kitiara—and her general, Bakaris, had fallen back upon Dargaard Keep, where they represented a significant threat. The good dragons had arrived here following that battle, on the day preceding Laurana's council of war. These mighty serpents, of gold and silver, brass, copper and bronze, had at last ended their exile from the war. Brought to Palanthas by Gilthanas and the great silver dragon called Silvara, they were anxious to exact vengeance against their evil cousins.

Though the numbers of dragons and troops in Laurana's force equaled a mere fraction of the total evil forces, she had the advantage of concentration—all of her forces were here, in the pass, while those of the enemy—the Red Wing, portions of the Green and White Wings, and the remnants of the Blue Wing—were scattered over Solamnia from Vingaard and Caergoth to Kalaman and Neraka. Also, a huge reserve army under the command of Emperor Ariakus himself had spent the winter encamped in Sanction. Recent rumors placed the dragonarmy on the march, however, though Laurana and her captains had no idea of its location or destination.

The time was night, a council fire flared high. Mellison

reports that its light was reflected in gold and silver gleams from the massive dragons crouched just beyond the human commanders.

"We can hold them here forever!" stated Sir Rose, opening the council. "With the dragons and the men of Palanthas to back us up, the knights will form an unbreakable wall!"

"Hold them, indeed," agreed Sir Patrick. "If they dare to attack again, we'll butcher them to the last scale-faced draconian! Don't you agree, general?" Grudgingly he turned to Laurana for confirmation. Of the Crown Knights, he had been most reluctant to accept her leadership—yet the orders of Gunthar Uth Wistan had thus far proven sufficient to steel him to his duty.

"I have no intention of holding them here, or anywhere!" declared Laurana, with that shake of her head that set her golden hair flowing about her shoulders.

"What is your plan?" inquired Markham, with his easy grin that somewhat lightened the tension.

"We attack." Laurana spoke the two words, and then paused to fix her eyes on each of her listeners. She seemed to grow in stature as the firelight flared across her fair skin, her almond-shaped eyes. "The Army of Solamnia will advance under the wings of the good dragons, seek out the dragonarmies, and destroy them!"

"Leave the pass unguarded?" sputtered Sir Rose. "After this great victory, you risk throwing everything . . . the lives, the—"

Laurana's reply was sharp and bitter. "I know very well the cost in lives!" she snapped with enough force to shut the mouth of the grizzled veteran. For a moment she closed her eyes. Mellison saw the sharp pain of memory etched across Laurana's face. Gilthanas placed a comforting hand on his sister's arm, but she shrugged it away. She took a breath and continued.

"Nothing could be more wasteful of those lives than for us to cower here, behind these walls, and give the dragonarmies time to concentrate their scattered forces. No, my captains, we won't wait for them to act. It is time this war came back against those who began it!"

"Where do we go, then?" inquired Sir Rose. "Do we advance south, toward Solanthus? Or eastward, to threaten the occupation forces at Vingaard? Both of these courses allow us this fortress as a base. Too, they keep the Vingaard River as a strong barrier between us and the bulk of the enemy—the option to fall back in the event of . . ." He did not complete his speculation; something in the general's eyes silenced him.

"Vingaard," Laurana announced. "But not as a threat—I mean to liberate it. As to the river, I want this entire army across it within a week."

"*Beyond* the Vingaard?" Patrick was shocked, but his eyes measured the elf woman with surprise and new appraisal. "Into the heart of the dragonrealms?"

"The dragonarmies will meet us there, in force," Markham said cautiously. "Do you intend to draw them into a battle? Destroy them on the field?"

"That will be an historic moment!" Lord Sword declared, his face flushing and his long mustaches bobbing at the prospect. A fierce light entered his eyes. "To drive our lances into the faces of those beasts, for once—instead of merely standing our ground!"

Laurana smiled, too, but it was a grim expression to Mellison. She thought it made the elf woman look much older. "Yes—I will draw them into battle. The first of many. Once we've crossed the river, I don't intend to rest until we reach the gates of Kalaman!"

"Kalaman!" Sir Rose sputtered so much that his mustaches floated out from his mouth. They all knew that the distant city was in desperate straits, following a long winter of isolation and siege. Still, hundreds of miles of enemy territory lay between themselves and Kalaman.

"You're mad!" barked Patrick.

Laurana allowed the insult to pass, but this time her brother stepped forward. "The good dragons give us a striking force that you knights can't begin to imagine!" countered the tall elf. "We cannot waste them!"

"What about Dargaard?" asked Markham, turning to Laurana. "That's a powerful bastion across your path—the Dark Lady is there in force, together with the dragons of her

Blue Wing. The ogres of Throtl are supported by green dragons, and they're certain to mass against your south flank."

"I intend to ignore Dargaard, for the time being. The ogres we'll meet, and defeat."

"They'll have the Green Wing to support them. And Emperor Ariakus has sent the Red Wing from Neraka as a reinforcement. Too, we don't have any idea where the reserve army has gone," argued Sir Rose.

"We have dragonlances," cried Gilthanas. "We can meet these serpents in the skies, finally, and defeat them!"

"The weapon, so far, has only proven itself in the closed confines of the tower!" Patrick growled back.

"That is true," Laurana agreed. "But I don't intend to fight all the dragons at once. That's why it's so important that we *move!*"

"But a major river crossing!" objected Patrick. "You can't imagine the difficulties! And if we're caught with the army divided—"

"Our dragons will screen the crossing. And I intend to reach the Vingaard too quickly for anything but a token force to stand in our way."

"But there's the fortress itself—Vingaard Keep has a massive garrison!" persisted Patrick. "Anywhere we cross puts us in easy reach of a counterattack!"

"That brings me to the next part of the plan," Laurana announced, pausing to make sure she had the attention of all the men. "Vingaard will be liberated—*tomorrow.*"

The knights, to a man, stared at the general in amazement. All knew that Vingaard Keep was three days' ride by horse.

At this point, the Council's voices grew hushed and confidential, so the rest of the conversation is lost to Mellison's diary—and to history. The results of this historic and clandestine conversation are known.

The following dawn, the skies over the High Clerist's Tower were filled with dragons—their metallic colors dappling the ground with moving reflections of the brilliant sunrise. Laurana, astride the huge gold dragon Quallathon, led the way. A wing of griffon cavalry, mounted with elven bowmen and lancers—lately arrived from Southern Ergoth—flew beside the great serpents. Altogether, two hundred of the half-hawk, half-lion beasts accompanied an equal number of dragons soaring southeast toward Vingaard—eighty miles away across the flat plain. Their bodies blackened the sky.

At the same time, the army moved out. Led by the knights on horseback, accompanied by the blue-garbed troops of Palanthas and a large and growing force of irregulars recruited from Solamnia and Ergoth, the soldiers of Laurana's command marched to the northeast. The diverging paths were obvious to all. The flying army was on its own, the battle would be won or lost long before the troops on the ground could arrive.

Gilthanas, in an extensive letter to Porthios, gives us a vivid picture of this assault—the first time the good dragons took the offensive in the war.

"Within four hours our dragons drew within sight of mighty Vingaard Keep, standing on the near bank of the river that bears the same name.

"For more than a year, the dragonarmies had held the fortress, and their presence formed a bleak shroud around the once-grand castle. Layers of soot clouded the walls, and rubble-strewn fields surrounded the high towers, where once thrived lush crops of grain.

"I never knew such exhilaration and excitement. Silvara tucked in her wings and plunged toward the city. Wind lashed my hair and stung my face. The ground approached with dizzying speed, and I felt a fierce joy.

"At last the dragonarmies would get a taste of the terror they had spread so wantonly across Ansalon. Silvara's challenging bellow thundered through the air, echoed by scores of silver and golden throats.

"The draconians lining the walls quivered and shook under the awe of dragonfear, and only ceased their trembling as they died. Clouds of horrific breath expelled by the good dragons swept the draconian ranks, slaying them where they stood. Blistering heat from the brass and gold dragons mingled with the lightning bolts spit by the bronze; spurts of acid from the copper dragons pooled on the paving stones beside the chilling blasts of ice spouting from the silver wyrms.

"A few evil dragons, mostly blues, had taken refuge in the city after the battle at Westgate. Now, these rose to meet us, spitting lightning bolts, carrying their riders into the fray. But even as they rose, the magic of the gold dragons smashed the leaders from the skies. Then a rank of knights led by Silvara and me, carrying dragonlances shining as bright as silver dragonwings, met the enemy and ripped into the blues.

"Silvara reached out with rending claws and tore the wing from one of the blues. I watched the crippled creature plunge to its death. Then a bolt of lightning crackled past my head. Quickly I raised my lance as Silvara shrieked. Her head, of silvered steel, struck the back of the blue wyrm and that serpent, fatally pierced, followed its fellow to the ground. The other good dragons whirled passed us, slaying the remainder of the blues before their deadly breath weapons could begin to tell.

"Within an hour, brother, the good dragons had settled to the rooftops and towers of the city, spewing their deadly breath while the griffon-mounted elves showered the remaining defenders with arrows. For the whole day the dragons remained perched on all the high places in the city, following the plan of our general."

Gilthanas was all for pursuing the enemy troops into their hiding holes, driving them from the city, but his sister insisted on patience. There would be no pursuit. Instead, the dragons of good would occupy every vantage point in the city, barring any draconian from appearing in the light of day.

This patience paid off in lives. Seeing that their hated enemies were not about to depart, the troops of the dragonarmy abandoned Vingaard Keep during the night. Some fled south, fearing the spring-swollen river as much as they did the good dragons. Many of these were humans, who hoped to blend into the populace. A great number of these, it is known from the records of the knighthood, joined the ranks of Laurana's army by the end of the campaign. Others stole what boats they could or, in the case of draconians, tried to use their wings to carry them across the deep torrent. (Fully half of the latter are believed to have perished in the attempt.) When the sun next rose over Vingaard Keep, the fortress was held by the good dragons and their elven allies.

The few humans who had survived the long and brutal occupation crept from their shadowed rooms into the sunrise. They caught sight of Laurana's hair, trailing from her helm like a pennant of streaming gold in her wake. Those long golden locks could be seen a mile away on the battlefield.

"Hail to the General of the Golden Banner!" they cried. Soon it became "Hail to the Golden General!"

And the Vingaard Campaign had begun.

Next I journey to that keep, Excellency, there to sit upon the banks of the river—and ponder the next example of Laurana's audacity, the crossing of the Vingaard.

In devotion, as ever,
Foryth Teel, Senior Scribe of Astinus

* * * * *

To the Great Astinus, Lorekeeper of Krynn,

I am here, now, at the shore of the Vingaard River. The season is spring, as it was when Laurana ordered her forces across—and I cannot but wonder at the courage and vision that compelled an army to ford its murky depths. Now, when the snow is melting in the Dargaard Mountains and along the north slopes of the Garnet Range, the river runs high and deep. It seems propelled by anger, roaring across this great plain toward the distant seaport of Kalaman, nearly two hundred miles away.

During its course, the river passes within a dozen miles of Dargaard Keep, yet in the next weeks Laurana would dare to bypass that dark bastion and press on to her destination—but I get ahead of myself. First, I must describe the crossing. The land troops of the Army of Solamnia reached the banks of the river after a three-day forced march from Westgate.

We know from the multiple sources that the good dragons, fresh from their victory at Vingaard, joined the land-bound army at the banks of the river, some forty miles north of the liberated fortress. The Vingaard is wide and deep here, navigable only by ferries—except in a dry summer, when a few fords appear. Such was not the case that spring, of course. Here, we see another example of the elven general's ingenuity—for she employed a tactic that no by-the-book Knight of Solamnia could have imagined in his most daring dreams.

She ferried the troops across the river—by air! One can imagine the shrill neighing of the knight's terrified horses as they were hoisted aloft, gently, in the claws of the largest of the great dragons. Or the poor, trembling foot soldiers, mounted six or eight to a dragon, eyes squeezed tightly shut, praying to the gods of good (or any others!) for their very survival.

It was still a long, slow process. Mellison records that her mistress camped at the shore of the river for three days—we can assume that this was the time required to cross. The baggage train, which had been light to begin with, was abandoned here. From now on the army would survive on the food it could capture or forage. A screen of flying griffons, mounted with elves, guarded the crossing.

The fears of the knights—that the army would be attacked by massive dragonforces in the midst of the crossing—proved unfounded, for two reasons. First, the rout of Vingaard Keep had sent the nearest enemy wing into chaotic flight; and second, the sheer speed of Laurana's march seemed to have taken the Highlords by complete surprise. We know from his own records, for example, that by the time Ariakus learned the Golden General had left Westgate Pass, the Army of Solamnia was already gathered on the east bank of the Vingaard.

One small force did try to disrupt the crossing. Highlord Toede sent six of his green dragons from Throtl to investigate the activities of Laurana's army. The beasts could have wreaked terrible havoc on the heavily laden good dragons, but the griffon-mounted elves intercepted them a few miles from the river. Nearly a quarter of the griffons and their riders fell during that skirmish in the skies. It was a tragic and irreplaceable loss, but none of the greens survived to pursue the attack. Gilthanas writes a long eulogy to the bravery of the griffon-mounted elves and even the official records of the Solamnian Knights, Excellency, include generous words about their sacrifice!

Her forces again assembled on the opposite bank of the river, Laurana was determined to maintain the speed and unpredictability of her advance. (It is ironic to note that this young elf maid grasped, intuitively, principles of warfare that veteran knights, too long hidebound by doctrine, resisted until the proof became too overwhelming to deny. Thank goodness for Laurana's persistence.)

Once again, it is the servant Mellison who provides our look into the planning of operations, for she served tea to Laurana and her captains as they planned their next move.

Present were the same five: Sir Markham, Sir Patrick, "Sir Rose," "Lord Sword," and Gilthanas of Qualinesti. Laurana announced her intention to move on Kalaman. Patrick protested. "But we know that Ariakus had ten thousand troops in Sanction! They could have been on the march for three weeks—and now you want to leave our flank unprotected. The river now guards us. If we march from here, we expose the whole army to an attack from the rear!"

"Our wagons are left behind," Laurana pointed out, coolly. "Therefore, the rear of our army is as easy to defend as the front—even more so, if the enemy expects to encounter a defenseless baggage train, but instead meets the steel of charging knights."

"True, true," noted Lord Sword. "But we move so far from the pass—Palanthas is all but defenseless."

"I realize that, my lord," Laurana explained patiently. "But I'm betting that the Highlords are no longer concerned with that city. Their attention must be riveted upon *us*! This army is a far greater threat than they have ever faced before. They'll need to concentrate and destroy us. Ariakus—and Kitiara too—will assume they have plenty of time for Palanthas after we've been destroyed."

"Are they wrong?" demanded Patrick.

"Only in the assumption that they'll *find* us!" Laurana retorted. "That's why it's so important to move quickly!"

"There will be opposition," Markham pointed out. "The

Red Wing is out there, and portions of two others—not to mention the reserve army."

"Of course. But with speed, we'll be able to meet these forces—and defeat them—one at a time. It's essential that we bring the Red Wing to battle before Ariakus can join with his allies!"

"But if you're wrong, you risk—"

"I risk *what*, Sir Patrick?" Laurana snapped. "Would you go back to the days of cowering behind the stone walls of your fortress, waiting for the enemy to attack? And if we win against that attack, then what—we wait for the next, and the next until our forces are depleted, our supplies gone? Better to stake this army on the hope of a *real* victory—one that will do more than protect Palanthas. We take the war into the heart of the dragonrealms! Only *then* will our enemies face the prospect of defeat!"

(Excellency, if Mellison did not exaggerate the words, I can only assume that the Golden General quite lost her temper. It is hard to imagine her using a term like "cower" to the proud knight. However, it seemed to have had the effect of silencing him, if nothing else.)

"We know that much of the Green Wing remains in Throtl," continued the elven princess. "Tomorrow, at first light, I will lead the dragons against them. If we can scatter the ogre ground forces, so much the better. The main body, in the meantime, will continue its march to the northeast. I want the Highlords to believe that Dargaard is our next destination."

"A bold plan, my general," Sir Rose noted, with a smile. "As you know, these plains were my home. I should warn you that the river narrows and deepens north of here. It presents a formidable obstacle to movement to our left."

"Thank you, Sir Knight," Laurana replied. "I, too, knew of this river—and, in fact, it will play a role in my plans."

If the princess revealed that role on this night, we don't learn of it from Mellison. The girl drifted off to sleep while the warriors discussed tactics into the early hours of predawn. Perhaps even now the elven princess foresaw the Battle of Margaard Ford and was drawing up her plans for that epic confrontation. But alas, we can only speculate!

My journeys, Your Grace, shall next take me along the foothills of the Dargaard Mountains. I will retrace the steps of Laurana's army as she moved east, south, and then north—always keeping the Highlords guessing.

Until that next message, I remain,
Your Devoted Servant, Foryth Teel

* * * * *

To the Great Astinus, Lorekeeper of Krynn,

The Army of Solamnia exploded across the plains, shocking the dragonarmies in a series of engagements. These were distinct and isolated clashes, some of them cavalry skirmishes, others dragonfights in the skies, and a few of them pitched battles pitting all of Laurana's troops against equal or greater numbers of the Dark Queen's minions.

The dragonarmies were forced to fight when they had planned to march. And when they planned to fight they found no opponents and were forced to march. Not until the final confrontation, at Margaard Ford, did the Highlords finally assemble an overwhelming force—and then they fought a battle at the very place Laurana had selected. But forgive me, Your Grace; again I precede myself.

First to challenge Laurana's advance was the portion of the Green Wing encamped in Throtl. Two dozen dragons and more than a thousand draconians—mostly vicious kapaks—formed the heart of this legion, supported by hundreds of ogres, honorless men, and more than three thousand hobgoblins.

These troops were ostensibly under the command of the Highlord Toede, though the records of that ignoble hobgoblin make no mention of the battle. Our best reports of the fight come from Gilthanas, and the interviews conducted by the knights with one Kadagh—an ogre who served as captain of one of the Green Wing companies.

Kadagh awakened to a clear, sunlit morning—unusual weather, here in the shadow of the Dargaard Mountains. Yet this day the eastern peaks and foothills were visible, etched in vivid detail as the ogre emerged from his tent and stretched the kinks out of his knotted muscles. Then, restless, his gaze drifted to the west.

He first thought that the gods had sprinkled gold dust through the skies. Gold gleamed in the sun, floated gently through the air. But ogres are pragmatic, and Kadagh quickly observed the specks of metal growing steadily larger. His bellow of alarm alerted the camp of the Green Wing to the danger.

Laurana and her dragons had caught the detachment of the Green Wing as it prepared to march in a delayed response to the Army of Solamnia's rampage across the plain. The green dragons squatted on the ground, saddled but riderless, as gold and silver and brass death came screaming from the skies. The few greens who leaped into the air were mercilessly smashed to ground and destroyed.

Gilthanas commanded his flyers to be utterly ruthless in this deadly strike against the enemy dragons—and it seems his orders were carefully followed. The dragonlances again proved their worth, although the numerical advantage of the good dragons made the outcome all but inevitable. In moments, the evil serpents had been slain; with tooth and claw and lance.

Just before the bloody end, however, Kadagh saw one stooped figure scramble into the saddle of a green dragon and urge the beast into the air. Flying low, ducking and weaving between trees and hillocks, the lone dragon and its rider vanished into the heights of the Dargaard Range, leaving the battle far behind. It was Lord Toede, providing an example of courage for his doomed army.

Laurana's dragons conserved their killing breath weapons for the attack against the draconians, ogres, and hobgoblins of Throtl's legion. Swiftly Kadagh assembled his company—brutish ogres, armored in plate mail and bearing great swords. They were the most formidable footsoldiers of the Green Wing, and records of both sides indicated they fought accordingly.

The ogres scattered into the ravines and thickets around the camp, fighting in small groups and rushing at any dragons careless enough to get caught on the ground. The gold dragons belched fire into the underbrush, and smoke and flame drifted across the battlefield. Kadagh himself led the charge against a brass dragon that had landed, exhausted, near a clump of brush. He leaped onto the creature's wing and felled the rider, a knight, with one blow of his great sword. Others of his company rushed at the dragon, and when the wyrm reared back, Kadagh plunged his blade into the base of its skull.

(This tale is more than mere ogre boasting, Your Grace. Gilthanas witnessed the entire incident. Silvara immediately pounced on the ogre, crushing him to earth and felling the rest of his company with a blast of her icy breath. So impressed were the elves with the ogre's valor, however, that they later returned him as a prisoner to Laurana's camp.)

The knights sought and slaughtered the monsters of the Green Wing for the rest of that grim and bloody day until the tattered remnants of the force finally slipped into the wilderness of the Dargaard Mountains.

It is interesting to note, Your Grace, that by dint of this tactic, Laurana left her own ground forces open to the same kind of attack by the blue dragons in Dargaard. She was bold enough to gamble (correctly, it turned out) that Kitiara was still too chastened by her defeat at the High Clerist's Tower to risk sending her most powerful forces into a possible trap.

After the Battle of Throtl, Laurana once again divided her army. She sent many of the dragons—all of the brass and bronze, with some of the copper—to guard the portion of her army that marched on the ground. The other dragons scattered across the plain, to all points of the compass, seeking the dragonarmies. Laurana knew that elements of the White Wing lay somewhere to the south, but she had no clue as to the location of the mighty Red Wing.

And still there was the presence of Ariakus's huge reserve wing, vanished since it had departed Sanction. Laurana dispatched a pair of the precious silver dragons toward that glowering seaport, determined to learn what she would about the reserve army's location.

When the scouting dragons discovered forces of the Dark Queen, they were to report the location of those troops to the Golden General. Under no circumstances were they to precipitate an attack. I surmise, Excellency, that these dragons performed the reconnaissances in the guise of soaring birds of prey. At least, the records of the dragonarmies show no sign that they knew they were under observation—and Laurana's assignment of the scouting to the golds, silvers, and coppers indicates a preference for those dragons who could polymorph themselves into the bodies of different creatures. And what better than a hawk or eagle, symbolically patrolling over the plains?

The soaring spies first spotted the strong contingent of the White Wing, larger than the Throtl Legion and including many sivak draconians (the only draconian, as Your Grace well knows, capable of true flight). Dragonarmy records show that this force had been ordered northward by Ariakus himself more than a week earlier. (After the battle at the Clerist's tower, the emperor had anticipated the need for additional forces in the plains, and issued the necessary orders.)

The White Wing was discovered by none other than Silvara, herself, as the great silver dragon flew a southwestward arc in her search. The force had just crossed the Dargaard River, and marched northward along the east bank of the Vingaard, placing it squarely across Laurana's line of retreat. The river here flows through the rock-carved channel noted by Markham—a gorge that is some twenty miles long.

(Silvara flew alone on this scouting mission. I submit, Your Grace, that the absence of Gilthanas from her back supports the idea that she flew in the body of a bird, rather than as a dragon.)

Laurana's response to the information was immediate and bold: she reversed her army's line of advance and urged the troops into a forced march straight into the advancing White Wing. Each scouting dragon, as it returned from its patrol, rejoined the army, until the Golden General again held all her dragons close to the body of the force. Within twenty-four hours, the Army of Solamnia was massed and focused on a single line of march, screened by a picket line of flying, griffon-mounted elves.

The White Wing, in contrast, had not yet located its foe, though it marched along Laurana's trail, and must have known that the Army of Solamnia had preceded it only by a matter of days. A wide screen of sivak draconians flew ahead of the wing, while the white dragons remained behind with the main body.

The following day near noon, the sivaks and elves came into sight of each other nearly a thousand feet above the ground. The armies advanced to meet on the bank of the Vingaard River, near the rapid channel called, simply, the Narrows. (That channel would give its name to the battle that occurred here.) The airborne skirmish was quickly reinforced by dragons on both sides, and by midafternoon the forces on the ground had formed parallel lines of battle.

Finally Laurana found the chance to unleash her horse-mounted knights, and the lancers of Solamnia added much glory to their names on this bloody afternoon. The Knights of the Rose led the charge, supported quickly by those of the Sword—and here, Excellency, we learn the name of the captain called so quaintly by Mellison "Sir Rose." He is Bendford Caerscion, and he led this thunderous advance from the saddle of his night-black charger. His report to Gunthar gives us a first-hand and thorough account of this pivotal melee.

"Eagerly the knights answered the call to attack—trumpets brayed and our restless steeds exploded into a gallop. Pounding hooves reverberated through the ground as the line of armored knights and horses gained unstoppable momentum. My heart swelled with pride—the moment culminated a lifetime of training and devotion. A heavy lance, well-couched at my right side, extended far past my warhorse's snorting head.

"The plain before me seethed with draconians. I saw their snapping jaws, heard them hissing in hatred and fear, as we knights stampeded closer. The reptilian horrors bore swords and shields. The few with spears lacked the wits to brace them to meet the charge. As our thunderous formation neared the draconians, several companies of baaz turned and fled—crashing into a rank of brutal sivaks who tried to whip them back to the fight.

"But it was too late. My knights ripped into the ragged line of draconians with scarcely a falter in their momentum. My lance pierced the body of a huge sivak, pinning the creature to the ground. I released my lance and drew my sword. The monster remained stuck on the lance, its wings flapping, feet kicking, like some monstrous insect pinned to a display board.

"The knights' charge smashed draconian after draconian to the ground, crushing their limbs with pounding hooves, for we were rumbling forward at a fast canter. I slashed this way and that with my blade, aiming for the heads of the monsters and leaving a dozen badly injured in my wake.

"Then we broke through, leaving the shattered remnants of the draconian force to scatter in panicked flight. I hauled back on my reins as soon as the enemy broke from the fight, but my horse—and most of the others—were so excited that they continued the frenzied race for nearly a mile.

"Our two companies of knights numbered less than three hundred in total, but the stampeding momentum of our charge split the draconian line in two. We whirled back and rode against a small contingent of hobgoblins mounted on great wolves. This rabble, too, was quickly scattered or destroyed.

"A shadow flashed over me as this melee ended in the enemy's rout. I felt a chill wind strike me and then, to my horror, I saw a trio of brave knights—riding in close formation—buried beneath the full weight of a diving white dragon. The monster bore men and horses to earth, and dispatched the riders with crushing blows of its great claws and rending teeth.

"Then the serpent's jaws gaped and it belched forth a swirling cloud of numbingly cold frost, slaying several more horses and riders in an instant. I urged my charger toward the monster, but the steady horse refused to go near—and then the dragon turned its attention to me. I prepared myself to die in that moment—but a new shadow flicked past, and in the next instant a huge silver dragon flashed overhead. Its rider—a golden-haired elf—thrust a heavy dragonlance through the white's wing, and then the great silver broke the wyrm's neck with a single bite.

"With a salute of thanks, I recognized Gilthanas—and then we two parted and rode on, seeking the scattered troops of the beleaguered enemy."

All this time the Golden General kept the Knights of the Crown—most numerous of the knightly orders—in reserve. Sir Patrick and Sir Markham no doubt chafed at this delay. It is perhaps well for the sensitivities of this historian that I find no exact record of their remarks, as they were forced to sit idle and watch the orders of the Sword and Rose acquit themselves with glory.

Meanwhile, the men of Palanthas met the charge of baaz draconians with pike and shield, while companies of irregular sword-and-buckler men harassed the flanks of the White Wing. In the sky, the battle raged fierce and costly for both sides. The powerful good dragons eventually slew the last of the whites and their riders, but not before nearly two dozen of them perished—including two silvers and a gold.

Then, as sunset began to cast its shadows across the field, Laurana sent in the Knights of the Crown—five hundred armored riders on eager steeds, charging with their lances, in a thunderous rush that swept the battered remnants of the White Wing from the field. By nightfall, the evil forces were in full retreat, though Laurana ordered a pursuit that continued into the following day. Only when she was convinced that the enemy troops were beyond reassembling did she order her army again to concentrate, turning about to resume the advance toward Dargaard and Kalaman.

From here, Excellency, I depart to follow in the path of that great march. My eventual destination is that great seaport—though on the way, I shall, of course, stop to examine the scene of Laurana's greatest triumph.

It is for this purpose, therefore, that tomorrow I embark for Margaard Ford.

Until that time I endeavor in the service of history,
    Foryth Teel

* * * * *

To the Great Astinus, Lorekeeper of Krynn,
    I return to the Vingaard River again, Excellency, as did

Laurana's army. It becomes increasingly clear to me how the Golden General employed this great flow of water as the keystone of her campaign—using it to screen her movements, defend her force, and—by crossing unexpectedly—surprise her enemy.

After the Battle of the Narrows, Laurana resumed her northeastward push, but misgivings clearly began to grow among the knights. Palanthas and the High Clerist's tower lay too far behind them, now, and the forces of the Dark Lady were known to be mustering at Dargaard.

The losses from this battle—the first pitched fight since the High Clerist's Tower—had been high. We can only guess at the heartache the Golden General must have felt. Did each fallen knight remind her of her dear friend—the stalwart Brightblade? Elves had fallen, and Laurana well knew that each of those deaths had cut short many centuries of life. And the human foot soldiers who had rallied to her cause—surely their loss, too, was as bitter a waste to the elf woman.

Mellison's diary tells us that Laurana retired early to her tent for the nights following that battle, foregoing the camaraderie that had begun to grow between the captains and their general. For three days the army marched steadily, but not frantically. Laurana made certain that the troops and dragons had opportunities to rest, that the horses could graze on the newly sprouted grass beginning to carpet the plain. Spring storms to the east shrouded the Dargaard Mountains, but the skies over the army remained clear.

Finally, on the fourth day after the Battle of the Narrows, the scouting dragons reported back. The Red Wing was on the march, and had been discovered to the southeast, advancing steadily toward Dargaard. Heavy rains accompanied by thick clouds and fog continued to mask the mountains for much of this time, and shortly after the marching column was sighted, it disappeared into the foothills. The Red Wing might as well have vanished, screened as it was by the weather against further observation.

That night, Laurana held another council of war—and again Mellison was present to record the first part of the discussions.

"We *must* take up a defensive position!" Sir Patrick urged. "I admit, my general, that your leadership has carried us to victories beyond my wildest dreams. But now— we *still* don't know where the Emperor's main body is. The clouds mask our entire right flank while we march in the open, day after day! The attack could come with barely an hour's warning. And if it catches us in line of march, we will be smashed and broken in detail!"

"Bah!" Gilthanas—undoubtedly nervous himself— exploded in a rare show of temper. "These dragons are not *defensive* creatures! If you tie them to one location, you deprive them of their strength. Can't you knights force that fact through your Oath-and-Measure-bound skulls?"

Sir Patrick stiffened, his hand going to the hilt of his sword, but the Golden General stepped smoothly between the two. Laurana did not involve herself in the quarrel. Instead, she turned to Lord Sword. "And you, my lord, do you have thoughts on this topic?"

That white-whiskered veteran sighed and shook his head. "I don't know what to believe any more, general. For a certainty you have shown us the value of speed and movement. But Sir Patrick makes a valid point. Without knowledge of the enemy's location, how can we know where to move?"

The elven princess pondered the lord's words, then turned to Sir Caerscion and Sir Markham, who had remained silent up until this point.

"And you, good sirs?" Laurana asked. "Do you counsel a stand here, on the plain?"

"I do, general," Sir Caerscion replied. "With a few days to prepare entrenchments, and a good scouting effort, we can make a strong position. The Dark Lady will find us and attack, but we will meet her forces well-rested and prepared to fight."

"But if we stop, the Highlord will be able to strike us with every weapon at her disposal. That includes the Red Wing—and we still don't know where the reserve army is. Whereas, if we keep moving we force the enemy to keep pursuing. It is far less likely that they will gather the concentration they could muster if we stopped." Markham's remarks provoked a scowl of angry disapproval from Sir Patrick.

Laurana smiled, pleasantly surprised by the young captain's observations. "*Exactly!* That's why we resume the march, tomorrow, but with a change in course."

"*Again!*" cried Patrick in exasperation. "If you must march, let us at least fall back on Palanthas!"

"We will, Sir Patrick. Only not quite that far. Our destination is the final battleground. And that—I mean to ensure—will be our own choosing."

Lord Sword gestured to the flat plains stretching away on all sides. "One patch of the grass is pretty much like another."

"For the most part," Laurana agreed. "But there are exceptions."

The others paused, curious to know what she would tell them next. Markham had a half-smile on his face. Lord Sword and Sir Caerscion waited with obvious apprehension. Gilthanas seemed bored and restless, his eyes drifting over to the great silver dragon resting beyond the fringes of the fire.

Sir Patrick, of course, scowled in preliminary displeasure. Finally he could hold his tongue no longer. "Exceptions?" he grumbled.

"Exactly," announced the Golden General. "Exceptions like rivers. That's why, as soon as we reach the near bank, we will again cross the Vingaard."

The council paused as the captains registered their surprise in raised eyebrows or shrewd squints. For once, however, the knights did not greet their general's plan with a chorus of objections—the advantages of her plan were obvious to all of them. Once they had crossed to the west bank—or the north, actually, for the river had already begun its broad sweep eastward toward Kalaman—they would place the river as barrier between them and the dragonarmies of the Red and Blue Wings.

"But don't we allow them the chance to concentrate their forces? We've labored long to avoid giving them the opportunity until now," ventured Sir Markham perceptively.

Laurana frowned. Her face, in the play of the slowly fading fire, took on again that look of age. Lines of strain lingered in shadows around her cheeks and her eyes.

"We do," she admitted. "My hope is that Ariakus and Kitiara will see their quarry slipping back to the safety of the High Clerist's Tower and come after us in a hurry. If the Red Wing reaches the river first, we can goad it into crossing before the reserve army or the Blue Wing can join up."

"And if they don't?" suggested Sir Patrick, belligerently.

"You were right in the observation you made before, Sir Patrick," Laurana said, causing the knight to clamp his mouth shut and blink his eyes in surprise. "The clouds over the Dargaard Range hide our foes from us. If we remain this far east, the entire assembled dragonarmy can strike us before we have time to react. That's why we need the river."

"Will we fly the troops across again?" asked Lord Sword, with a worried look. "That was a slow process, and we couldn't expect to do it uninterrupted a second time."

"We'll have to," Sir Caerscion noted. "There is a ford in the bend of the River—Margaard Ford, I believe it's called—but it's certain to be too dangerous to use at this time of year. The current would carry an armored knight and his warhorse away, not to mention the poor blighters on foot."

"It may be that we can use the ford. I won't know until tomorrow. I am weary, gentlemen. I bid you good night." Laurana turned away, and only Mellison saw the smile that creased the general's lips. By her remark about the ford, it was obvious Laurana's plan was already in her mind, though she did not share it with anyone.

So the army once more broke camp before the dawn, turning back toward the Vingaard. The mighty river, no more than ten miles away, to the northwest, was swollen by the spring melt. By the end of a single day of marching, the entire army reached the bank—but even before then, Laurana had embarked upon the next part of her plan.

As the army marched toward Margaard Ford, the Golden General dispatched her brass and bronze dragons to the edge of the cloud bank, there to patrol and watch for signs of the emerging dragonarmies. Meanwhile, Laurana, mounted on her gold dragon, flew southward, toward the tightest bottleneck of the Narrows. She took all of the silver dragons with her, including the mighty Silvara with her brother Gilthanas astride.

"We followed her without question," Gilthanas reported to his brother, Porthios, by letter. "By this time, our faith in Laurana was absolute—even the gruff captains of the knightly orders had begun to treat her with a 'measure' of respect!

"I have traveled along the bank of the Narrows, and there can be no doubt as to the site Laurana selected for the work of the silver dragons: gray walls of granite rise a hundred feet on either side of the river, forcing the wide Vingaard through a ravine merely two hundred feet wide. In spring, the swollen river becomes an angry torrent, cascading through a forest of boulders, its waters churned into a chaotic maelstrom.

"Less than half a mile beyond, the gorge walls fall away and the river returns to its wide, deceptively placid flow. It remains thus tamed throughout its course to Margaard Ford, some fifty miles to the north of the Narrows. In the spring, at the time of the battle, the water was at its highest, raging around the crests of the boulders that dot the bed, roaring angrily against anything daring enough to enter this channel.

"But the silver dragons entered, and they *landed* on these boulders—fighting for purchase on the slick rocks, some of the serpents slipping into the water and splashing back into the air after being swept far downstream. Finally, some perched on the wave-swept crests of stone, others crouched on the rocky banks. Their long necks stretched downward to the water, the great serpents awaited the further commands of their Golden General.

"Laurana gave the order. The silver dragons breathed upon the waters; their maws gaping wide, their lungs pulsing with the most potent and deadly of a silver serpent's horrific attacks: a blast of icy frost that casts its chilling grip across everything that lies in its path and magically penetrates the target, sapping every vestige of heat. It is an attack that will drive life from mortal limbs, kill fragile leaves even as the force of the blast shatters the brittle rock into frosty dust. It will turn water, instantly, to ice.

"Once and then again, each dragon expelled his powerful breath. The Vingaard River froze solid in its bed. A belt of ice, extending to the bottom and anchored firmly in the great rocks of the river bed, dammed the river's flow. As the pressure of surging water rose, waves poured over the top of the frozen barrier and the dragons breathed again, building the ice dam higher and higher.

"The channel behind this bottleneck was much wider than the choke-point, and much deeper. The waters of the Vingaard gathered there, swirling and tossing, surging over their banks and spreading outward. Although the lake thus formed expanded steadily, the wall of ice—thickly built and firmly centered in its frame of granite bedrock—held back the pressure.

"Below the dam, the mighty Vingaard began to dwindle to a trickle, seeping between sodden banks. Fifty miles north of the Narrows, downstream of the dam, the Army of Solamnia reached Margaard Ford at nightfall, to find the water still too high to cross safely.

"That night the brass dragons returned with word: the dragonarmies were on the march. The Red and Blue Wings had joined forces with the powerful reserve wing, which must have been marching northward from Sanction for weeks, concealed by the crest of the Dargaard Mountains and the clouds beyond."

Indeed, Excellency, we know from dragonarmy records that Ariakus had put the formation into action weeks before—even preceding the defeat at the High Clerist's Tower. Although initially the Emperor himself commanded this formation, by this time in the campaign, command had been turned over to General Bakaris.

Now the entire force advanced under a swarming flock of blue and red dragons—the mightiest of evil dragonkind—bound to destroy the Army of Solamnia. To the captains of the knights, who received these reports with their backs to an apparently impassable ford, the news must have seemed dire, indeed.

Nevertheless, the Golden General met her captains there and told them they would cross in the morning. We have no record of their reactions, but surely any misgivings they held faded away as the river level fell steadily during the night. By dawn, the ford was a collection of puddles spotting a smooth, gravelly path. The Army of Solamnia marched across it in a matter of hours, while copper dragons kept watch over the advancing wings of the dragonarmies.

The spying copper dragons dived and circled on the horizon, evading the blues and reds that frequently soared out to drive them away. Finally, Bakaris realized that such futile skirmishes only tired his dragons needlessly. He decided to conserve their strength and allow his enemies to maintain their airborne spies in peace.

Bakaris managed to avoid the mistakes of the other commanders who had thus far faced the Golden General. He maintained the concentration of his forces during the advance, refusing to be distracted by anything except his goal: the Army of Solamnia. He marched with considerable speed, making record time for even the normally fast-moving draconian forces. And he wasted no time deploying for battle when the enemy was at last located.

His skill, determination and, of course, the size of his force, made him a very dangerous opponent. He drew close to Laurana's army with shocking speed. By dawn, the morning after the Army of Solamnia had crossed the Vingaard, the advance elements of the dragon wings were visible on the horizon to scouts on dragonback. The dragonarmies would reach the dry ford sometime around the middle of the day. The captains heard the reports of the vast numbers of the enemy and were dismayed. Defeat seemed inevitable.

But Laurana had a final element to her plan, a part she kept secret to the last possible moment, fearing enemy spies. Some of the hidebound knights—who refused to recognize an innovative tactic until it all but knocked them out of their saddles—must have guessed what it was. Still, concern grew through the camp as dawn passed into full daylight. The battle was six hours away, and no barrier stood between the armies—yet Laurana retained all of her dragons in the camp.

Mellison relates that the captains gathered privately, muttering with concern as the sun rose steadily into the sky. They had just agreed that Sir Markham should go to the general when Laurana surprised them by calling them to her tent.

"I'll be leaving now, for a short time. I'll be taking most of the dragons with me."

The knights were certainly astounded by this pronouncement. If any of them mustered the wits for a reply, it has been lost to history.

"I'll leave you the silvers and the coppers. Form a line of defense along the riverbank. By tonight, we'll have opened the road to Kalaman . . . or to the Abyss."

The knights argued vehemently, but the Golden General held firm. She seemed unusually somber—perhaps even severe—as they watched her mount Quallathon. Gilthanas stood beside her and clasped her hand for a moment. Then, turning toward the army of metallic dragons around her, Laurana signalled with a wave of her hand. The great flight of brass, bronze, and gold dragons sprang into the air. The morning sun flashed on their wings as the monstrous serpents soared aloft, riding the updrafts. Lifting themselves above the trees, they bore south, along the line of the empty riverbed below.

Shortly after, from the riverside entrenchments, the dragonarmy came into sight. Bakaris proved as aggressive on the battlefield as he had been in the march. His dragons—massive waves of red and blue serpents bellowing their challenges through the skies—slashed into the silver and copper dragons protecting the Army of Solamnia. Gilthanas and Silvara, together as always, fought in the great aerial melee. He wrote to Porthios.

"I saw a dozen good dragons fall in the first pass, wings seared off by fiery breath, wounds gaping in their flesh, ripped by the lightning bolts of the blue. Silvara wheeled sharply, ducking below the crackling lightning bolt spit by a great blue dragon. I raised my lance, tearing the wyrm's wing as it whirled past. The two dragons met with a brutal crash, slashing at each other with rending talons as we plummeted toward the ground.

"The dragons split apart at the last instant, both of them torn and bleeding. Silvara struggled to regain altitude. I lost sight of my enemy in the chaos of the smoky sky, but drove my lance through the belly of a small red that attacked us from overhead. Mortally wounded, the dragon and its doomed rider plunged to earth, bellowing smoke and fire in a spiralling trail."

Yet such victories were rare. Gilthanas saw many corpses of silver and copper sprawled across the landscape below. Finally, after a half hour of savage battle, the elf was forced to accept the grim truth: the good dragons had lost this fight. More than half of them had perished.

Hellish fireballs spewed by the red dragons continued to erupt. Crackling bolts of lightning spit by the blues still crisscrossed the skies, rending copper wings and scorching scales of silver. The numbers made the outcome inevitable, and ultimately Gilthanas and Silvara were forced to order the surviving good dragons to retreat.

During the course of the screaming fight in the sky, Bakaris's ground troops quickly reached the bank of the ford. Hordes of goblins and hobgoblins, mounted upon howling wolves, immediately charged across the dry passage.

Sir Markham, commanding a large force of the knights, watched them approach. He writes: "The frenzied din of the snarling canines and their equally vociferous riders rolled across us—a cacophony of chaos. They rushed forward with astonishing speed, splashing through the shallow pools that were the only remnants of the once-flooding Vingaard."

Markham held his riders back from the west bank of the ford. When the charging wolfpack reached the halfway mark of the crossing, the knight gestured to his signalmen. Trumpets brayed, and a line of armored horses thundered toward the riverbank. The goblins and their snarling wolves scrambling onto the near bank were met by the crushing advance of the heavily barded warhorses and fully armored cavalry. Markham continues:

"My horse pitched and bucked in the midst of a swirling melee. Wolves snapped at my steed's flanks, drawing blood in many places. But a number of the beasts fell with skulls crushed or backs broken by the powerful kicks of the charger's hooves.

"No sooner had the snarling wolves launched into desperate battle with my knights than three thousand kapak draconians surged across the ford in support. Shrieking and hissing in their hideous tongue, the reptilian scourges flapped their wings madly, hastening the speed of their advance into an unnerving rush.

"Their charge was met by the pikemen of Palanthas, who stood in a three-rank line along the shore. The steely heads of their weapons ripped into the lizardlike attackers. Though the momentum of the charge staggered the line with its impetus, the men held against a breach. Savage and snarling, the formation of draconians crowded against the bank of the ford."

Bakaris here began to reveal his own plan—he hurled the rest of the draconian forces into the attack, holding only his companies of ogres in reserve. At the same time, the evil wyrms appeared in the skies overhead, having defeated the silver and copper dragons. The Dragonarmy general mounted his own dragon—a powerful blue.

Before he rode aloft he sent his field report by courier to Kitiara.

"The time to finish this is *now*—we own the skies over the field! I join my dragonriders, and we shall waste no time in driving onto the Knights of Solamnia, and the pathetic footmen of Palanthas and Ergoth—all of whom stand defenseless against the onslaught!"

Markham's knights had finally driven the last of the wolfriders back; nearly half of the vicious carnivores and their riders lay dead on the riverbank. Now, however, a newer—and far greater—menace approached.

The knight looked upward in raw, frustrated fury as he saw the green and blue forms fill the sky overhead—a sky devoid of metallic colors. The evil serpents tucked their wings, and Markham felt that every one of the beasts glared straight at *him*. The wyrms fanned into a broad line, spreading to strike the entire army.

The lines of pikemen and knights on the riverbank wavered as the dragonfear swept across them. Markham cursed and shouted, even using the flat of his sword to try and muster shaken footmen—but to no avail. Whole companies broke, fleeing blindly away from the ford, panicked beyond reason by the great, circling serpents above. Fireballs of dragonbreath and searing lightning bolts landed with enormous blasts, eliminating entire ranks and melting the stony bank. Screams of the dying mingled with the terrified wails of panicked men—veterans and rank recruits alike quailed at the dreadful attack. In mere seconds, most of the Army of Solamnia had broken and fled, leaving the ford unguarded.

Excellency, I must here remark upon the fact that, if the evil dragons had not expended so much of their limited breath weapons against Gilthanas and his flight, the carnage would have been many times worse. Nevertheless, in moments, the Army of Solamnia teetered at the brink of total collapse.

Laurana, meanwhile had flown southward with all speed—the timing of her activities was crucial. Soon the flight of good dragons and their Golden General came to the Narrows, where the ice dam had swelled from the overnight pressure of the great river. A vast new lake spread across the plains to each side. Before the huge sheet of white, glistening in the sunlight, but not melting in the cool spring air, Laurana and Quallathon settled to earth. The other golds and brass dragons also dropped, landing on the rocky riverbed. The bronze dragons circled overhead, watchful for any interference from the dragonarmies.

Again the Golden General turned the breath of her dragons onto the River Vingaard—but this time in the form of heat. Explosive fireballs belched forth from the golds; from the brass came blistering waves of scorching wind. The searing breath weapons swept across the frozen surface, assailing with arcane heat the same waters that had earlier suffered the onslaught of cold.

With convulsive force the great sheets of ice cracked and splintered, shifting and breaking under the rapid change of temperature. Huge chunks broke free, white mountains tumbled into the surging water. With a rush, the dam broke away. The waters of the Vingaard thundered forth, many

times more powerful than they had been even at the height
of the spring flood.

* * * * *

The huge, newly-formed lake roared through its new
outlet, carrying massive pieces of ice, like jagged daggers,
in the forefront of the advancing tide. Rocks that had rested
in the river bed for a century ripped free in the space of a
minute, rumbling along with the flow like great engines of
war.

Above the water flew the dragons of gold, brass, and
bronze. They soared northward now, racing the torrent—
but only barely matching it in speed. Thus, both the waters
and the good dragons reached Margaard Ford at the same
time, little more than two hours after the dam had collapsed.

Nevertheless, according to Gilthanas, the situation stood
at the brink of disaster. His silvers still wheeled in the sky,
forced back from the fight—and sadly reduced in numbers.
He had all but given up hope of victory, when he saw the
glint of sunlight on gilded wings.

Laurana's mighty gold dragons bellowed a challenge,
echoed by a hundred throats of gold and brass and bronze.
And below the wings of gleaming metal surged a maelstrom
of frothing white, capped by the icebergs and boulders.

The waters swept through Margaard Ford with all the impact of a tidal wave, drowning and crushing the enemy
troops trapped there. At the same time, the dragons of
Laurana and Gilthanas tore into the blues and reds. The evil
serpents fought desperately, but the vengeful attackers
swiftly slashed the enemy from the skies in the greatest aerial melee of the war. By my calculations, Excellency, it
seems likely that nearly four hundred dragons fought in the
air over Margaard Ford!

It is worth noting, Excellency, that Bakaris himself was
taken captive in this airborne clash. He ended the fight
clinging for his life to the mane of a bronze dragon after his
own mount had fallen. It was the famed hill dwarf Flint
Fireforge, together with his squire, who rode the bronze.

This was Fireforge's last flight on dragonback. He vowed everafter to keep his boots firmly on the ground.

The waters of the Vingaard slowly settled to their normal levels. We'll never know how many bodies they carried along their route to Kalaman and the sea. The few surviving troops belonged to the Blue Wing, and they hastened back to Dargaard Keep, where the Dark Lady still held her fortress.

The last of the dragonarmies had been driven from the plains, and Laurana slowed the pace of her march somewhat, to rest her weary army as it at last approached long-forsaken Kalaman. That city had endured a bleak winter of isolation and siege, and so it was only proper that their liberator and heroine should pass through the city gates to commence the Festival of Spring Dawning.

That event concludes the tale of the Vingaard Campaign. I hope Your Grace will forgive the addition of several of my conclusions that, I feel certain, can be comfortably established within the boundaries of objectivity.

It is interesting to note that the Dark Lady, Highlord Kitiara, was sentenced to death by Lord Ariakus for her failures in this campaign. When he arrived at Dargaard to carry out the sentence, however, Kitiara was able to persuade the Emperor that much of the campaign had passed according to her "plan."

It is true that her life was spared, but my own suspicion is that this is due more to her "friend," the Death Knight Lord Soth, than to any lapse in Ariakus's judgment. It is hard to imagine the campaign being viewed by the Emperor as anything but a monstrously disastrous defeat.

In retrospect, Grand Master Gunthar Uth Wistan's appointment of Laurana as the army's commander stands clearly vindicated. The Golden General proved capable of initiative and audacity far beyond what any Knight of Solamnia could have mustered. In fact, her use of dragon breath for strategic purposes (damming the river) clearly shows how she managed to outwit even her battle-seasoned opponents—no Highlord used the dragons for any purpose other than a tactical application on the battlefield.

In conclusion, Lauralanthalasa of Qualinesti must clearly

stand alongside Kith-Kanan, Vinas Solamnus, and Huma himself as one of the greatest generals of Krynn.

In gratitude, I shall remain heretofore,
Foryth Teel, Senior Scribe of Astinus

The Story That Tasslehoff Promised He Would Never, Ever, Ever Tell

Margaret Weis and Tracy Hickman

CHAPTER ONE

SO I GUESS YOU'RE WONDERING WHY I'M TELLING you this, since I promised not to. I'm sure Tanis wouldn't mind, seeing that it's you. I mean, you've heard the other stories, all about the War of the Lance and the Heroes of the Lance (of which I, Tasslehoff Burrfoot, am one) and how ten years ago we defeated the Dark Queen and her dragons. This is just one more story, one that never was told. As to why it was never told, you'll find that out when I get around to the part about promising Fizban.

It all began about a month ago. I was traveling up the Vingaard River, heading for Dargaard Keep. You've heard the stories about Dargaard Keep, how it's cursed and Lord Soth is supposed to haunt it. I hadn't seen Lord Soth in a while—he's a death knight and while we're not exactly friends, he is what you might call a close personal acquaintance. I was thinking about him one night and how he very nearly killed me once. (I don't harbor a grudge; death knights have to do these things, you see.) And it occurred to me that he might be bored, what with having nothing to do for the past ten years, ever since we defeated the Dark Queen, except haunt people.

Anyway, I thought I'd go find Lord Soth and fill him in on Recent Events and maybe he'd glare at me with his fiery eyes, and make me go all wonderfully cold and shivery inside.

I was on my way to Dargaard Keep when I stopped over in a little town that I can show you on my map, though I can't remember the name. They have a very nice jail there. I know, because I was spending the night in it, having become involved in an argument with a butcher over a string of sausages that had followed me out of his shop.

I tried to point out to the butcher that they must be magical sausages, because I couldn't think of any other way they would have ended up trailing after me like that. I thought he'd be pleased, you know, to realize he had the power to make magical sausages. And if I did eat two of them, it was just to find out if they did anything magical in the stomach. (They did, but I don't think that counts as magic. I'll have to ask Dalamar.) To make a long story short, he was not pleased to hear he had magical sausages and I was taken away to jail.

Things have a way of working out, though, as my grandmother Burrfoot used to say. There were a whole lot of other kender in the jail. (Quite a remarkable coincidence, don't you think?) We had a very agreeable time together, and I caught up on all the news of Kendermore.

And I found out that someone had been looking for me!

He was a friend of a friend of a friend and he had an important message for me. Just think! An Important Message. Kender all over Ansalon had been told to give it to me if they ran into me. This was the Important Message.

"Meet me at the Silver Dragon Mountain during this anniversary. Signed, FB."

I must say that I thought the message a bit confused, and I still think it probably lost something over having been passed around by so many people. But my friends assured me that was exactly how they'd heard it or close enough as not to make any difference. I knew right off who FB was, of course, and you must, too. (Tanis did. I could tell that from the groan he gave when I mentioned it.) And I knew where the Silver Dragon Mountain was. I'd been there before, with Flint and Laurana and Gilthanas and Theros Ironfeld and Silvara before we knew she was a silver dragon herself. You remember that story, don't you? Astinus wrote it all down and called it Dragons of Winter Night.

I was puzzling over this message and wondering what anniversary it was talking about, when the kender who gave it to me said that there was another part to it.

"Repeat the name Fizban backwards three times and clap your hands."

That sounded like magic to me and I am extremely fond of magic. But, knowing Fizban as I did, I thought it wise to take precautions. I told the other kender in the cell with me that this message was from a rather fuddled old wizard and that the spell might be Quite Interesting and that maybe I should wait until we were all out of jail in the morning.

But the other kender said that, while it would be a shame to blow up this nice jail, if I did blow it up, they didn't want to miss it. They all gathered around and I began.

"Nabzif, Nabzif, Nabzif!" I said quickly, kind of holding my breath, and I clapped my hands.

Poof!

Once I cleared away the smoke, I discovered I was holding a scroll. I unrolled it quickly, thinking it might be another spell, you see. But it wasn't. The other kender were considerably disappointed and rather miffed that I hadn't blown up either the jail or myself. They went back to comparing jails in other parts of Solamnia. I read what I was holding in my hands.

It turned out to be an invitation. At least I think that's what it was. It was hard to tell, what with all the burn holes and smudges and smears of what smelled like grape jelly.

The writing was very pretty and elaborate. I can't copy it, but this is what it said (I'm including smudges and blots):

A Celebration of the Tenth Anniversary of the
(Blot)of the Dragonl(smudge)
to be held at the
Silver Dragon Mountain
Yuletime.
Hero of the Lance
Your Presence is Most Earnestly Requested.
We Honor the Knight of Solamnia
Who First Did Battle with the (blob, blot),
Sir (smear and tarbean tea-stain)ower

It was signed *Lord Gunthar Uth Wistan.*

Well, of course, this explained everything (not counting the blots). The knights were holding a celebration in honor of something, probably the War of the Lance. And, since I'm one of the Heroes, I was invited! This was incredibly exciting. I put off my visit to Lord Soth (I hope he understands, if he reads this), let myself out of jail with a key I found in my pocket, and headed immediately for Silver Dragon Mountain.

It used to be you couldn't find Silver Dragon Mountain, but after the War, the knights turned it into a Monument and fixed the roads so that they could get to it easier. They left the Ruined Keep ruined. I traveled past it and wandered through the Woods of Peace awhile, then I stopped to admire the hot springs that boil just like Tika's tea kettle and I crossed the bridge where I saw the statues that looked like my friends, only they were just statues now. Probably because of the Monument. And then I came to Foghaven Vale.

Foghaven Vale has a lot to do with the rest of my story, so I'll tell you about it, in case you've forgotten from the last time I was there.[1] The Hot Springs mixing with the water of the Cool Lake makes fog so thick that it's hard to see your topknot in front of your nose. No one used to know where this Vale was, a long time ago, except Silvara and the other silver dragons, who guarded Huma's Tomb, the final resting place of a truly great knight from long, long ago. His tomb is there, only he isn't.

At the north end of Foghaven Vale stands Silver Dragon Mountain. You can get into the mountain through a secret tunnel inside Huma's Tomb. I know, because I accidentally fell into it and got sucked up the statue dragon's windpipe. That's where I found Fizban after he was dead, only he wasn't.

And it was in this mountain that Theros Ironfeld forged the dragonlances. And that's why it's a Monument.

Every year at Yuletime the knights come to the Silver

---

[1]*Dragons of Winter Night*, Dragonlance Chronicles, Volume 2. Available in the Library at Palanthas, which is a very nice city to visit, especially since they've cleaned up after the dragons. The library is one block south and two east of the jail. You can't miss it.

Dragon Mountain and Huma's Tomb and they sing songs of Huma and of Sturm Brightblade—a very good friend of mine! They "tell tales of glory by day, and spend the night on their knees in prayer before Huma's stone bier." Those quotes are from Tanis.

I knew about this, but I'd never been invited to come before, probably because I'm not a knight. (Though I would really like to be, someday. I know a story about a half-kender who was almost a knight. Have you heard it? Oh, all right.) I guess I was invited this year because this year was special, being the tenth anniversary of Something that I couldn't read for the blot. But I didn't care what it was, as long as there was to be a big party in honor of it.

I was traipsing through the fog of Foghaven Vale, wondering where I was (I had wandered off the path), when I heard voices. Naturally, I stopped to listen and while stopping to listen I may have sneaked behind a tree. (This is not snooping. It is called "caution" and caution is conducive to a long life. Something Tanis is very big on. I'll explain later.)

This is what I heard the voice say.

" 'The tenth anniversary is to be a reverent, solemn, holy time of rededication for all good and righteous people of Krynn.' " It was Tanis! I was sure it was his voice, only he was talking in a Lord Gunthar-kind of tone. Then Tanis said in his own voice, "Crap. It's all a lot of crap."

"What?—" said another voice, and I knew that voice was Caramon's, and he sounded the same dear old confused Caramon as always. I couldn't believe my luck.

"Tanis, my dear," came a woman's voice and it was Laurana! I knew that because she's the only one who ever calls Tanis *my dear*. "Don't talk so loudly."

"But what?—" That was Caramon again.

"No one can hear me," said Tanis, interrupting. He sounded really irritated and in a Bad Mood. "This damn fog muffles everything. The truth is that the knights are having political problems at home. That draconian raid on Throtl touched off a riot in Palanthas. People think the knights should go into the mountains and wipe out the draconians and the goblins and anything else that doesn't wipe them out first. It's all the fault of this new group of boneheads who say we should go back to the golden days of the Kingpriest!"

"But doesn't Lady Crysania—" Caramon tried again.

"Oh, she reminds people of the truth," Tanis told him. "And I think most understand. But the fanatics are gaining converts, especially when the refugees come forward and tell their tales of Throtl in flames and goblins killing babies. What no one seems to realize is that the knights couldn't possibly raise an army large enough to go into the Khalkists, even if they did ally with the dwarves. The rest of Solamnia would be left defenseless, which is probably just exactly what these goblins raids are trying to accomplish. But these fools don't want to listen to reason."

"Then why are we—"

"—here? That's why," Tanis answered. "The knights are turning this into a public spectacle in order to remind everyone how truly great and wonderful we are. Are you sure we're going the right direction?"

I could see them now from where I was hiding. (Caution, not snooping.) Tanis and Caramon and Laurana were riding on horses, and an escort of knights was riding behind— a long way behind. Tanis had reigned in his horse and was looking around like he thought he was lost, and Caramon was looking, too.

"I think—" Caramon began.

"Yes, dear," said Laurana patiently. "This is the trail. I came this way before, remember?"

"Ten years ago," Tanis reminded her, turning to look at her with a smile.

"Yes, ten years," she said. "But I'm not likely to ever forget it. I was with Silvara and Gilthanas . . . and Flint. Dear old Flint." She sighed and brushed her hand across her cheek.

I felt a snuffle coming on, so I kept behind the tree until I could choke it back down. I heard Tanis clear his throat. He shifted uncomfortably in his saddle and moved closer to Caramon. Their horses were nose to nose and almost nose to nose with me.

"I was afraid this would happen," Tanis said quietly. "I tried to talk her out of coming, but she insisted. Damn knights. Polishing up their armor and their memories of glory from ten years ago, hoping that people will remember the battle of the High Clerist's Tower and forget the Sacking of Throtl."

Caramon blinked. "Was Throtl really?—"

"Don't exaggerate, Tanis," said Laurana briskly, riding up to join them. "And don't worry about me. It's good to be reminded of those who have gone before us, who wait for us at the end of our long journey. My memories of my dear friends aren't bitter. They don't make me unhappy, only sad. It is our loss, not theirs." Her eyes went to Caramon as she spoke.

The big man smiled, nodded his head in silent understanding. He was thinking of Raistlin. I know because I was thinking of Raistlin, too, and some fog got into my eyes and made them go all watery. I thought about what Caramon had put on the little stone marker he set up in Solace in Raistlin's honor.

One granted peace for his sacrifice. One who sleeps, at rest, in eternal night.

Tanis scratched his beard. (His beard has little streaks of gray in it now. It looks quite distinguished.) He looked frustrated.

"You'll see what I mean when we get there. The knights have gone to all this trouble and expense, and I don't think it's going to help matters. People don't live in the past. They live in the present. That's what counts now. The knights need to do something to bolster our faith in them now, not remind us of what they were ten years ago. Some are beginning to say it was all wizard's work back then anyway. Gods and magic." He shook his head. "I wish we could forget the past and get on with the future."

"But we should remember the past, honor it," said Caramon, actually managing to finish a complete sentence. He wouldn't have managed that—Tanis was so worked up—only Tanis had been forced to stop talking by a sneeze. "If people are divided now, then it seems that we should remind them of a time they came together."

"If it would do that, it might be of some worth," Tanis muttered, sniffing. He was searching through his pockets, probably for a handkerchief. He's quite careless about losing things. I know because I was holding onto his pack at the time.

Here's how it happened that I had his pack. I had stepped out from behind the tree, ready to surprise him. I caught hold of the pack, which had been tied (not very well) onto the back of the saddle. Suddenly the pack bounced loose and came off in my hand. I would have said something to him then, but he was talking again and it wouldn't have been polite to interrupt. So I took the pack and stepped back behind the tree and looked inside it to see if it was really his and not someone else's by mistake.

"But the knights won't do anything except wallow in the past," Tanis was saying. "Mark my words. Have you heard that latest song they've made up about Sturm? Some minstrel sang it for us the other night, before we left. I laughed out loud."

"You deeply offended him," said Laurana. "He wouldn't even stay the night. And there was no need to follow him out to the gate, yelling at him."

"I told him to sing the truth next time. Sturm Brightblade wasn't a paragon of virtue and courage. He was a man and he had the same fears and faults as the rest of us. Sing about that!"

Tanis sneezed again. "Blast this damp! The cold eats into the bone. And we'll be spending the night on our knees in a mouldy old tomb. Where the blazes did I put my handker—"

Well, of course, it was in his pack.

"Is this it, Tanis? You dropped it," I said, coming out of the fog.

Once they were over being amazed, they were all very happy to see me. Laurana hugged me (she is so beautiful!) and they asked me where I was going and I told them and then they didn't look so happy.

"You were supposed to invite him to come," said Laurana.

(She either said that or "You *weren't* supposed to invite him to come." I wasn't certain. She was talking so softly I had to strain my ears to hear.)

"I didn't," said Tanis, and he glared at Caramon.

"Not me!" said the big man emphatically.

"Oh, don't worry," I said, not wanting them to feel bad that they'd each forgotten to invite me. "I have my own invitation. It found me, so to speak." And I held it up.

They all stared at it and looked so amazed and astonished that I thought I better not say who had sent it to me. Like I said, Tanis always groans whenever I mention Fizban.

Tanis said something in a low voice to Caramon that sounded like, "It will only make things worse if we try to get rid of him . . . follow us . . . this way, keep an eye on him."

I wondered who it was they were talking about.

"Who are you talking about?" I asked. "Who'd follow you? Keep an eye on who?"

"I'll give you three guesses," Tanis growled, holding out his hand to me and pulling me up to ride behind him.

Well, I spent the rest of the trip to the Silver Dragon Mountain guessing, but Tanis said I never got it right.

CHAPTER TWO

"I asked you not to bring the kender," said Lord Gunthar.

He thought he was talking in a low voice, but I heard him. I looked around, wondering where this other kender was that they were talking about.

I knew it couldn't be me, because I'm one of the Heroes of the Lance.

We were standing in the Upper Gallery that is inside the Silver Dragon Mountain. It is a large room with dragonlances all around one end and it is meant for formal celebrations like this one. We were all of us dressed in our very best clothes because, as Tanis said, this was a reverent and solemn occasion. (I was wearing my new purple leggings with the red fringe that Tika sewed for me and my buckskin shirt with the yellow and orange and green bead work that was a gift from Goldmoon.)

There were lots of knights in their shining armor and Caramon (Tika was home with the babies) and Laurana were there and some other people I didn't know. Lady Crysania was expected any minute. It was very exciting, and I wasn't the least bored, or I wouldn't have been if I could have walked around, talking to people. But Tanis said I was to stay close to him or to Caramon or Laurana.

I thought it was sweet that they wanted me close by them that much, and so I did what Tanis said, though I pointed out that it would be more polite if I were to mingle with the other guests.

Tanis said that on no account was I to mingle.

"I didn't bring him," Tanis was telling Lord Gunthar. "Somehow or other he got hold of an invitation. Besides, he has a right to be here. He's just as much as hero as any of us. Maybe more."

Again I wondered who Tanis was talking about. This person sounded like an interesting fellow to me. Tanis was going to say more except he sneezed. He must have caught a really nasty cold out there in Foghaven Vale. (I've often wondered why we say "you've caught a cold." I mean, no one I ever knew went out after a cold. And I never heard of anyone going cold-chasing. It seems to me that it would make more sense to say the cold's caught you.)

"Bless you," Lord Gunthar said, then he sighed. "I suppose there's no help for it. You'll keep an eye on him, won't you?"

Tanis promised he would. I gave him his handkerchief. Odd, the way he kept losing it. Lord Gunthar turned to me.

"Burrfoot, my old friend," he said, putting his hands behind his back. A lot of people have a habit of doing that when we're introduced. "So glad to see you again. I hope the roads you travel have been sunny and straight." (That is a polite form of greeting to a kender and I thought it very fine of the knight to use it. Not many people are that considerate.)

"Thank you, Sir Gunthar," I said, holding out my hand.

He sighed and shook hands. I noticed he was wearing a very nice set of silver bracers and a most elegant dagger.

"I hope your lady wife is well?" I asked, not to be outdone in politeness. This was, after all, a Formal Occasion.

"Yes, thank you," said Gunthar. "She . . . um . . . appreciated the Yule gift."

"Did she?" I was excited. "I'm really glad she liked it. I always think of the time Fizban and I spent Yule at your castle, right after . . . er . . . after . . ."

Well, I almost told the story I wasn't supposed to tell, right there! Which would have been terrible! I caught myself in time.

"I—I mean right before the Council of Whitestone. When I broke the dragon orb. And Theros smashed the rock with the dragonlance. Has she used it yet?"

"The lance?" Gunthar seemed somewhat confused.

"No, no, the Yule present," I corrected him.

"Well . . . that is . . ." Gunthar looked embarrassed. "The wizard Dalamar advised us that we shouldn't . . ."

"Ah, so it *was* magical." I nodded. "I had a feeling it might be. I wanted to try it myself, but I've had a couple of experiences with magic rings and while they've certainly been interesting experiences, I didn't feel like being turned into a mouse or being magicked into the castle of an evil wizard just at that particular time. It wasn't convenient, if you know what I mean."

"Yes," said Lord Gunthar, tugging on his moustaches. "I understand."

"Plus, I think we should share experiences like that. It's selfish to keep them all to ourselves. Not that I'd want your lady wife to be magicked into the castle of an evil wizard. Unless she really felt inclined for the trip, that is. It does make a nice change of pace. For example, did I ever tell you about the time that I was—"

"Excuse me," said Lord Gunthar. "I must go welcome our other guests."

He bowed, checked to see that he was still wearing his bracers, and left.

"A very polite man," I said.

"Give me the dagger," Tanis said, sighing.

"What dagger? I'm not carrying a dagger."

Then I noticed I *was* carrying a dagger. An elegant dagger decorated with roses on the hilt. Imagine my surprise!

"Is this yours?" I asked wistfully, because it was such a truly elegant dagger.

"No, it belongs to Lord Gunthar. Hand it over."

"I guess he must have dropped it," I said, and gave it to Tanis. After all, I have my own dagger, which I call Rabbitslayer, but that's another story.

Tanis turned to Caramon, saying something about tying someone's hands and head up in a sack. That sounded extremely interesting, but I didn't hear who it was they were talking about because I suddenly saw someone I wasn't expecting to see.

Someone I didn't want to see.

Someone I wasn't supposed to see.

I felt very strange for a moment, kind of like you feel right after you've been clunked in the head and right before you see all the stars and bright lights, then everything goes dark.

I looked at him very closely. And then I realized it couldn't have been him because he was too young. I mean, I hadn't seen this knight for ten years and I guess he must have aged during that time. So I was feeling a little better, when I saw the other knight. He was standing a little ways behind the first man I'd seen. Then I realized that the younger man must be his son. I still hoped I might be wrong. It had been ten years, after all.

I tugged on Tanis's sleeve.

"Is that Owen Glendower over there?" I asked, pointing.

Tanis looked. "No, that's Owen's son, Gwynfor. Owen Glendower is the one standing in back, over by the lances." Then he looked at me and he frowned. "How do you know Owen Glendower? I didn't meet him until after the war was over."

"I don't know him," I said, feeling sicker than ever.

"But you just said his name and asked me if that was him."

Tanis is thick-headed, sometimes.

"Whose name?" I asked, truly miserable.

"Owen Glendower's!"

I didn't think Tanis should shout on a Formal Occasion and I told him so.

"Never heard of him," I added. And then, to make matters worse, in walked Theros Ironfeld!

Do you know who Theros Ironfeld is? I'm sure you do, but I think I should mention it, in case you've forgotten. Theros is the blacksmith with the silver arm who forged the dragonlances from the magical pool of dragonmetal that some people think is under the Silver Dragon Mountain.

"Theros, too!" I was having trouble breathing.

"Yes, of course," Tanis said. "It is the tenth anniversary of the Forging of the Lance. Didn't you know that? It says so right on your invitation. We're meeting here to honor Sir Owen Glendower, the first knight who ever used the dragonlance against a dragon."

It didn't say that on *my* invitation! I fished it out of my pouch and looked at it again. My invitation said we were honoring *Sir* (Splot)*ower*.

Well, let me tell you it was a wonder I didn't fall down on the spot in a state of nervous prostration. (I'm not certain what that is, but it describes the way I felt.)

"I'm not feeling very good, Tanis," I said, putting one hand to my forehead and the other to my stomach, for they both were acting very queer. "I think I'll go lie down."

I meant to leave, truly. I was going to get as far from that Silver Dragon Mountain as possible. Only I didn't tell Tanis that, because he and Laurana and Caramon had all been so glad to see me and were so nice about wanting me around. I didn't want to hurt their feelings.

But Tanis took hold of my arm and said, "No, you're staying with me, at least until after the ceremony."

That was awfully good of him, if inconvenient and uncomfortable for me. I decided maybe I could get through the ceremony, especially if Owen Glendower didn't talk to me, and I suspected that he wouldn't want to talk to me anymore than I wanted to talk to him. Tanis said all I would have to do was go up with him when my name was called out by Lord Gunthar as one of the Heroes of the Lance. I wasn't to say anything, just bow and look honored.

Then the knights would sing and go off to pray at Huma's Tomb and, since I wasn't permitted to go there (which I don't know why since I was there several times before, as you'll hear), I could leave and maybe we'd go have dinner.

I didn't feel at all hungry, but I told Tanis that would be fine with me. And I hid behind Caramon (six kender could hide behind him), so that Owen wouldn't see me, and I hoped it would all be over soon. I was so nervous I'd forgotten to ask Lord Gunthar about Fizban, who hadn't come anyhow.

The ceremony started. Lord Gunthar and all the dignitaries lined up in front of the dragonlances that stand all around the front end Upper Gallery. I heard the beginning of Lord Gunthar's speech. This was it:

"We knights come to rededicate ourselves to continue the fight against the evil that exists still in the world.

"For the Queen of Darkness wages unceasing eternal war against the powers of good. Though her dragons have retreated to hidden places, they continue to ravage the land. Her armies of goblins and draconians and ogres and other wicked creatures rise up from dark places to slaughter and burn and plunder."

This was interesting and I began to breathe easier, but right then he started going on about the magic of the dragonlances that had been blessed by Paladine himself and how the magic dragonlances had been responsible for defeating the Dark Queen's dragons. The more Lord Gunthar talked like this, the worse the queer feeling in my stomach grew.

Then I was hot and cold, both at the same time, which might sound entertaining to you, but I can assure you it isn't. Take my word. It's very uncomfortable. Then the room began to bulge in and out.

Lord Gunthar introduced Theros Ironfeld and talked about how he forged the magical lance. Then Lord Gunthar brought forth Sir Owen Glendower.

"The first knight ever to use the dragonlance in battle."

And someone gave a kind of strangled choke and tumbled down on the floor in what Tanis said was a fit, but which I think was a state of nervous prostration. At first I thought it was me, but I realized it wasn't, because I was on my feet.

It was Sir Owen Glendower.

That put an end to the ceremony real quick.

I could have left then, because Tanis let loose of me and ran over to Owen. Everyone was running over to Owen—to see him having his fit, I suppose. I'm sure it must have been exciting, to judge by the sounds he was making—

gurgling and thrashing about on the floor—and I would have liked to have seen it myself, except I wasn't certain that I wouldn't be having a fit of my own any minute.

"Stand back!" cried Caramon. "Give him air."

Poor Caramon. As if he thought we'd suck up all the air in that big chamber and not leave any for Owen to have his fit with. But everyone did what Caramon said (they generally do, I've noticed, especially when he flexes his arm muscles) and they all backed up, except for Owen's son, who was kneeling beside his father and looking terribly worried and anxious.

Lady Crysania . . . (Did I mention she was there now?) Anyway, Lady Crysania (she was there) knelt down and put her hands on the knight's head and she prayed to Paladine and Owen Glendower quit flopping around. But I couldn't see that he'd improved much. He was lying still as death and his breathing sounded real funny—when he remembered to breathe at all.

"He needs rest and quiet," said Lady Crysania. "No, it would be better not to move him. We must keep him warm. Make a pallet for him here."

They all piled up cloaks and furs and Theros and Caramon lifted the knight very, very gently and laid him on the pallet. Laurana covered him up with her own fur cape. Gwynfor sat down beside his father and held his hand.

Tanis said something in a low voice to Lord Gunthar. Lord Gunthar nodded his head and announced that this might be a convenient time for the knights to all go down to the tomb and pray and rededicate themselves to fighting evil. The knights thought so, too, and off they went. That cleared a lot of people out of the room.

Lord Gunthar next said that he thought all the other guests should go to dinner, and Caramon saw to it that the other guests did, whether they wanted to or not. That cleared out about everyone else. I couldn't go to the Tomb and I wasn't hungry and my legs felt wobbly, so I stayed.

"Will my father be all right?" Gwynfor was asking Lady Crysania. Theros Ironfeld was standing over Owen, looking down at the knight with the grimmest expression I'd ever seen Theros wear.

"Yes, my lord," Crysania said, turning in the direction of Gwynfor's voice. (Lady Crysania is blind. That is another interesting story, only kind of sad, so I won't tell it here.) "He is in Paladine's hands."

"Perhaps we should leave," suggested Tanis.

But Lady Crysania shook her head. "No. I would like you all to stay. There is something very wrong here."

I could have told her *that*!

"I've done what I could to heal him, but Sir Glendower's affliction isn't in his body. It's in his mind. Paladine has given me to know that there is a secret locked inside the knight, a secret he's been carrying by himself for a long, long time. Unless we can discover the secret and free him of it, I'm afraid he will not recover."

"If Paladine's given you to know the knight has a secret, why doesn't Paladine just tell you what the damn secret is?" Tanis asked, and he sounded a bit testy. He gets put out at the gods sometimes.

Laurana cleared her throat and gave him one of Those Looks that married people give each other sometimes. One reason I've never been married myself.

"Paladine has done so," said Lady Crysania with a smile.

And you may believe this or not, but she turned her head and looked straight at me, even though she couldn't see me and she couldn't have had any idea that I was in the room for I was being as quiet as the time I accidentally turned myself into a mouse.

"Tasslehoff!" Tanis said, and he didn't sound at all pleased. "Do you know anything about this?"

"Me?" I asked, looking around. I didn't think it likely he could have been talking to any other Tasslehoff, but I could always hope.

He meant me, however.

"Yeeessss," I said, drawing out the word a long time, as long as possible, and not looking at him. I don't like it when he looks so stern. "But I promised not to tell."

Tanis sighed. "All right, Tas. You promised not to tell. Now I'm certain you must have told this story a dozen times since then so it won't hurt if you tell it—"

"No, Tanis." I interrupted him, which was not very polite, but he truly had it all wrong. I looked up at him and I was extremely solemn and serious. "I haven't told. Not ever. Not anyone. I promised, you see."

He stared at me real hard. Then his eyes crinkled. He looked worried. Kneeling down, he put his hand on my shoulder. "You haven't told anyone?"

"No, Tanis," I said, and for some reason a tear slid out of my eye. "I never have. I promised him I wouldn't."

"Promised who?"

"Fizban," I said.

Tanis groaned. (I told you, he always groans when I mention FB.)

"I, too, know," said a voice unexpectedly.

And at this we all turned to look at Theros. And he was as grim and dour and stern as I've ever seen Theros, who is usually quite nice, even if he does pick me up by the top-knot sometimes, which isn't at all dignified.

"Sir Owen Glendower and I have discussed it between ourselves, often, each looking for his own truth. I have found mine. And I thought he had found his. Perhaps I was wrong. It is not for me to tell his tale, however. If he had wanted it told, he would have done so before now."

"But surely," Tanis said, growing more irritated than ever, "if the man's life is at stake . . ."

"I can tell you nothing," Theros said. "I wasn't there." He turned and stalked out of the Upper Gallery.

Which left me. You see, I *was* there.

"C'mon, Tas," said Caramon in that wheedling way of his that makes me feel like I'd like to hit him sometimes. "You can tell me."

"I promised not to tell anyone," I said. They were all standing around me now, and I had never in my life felt more miserable, except maybe when I was in the Abyss. "I promised Fizban I wouldn't."

Tanis started to get red in the face and he would have yelled at me for sure but two things—a sneeze and Laurana digging her elbow into his ribs—put a stop to it. I didn't even remember to give him his handkerchief, I was so unhappy.

Lady Crysania came over to me and put out her hand and

touched me. Her touch was soft and gentle. I wanted to run into her arms and cry like a big baby. I didn't, because that wouldn't have been dignified for a kender my age and a hero, to boot, but I wanted to, most desperately.

"Tas," she said to me, "how did you happen to come here?"

I thought that was a strange question, since I was invited, so I told her about the sausages and the jail and the message and the invitation from Fizban.

Tanis groaned and sneezed again.

"Don't you see, Tasslehoff?" asked Lady Crysania. "It was Fizban who sent you here. You know who Fizban really is, don't you?"

"I know who he *thinks* he is," I said, because Raistlin told me once that he wasn't really certain himself if the wacky old wizard was telling the truth or not. "Fizban thinks he's the god Paladine."

"Whether he is or he isn't"—Lady Crysania smiled again—"he sent you here for a reason, you may be sure. I think he wants you to tell us the story."

"Do you?" I asked hopefully. "I'd like to, because it's been weighing on my mind."

I handed Tanis his handkerchief and gave the matter some thought. "But you don't know that for sure, Lady Crysania," I said, starting to feel miserable again. "I'm always *not* doing the right thing. I wouldn't want to not do the right thing now."

I thought some more. "But I wouldn't want Sir Owen to die either."

I had an idea. "I know! I'll tell you all the secret, then you can tell me whether or not I should tell anyone. And if you say I shouldn't, then I won't."

"But Tas, if you tell us—" Caramon began.

At which point Laurana gave him a nudge on one side and Tanis gave him a nudge on the other, so that Caramon coughed and was all sort of nudged out, I guess, because he didn't say anymore.

"I think that is very wise," said Lady Crysania, and she said she wanted to keep near Owen Glendower, so we all followed her. There weren't any chairs. We sat down on the floor in a circle, with Lady Crysania keeping beside Owen and everyone else around her and me opposite.

And it was there, sitting on the floor next to Owen Glendower, stretched out in his armor on the fur cloaks, that I told the story I had sworn by my topknot I would never, ever, ever tell.

I took hold of my topknot and held it fast, because I thought this might be the last time I'd ever see it.

CHAPTER THREE

Well, I'm certain you must remember the part in the old story where most of us went to the Silver Dragon Mountain. There was me and Flint and Laurana and her brother Gilthanas and Theros Ironfeld and Silvara, the silver dragon, except we didn't know she was a silver dragon then.

Silvara took us to the Silver Dragon Mountain on purpose to find the dragonlances and to tell us how to forge them. But once we got there, she began to have second thoughts about telling us, because of the oath the good dragons had taken.

It's all very complicated and doesn't have anything much to do with my story, but it sets the scene for you, so speak. While we were inside Huma's Tomb, Silvara cast a spell on everyone, except she missed me, because I was hiding under a shield. I went to get help for my friends, who were under her sleep spell, and I got sucked up inside the Silver Dragon Mountain. And it was there that I found Fizban, who was dead. Only he wasn't.

I brought him down, and he had a talk with Silvara. It was after that talk that she decided to tell everyone who she was really. And she led Theros Ironfeld to the pool of dragonmetal that would be used to forge the lances. Only that comes later. Where I'm starting now is the part right after Fizban had the talk with Silvara. He'd decided that he had to leave.

"Good-bye, good-bye," Fizban told us. We were all inside Huma's Tomb, in the Silver Dragon Mountain. "Nice seeing you again. I'm a bit miffed about the chicken feathers"—(I could explain that part but it would take too long. Astinus has it written down in his Chronicles[2].)—"but no hard feelings."

Then Fizban glared at me.

"Are you coming?" he demanded. "I haven't got all night."

The chance to travel with a wizard! Especially a dead wizard! I couldn't pass it up. (Though I guess he wasn't really dead but none of us were sure of that at the time, especially Fizban.)

"Coming? With you!" I cried.

I was all excited and would have left right then and there, but it occurred to me that if I left, who would look out for everyone else in the group? (If I had known then that Silvara was really a silver dragon, I wouldn't have felt so bad, but I didn't.) I had no idea what sort of trouble my friends would get into without me. Especially Flint, my best friend, the dwarf.

Flint was truly a wonderful person and had many good qualities, but—since I have to be honest—I thought he lacked a bit in the common-sense line. He was constantly getting into trouble and it was me who was always having to drag him out.

But Fizban promised me that Flint and the rest of my friends would be fine without me and that we'd see them again in Famine Time, which was coming up soon. So I grabbed my pack and my pouches and off Fizban and I went together on an adventure.

An adventure that I never told anyone about until now.

THE STORY I NEVER TOLD

"Where are we going?" I asked Fizban, after we'd left Huma's Tomb far, far behind us.

The wizard was moving in a tremendous hurry, huffing and puffing and stomping down the trail, his arms flying, his hat pulled low over his forehead, his staff thumping the ground.

---

[2]*Dragons of Autumn Twilight*, Dragonlance Chronicles, Volume 1.

"I don't know," he said fiercely, and walked faster than ever.

This struck me as a bit odd. I mean, I've set off on journeys to places that I didn't know precisely where I was going but I never rushed to get there. I took my time. Enjoyed the scenery. Which is maybe why we were traveling so fast, because at that point there wasn't much scenery to enjoy. We hadn't gone very far when—smack—we walked right into Foghaven Vale.

I suppose you're wondering about that *smack* sound. Maybe you think *squish* might be more appropriate for talking about walking into fog. Or perhaps *whoosh*. But I thought "smack" at the time because that's what it felt like. Smack into a gray-white wall of fog. It was thick. Extremely thick. I know because I held my hand up to my face and walked right into it myself. I wondered if the fog had thickened up on purpose in our honor.

"Drat!" said Fizban, waving his arms. "Get out of my way! Can't see a confounded thing. What's the meaning of this? No respect for the aged! Absolutely none at all."

He stood there waving his arms and shouting at the fog. I watched a while as best I could for not being able to see him all that well. But it seemed to me that the more he shouted the thicker the fog got—sort of an "I'll Show You, Old Man!" type of reaction. And my topknot was soaking wet and dripping water down the back of my shirt, and my shoes were slowly filling up with oozing muck—all of which was very entertaining for a while, but soon lost a lot of its charm.

"Fizban," I said, going up to tug on his sleeve.

I guess I startled him, coming up on him suddenly out of the fog like that.

At any rate, he apologized very handsomely for hitting me on the nose with his staff and helped pick me up out of the muck and patted my head until it quit ringing. And we thought at first my nose was broken, then decided it wasn't and when the bleeding stopped, we started on our way again.

We walked and we walked. Finally, Fizban said he thought the fog had let up considerably. The result, he said, of a marvelous spell he'd cast on it. I didn't think it was polite to contradict him and besides I could almost sort of see the grass under my feet if I bent down and looked for it, so I figured he must be right. But we slowed our pace quite a bit, especially after Fizban walked *blam* into the tree.

It was either right before or right after he set the tree on fire that we came to Huma's Tomb.

It was daylight now. (We'd spent the night getting here.) The fog lifted just enough for us to see where we were, which I thought was quite sneaky of the fog. Almost like it was laughing at us.

I must tell you I was somewhat disappointed to see Huma's Tomb again. Not that it isn't a wonderful place. It is. Huma's Tomb, for those who haven't made the pilgrimage there, is really a temple. It is rectangular in shape and made out of black rock that Flint called obsidian. The outside is carved all over with knights fighting dragons and it is a very solemn and reverent place.

Inside is Huma's bier where they laid his body to rest. And his shield and sword are still there, but his body isn't. The Tomb is sad because it makes you think about your life and how you wish you'd done things better. But it's a good kind of sad because you realize that there's still the rest of your life for you to change and make better.

That was how I felt when I *first* saw Huma's Tomb, but now maybe all the fog was making it look different. All I felt now was the kind of sad that doesn't make you feel good inside.

"Ah, ha!" Fizban shouted. "I know where I am."

"Huma's Tomb," I said.

"No!" He was thunderstruck. "Didn't we just leave here?"

"Yes. We must have been walking in circles. Maybe I'll go say good-bye to Flint, while I'm here," I said, and started to climb the stairs.

"No, no," Fizban said quickly, grabbing hold of me. "They're not there. All gone inside the Silver Dragon Mountain. Silvara's taken them to the magical pool of dragonmetal, used to forge the magical dragonlances. Come along. We have other fish to fry."

Well, I had to admit that the temple did look dark and

deserted now. And fried fish sounded good. So we set out.

We hadn't taken two steps before the fog came back, only this time it was mixed with smoke from the smoldering tree and I couldn't see the grass beneath my feet. I couldn't see my feet.

We walked and walked and walked and stopped and rested and ate dinner. We began to walk again and Fizban told me what a marvelous tracker he was, much better than Riverwind, and how he (Fizban) never ever got lost and how he always kept the wind on his right cheek so moss wouldn't grow on his north side. And then we came to Huma's Tomb. The second time.

"Ah! ha!" cried Fizban, charging out of the fog, and stubbed his toe on the stairs leading up to the temple.

When he saw where we were (for the second time), he shouted. "You again!" He scowled and shook his fist at the temple. And he kicked the stairs with the same toe he used to bump into them.

Fizban hopped around on one foot and yelled at the stairs, which was fun to watch for a while, but must have got pretty boring later on because the next thing I knew I was asleep.

What I mean to say is that the next thing I knew I was awake, but I must have fallen asleep in order to have woken up, mustn't I? I think I slept for a considerable length of time because I was all stiff and sore from lying on the slick, black stairs, and I was wet and cold and hungry.

"Fizban?" I said.

He wasn't there.

I felt sort of creepy, maybe because the Tomb was sort of creepy. My stomach twisted up, because I was afraid something might have happened to Fizban and, to be honest, this fog was starting to make my skin shiver, as Flint would say. Then I heard him snore. (Fizban.) He was sleeping on the grass with his injured foot propped up on a step and his hat over it (his foot).

I was very glad to see him and guess I startled him, waking him up suddenly with a yell like that. He apologized for letting off the fireball, and we were able to have a hot breakfast, due to the fact that another tree was burning.

He said that my eyebrows would grow back any day.

After breakfast, off we went again—Fizban with his foot wrapped up in a dish towel I'd found in my pouch. We walked around in the fog for I forget how long except I remember eating again and sleeping again and then we came to Huma's Tomb.

For the third time.

I don't mean to offend any knights when I say this, but I was beginning to be a little bored at the sight of it.

"This does it," Fizban muttered, and he started to roll up his sleeves. "Follow us, will you!"

"I don't think it's following us," I pointed out, and I'm afraid I spoke pretty sharp. "I think we're following it!"

"No!" Fizban looked amazed. Then confused. "Do you think so?"

"Yes," I snapped, wondering if my eyebrows would truly grow back and wishing I could see what I looked like without them. In fact, I was wishing I could see anything, besides Huma's Tomb and fog and burning trees.

"Then you don't think I should let loose with a real rip-snorter of a spell and blow it sky high?" he asked, in a kind of wistful tone.

"I don't think the knights would like that," I pointed out testily. "And you know how they can be."

(No offense. I don't mean all knights. Just some knights.)

"Besides," I continued, "Huma might come back and be really put out to find that someone blew up his Tomb while he was gone. And I can't say that I'd blame him."

"No, I suppose not," said Fizban, unhappily. "Maybe I could just blow up the stairs?"

"How will Huma get up to the door if the stairs are gone?"

"I see your point." Fizban heaved a sigh.

"You know, Fizban," I said sternly (I decided I had to be stern), "this has been a lot of fun. Really. It's not everyday I get my nose almost broken and both my eyebrows singed off and watch you set fire to two trees and see Huma's Tomb in the fog three times (four for me) but I think we've done just about everything exciting there is to do around here. It's time to move on. *Wherever it is we're going.*" I said the last words in an extra firm tone, hoping he'd take the hint.

Fizban muttered around awhile and did a few magic tricks that were kind of interesting, like shooting off some white and purple stars. He asked me how I liked that one and would I like to see some more?

I said no.

Then he got real flustered and took off his hat and took off the dish towel from around his hurt foot and put his hat back on, only he put it on his foot and put the dish towel over his head.

Suddenly he said, "I've got it! A spell—"

"Wait! Not yet!" I cried, jumping up and covering my face with my hands.

"A spell that will take us right where we want to go!" he shouted triumphantly. "Here, grab hold of my sleeve. Hang on tight, there's a good lad. Keep your hand out of my pouch. Wizard-stuff in there. And some rather fine liverwurst. Ready? Here we go!"

Well, I thought. Finally! At last!

I grabbed hold of Fizban's sleeve and he spoke some words that sounded like spiders crawling around inside my head. Everything went blurry and I heard a sound like wind blowing in my ears.

And when I opened my eyes, there we were.

Inside Huma's Tomb.

CHAPTER FOUR

"Fizban!" I said and this time I was stern *and* firm. "Did you mean to do that?"

"Yes," he said, twisting the dish towel in his hands and sneaking peeks around the room. "Got us right where I wanted. Uh, do you happen to know where that might be? Just testing you," he added quickly.

I'm afraid I shouted. "We're in Huma's Tomb!"

"Oh, dear," he said.

Well, by this time I'd had enough. "I hate to hurt your feelings, Fizban, but I don't think you're much of a wizard and—"

I didn't finish that because Fizban's eyebrows (*he* still had eyebrows) came together and got real bristly and stuck out over his nose and he looked suddenly very fierce and angry. I was afraid he was angry at me, but as it turned out, he wasn't.

"Enchantment!" he cried.

"What?" I didn't know what we were talking about.

"Enchantment!" he said again. "We're under an enchantment! We're cursed!"

"How marvelou—I m-mean, how awful," I stammered, seeing his fierce look grow even fiercer. "Who . . . who would put us under an enchantment?" I asked in very polite tones.

"Who else? The Dark Queen." He glared at me and stomped around the tomb. "She knows I'm after the dragon orb and she's trying to thwart me. I'll fix her. I'll . . . (mumble, mumble, mumble)."

I put the mumbles in because I really couldn't make out what Fizban said he was going to do to the Dark Queen if he ever got his hands on her. Or if I did at the time I can't remember now.

"Well," I said briskly, hopping up. "Now that we know we're cursed and under an enchantment, let's leave and get on with our journey."

Fizban bristled at me. "That's just it, you see. We can't leave."

"Can't leave?!" My heart sank down to the hole in my sock. "You mean . . . we're . . . "

"Trapped," said Fizban gloomily. "Doomed forever to wander in the fog and always come back here, where we started. Huma's Tomb."

"Forever!"

My heart oozed right out of the hole in my sock and ended up in my shoe. A snuffle rose up in my throat and choked me. "I'm very glad you're not dead anymore, Fizban, and I'm truly quite fond of you, but I don't want to be trapped in a cursed enchantment in a tomb with you forever! Why, what would Flint do without me? And Tanis? I'm his advisor, you know. You have to get us out of here!"

I'm afraid I went a bit wild, just because I was so tired of being in this Tomb and of the fog and everything. I grabbed hold of Fizban's robes and the snuffle turned into a whimper, then into a wail, and I lost control of myself for a fairly good stretch of time.

Fizban patted my topknot and let me cry into his robes, then he slapped me on the back and said to brace myself and keep a stiff upper torso. He was going to offer me his handkerchief to wipe my nose only he couldn't find it. Fortunately, I found it and so I used it and felt some better. Funny, the way getting those snuffles and wails out of your insides makes you feel better.

And I was so much better that I had an Idea.

"Fizban," I said, after giving the matter thought, "if the Dark Queen has put us under an enchantment, it must mean she's watching us—right?"

"You betcha!" he said, and he looked around quite fierce again.

It occurred to me then that maybe I shouldn't talk so loud because if she was watching us she might be listening to us, too. So I crept over to Fizban and, once I found his ear under all that hair, I whispered into it, "If she's watching the front door, why don't we sneak out the back?"

He looked sort of stunned, then he blinked and said, "By George! I have an idea. If the Dark Queen's watching the front door, why don't we sneak out the back?!"

"That was my idea," I pointed out.

"Don't be a ninny!" he said, miffed. "Are you a great and powerful wizard?"

"No," I was forced to admit.

"Then it was my idea," he said. "Hang on."

He grabbed hold of my topknot and I grabbed hold of his robes and he spoke some more of those spider-leg words. The Tomb got blurry and wind rushed around me and I was dizzy and turned every which way. All in all quite a delightful sensation. And then everything settled down and I heard Fizban say "oops" in a kind of way that I didn't like much, having said it myself a time or two on occasion and knowing what it meant.

I opened my eyes kind of cautiously, thinking that if I saw Huma's Tomb again I'd be upset. But I didn't. See Huma's

Tomb, that is. I opened my eyes wide and my mouth opened at the same time to ask where we were, when suddenly a hand clapped over my mouth.

"Shush!" said Fizban.

His whiskers tickled my cheek, and, before I knew what was happening, he'd lifted me clean off my feet and was dragging me backward into a really dark part of wherever it was we were.

"Mish, muckgup, whursh blimp," I said. What I meant to say was, "But, Fizban, that's Flint!" only it sounded like the other since he had his hand over my mouth.

"Quiet! We're not supposed to be here!" he hissed back at me, and he looked incredibly angry and not at all pleased with either me or himself and probably the Dark Queen, too. So I kept quiet.

Though of course what I really wanted to do was to shout, "Hey, Flint! It's me, Tas!" 'cause I knew the dwarf'd be really glad to see me.

He always is, though he pretends he isn't, because that's the way dwarves are. And Theros Ironfeld was with Flint, too, and I knew Theros would be glad to see me because just a while back up in Huma's Tomb he'd saved me from falling into a hole and ending up on the other side of the world.

With Fizban's hand clapped tight over my mouth and his whiskers tickling me I didn't have much else to do except look. So I looked. We were in what appeared to be a blacksmith's shop, only it was the largest and finest blacksmith's shop I'd ever seen in my entire life. And I guessed then that this blacksmith's shop must be making Theros happy because he is the finest blacksmith I'd ever known in my life. He and this shop just seemed to go together.

There was an anvil bigger than me and a forge with a bellows and a lake of cold water that you put the hot metal in to hear it hiss and see steam rise up and when the metal comes out it's not hot anymore.

But the most wonderful thing was a huge pool of what looked like molten silver that gave off a most beautiful light. It reminded me of Silvara's hair in the light of Solinari, the silver moon. That silver light was the only light in the forge and it seemed to coat everything with silver, even Flint's beard. Theros's black skin shone like he'd been standing out in the moonlight. And his silver arm gleamed and glistened and it was so lovely and wonderful that I felt a snuffle come up on me again.

"Shhhh!" Fizban whispered.

I couldn't have talked now anyhow, what with the snuffle, and he knew that, I guess, because he let loose of me. We stood quietly in the shadows and watched. All the time Fizban was muttering that we shouldn't be here.

While Fizban muttered to himself—trying to remember his spell, I suppose—I fought the snuffle and listened to Flint and Theros talk. For awhile I was too busy with the snuffle to pay much attention to what they were saying, but then it occurred to me that neither of them looked very happy, which was odd, considering that they were down here with this wonderful pool of silver. I listened to find out why.

"This is what I'm to use to forge the dragonlances?" asked Theros, and he stared into the pool with a very a grim expression.

"Yes, lad," said Flint, and he sighed.

"Dragonmetal. Magical silver."

Theros bent down and picked up something from a pile of somethings lying on the floor. It was a lance, and it gleamed in the light of the silver pool, and it certainly seemed very fine to me. He held it in his hand and it was well-balanced and the light glinted off its sharp spearlike point. Suddenly, Theros's big arm muscle bunched up and he threw the lance, hard as he could, straight in to the rock wall.

The lance broke.

"You didn't see that!" Fizban gasped and clapped his hand over my eyes, but, of course, it was too late, which he must have realized, cause he let me look again after I started squirming.

"There's your magical dragonlances!" Theros snarled, glaring at the pieces of the shattered lance.

He squatted down at the edge of the pool, his big arms hanging between his knees and his head bowed low. He

looked defeated, finished, beaten. I had never seen Theros
look that way, not even when the draconians had cut off his
arm and he was near dying.

"Steel," he said. "Fair quality. Certainly not the best.
Look how it shattered. Plain ordinary steel." Standing up,
he walked over and picked up the pieces of the broken
lance. "I'll have to tell the others, of course."

Flint looked at him and wiped his hand over his face and
beard, the way he does when he's thinking pretty hard and
pretty deep. Going over to Theros, the dwarf laid a hand on
the big man's arm.

"No, you won't, lad," he said. "You'll go on making more
of these. You'll use your silver arm and say they're made of
dragonmetal. And you won't say a word about the steel."

Theros stared at him, startled. Then he frowned. "I can't
lie to them."

"You won't be," Flint said, and he had That Look on his
face.

I knew That Look. It was like a mountain had plunked
down right in the middle of the path you want to walk on.
(I heard that actually happened, during the Cataclysm.)
You can say what you like to it, but the mountain won't
move. And when the mountain won't move it has That
Look on its face.

I said to Theros, under my breath, *You might as well give
up right now, because you'll never budge him.*

Flint was going on. "We'll take these lances to the knights
and we'll say, 'Here, lads, Paladine has sent these to you. He
hasn't forgotten you. He's fighting here with you, right
now.' And the faith will fill their hearts and that faith will
flow into their arms and into their bright eyes and when
they throw those lances it will be the strength of that faith
and the power of their arms and the vision of their bright
eyes that will guide these lances into the evil dragons' dark
hearts. And who's to say that this isn't magic, perhaps the
greatest magic of all?"

"But it isn't true," argued Theros, glowering.

"And how do you know what is true and what is not?"
Flint demanded, glowering right back, though he only came
up to Theros's waist. "Here you stand, alive and well with

the silver arm, when you should—if you want truth—be lying dead and moldering in the ground with worms eating you.

"And here we are, inside the Silver Dragon Mountain, brought here by that beautiful creature who gave up everything, even love itself, for the sake of us all, and broke her oath and doomed herself, when—if you want truth—she could have magicked us all away and never said a word.

"Now I'll tell you what we're going to do, Theros Ironfeld," Flint went on, the stubborn look on his face getting stubborner. He rolled up his sleeves and hitched up his pants. "We're going to get to work, you and I. And we're going to make these dragonlances. And we're going to let the truth each man and woman carries in his or her own heart be the magic that guides it."

Well, at this point Fizban got the snuffles. He was dabbing his eyes with the end of his beard. I guess I wasn't much better. We both stood there and snuffled together and shared a handkerchief that I happened to have with me and by the time we were over the snuffles Flint and Theros had gone away.

"What do we do now?" I asked. "Do we go help Flint and Theros?"

"A lot of help you'd be," Fizban snapped. "Probably fall into the dragonmetal well. No," he said, after chewing on the end of his beard, which must have been quite salty from his tears, "I think I know how to break the enchantment."

"You do?" I was truly glad.

"We've got to grab a couple of those lances." He pointed to the pile of lances lying by the pool.

"But those don't work," I reminded him. "Theros said they don't."

"What do you use these for?" Fizban demanded, grabbing hold of my ears and giving them a tug that brought water to my eyes. "Doorknobs? Weren't you listening?"

Well, of course, I had been. I'd heard every word and if some of it wasn't exactly clear that wasn't my fault and I don't know why he had to go and pull my ears nearly off my head, especially after he'd already almost broken my nose and burned off my eyebrows.

"If you ask Theros nicely I'm sure he'd lend you a couple of lances," I said, rubbing my ears and trying not to be mad. After all, Fizban had gotten me caught in an enchantment and, while it was a dull and boring enchantment, it was an enchantment nonetheless and I felt I owed him something. "Especially since they don't work."

"No, no!" Fizban muttered, and his eyes sparkled in quite a cunning and sneaky manner. "We won't bother Theros. He's over firing up the forge. You and I'll just sneak in and borrow a lance or two. He'll never notice."

Now if there's one thing I'm good at, it's borrowing. You won't find a better borrower than me, except maybe Uncle Trapspringer, but that's another story.

Fizban and I sneaked out of the shadows where we'd been hiding and crept quiet as mice over to where the lances lay by the shining pool of silver. Once I got close to the lances, I had to admit they were beautiful things, whether they worked or not. I wanted one very badly and I was glad Fizban had decided he wanted one, too. I was a bit uncertain, at first, as to how we were going to make off with them, for they were long and big and heavy, and I couldn't very well stuff one in my pouch.

"I'll carry the butt-end," said Fizban, "and you carry the spear-end. Balance it on our shoulders, like this."

I saw that would work, though I couldn't quite balance my end on my shoulders, since Fizban's shoulders are higher than mine. But I held my end up in the air and Fizban managed the butt-end. We lifted up two of the lances and ran off with them.

And while we were running, Fizban said some more of those spider-foot words and the next thing I knew I was running straight into . . .

You guessed it. Huma's Tomb.

CHAPTER FIVE

"Oh, now, really!" I began, quite put out.

But I didn't get the rest of my sentence finished, which was probably just as well, since it would have most likely made Fizban angry and he might have sent my topknot to join my eyebrows.

The reason I didn't get the rest of my sentence finished was that we weren't alone in Huma's Tomb anymore. A knight was there. A knight in full battle armor and he was kneeling beside the bier in the silver moonlight, with tears rolling down his cheeks.

"Thank you, Paladine!" he was saying, over and over again in a tone that made me feel I'd like to go off somewhere and be very, very quiet for a long time.

But the lances were growing extremely heavy, and I'm afraid I dropped my end, which caused Fizban to overbalance and nearly tumble over backward, and he dropped his butt-end. Which meant we both dropped the middles. The lances fell to the stone floor with quite a remarkable-sounding clatter.

The knight nearly leapt out of his armor. Jumping to his feet, he drew his sword and whipped right around and glared at us.

He had taken off his helmet to pray. He was older, about thirty, I guess. His hair was dark red and he wore it in two long braids. His eyes were green as the vallenwood leaves in Solace, where I live when I'm not out adventuring or residing in jails. Only his eyes didn't look green as leaves just at the moment. They looked hard and cold as the ice in Ice Wall.

I don't know what the knight expected—maybe a dragon or at least a draconian, or possibly a goblin or two. What he obviously didn't expect was Fizban and me.

The knight's face, when he saw us, slipped from fierce into muddled and puzzled, but it hardened again right off.

"A wizard," he said in the same tone of voice he might have said "ogre dung." "And a kender." (I won't tell you what *that* sounded like!) "What are you two doing here? How dare you defile this sacred place?"

He was getting himself all worked up and waving his sword around in a way that was quite careless and might have hurt somebody—namely me, because I was suddenly closest, Fizban having reached out and pulled me in front of him.

"Now wait just a minute, Sir Knight," said Fizban, quite bravely, I thought, especially since he was using me for a shield, and my small body wouldn't have done much to stop that knight's sharp sword, "we're not defiling anything. We came in here to pay our respects, same as you, only Huma was out. Not in, you see," the wizard added, gesturing vaguely to the empty bier. "So we . . . er . . . decided to wait a bit, give him a chance to come back."

The knight stared at us for quite a long time. He would have stroked his moustaches, I thought, like Sturm did when he was thinking hard, except that this knight didn't have any moustaches, yet. Only the beginnings of some, like he was just starting to grow them out. He lowered the sword a little, little bit.

"You are a white-robed wizard?" he asked.

Fizban held out his sleeve. "White as snow." Actually it wasn't, having been draggled through the mud and spotted with blood from my nose and slobber from both of us and ashes from the burning tree and some soot we'd picked up in the dragonlance forge.

Fizban's robes didn't impress the knight. He raised his sword again and his face was extremely grim. "I don't trust wizards of any color robe. And I don't like kender."

Well, I was just about to express my opinion of knights, which I thought might help him—(Tanis says we should come to know our own faults, to be better persons)—but Fizban grabbed hold of my topknot and lifted me up like you pick up a rabbit by the ears and shuffled me off to one side.

"How did you find this sacred place, Sir Knight?" Fizban asked, and I saw his eyes go cunning and shrewd like they do sometimes when they're not vague and confused.

"I was led here by the light of the fire of two burning trees and a celestial shower of white and purple stars . . ." The knight's voice faded to an awed breath.

Fizban smirked at me. "And you said I wasn't much of a wizard!"

The knight appeared dazed. He lowered his sword again. "You did that? You led me here purposefully?"

"Well, of course," said Fizban. "Knew you were coming

all along."

I was about to explain to the knight about my singed eyebrows and even offer to show him where they'd been, in case he was interested, but Fizban accidently trod on my foot at that moment.

You wouldn't think one old man, especially one who looks as frail and skinny as Fizban, could be so heavy, but he was. And I couldn't make him understand that he was standing on my foot—he kept shushing me and telling me to have respect for my elders and that kender should be seen and not heard and maybe not even seen—and by the time I managed to pull my foot out from under his, he and the knight were talking about something else.

"Tell me exactly what happened," Fizban was saying. "Very important, from a wizard's standpoint."

"You might tell us your name, too," I suggested.

"I am Owen of the House of Glendower," said the knight but that was all he would tell us. He was still holding his sword and still staring at Fizban as if trying to decide whether to clap him heartily on the shoulder or clout him a good one on the headbone.

"I'm Tasslehoff Burrfoot," I said, holding out my hand politely, "and I have a house myself, in Solace, only it doesn't have a name. And maybe I don't even have a house anymore now," I added, remembering what I'd seen of Solace the last time I was there and growing kind of sad at the thought.

The knight raised his eyebrows (*he* had eyebrows) and was staring at me now.

"But that's all right," I said, thinking Owen Glendower might be feeling sorry for me because my house had most likely been burned down by dragons. "Tika said I could come live with her, if I ever see Tika again," I added, and that made me sadder still, because I hadn't seen Tika in a long time either.

"You came all the way from Solace?" asked Owen Glendower, and he sounded no end astonished.

"Some of us came a lot farther than that," Fizban said solemnly, only the knight didn't hear him, which was probably just as well.

"Yes, we came from Solace," I explained. "A large group of us, only some of us aren't with us anymore. There was Tanis and Raistlin and Caramon and Tika, only we lost them in Tarsis, and that left Sturm and Elistan and Derek Crownguard and they went to—"

"Derek Crownguard!" Owen gasped. "You traveled with Derek Crownguard?"

"I'm not finished," I said, eyeing him sternly. "And it isn't polite to interrupt. Tanis says so. Inside there's Laurana and Flint and Theros—"

"But it's Sir Derek I'm searching for," said the knight, completely ignoring me. (I'm not certain but I believe that ignoring people is against their knightly code, though Sturm often ignored me, now that I come to think of it. But Tanis says that if ignoring kender isn't in the Measure it should be.)

"I'm a courier from Lord Gunthar and I've been sent to find Sir Derek—"

"You've just missed him," I said, and tried to look sad about it, though I wasn't, not in the least. "He went off with the dragon orb."

"The what?" Owen stared at me.

"Dragon *herb*," said Fizban, giving me a tug on the topknot that made tears come to my eyes. "Similar to wolfbane. Only different."

Well, I had no idea what he was talking about, but it wasn't important anyway and I could see Owen was getting a bit impatient. So I went on.

"I don't know why you were looking for him. Derek Crownguard is *not* a nice person," I informed him.

"Describe him to me," said Owen.

"Don't you know him?" I asked, amazed. "How can you find him if you don't know him?"

"Just describe him, kender," growled the knight.

"Tasslehoff Burrfoot," I reminded him. Obviously he'd forgotten. "Well, Derek's mad at most everyone all the time and he's not at all polite and I don't think he has much common sense either, if you want my opinion."

Well, as it turned out, Owen didn't want my opinion; what he wanted was a description of what Derek looked like, not what he acted like, so I gave him that, too. My description seemed to please him, only it was hard to tell, because he was so confused.

"Yes, that's Derek Crownguard," he said. "You've described him perfectly. You must be telling the truth."

He thought another moment, then looked at Huma's bier, to see if it might help, and it looked very peaceful and beautiful in the moonlight. (If you are wondering why there was moonlight when there should have been fog, keep listening and I'll explain later on when the moonlight has its proper turn.)

"I was sent to find Derek Crownguard," Owen said, talking slowly, as if he might decide to stop any moment and take back everything he'd just said. "I have . . . dispatches for him. But I lost his trail, and I prayed to Paladine to help me find it again. That night, in a dream, I was told to seek Huma's resting place. I didn't know where it was—no one knows. But I was told that if I studied Solinari, on a cloudless night, I would see a map on the moon's surface. The next night, I did so. I saw what appeared to be a map of my homeland, Southern Ergoth. I have walked these mountains and valleys thirty years, yet I never knew this place existed. I followed Solinari's guidance, but then fog overtook me. I could no longer see the moon.

"The path led into a valley inside the mountains and vanished. I could not find my way out and have wandered about for days, perhaps. I'm not sure how long: time has lost all meaning to me. Then I saw a fire, burning in the distance. I followed it, thinking that I should at least find someone to guide me back to the trail. Then it went out and I was lost again. Then another fire and then clouds of purple stars and then I discovered this holy place, Huma's Tomb. And you."

Looking at us, he shook his head and I could tell we weren't exactly what he'd been praying to Paladine to find.

"But, if my Lord Crownguard left with the dragon orb, what are you two doing here?" he asked, after he'd stared at us longer than was really polite. "Why did you stay behind?"

"We're under an enchantment," I said. "Isn't it exciting?

317

Well, to be honest, not all that exciting. Actually it's been pretty boring, not to mention cold and icky and damp. The Dark Queen has put us under a spell, you see. And we can't get out of here because every time we leave we keep coming back. And we have to get out of here because we're on a Very Important Mission to . . . to . . . "

I stopped because I wasn't quite sure what our Important Mission was.

"Lord Gunthar. Important mission to Lord Gunthar," said Fizban. "Must see him right away. Most urgent."

"You're under black enchantment?" Owen pulled back from us both, raised his sword, and laid his hand on Huma's bier.

"Well, now. As to the enchantment part." Fizban scratched his head. "It could be that I exagger—"

"Oh, yes!" I averred. (I'm fond of that word, averred.) "The Dark Queen is most dreadfully afraid of Fizban, here. He's a great and powerful wizard."

Fizban blushed and took off his hat and twirled it around in his hands. "I do my best," he said modestly.

"Why did you send for me?" Owen asked, and he still seemed suspicious.

Fizban appeared somewhat at a loss. "Well, I . . . you see . . . that is . . ."

"I know! I know!" I cried, standing on my tiptoes and raising my hand in the air. Of course, anyone who's ever been a child knows the reason, but maybe knights were never children or maybe he didn't have a mother to tell him stories like my mother told me. "Only a true knight can break our enchantment!"

Fizban breathed a deep sigh. Taking off his hat, he mopped his forehead with his sleeve. "Yes, that's it. True knight. Rescue damsels in distress."

"We're not damsels," I said, thinking I should be truthful about all this, "but we are in considerable distress, so I should think that would count. Don't you?"

Owen stood beside Huma's bier, eyeing us, and he still seemed confused and suspicious—probably because we weren't damsels. I mean, I could see how that would be disappointing, but it wasn't our fault.

"And there's these dragonlances," I said, waving my hand at them, where we'd dropped them, on the floor at the back of the temple. "Only they don't—"

"Dragonlances!" Owen breathed, and suddenly, it was like Solinari had dropped right down out of the sky and burst on top of the knight. His armor was bright, bright silver and he was so handsome and strong-looking that I could only stare at him in wonder. "You have found the dragonlances!"

He thrust his sword in its sheath and hurried over to where I'd pointed. At the sight of the two lances, lying on the floor in the moonlight, Owen cried out loudly in words I didn't understand and fell down on his knees.

Then he said, in words I could understand, "Praise be to Paladine. These are dragonlances, true ones, such as Huma used to fight the Dark Queen. I saw the images, carved on the outside of the Temple."

He rose to his feet and came to stand before us. "Now I know that you speak the truth. You plan to take these lances to Lord Gunthar, don't you, Sir Wizard? And the Dark Queen has laid an enchantment on you to prevent it."

Fizban swelled up with pride at being called Sir Wizard and I saw him look at me to make certain I noticed, which I did. I was very happy for him because generally he gets called other things that aren't so polite.

"Why, uh, yes," he said, puffing and preening and smoothing his beard. "Yes, that's the ticket. Take the lances to Lord Gunthar. We should set out right away."

"But the lances don't—" I began.

"—shine," said Fizban. "Lances don't shine."

Well, before I could mention that the lances not only didn't shine but didn't work either, Fizban had upended one of my pouches, causing my most precious and valuable possessions in the whole world to spill out all over the floor. By the time I had everything picked up and resorted and examined and wondered where I'd come by a few things that I didn't recognize, Fizban and Owen were ready to leave.

Owen Glendower was holding the lances in his hand— did I mention that he was very strong? I mean, it took Fizban and me both to carry them, and here this knight was holding two of them without any trouble at all.

I asked Fizban about this but he said it was reverence and thankfulness that gave the knight unusual strength.

"Reverence and thankfulness. But we'll see about that as we go along," muttered Fizban, and I thought he looked cunning again.

Owen Glendower said good-bye to Huma and was very unhappy over leaving the Tomb.

"Don't worry," I told him. "If you haven't broken the enchantment, we'll be back."

"Oh, he's broken it, all right," said Fizban, and we all trooped out the door and into the moonlight.

And then I realized that it *was* moonlight. (I told you I'd tell you all this when it came its proper turn in the story, and this is it.) The fog was gone and we could see the Guardians and the Bridge of Passage and behind us the Silver Dragon Mountain. And Owen was so fascinated that we almost couldn't drag him off. But Fizban reminded him that the dragonlances were the "salvation of the people" and this got the knight moving.

He'd had a horse, but somehow or other he'd lost it. He said that when we reached civilized lands we'd find other horses to ride and that would get us to Lord Gunthar's faster.

I considered telling him that Fizban could get us all to Lord Gunthar's much, much faster, if he wanted to cast one of his spells on us. Then I thought that with Fizban's spells, all things considered (especially my eyebrows), we might end up in the middle of the Hot Springs. And maybe Fizban thought the same thing because he didn't mention his spells either. So we set off, with Owen Glendower carrying the dragonlances and me carrying my pouches and Fizban carrying a tune, sort of.

And, praise be to any and all of the gods, we did *not* go back to Huma's Tomb!

CHAPTER SIX

Let me point out right here and now that it wasn't my fault we ended up in the Wasted Lands. I had a map and I told Fizban and Sir Owen we were heading the wrong direction. (It was a perfectly good map: if Tarsis By the Sea chose to get itself landlocked, I don't see how anyone can blame me for it!)

It was night. We were wandering around in the mountains when we came to a pass. I told Fizban that we should go left. That would lead us out of the mountains and take us to Sancrist. But Fizban scoffed and said my map was outdated (outdated!) and Owen Glendower vowed he'd shave his moustaches before he ever took advice from a kender. (Which seemed a fairly safe vow to me, considering that he didn't have all that much yet to shave.) This after he'd admitted that he'd gotten himself all turned around in Foghaven Vale and wasn't real sure where he was now!

He said that we should wait until morning and that when the sun came up we'd know what direction to take, but Fizban said he had a feeling in his bones that the sun wouldn't come up in the morning, and, by gosh, he was right. The sun didn't come up or if it did we missed it what with the snow and all.

So we turned right when we should have turned left and came to the Wasted Lands and the adventure, but this isn't the adventure's proper place in the story yet, so it'll have to wait its turn.

I could tell you about the days we spent traveling through the mountains in the snow but, to be honest, that part wasn't very exciting . . . if you don't count Fizban accidentally melting our snow shelter down around us one night while he was trying to read his spell book by the light of a magical candle that turned out to be more magic than candle. (I got to keep the wick)

One nice thing about that time was traveling with Owen Glendower. I was getting to like the knight a lot. He said he didn't even mind being around me much (which may not sound very gracious to you but is a lot more than I expected).

"Probably," he said, "because I don't have many valuables to lose."

I didn't quite understand that last part, especially since he kept losing what he said was his most treasured possession: a very beautiful little painting of his wife and son that he carried in a small leather pouch over his left breast underneath his armor.

He discovered it missing one night when we were relaxing in our snow shelter (the one Fizban melted) and we all hunted for the painting most diligently. It was right when Owen said he was going to turn me upside down and maybe inside out if I didn't give it back to him that Fizban happened to find the painting inside my shirt pocket.

"See there," I said, handing it back to Owen, "I kept it from getting wet."

He wasn't the least appreciative. For a minute I thought he was going to throw me out off the side of the mountain and for a minute he thought he was going to, too. But after a while he calmed down, especially when I told him that the lady inside the painting was one of the prettiest ladies I'd ever seen, next to Tika and Laurana and a certain kender maid I know whose name is engraved forever on my heart. (If I could remember it, I'd tell you, but I guess that it isn't important right now.)

Owen sighed and said he was sorry he shouted at me and he wasn't really going to slit my pockets or maybe my gut, whichever came first. It was only that he missed his wife and son so much and was so very worried about them because he was here in the snow with us and the dragonlances, and his wife and son were back in their house alone without him.

Well, I understood that, even if I didn't have a wife or a son or a house anymore. We made an agreement then and there. If I found the painting I was to give it right back to him immediately.

And it was amazing to me that he lost that painting as often as he did, considering how much it meant to him. But I didn't mention this to him, because I didn't want to hurt his feelings. As I said, I was beginning to like Owen Glendower.

"Life hasn't been easy for my lady wife," he told us one other night while we were thawing out after having spent the day trekking about lost in the snow. "From what you've told me about your friend Brightblade, you know how the knights have been persecuted and reviled. My family was driven from our ancestral home years ago, but it was a point of honor among us that someday we would return to claim it. Our holdings have passed from one bad owner to the next. The people in the village have suffered under their tyrannies and though they were the ones who drove us out, they have more than paid for that now.

"I worked as a mercenary, to keep body and soul alive, and to earn the money to buy back lawfully what had been stolen from us. For I would be honorable, though the thieves that took it were not.

"At last, I was able to save the necessary sum. I am ashamed to say that I was forced to keep my identity as a knight secret, lest the owners refuse to sell to me."

He touched his moustaches as he said this. They were coming out fairly well, now, and were dark red as his hair.

"As it was, the thieves made a good bargain, for the manor was crumbling around their ears. We have repaired it ourselves, for I could not afford to hire the work done. The villagers helped. They were glad to see a knight return, especially in these dangerous times.

"My wife and son toiled beside me, both doing far more than their share. My wife's hands are rough and cracked from breaking stone and mixing mortar, but to me their touch is as soft as if she wrapped them in kid gloves every night of her life. Now she stands guard while I am gone, she and my boy. I did not like to leave them, with evil abroad in the land, but my duty lay with the knights, as she herself reminded me. I pray Paladine watches over them and keeps them safe."

"He does," said Fizban, only he said it very, very softly, so softly that I almost didn't hear him. And I might not have if I hadn't felt a snuffle coming on and so was searching in his pouch for a handkerchief.

Owen could tell the most interesting stories about when he was a mercenary and he said I was as good a listener as his son, though I asked too many questions.

We went on like this and were really having a good time and so I guess I have to admit that I didn't really mind that we took the wrong way. We'd been wandering around lost for about four days when it quit snowing and the sun came back.

Owen looked at the sun and frowned and said it was on the wrong side of the mountains.

I tried to be helpful and cheer him up. "If Tarsis By the Sea could move itself away from the sea, maybe these mountains hopped around, too."

But Owen didn't think much of my suggestion. He only looked very worried and grim. We were in the Wasted Lands, he said, and the bay we could see below us (Did I mention it? There was a bay below us.) was called Morgash Bay, which meant Bay of Darkness and that, all in all, we were in a Bad Place and should leave immediately, before it Got Worse.

"This is all your fault!" Fizban yelled at me and stamped his foot on the snow. "You and that stupid map."

"No, it isn't my fault!" I retorted. (Another good word—retorted.) "And it isn't a stupid map."

"Yes, it is!" Fizban shouted and he snatched his hat off his head and threw it on the snow and began to stomp up and down on top of it. "Stupid! Stupid! Stupid!"

Right then, things Got Worse.

Fizban fell into a hole.

Now, a normal person would fall into a normal hole, maybe twist an ankle or tumble down on his nose. But no, not Fizban. Fizban fell into a Hole. Not only that but he took us into the Hole along with him, which I considered thoughtful of him, but which Owen didn't like at all.

One minute Fizban was hopping up and down in the snow calling me a doorknob of a kender (That wasn't original, by the way. Flint yells that at me all the time.) and the next the snow gave way beneath his feet. He reached out to save himself and grabbed hold of me and I felt the snow start to give way beneath my feet and I reached out to save myself and grabbed hold of Owen and the snow started to give way beneath his feet and before we knew it we were all falling and falling and falling.

It was the most remarkable fall, and quite exciting, what with the snow flying around us and cascading down on top of us. There was one extremely interesting moment when I thought we were going to all be skewered on the dragonlances that Owen had been carrying and hadn't had time to let go of before I grabbed him. But we weren't.

We hit bottom and the lances hit bottom and the snow that came down with us hit bottom. We lay there a little bit, catching our breath. (I left mine up top somewhere.) Then Owen picked himself up out of a snowbank and glared at Fizban.

"Are you all right?" he demanded gruffly.

"Nothing's broken, if that's what you mean," Fizban said in a sort of quavery-type voice. "But I seem to have lost my hat."

Owen said something about consigning Fizban's hat to perdition and then he pulled me out of a snowbank and stood me up on my feet and picked me up when I fell back down (my breath not having made it this far yet) and he asked me if I was all right.

I said yes and wasn't that thrilling and did Fizban think there was the possibility we could do that again. Owen said the really thrilling part was just about to begin because how in the name of the Abyss were we going to get out of here?

Well, about that time I took a good look at where we were and we were in what appeared to be a cave all made out of snow and ice and stuff. And the hole that we'd fallen through was a long, long, long way up above us.

"And so are our packs and the rope and the food," said Owen, staring up at the hole we'd made and frowning.

"But we don't need to worry," I said cheerfully. "Fizban's a very great and powerful wizard and he'll just fly us all back up there in a jiffy. Won't you, Fizban?"

"Not without my hat," he said stiffly. "I can't work magic without my hat."

Owen muttered something that I won't repeat here as it isn't very complimentary to Fizban and I'm sure Owen is ashamed now he said something like that. And he frowned and glowered, but it soon became obvious that we couldn't get out of that hole without magic of some sort.

I tried climbing up the sides of the cave walls, but I kept sliding back down and was having a lot of fun, though not getting much accomplished, when Owen made me stop after a whole great load of snow broke loose and fell on top of us. He said the whole mountain might collapse.

There was nothing left to do but look for Fizban's hat.

Owen had dug the dragonlances out of the snow and he said the hat might be near where they were. We looked, but it wasn't. And we dug all around where Fizban had fallen and the hat wasn't there either.

Fizban was getting very unhappy and starting to blubber.

"I've had that hat since it was a pup," he whimpered, sniffing and wiping his eyes on the end of his beard. "Best hat in the whole world. Prefer a fedora, but they're not in for wizards. Still—"

I was about to ask who was Fedora and what did she have to do with his hat when Owen said "Shush!" in the kind of voice that makes your blood go all tingly and your stomach do funny things.

We shushed and stared at him.

"I heard something!" he said, only he said it without any voice, just his mouth moved.

I listened and then I heard something, too.

"Did you hear something?" asked a voice, only it wasn't any of our voices doing the asking. It came from behind a wall of snow that made up one end of the cave.

I'd heard that kind of voice before—slithery and hissing and ugly. I knew right off what it was, and I could tell from the expression on Owen's face—angry and loathing—that he knew too.

"Draconian!" Owen whispered.

"It was only a snowfall," answered another voice, and it boomed, deep and cold, so cold that it sent tiny bits of ice prickling through my skin and into my blood and I shivered from toe to topknot. "Avalanches are common in these mountains."

"I thought I heard voices," insisted the draconian. "On the other side of that wall. Maybe it's the rest of my outfit."

"Nonsense. I commanded them to wait up in the

mountains until I come. They don't dare disobey. They better not disobey, or I'll freeze them where they stand. You're nervous, that's all. And I don't like dracos who are nervous. You make me nervous. And when I get nervous I kill things."

There came a great slithering and scraping sound and the whole mountain shook. Snow came down on top of us again, but none of us moved or spoke. We just stared at each other. Each of us could match up that sound with a picture in our minds and while my picture was certainly very interesting, it wasn't conducive to long life. (Tanis told me once I should try to look at things from the perspective of whether they were or were not conducive to long life. If they weren't, I shouldn't hang around, no matter how interesting I thought it might be. And this wasn't.)

"A dragon!" whispered Owen Glendower, and he looked kind of awed.

"Not conducive to long life," I advised him, in case he didn't know.

I guess he did, because he glared at me like he would like to put his hand over my mouth but couldn't get close enough, so I put my own hand over my own mouth to save him the trouble.

"Probably a white dragon," murmured Fizban, whose eyes were about ready to roll out of his head. "Oh, my hat! My hat!" He wrung his hands.

Perhaps I should stop here and explain where we were in relation to the dragon. I'm not certain, but I think we were probably in a small cave that was right next to an extremely large cave where the dragon lived. A wall of snow separated us and I began to think that it wasn't a very thick wall of snow. I mean, when one is trapped in a cave with a white dragon, one would like a wall of snow to be about a zillion miles thick, and I had the unfortunate feeling that this one wasn't.

So there we were, in a snow cave, slowly freezing to death (did I mention that?) and we couldn't move, not a muscle, for fear the dragon would hear us. Fizban couldn't work his magic because he didn't have his hat. Owen didn't look like he knew what to do, and I guess I couldn't blame him because he'd probably never come across a dragon before now. So we didn't do anything except stand there and breathe and we didn't even do much of that. Just what we had to.

"Go on with your report," said the dragon.

"Yes, O Master." The draconian sounded a lot more respectful, probably not wanting to make the dragon nervous. "I scouted the village, like you said. It's fat—lots of food laid in for the winter. One of those (the draconian said a bad word here) Solamnic Knights has a manor near it, but he's off on some sort of errand."

"Has he left behind men-at-arms to guard his manor?"

The draconian made a rude noise. "This knight's poor as dirt, Master. He can't afford to keep men-at-arms. The manor's empty, except for his wife and kid."

Owen's face lost some of its color at this. I felt sorry for him because I knew he must be thinking of his own wife and child.

"The villagers?"

"Peasants!" The draconian spit. "They'll fall down and wet themselves when our raiding parties attack. It'll be easy pickings."

"Excellent. We will store the food here, to be used when the main force arrives to take the High Clerist's Tower. Are there more villages beyond this?"

"Yes, O Master. I will show you on the map. Glendower is here. And then beyond that there are—"

But I didn't hear anymore because I was afraid suddenly that Owen Glendower was going to fall over. His face had gone whiter than the snow and he shook so that his armor rattled.

"My family!" he groaned, and I saw his knees start to buckle.

I can move awfully quietly when I have to and I figured that this was one time I had to. I crept over to him, put my arm around him, and propped him up until he quit shaking.

He was grateful, I think, because he held onto me very tightly, uncomfortably tightly (did I mention he was really strong) and my breath almost left me again before he relaxed and let loose.

By now some blood had come back into his cheeks and he didn't look sick anymore. He looked grim and determined and resolved, and I knew then and there what he was planning to do. It was not conducive to a long life.

The dragon and draconian had gone into a rather heated discussion over which village they should burn and pillage and loot next after Glendower.

I took advantage of the noise they were making to whisper to Owen, "Have you ever seen a dragon?"

He shook his head. He was tightening buckles on his armor and pulling at straps and things and, having seen Sturm do this before a battle, I knew what it meant.

"They're huge," I said, feeling a snuffle coming on, "and extremely big. And enormous. And they have terrible sharp teeth and they're magical. More magical than Fizban. More magical than Raistlin, even, only you don't know him, so I guess that doesn't mean much. And the white dragons can kill you by just breathing on you. I know because I met one in Ice Wall. They can turn you into ice harder than this mountain and kill you dead."

I said all this, but it didn't seem to make any impression on Owen Glendower. He just kept buckling and tightening and his face got more and more cold and determined until I begin to think that it might not make much difference if the white dragon breathed a cone of frost on the knight because he looked already frozen to me.

"Oh, Fizban!" I'm afraid I may have whimpered a bit here, but I truly didn't want to see Owen turned into part of this mountain. "Make him stop!"

But Fizban was no help. The wizard got that crafty, cunning look on his face that makes me feel squirmy, and he said, real soft, "He can do it. He has the dragonlances!"

Owen lit up. He stood tall and straight and his eyes shone bright green, fueled from inside by a beautiful, awful, radiant light.

"Yes," he said in a reverent voice, like he was praying. "Paladine sent the lances to my hand and then sent me here, to save my family. This is Paladine's work."

Well, I felt like telling him, No, it wasn't Paladine. It was just an old, skinny, and occasionally fuddled wizard who got us into this by falling into a hole. But I didn't. I had more important things on my mind.

Like the dragonlances.

I looked at them lying in the snow, and I could hear Theros's voice in my head. And I looked at Owen, standing so tall and handsome, and I thought about the painting of his wife and child and how sad they'd be if he was dead. Then I thought that if he was dead they'd be dead, too. And I heard Theros's voice again in my head.

Owen reached down and picked up one of the dragonlances and before I could stop it, a yell burst out of me.

"No! Owen! You can't use the dragonlances!" I cried, grabbing hold of his arm and hanging on. "They don't work!"

CHAPTER SEVEN

Well, at that moment, a whole lot of things happened at once. I'll try to keep them straight for you, but it was all pretty confusing and I may put some things not in quite the right order.

Owen Glendower stared at me and said, "What?"

Fizban glared at me and snapped, "You fool kender! Keep your mouth shut!"

The draconian probably would have stared at me if it could have seen me through the wall of snow and it said, "I heard that!"

The dragon shifted its big body around (we could hear it scraping against the walls) and said, "So did I! And I smell warm blood! Spies! You, draco! Go warn the others! I'll deal with these!"

Wham!

That was the dragon's head, butting the ice wall that separated us. (Apparently, the wall was much thicker and stronger than I'd first supposed. For which we were all grateful.) The mountain shook and more snow fell down on top of us. The hole at the top grew larger—not that this was much help at the moment, since we couldn't get up there.

Owen Glendower was holding the dragonlance and staring at me. "What do you mean—the lances don't work!"

I looked helplessly at Fizban, who scowled at me so fiercely that I was afraid his eyebrows would slide right off his face and down his nose.

Wham!

That was the dragon's head again.

"I have to tell him, Fizban!" I wailed. And I spoke as quickly as I could because I could see that I wasn't going to have time to go into a lot of detail. "We overheard Theros Ironfeld say to Flint that the lances aren't special or magical or anything—they're plain ordinary steel and when Theros threw one against the wall it broke—I saw it!"

I stopped to suck in a big breath, having used up the one I'd taken to get all that out.

And then I used the next breath to shout, "Fizban! There's your hat!"

The dragon's head-whamming had knocked over a snow bank and there lay Fizban's hat, looking sort of dirty and crumpled and nibbled on and not at all magical. I made a dive for it, brought it up and waved it at him.

"Here it is! Now we can escape! C'mon, Owen!" And I tugged on the knight's arm.

Wham! Wham! That was the dragon's head twice.

Owen looked from the shaking wall (We could hear the dragon shrieking "Spies!" on the other side.) to me, to the lance, to Fizban.

"What do you know about this, Wizard?" he asked, and he was pale and breathing kind of funny.

"Maybe the lance is ordinary. Maybe it is blessed. Maybe it is flawed. Maybe you are the one with the flaw!" Fizban jabbed a finger at Owen.

The knight flushed deeply, and put his hand to his shaven moustaches.

Wham! A crack shivered up the wall and part of a huge dragon snout that was white as bleached bone shoved through the crack. But the dragon couldn't get its whole mouth through and so it left off and started butting the ice again. (That ice was much, much stronger than I'd first thought. Very odd.)

Owen stood holding the dragonlance and staring at it, hard, as if he was trying to find cracks in it. Well, I could have told him there wouldn't be any, because Theros was a master blacksmith, even if he was working with ordinary steel, but there wasn't time. I shoved Fizban's hat into the wizard's hand.

"Quick!" I cried. "Let's go! C'mon, Owen! Please!"

"Well, Sir Knight?" said Fizban, taking his hat. "Are you coming with us?"

Owen dropped the dragonlance. He drew his sword. "You go," he said. "Take the kender. I will stay."

"You, ninny!" Fizban snorted. "You can't fight a dragon with a sword!"

"Run, Wizard!" Owen snarled. "Leave while you still can!" He looked at me and his eyes shimmered. "You have the painting," he said softly. "Take it to them. Tell them—"

Well, I never found out what I was supposed to tell them because at that moment the dragon's head punched right smack through the ice wall.

The cave we were trapped in was smallish compared to the dragon, and the wyrm could only get its head inside. Its chin scraped along the floor and its snaky eyes glared at us horribly. It was so huge and awful and wonderful that I'm afraid I forgot all about its not being conducive to long life and mine would have ended then and there except Fizban grabbed hold of me by the collar and dragged me against the far wall.

Owen staggered backward, sword in hand, leaving the dragonlances in the snow. I could tell that the knight was fairly well floored at the immensity and sheer terribleness of the dragon. It must have been obvious to him right then that what Fizban said was right. You can't fight a dragon with a sword.

"Work some magic, Wizard!" Owen shouted. "Distract it!"

"Distract it! Right!" Fizban muttered and, with a great deal of courage, I thought, the old wizard leaned out from around me (I was in front of him again) and waved his hat in the dragon's general direction.

"Shoo!" he said.

I don't know if you're aware of this or not, but dragons don't shoo. In fact, being shooed seems to have an irritating effect on them. This one's eyes blazed until the snow started melting around my shoes. It began to suck in a deep, deep, deep breath and I knew that when it let that breath out we'd all be permanently frozen statues down here beneath the mountain forever and ever.

The wind whistled and snow whirled around us from the dragon's sucking up all the air. And then, suddenly, the dragon went "Ulp!" and got an extremely startled and amazed look in it eyes.

It had sucked up Fizban's hat.

Fizban had been waving his hat at the dragon, you see, and when the dragon started sucking up air it sucked the hat right out of Fizban's hand. The hat whipped through the air and in between the dragon's fangs and the "Ulp!" was the hat getting stuck in the dragon's throat.

"My hat!" wailed Fizban, and he swelled up until I thought he was going to burst.

The dragon was tossing its head around, choking and wheezing and coughing and trying to dislodge the hat. Owen dashed forward, not bothering to take the time to give the knight's salute to an enemy, which I thought was sensible of him, and stuck his sword (or tried to stick it) in the dragon's throat.

The sword's blade shivered and then shattered. The dragon lashed out at Owen, but it couldn't do much except try to thump him on the head since it was still trying to breathe around the hat. Owen stumbled away and slipped and fell in the snow. His hand landed on the dragonlance.

It was the only weapon we had except for my hoopak, and I would have offered him the hoopak at the time only I forgot I had it. This was all so thrilling.

"Save my hat!" Fizban was shrieking and hopping up and down. "Save my hat!"

Phuey!

The dragon spit out the hat. It flew across the cave and hit Fizban in the face and flattened him but good. Owen leapt to his feet. He was shaking all over, his armor rattled, but he lifted the dragonlance and threw with all his might.

The dragonlance struck the dragon's scaly hide and broke into about a million pieces.

The dragon was sucking in its breath again. Owen slumped. He looked all defeated and hurting. He knew he was going to die, but I could tell that didn't matter to him. It was the thought that his wife and little boy and maybe all those villagers too were going to die that was like a spear in his heart.

And then it seemed to me that I heard a voice. It was Flint's voice, and it sounded so close that I looked all around, more than half-expecting to see him come dashing at me, all red in the face and bellowing.

"You doorknob of a kender! Didn't you hear anything *I* said? Tell him what I told Theros!"

I tried to remember it and then I did remember it and I began to babble, "When you throw the lance, it will be the strength of your faith and the power of your arm and the vision of your eye that will guide the lances into the evil dragon's dark heart. That's what Flint said, sort of, Owen, except I changed it a little. Maybe I was wrong!" I shouted. "Try the other lance!"

I don't know whether he heard me or not. The dragon was making a lot of noise and snow was falling and swirling around us. Either Owen did hear me and took my advice (and Flint's) or else he could see as plain as the hat on Fizban's face that the lance was our last and only hope. He picked it up and this time he didn't throw it. This time he ran with it, straight at the dragon, and with all his strength and might and muscle he drove the lance right into the dragon's throat.

Blood spurted out, staining the white snow red. The dragon gave a horrible yell and flung its head from side to side, screaming in pain and fury. Owen hung onto the lance, stabbing it deeper and deeper into the dragon. The lance didn't break, but held straight and true.

Blood was all over the place and all over Owen and the dragon's shrieks were deafening. Then it made a terrible kind of gurgling sound. The head sank down onto the bloody snow, shuddered, and lay still.

None of us moved—Fizban because he was unconscious

and Owen because he'd been battered about quite a bit by the dragon's thrashing, and me because I just didn't feel quite like moving at the time. The dragon didn't move, either, and it was then I realized it was dead.

Owen crouched on his hands and knees, breathing heavily and wiping blood out of his face and eyes. Fizban was stirring and groaning and mumbling something about his hat, so I knew he was all right. I hurried over to help Owen.

"Are you hurt?" I cried anxiously.

"No," he managed and, leaning on me, he staggered to his feet. He took a stumbling step backward, like he didn't mean to, and then caught himself, and stood gasping and staring at the dragon.

Fizban woke up and peered around dazedly. When he saw the dragon's nose lying about a foot from him, he let out a cry, jumped to his feet in a panic, and tried to climb backward through a solid wall.

"Fizban," I told him. "The dragon's dead."

Fizban stared at it hard, eyes narrowed. Then, when it didn't move and its eyes didn't blink, he walked over and kicked it on the snout.

"So there!" he said.

Owen could walk some better now, without using me for a crutch. Going over to the dragon, he took hold of the dragonlance and jerked it out of the dragon's hide. That took some doing. The lance had bit deep and he'd buried it almost to the hilt. He wiped the lance in the snow, and we could all see that the tip was sharp and finely honed as ever, not a notch or crack anywhere. Owen looked from the good dragonlance to the broken dragonlance, lying in pieces underneath the dragon's chin.

"One broke and one did what no ordinary lance could do. What is the truth?" Owen looked all puzzled and confused.

"That you killed the dragon," said Fizban.

Owen looked back at the lances and shook his head. "But I don't understand . . ."

"And whoever said you would. Or were entitled to!" Fizban snorted. He picked up his hat and sighed. The hat didn't even look like a hat anymore. It was all scrunched and mushed and slimy.

"Dragon slobber," he said sadly. "And who'll pay for the dry cleaning?" He glared round at us.

I would have offered to pay for it, whatever it was, except I never seem to have much money. Besides neither Owen nor I were paying attention to Fizban right then. Owen was polishing up the good dragonlance and when he was done with that, he gathered up the pieces of the flawed dragonlance and studied them real carefully. Then he shook his head again and did something that didn't make much sense to me. He very reverently and gently put the pieces of the broken dragonlance all in a heap together, and then wrapped them up in a bundle and tied it with a bit of leather that I found for him in one of my pouches.

I gathered together all my stuff, that had gotten sort of spread out during the running and jumping and hat-waving and dragon-fighting. By that time Owen was ready to go and I was ready to go and Fizban was ready to go and it was then I realized we were all still stuck down in the cave.

"Oh, bother," muttered Fizban, and walking over to the back part of the cave, he kicked at it a couple times with his foot, and the wall tumbled right down.

We were staring out into bright sunshine and blue sky and when we quit blinking we saw that what we'd thought was a wall wasn't. It had only been a snow bank, and I guess we could have walked out anytime at all if only we'd known it was there.

Well, Owen gave Fizban a really odd look.

Fizban didn't see it. He stuck his maltreated hat in a pocket of his robes, picked up his staff, which had been lying in the snow waiting for him, I guess, and walked out into the sun. Owen and I followed; Owen carrying the dragonlances and me carrying my most precious possessions.

"Now," said Fizban, "the kender and I have to travel to Lord Gunthar's, and you, Owen Glendower, have to return to your village and prepare to face the draconian raiding party. No, no, don't mind us. I'm a great and powerful wizard, you know. I'll just magic us to Lord Gunthar's. You haven't got much time. The draconian ran off to alert its troops. They'll move swiftly now. If you go back into the dragon's lair, you'll find that the cave extends all the way through to the other side of the mountain. Cut your distance in half and it will be safe traveling, now that the dragon's dead.

"No, no, we'll be fine on our own. I know where Lord Gunthar's house is. Known all along. We make a left at the pass instead of a right," he said.

I was about to say that's what I'd said all along, only Owen was obviously real anxious to get on his way.

He said good-bye and shook hands with me very formally and politely. And I gave him back the painting and told him—rather sternly—that if he thought so much of it he should take better care of it. And he smiled and promised he would. And then he shook hands with Fizban, all the time looking at him in that odd way.

"May your moustaches grow long," said Fizban, clapping Owen on both shoulders. "And don't worry about my hat. Though, of course, it will never be the same." He heaved a sad sigh.

Owen stood back and gave us both the knight's salute. I would have given it back, only a snuffle took hold of me right then, and I was looking for a handkerchief. When I found it (in Fizban's pouch) Owen was gone. The snuffle got bigger and it probably would have turned into a sob if Fizban hadn't taken hold of me and given me a restorative shake. Then he raised a finger in the air.

"Tasslehoff Burrfoot," he said, and he looked very solemn and wizardly and so I paid strict attention, which I must admit sometimes I don't when he's talking, "you must promise me that you will never, ever, ever, tell anyone else about the dragonlances."

"What about them?" I asked, interested.

His eyebrows nearly flew up off his head and into the sky, which is probably where my eyebrows were at the moment.

"You mean . . . um . . . about them not working?" I suggested.

"They work!" he roared.

"Yes, of course," I said hurriedly. I knew why he was yelling. He was upset about his hat. "What about Theros? What if he says something? He's a very honest person."

"That is Theros's decision," said Fizban. "He'll take the lances to the Council of Whitestone and we'll see what he does when he gets there."

Well, of course, when Theros got to the Council of Whitestone, which—in case you've forgotten—was a big meeting of the Knights of Solamnia and the elves and some other people that I can't remember. And they were all ready to kill each other, when they should have been ready to kill the evil dragons, and I was only trying to prove a point when I broke the dragon orb (That's *orb* not *herb!*) and I guess they would have all been ready to kill me, except Theros came with the dragonlances and he threw a lance at the Whitestone and shattered it—the stone, not the lance— so I guess he had decided the lances worked, after all.

Fizban took his slobbered-on hat out of his pocket and perched it gingerly on his head. He began to hum and wave his hands in the air so I knew a spell was coming on. I covered my face and took hold of his sleeve.

"And what about Owen?" I asked. "What if he tells the other knights about the lances?"

"Don't interrupt me. Very difficult, this spell," he muttered.

I kept quiet or at least I meant to keep quiet, but the words came out before I could stop them, in the same sort of way a hiccup comes out, whether you want it to or not.

"Owen Glendower's a knight," I said, "and you know how knights are about telling the truth all the time. He's bound by whatever it is that knights are bound by to tell the other knights about the lances, isn't he?"

"If he does, he does. It's his decision," said Fizban. And he was suddenly holding a flapping black bat in his hand. "Wing of bat!" he shouted at nobody that I could see. "Not the whole damn . . . " Muttering, he let the bat loose, glared at me, and sighed. "Now I'll have to start over."

"It doesn't seem to me very fair," I commented, watching the bat fly into the cave. "If it's Theros's decision to tell or not to tell and Owen's decision—then it should be my decision, too. I mean whether or not to say anything about the lances. Working," I added.

Fizban stopped his spell casting and stared at me. Then his eyebrows smoothed out. "By gosh. I believe you've caught on at last. You are absolutely right, Tasslehoff Burrfoot. The decision will be yours. What do you say?"

Well, I thought and I thought and I thought.

"Maybe the lances aren't magical," I said, after thinking so hard that my hair hurt. "Maybe the magic's inside us. But, if that's true, then some people might not have found the magic inside themselves yet, so if they use the lances and think that the magic is outside themselves and inside the lances, then the magic that isn't inside the lances will really be inside them. And after a while they'll come to understand—just like Owen did, though he doesn't—and they'll look for the magic inside and not for the magic outside."

Fizban had the sort of expression that you get on your face when you're sitting in a rope swing and someone winds the rope up real tight, then lets it loose and you spin round and round and throw up, if you're lucky.

"I think I better sit down," he said, and he sat down in the snow.

I sat down in the snow and we talked some more and eventually he knew what I was trying to say. Which was that I would never, ever, ever say anything to anybody about the dragonlances not working. And, just to make certain that the words didn't accidentally slip out, like a hiccup, I swore the most solemn and reverent oath a kender can take.

I swore on my topknot.

And I want to say right here and now, for Astinus and history, that I kept my oath.

I just wouldn't be me without a topknot.

CHAPTER EIGHT

I finished my story. They were all sitting in the Upper Gallery, next to poor Owen Glendower, listening to me. And they were about the best audience I'd ever had.

Tanis and Lady Crysania and Laurana and Caramon and Owen's son and Lord Gunthar all sat staring at me like they'd been frozen into statues by the white dragon's frost breath. But I'm afraid the only thing I was thinking about then was my topknot shriveling up and falling off. I was hoping it didn't, but that's a risk I figured I had to take. I just couldn't let Owen Glendower die of a fit when telling this story might help him, though I didn't see how it could.

"You mean to say," said Lord Gunthar, his moustaches starting to quiver, "that we fought that entire war and risked our very lives on dragonlances that were supposed to be magical and they were just ordinary lances?"

"You said it," I told him, hanging onto my topknot and thinking how fond I was of it. "I didn't."

"Theros of the Silver Arm knew they were ordinary," Lord Gunthar went on, and I could see him getting himself all worked up over it. "He knew the metal was plain steel. Theros should have told someone—"

"Theros Ironfeld knew, and Theros Ironfeld split the Whitestone with the dragonlance," Lady Crysania said coolly. "The lance didn't break when he threw it."

"That's true," said Lord Gunthar, struck by the fact. He thought this over, then he looked angry again. "But, as the kender reminded us, Owen Glendower knew. And by the Measure he should have told the Knight's Council."

"What did I know?" asked a voice, and we all jumped up to our feet.

Owen Glendower was standing up in the middle of the pile of cloaks and, though he looked almost as bad as he had when he was fighting the dragon, he had at least come out of his fit.

"You knew the truth, Sir!" said Lord Gunthar, scowling.

"I came to know the truth—for myself. But how could I know it for any other? That was what I told myself and what I believed until . . . until . . ." He glanced at his son.

"Until I became a knight," said Gwynfor.

"Yes, my son." Owen sighed, and stroked his moustaches that were extremely long now, though they weren't red so much as mostly gray. "I saw you with the lance in your hand and I saw again the lance—the first lance I threw—

shatter and fall to pieces in front of my foe. How could I let you go to battle the evil in this world, knowing as I did that the weapon on which your life depended was plain, ordinary? And how could I tell you? How could I destroy your faith?"

"The faith you feared to destroy in your son was not in the dragonlance, but in yourself, wasn't it, Sir Knight?" Lady Crysania asked, her sightless eyes turning to see him.

"Yes, Revered Daughter," answered Owen. "I know that now, listening to the kender's story. Which," he added, his mouth twisting, "wasn't precisely the way it all happened."

Tanis eyed me sternly.

"It was so, too!" I said, but I said it under my breath. My topknot didn't appear to be going anywhere for the time being and I intended to keep it that way.

"It was my faith that faltered the first time," Owen said. "The second, my heart and my aim held true."

"And so will mine, father," said Gwynfor Glendower. "So will mine. You have taught me well."

Gwynfor threw his arms around his father. Owen hugged his son close, which must have been hard to do with all the armor they were wearing, but they managed. Lord Gunthar thought at first he was going to keep being mad, but then, the more he thought about it, the more I guess he decided he wouldn't. He went over to Owen and they shook hands and then they put their arms around each other.

Laurana went to get Theros, who'd walked out of the room, you remember. He was awfully gruff and grim when he first came back, as if he thought everyone was going to yell at him or something. But he relaxed quite a bit when he saw that Owen was walking around and smiling, and that we were all smiling, even Lord Gunthar—as much as he ever smiles, which is mostly just a twitch around the moustaches.

They decided to go on with the ceremony of the Forging of the Lance, but it wasn't going to be a "public spectacle" as Tanis put it, when he thought Lord Gunthar wasn't listening. It was going to be a time for the knights to rededicate themselves to honor and courage and nobility and self-sacrifice. And now it would have more meaning than ever.

"Are you going to tell them the truth about the lances?" Laurana asked.

"What truth?" asked Lord Gunthar and for a moment he looked as crafty and cunning as Fizban. Then he smiled. "No, I'm not. But I am going to urge Owen Glendower to tell his story to them."

And with that he and Owen and Gwynfor left (Owen said good-bye to me very politely) and went down to Huma's Tomb, where all the other knights were getting ready to fast and pray and rededicate themselves.

"His story!" I said to Tanis, and I must admit I was a bit indignant. "Why it's my story and Fizban's story just as much as it is Owen's story."

"You're absolutely right, Tas," said Tanis seriously. One thing I do like about Tanis is that he always takes me seriously. "It is your story. You have my permission to go down into Huma's Tomb and tell your side of it. I'm certain that Lord Gunthar would understand."

"I'm certain he better," I said loftily.

I was about to go down to Huma's Tomb, because I was afraid Owen would leave out a lot of the very best parts, only about then Caramon came up to us.

"I don't understand," he said, his big face all screwed up into thought-wrinkles. "Did the lances work? Or didn't they?"

I looked at Tanis. Tanis looked at me. Then Tanis put his arm around Caramon's shoulders.

"Caramon," he said. "I think we better have a little talk. We used the lances, and we won the war because of them. And so you see . . ."

The two of them walked off. And I hope Caramon understands the truth about the lances now, though I think it's more likely that he just caught Tanis's cold.

I was on my own, and I started once again to go down to Huma's Tomb when the thought occurred to me.

Huma's Tomb. Again.

Now, please don't misunderstand, all you knights who read this. Huma's Tomb is a most wonderful and solemn and sorrowful and feel-sad-until-you-feel-good kind of place.

But I'd seen about all of it I wanted to see in one lifetime.

Right then I heard Tanis sneeze, and I figured he'd need his handkerchief, which he'd left behind in my pocket, so I decided I'd go take it to him instead.

And I figure that about now Owen Glendower must be looking for that little painting of his that he keeps losing. I plan to give it right back to him . . . when he leaves Huma's Tomb.